ZANE P

Retribution

Dear Reader:

Cairo is on a continuous roll of entertainment with his raw brand of erotica and memorable characters. We first met Pasha, the diva fascinated with oral sex, in *Deep Throat Diva*. Now the salon owner of Nappy No More returns with a vengeance, determined to destroy those who have wronged her: from the team of hooded kidnappers who took turns abusing her to women who have betrayed her in some fashion.

Despite her unfaithfulness—although she doesn't consider what she does as cheating—while her hubby, Jasper, is in lockup, Pasha is viewed as a heroine. She doesn't slow her roll during his incarceration and gains a reputation for her skills. Men constantly crave to experience her favorite hobby.

She manages to satisfy their desires, but she never loses focus. Her vicious mission is to pay back the culprits in her path, one by one.

Thanks for giving *Retribution* support and look out for *Ruthless*, the next title in the series. Make sure to check out Cairo's other titles: *The Kat Trap, The Man Handler, Daddy Long Stroke, Kitty-Kitty, Bang-Bang, Man Swappers, Big Booty, Slippery When Wet* and the e-book, *The Stud Palace*. Thanks also for supporting the authors of Strebor Books. We truly appreciate the love. You may contact me at www.facebook.com/AuthorZane or via email at Zane@eroticanoir.com.

Blessings,

Zane

Publisher
Strebor Books
www.simonandschuster.com

ZANE PRESENTS

Retribution

A NOVEL BY

CAIRO

SBI

STREBOR BOOKS

NEW YORK LONDON TORONTO SYDNEY

Strebor Books
P.O. Box 6505
Largo, MD 20792
http://www.streborbooks.com

ISBN 978-1-59309-511-6
ISBN 978-1-4767-3357-9 (ebook)
LCCN 2013950687

First Strebor Books trade paperback edition March 2014

Cover design: www.mariondesigns.com
Cover photograph: © Keith Saunders/Marion Designs

10 9 8 7 6 5 4 3 2 1

Manufactured in the United States of America

For information regarding special discounts for bulk purchases,
please contact Simon & Schuster Special Sales at 1-866-506-1949
or business@simonandschuster.com

The Simon & Schuster Speakers Bureau can bring authors to your live event.
For more information or to book an event, contact the Simon & Schuster Speakers
Bureau at 1-866-248-3049 or visit our website at www.simonspeakers.com.

This book is dedicated to all the dick suckers in the room
who love givin' that bomb-ass head & to all
The Deep Throat Diva *fans who have waited patiently*
for Pasha to bring it to Jasper's head.
Well, guess what? She's baaaaaaaaack!
And this time she's suckin' dick for a cause!
Swallow the heat 'n' enjoy the cream!
This one's for you!

ACKNOWLEDGMENTS

Aiight, my Juice Lovas 'n' freaks, I'ma keep it short 'n' sweet this time. Nine books in 'n' countin'. Don't sleep on ya boy, I'm still pushin' out the heat, one stroke at a time!

To the sexually liberated and open-minded: Thanks for continuin' to wave ya freak flags, ridin' this hot, *nassy* wave with me, and gettin' down with the juice. Let's keep it wet, keep it sticky, and always keep it ready! The Cairo Movement is here to stay!

To all the Facebook beauties 'n' cuties and cool-ass bruhs who make this journey mad fun: Real rap. Y'all my muthaeffen peeps! Thanks for vibin' with ya boy! And, uh, I'm still waitin' for some'a you to run me some of them sex tapes y'all got hidden. I ain't playin'. I wanna watch! LOL

To all the silent-haters, close-minded & sexually repressed peeps: Eat my nut sac! It's filled wit' lots of hot thick, sticky cream just for you. Maybe that'll help open ya unclog ya sexually constipated asses.

To Zane, Charmaine, Yona and the rest of the Strebor/Simon & Schuster team: As always, I hope you all know how much ya boy appreciates the never-ending luv!

To the members of *Cairo's World:* Uh, yeah, yeah, yeah...I already know I still haven't been handlin' thangs over on the other side like I said I would. I'ma get the flames *turnt* up for y'all nassy-asses real soon; real spit.

And, as always, to the naysayers: Here's another joint for you to pop shit about. You already know it's because of you that I keep it raw, hot 'n' oh-so *nassy!* Keep juicin' the haterade, my peeps. It keeps me horny and keeps me strokin' out that hotness! Lick them fingers or keep it movin'. Either way, I ain't goin' anywhere!

One luv—

Cairo

2011

I, Jasper Edwin Tyler, take you, Pasha Nivea-Alona Allen, to be my wedded wife. To have and to hold from this day forth. That's real, yo. From da moment I laid my eyes on you, baby, I knew you were da one for me. You are my soulmate, baby. My e'erything. My heart beats and bleeds for you. And together we are forever connected as one. You are my joy, my guidin' light. Da wind beneath my wings, yo. I pledge my love to you, baby. No woman has ever inspired me, loved me, or treated me da way you do. I need you like I need air, baby. And I ain't ever lettin' you go. I lay down my life for you. I promise to love you, protect you, respect you, and be da man you need me to be. The love I have for you is forever, Pasha, ya heard? 'Til death *do us part...*"

"I, Pasha Nivea-Alona Allen, take you...Jasper Edwin Tyler... to be my...wedded...husband. With each w-w-waking breath, I-I...p-p-promise...to l-l-love you unconditionally, to f-f-for... give...you without reservation, to r-r-respect you...and be the w-w-woman...you n-n-need me to be. I s-s-shed these tears for you and with you. I give you...a-all of m-m-me, Jasper. In the joys and sorrows, in the good times and the bad times—from this day forward, I pledge my love to you. A commitment made in l-l-love, k-k-kept in faith, and e-e-eternally m-m-made anew...."

One

Every bitch has a past. A present. And more than one story to tell…

"Aaaaah, shit yeah. Goddamn, baby, you know how to suck this dick…fuck, aaah, shit…uhhh, motherfuck. Damn. Mmmm…Ummmph…Yeah, get up on them balls, baby…aaaah, shit…wet them balls up…uhhh, put that dick back in ya mouth, baby…"

I grin as the head of his throbbing dick is engulfed in the warm, wetness of my mouth. My mouth becoming a quick replacement for the juicy wet pussy it craves to be deep inside of. Oh, yes…I'll be riding down on his hard dick for the second time tonight, but right now, sucking another hot nut out of him is my only mission.

I swallow him down to the base, my nose pressed into his musky, sweat-and-pussy-scented pubic hairs, as I grab his balls and pull them up, extending my tongue and licking them.

I gulp him and let my throat muscles massage the head of his dick. He pushes his hips into my face. Fucks my throat in slow deep thrusts. Most bitches are born with only one cunt. I'm one of the fortunate to have been blessed with two: the one between my smooth, beautiful thighs, and the one in the back of my throat. Sucking dick wets my pussy and sets my insides on fire.

"Oh shit, oh shit, oh shit…Motherfuck, yo…damn…uh, fuck…sssssssssssshiiiiiit…you got the head game on lock, baby…aaaah, fuck!"

I grin to myself. *Of course I do. I'm not the Deep Throat Diva for nothing.*

I slowly pull off his dick, sucking all the way up, then licking up and down the sides of the shaft. I tongue his piss slit, lapping at the sticky precum as it oozes out. I look up at him, watching him watching me as I make love to his dick and balls with my mouth, lips, tongue and hands. I reach up and play with his nipples. They're dark chocolate pebbles, hard with desire. I pinch them, giving him my specialty no-hands dick throat action, bobbing my head up and down, taking him deep into my mouth, gulping down every thick inch of him.

He moans. "Damn, baby…mmmph…you got my head spinnin', yo…ooooh, shit, shit, shit…"

I pull his dick from out of my throat, then inch up over his body and press my lips to his, slipping my tongue into his mouth, giving him a taste of what I taste. His hard cock. His sticky precum. His tongue greets mine and we engage in a round of deep, tongue-probing kisses until I finally break away, breathlessly and greedy for more dick. I kiss the side of his neck, my wet tongue trailing along his skin, my mouth running down his chiseled body, swirling my tongue over each of his nipples before journeying down to his stomach, dipping my tongue into his navel. I tease him with my lips and tongue. Make him beg me to take his dick back into my mouth.

"Get back on that dick, baby. Wrap them sexy-ass lips around it…"

I grin, looking back up at him as I run my tongue along the shaft, right side first, then the left side. "Buckle up, baby," I whisper. I lick around his balls. "I'm about to give you the dick sucking of your life."

"Yeah, suck my shit…"

I swallow him again, sucking faster and harder, giving him the vacuum deluxe. His dick engulfed in my mouth, my lips wrapped tightly around the base of it with a bunch of spitting and slurping and gulping—my jaws milking him, as I rapidly bob my head up and down, my soft lips sucking up the length of his shaft, then back down with each slurp.

"Aaaah, fuck…you gonna make me bust this nut…uhhh, mmmm… you want me to bust this thick nut down in ya throat, baby? You like that good dick, don't you? Aaaah, shiiiit, yeah…suck that shit… You want Daddy's hot nut…?"

With a mouth full of dick, all I can do is grunt and massage his balls to edge him on. I give him one hell of a porn star performance. Pulling his dick out, then spitting all over it. I give it to him wet and sloppy, the way he loves it. I run my hands along his hard body, reach up and pinch his nipples, then glide them back down over his skin, my nails lightly grazing his flesh.

I increase the suction on his dick, wrapping my hands along the back of his muscular thighs—the way I did the first time I had him stretched out in a hotel bed, giving him my no-hands-all-neck-and-throat action, ramming his dick in and out of my throat.

I can barely hear his moans over the wet, gushy, slopping sounds coming out of the back of my throat. I slow my pace. Pull him out of my throat and suckle his cockhead, swirling my tongue over it, lapping at the ever-flowing precum seeping out. Halfway up his dick, I wrap my right hand around the base of his shaft and pump while I continue working over the top half of his dick with my mouth. Slowly bobbing and pumping into a groove that has him clutching the sheets, his toes opening and closing.

He begs me to take him deep in my throat again. He's ready to nut. But I want to keep teasing him. Want to keep edging him. I flick my tongue over the head of his dick, run my tongue around the rim of it, swirling back up to his slit.

"Goddamn, baby…fuck! Let me get that throat…"

I tongue around the head some more, then slide it to the underside of his pulsing shaft. Ooooh, I love how thick it is. Love how his vein swells. Slowly…so very slowly, I lick down to the base, to his sac, licking under them. I kiss them, lick a circle around them, then pull each one into my mouth, gently sucking his balls.

He grips my head, grinds his balls into my mouth, his dick bouncing and throbbing against my forehead. He grabs it, attempts to stroke it. But I yank his hand back.

I knew the very first time I sucked his thick, juicy dick up on the third level of that parking garage in his tinted SUV, then swallowed his creamy nut and looked up into his hazel eyes that I had opened Pandora's box for the both of us. I knew the first time I let him eat my pussy, the first time we were in the sixty-nine position, the first time I contemplated giving him some of this pussy, the first time he kissed me, that I was at a point of no return with him.

I climb up on top of him. Position his dick in the center of my slick pussy. Then lean in and whisper in his ear, "You ready to fuck this pussy?"

He grabs my hips, thrusts upward. Attempts to stab his dick into my wetness. "Yeah. You already know what it is." I press my lips to his again. Our tongues meet. And our kiss ignites another burst of flames inside of me as I reach in back of me and guide the head of his dick in. I ease it in between the lips of my pussy. Fuck the tip of his dick. Raw. I roll my hips nice and slow until I am sitting all the way down on his dick. I lift my hips up halfway, slam back down, then rodeo fuck him, serving him up a dish of hot, naked pussy.

He grunts.

I moan.

He moans.

I grunt.

He cups my ass. Thrusts his hips up into me. We find a rhythm and fuck each other as if it's our last night on this earth. Shit, if we ever get caught it just might be his. Still, we both know we're playing a very dangerous game.

"Aaaah, fuck…ooooh, shit, baby…I love fuckin' this pussy…"

"Yeah, daddy…fuck this slutty pussy…oooh, yes…"

"Uhhh…uhhh…shit…fuck…I'm gettin' ready to bust…"

I quickly lift up off his cum-coated dick, my pussy juices sliding down his shaft and wrap my mouth over it, sucking the nut out of him. The head of his dick hits my tonsils as I swallow him all the way in, dick and nut down into my throat.

And it's good to the last damn drop!

I pull his dick from out of my neck. Lick it clean. Then smack my lips together as he dozes off, lightly snoring.

*A hard, horny dick has no conscience. It'll fuck a bitch over
if she lets it...*

I ease out from under the rumpled sheets, still damp with sweat
and cum from an all-night suck-and-fuck-athon, grabbing my
buzzing cell while slipping on my silk robe. I quietly slide
open the balcony door, then step out into the early morning light.
I slide the door shut behind me, rolling my eyes the minute I hear
his voice. *I hate everything this motherfucking nigga stands for!*

"Yo, what da fuck is you doin', yo? I been callin' ya ass all muthafuckin' night, yo. Don't have me bust yo' ass, Pasha. Word up. Let
me find out you back on ya bullshit, ya heard?"

This nigga's crazy.

Shit, he's *always* been fucking crazy! But it's gotten worse.

I suck my teeth. "And what are you gonna do, Jasper, kill me this
time?" I say sarcastically. Although I'm half-joking, half serious,
knowing that if he could body me, he would. But as it stands right
now, I'm worth more to him alive than I am dead; particularly since
everything—the house, the cars, the bank accounts, and the busi-
nesses he now own—is in my name. A smart nigga wouldn't be so
caught up in the material shit. But Jasper is. And as insurance in
case this happy-handed nigga ever decides to really toe-tag me,
I've made sure my son is the sole beneficiary of everything and I've
assigned my attorney as the executor of my estate.

Jasper will be left with nothing, if I can help it.

"Yo, fuck outta here. I'ma bust yo shit, that's what. You already know what it is, yo. Now act fuckin' stupid if you want, ya heard? I keep…"

I shake my head. His threats are of no longer any consequence to me. And to think I once loved his ass with everything in me. There was a time—before the prison bid, before all of the cheating, before the lies, before everything else happened between us—when I believed that Jasper was the only man for me. I thought I would love him forever. Mmmph. What a goddamn joke!

Ain't shit forever! Not love, not life…nothing!

All I have in me for this nigga is contempt. I hate his black ass. The way he looks at me, the way he smells, the way he touches me, makes my skin crawl. Jasper's a grimy, ruthless motherfucker. And I hate him. I know he's my son's father—and there's nothing I can do about that. But, God forgive me. Sometimes I wish this nigga dead for what he did to me. This dirty nigga had me locked up and tied up and gagged down in some dusty-ass basement. Then let his goons violate me. Yeah, I did my dirt while he was on lock. But what this dirty nigga did to me is unthinkable, unconscionable. It haunts me. And it's some shit I can't, I won't, ever forgive him for.

No, a snake nigga like Jasper has to be dealt with, carefully.

"Don't have me fuck you up, yo…If I ever find out you playin' me, yo…I'ma fuck you up…to teach you a lesson…"

I knew my transgressions—sucking a string of random dicks while Jasper was incarcerated—would cost me. I had gotten greedy. I let it consume me. Let it become an obsession. And instead of quitting while I was ahead, I let my thirst for dick and cum control me. And, as a result, I kept posting ads on that godforsaken website Nastyfreaks4u.com, soliciting men who sought out getting some anonymous head. And with the promise of providing a toe-curling experience and giving men some of the best mouth, tongue, and throat work around, I started living up to my screen name, *Deep Throat Diva*, throat-swabbing niggas like there was no tomorrow.

Problem is, niggas started getting strung out. Some crazy nigga started harassing me. Another started stalking me. Then the nigga tried to snatch me up in my own yard. I had to fight the nigga off of me. Had my next-door neighbor not pulled up when he had, I don't know what that crazy nigga might have done to me. And of course I refused to call the police. I couldn't.

What was I going to tell them? "Hi. I'm known as Deep Throat Diva in cyberland. I post ads online to suck dick, and I sucked this nutty nigga crazy. Oh...and by the way, my fiancé—who's been locked up for almost five years—can't ever find out that the woman he wants to marry is a cum guzzler or he'll beat the shit out of me."

Really?

You think?

Umm, no thank you. That was news I didn't want out. It was info I had hoped to sweep up into a tiny box of lies and keep locked away before Jasper got home. But it didn't happen that way. Something went tragically wrong. Someone got up in Jasper's ear. And the shit blew up in my face.

Now wait. You judgmental bitches can think what you want about me. I *loved* Jasper. My dick sucking had nothing to do with how I felt about him at that time. There was no emotional connection to any of them niggas I sucked. All they were were a bunch of hard dicks. It was all about what I needed/wanted to fill a sexual void. I had no intentions of ever fucking anyone other than Jasper.

And, at the time—somewhere stuck in between my neglected libido and loneliness—I concocted this twisted fantasy of believing that as long as I didn't give up my pussy to any other nigga that Jasper and I could live happily-ever-after once he was finally released from prison. And he'd be none the wiser to know that the lips he kissed were the same lips that stayed wrapped around a bunch of different dicks and had been glazed with more nuts than I care to remember.

But it didn't work out that way for me. My happily-ever-after didn't turn out so happy for me after all. And I'm sure you know, or can at least imagine, how the rest of the story ended for me.

If Jasper would have just beat the shit out of me, I could have handled it, deservingly. I would have worn my ass whooping proudly, knowing I caused it. And maybe things with us would be different. Maybe he would have found it in his heart to forgive me. Maybe we could have moved on from it. I don't know.

What I do know is, after what that bastard did to me. Whatever love I had for him has turned into deep seething contempt. Everything I believed in, held on to, was shattered the moment Jasper leaned over my hospital bed, smirking. His eyes still haunt me. The way he stared into me, cold and calculating. The whole time I was missing, I had hoped and prayed that he'd be out looking for me, that he'd be stricken with worry. And all the while that motherfucker knew where I was. Because *he* was behind it all.

No one has any idea what happened to my spirit down in that basement.

The humiliation.

The fear.

The disrespect.

Somewhere in between the second or third dick shoved into my mouth, I lost pieces of me. By the fifth dick, everything inside of me snapped. I was broken. By the sixth dick, I became numb. I crumbled up and died inside.

Jasper did that to me.

Okay, I did that to me.

Still…I didn't deserve *that!*

Anyway. It was only supposed to be temporary—posting ads, only something to do until Jasper came home. That's what I kept telling myself every time I posted an ad. Cheating—well, *fucking*, on Jasper wasn't a thought for me like I said. But celibacy was taking its toll on me. How was I supposed to go five fucking years without dick? I missed the feel of a hard dick—his hard dick. My pussy *ached* for it. But I stayed true the best way I could.

I had promised Jasper before he had gone to prison that I wouldn't let another nigga fuck me while he was locked up. Still a bitch like me needed something more than an assortment of dildos and vibrators to fuck to take the edge off, until Jasper was released from prison. So I posted—what was supposed to be a one-time thing—a sex ad looking for men who wanted throat work. I didn't think I would get swamped with replies from men from all walks of life—some married, some single, some shacking with women, some freakier and kinkier than others—looking for a good dick suck.

So what started out as mere curiosity and a means to an end quickly became an obsession.

My guilty pleasure.

My dirty little secret.

Dick sucking consumed me.

And there was a hefty price to pay. But I didn't think it would almost cost me my life. Okay, okay, I'm lying. I *knew* I was playing with fire, taking dangerous risks creeping out in the middle of the night and sucking random niggas off in their cars in parking lots, parks, or motel rooms. I *knew* Jasper would kill me if he ever found out. And I believe he would have bodied me if I hadn't been pregnant with our son at the time. Still…that didn't stop him from degrading me, then beating the shit out of me, almost to death, no less—even though I was pregnant. And he knew it.

I can still remember the shit as if it were yesterday.

"Remember she's not to be hurt…"

"No doubt, I'll just rough the bitch up a bit…"

"C'mon, man…chill out wit' all that…she's pregnant…"

I can still hear their voices, deep and unrecognizable, in my head. *"Bitch, if you so much as flinch, I'ma dead ya ass right here…Now do what I tell you and I won't haveta spill ya pretty lil brains out all over this concrete…"*

I can still feel their hands on me. The niggas who snatched me up that night at the mall. My hair being violently pulled and my head snapped back. I can still hear the click of the gun, pressing against my temple.

"…I promise you. On e'erything I love. I will kill you, bitch…"

I continue replaying pieces of that night in my mind. I fight back. Attempt to get away. And, then…in one swift motion there's a blade pressed up under my throat.

"…I'ma slice ya muthafuckin' throat, ya heard?"

Three

A lie is never a lie, until you get caught in it...

I blink.

"...Pasha, *what da fuck, yo?!*" Jasper shrieks in my ear, jolting me back to the present. "You hear me talkin' to ya ass?"

I gaze out into the Pacific Ocean, breathing in the morning breeze while taking in layers of orange, red, and yellow as the sun rises from the horizon. Sometimes I wish I could blink my eyes three times and make this nigga disappear for good. I swear. If I were a snitch-type bitch, I'd have his ass set up and feed his ass to the feds. They've been watching his slick-ass every since he got released from prison. And he knows this. But his dumbass is still caught up in that life, thinking he can't be touched.

I understand the game. It's hard to get out of. I know the risks that are involved. Someone's bound to get at you at some point, whether it's the feds, some jealous-ass hater, or a hungry nigga looking for a come-up. Either way, when your time's up, it's up.

And I recognize it was Jasper's drug money that made it possible for me to open my salon, Nappy No More, ten years ago. Jasper believed in my vision. He footed the bill, no questions asked. And in less than three years I quadrupled his investment, even wrote him a check for the full amount, although he refused to take it.

Still, I wanted him to be clear that my salon was *mine*—free and clear, period. Not his. Or ours. Mine.

I let him know, I didn't want to keep feeling like he had claims to my shit. Reluctantly, he took the check, popping shit about only taking it to shut me up. He didn't cash the shit, of course. But I made it clear that whether he cashed it or not, I didn't owe him shit where my salon was concerned. Now here we are ten years later, and it's my hard-earned money this go-round that'll be opening up Nappy No More II out here on the West Coast as soon as the deal is sealed.

So, again, I don't need the nigga. So, why am I still with him?

Because I'm not leaving him until he pays for what he's done to me. Until I take him for every-goddamn-thing he's worth. And my staying has *nothing* to do with the threat of him *killing* me. I'm beyond that. Like I said earlier, once this nigga no longer *thinks* he needs me, I'm good as dead the next time I'm caught with another nigga's dick in my throat. Still, as far as I'm concerned, he owes me for all of my pain and suffering. And he's going to pay in more than one way.

In the meantime, I suffer and plot in silence.

A stack here, a stack there; bit-by-bit until I have every motherfucking dime of his, or at least most of it. I know Jasper's no fool when it comes to his paper. So I already know he has a load of money tucked somewhere other than in the safe tucked behind a wall panel in his walk-in closet, or the one that's built into the floor of our pool house—the one he *thinks* I don't know about. Jasper's money is long. And so is his ego and temper. So as long as I *play* along with his sick mind games and need for control, I still benefit from his drug dealing, and whatever other dirty shit he's into.

Again, not that I need it. But I *want* it. I deserve it. The jewels, the furs, the shopping sprees—all financed by him. Still, it all comes with a price to pay. Jasper's unpredictable mood swings. His paranoia. His jealousy. His abuse.

Am I scared of him?

There's no easy answer to that. Jasper's unstable. But the one thing I know is, this nigga's *in love*—okay, *obsessed*—with my pussy. And, yeah…Beating me almost to death for sucking dick—okay, *dicks*—is one thing, but putting me in a body bag isn't where he's at—not yet. And as long as I keep sucking and fucking him and stroking his fragile ego, I'm good for now.

Still…every time I feel this nigga looking at me, I feel as if he's staring right through me. His dark eyes are cold and cutting. I can tell the nigga's always thinking. Always trying to catch me slipping. So, because of that, *yes*, I'm afraid—very.

But not enough—as you can see—to stop what I'm doing. The knots in my stomach are a constant reminder that I married the devil, and he's been fucking me raw ever since.

Still, I play my position.

But one of these days, very soon, this nigga's got it coming to him. Every dirty thing he's ever done is going to come back to him. And I'm going to be the one he's looking at before his black ass gets dropped. I'm going to be the one who spits in his face when it happens. I promise you. Before his lights get shut, I'll be the last bitch he sees.

"I'm so fuckin' relieved you and the baby are aiight….If I woulda lost you and my seed, I'da lost it for real, yo. We connected, baby….For life."

As hard as I've tried blocking everything out, I can't. His voice. The look in his eyes, the way the motherfucker smirked when he saw it in my own eyes. That I knew.

"*...and if I find out you been playin' me, yo; that you had another nigga's dick up in you, I'ma beat the dog shit outta ya ass, you dig?*"

It was him.

"*I know what you're thinkin', baby...It's over wit', baby...all that shit you were doin'...I warned you, Pasha. I told you don't fuckin' play me, yo.*"

They knew I was pregnant, because Jasper had told them. But I didn't know it then. I had no clue he was behind any of that sordid shit until I woke up in the hospital and he was there by my bedside—tears streaming from his eyes, concern painted on his weary face, pretending.

I mean, I knew he had a vicious streak.

Knew he could be violent.

Yet, to think he'd go to that extreme to do what he did, to be willing to pimp me out to a bunch of his niggas and let them disrespect me.

Let them take turns fucking my throat.

And smacking me around.

No. Jasper wouldn't ever have any of that shit done to me. Not the man I loved. Not the father of my child. I couldn't imagine it.

Then, again...I'm sure he didn't expect the woman he loved, the woman carrying his child, to be practically running a community dick-sucking center behind his back, either.

Anyway. I finally saw the truth in his eyes when he hovered over my hospital bed. Realization. That he was behind the attack. And, every since that awful night—the night I was kidnapped out in the parking garage of The Mall at Short Hills, nothing for me has ever been the same.

I warned you, Pasha. Told you don't fuckin' play me, yo."

I bring my attention back to the idiot on the other end of the line. "What is it, Jasper?"

"What da fuck you mean, 'what is it'? I asked you what da fuck is you doin', yo? I'm talkin' to ya silly ass 'n' you actin' like you iggin' a muhfucka."

I sigh, glancing over my shoulder looking back into the suite. I want another round of dick from the man sleeping under the covers before I have to make the twenty-minute drive back to my condo in L.A.

I eye Mr. Thick-Seven-And-A-Half as he stirs. He rolls over onto his back, pulling back the white sheet. His dick springs upward. And my mouth instantly waters. He stretches his long legs out, then grabs his hard dick and strokes it. He sees me watching him.

I knew the first time I let him bust his creamy nut in my mouth and I swallowed him down to the last drop that I would keep sucking him. I knew sucking his thick chocolate dick would become my guiltiest pleasure. I just didn't think I would be fucking him, too. But here I am. In Santa Monica with my pussy sore from the pounding he put on me into the wee hours of the morning; his raw dick deep inside of me, fucking what's only on loan to him.

Later tonight, he'll be going back to his *wifey* and two children, playing the loving man and doting daddy. And, tomorrow, I'll be going back to Jasper's crazy ass.

"Actually, Jasper," I finally say. "If you really wanna know. I *was* iggin' you. It's too early in the morning for this shit. I'm in Los Angeles, nigga. Where I've been for the last week, getting shit ready for the final phase of opening *my* new salon."

"Yo, who da fuck is you snappin' at like that, huh?"

I blow out a frustrated breath. "You know what, Jasper? I'm sick of you always coming at me all crazy. Do me a favor. Why don't you go fuck one of your side bitches and leave me the fuck alone? I'll see you when I get home."

"*Bitch*, is you fuckin' serious, yo? Put my muthafuckin' son on the phone."

"He's asleep. And I'm not waking him. If you want to talk to Jaylen, I'll call you back when he wakes up. Now goodbye."

I end the call before he can say anything else. I slide back the glass door, then step in, leaving the door open as the ocean's breeze eases in. "You ready for some more of this pussy?" I untie my robe and let it slide off my shoulders.

He grins. "You already know the answer to that. Come over here and wet this dick, baby."

A devious smile eases over my lips. "What you want, first, this throat or pussy?"

I crawl in between his legs. I stroke his dick with my hand, licking around his balls, the pungent scent of sweat and fucking still clinging to them. "Both," he says as I slip the head of his dick into my mouth. My body shivers the minute the head of his dick hits the back of my throat. "Awwww, fuck yeah…Suck that dick, baby…"

The bitch you think has your back, is the same bitch who'll snake you...

8 A.M., I'm heading north on I-10 toward L.A., relieved there is no traffic. Los Angeles's traffic is usually horrible no matter which highway you're on, or what time of the day it is. But, this morning, it's smooth sailing, probably because it's early on a Saturday morning. As bad as I wanted to stay wrapped up in Thick Seven's arms, I couldn't. He has shit to do. And so do I. Getting back to my son, that is.

Jaylen's been my saving grace. He's the reason I haven't lost my mind fucking around with Jasper. Even, after the kidnapping, I kept it together—for his sake. He needed me to be strong so that I could carry him to full-term. The doctors had said I was at high risk for delivering him months early due to the stress and trauma of what I had been through. My baby's life depended on me being strong. But it wasn't easy.

I had shed my tears, while never letting anyone else see me break. Not even Jasper's snake-ass. The nigga knew he had me shook. He had seen it in my eyes. But I'd be damn if he'd ever see me shed a tear over it. No, those tears were reserved for when he left the hospital at night.

I spent two weeks in the hospital. And the whole time I was laid up in that bed with tubes and monitors all hooked up to me, I refused to talk to the police. Refused to give them any information surrounding what had happened to me. I refused visitors. I didn't want to see anyone. Or let anyone see me like *that*—all banged up and broken, all swollen and bruised. Not even my Nana, whom I love dearly. Not even Felecia who at the time I *loved* like a sister— up until I learned that that phony, two-faced bitch was talking shit about me behind my back. After all I've done for that bitch. And that's how she repays me. Kicking my back in, then smiling in my face.

My gut always told me to watch that bitch, which is probably why I never confided in her like I used to when we were growing up. Everyone always said when we were growing up that Felecia was jealous of me. But I didn't want to believe it. Felecia had the same opportunities as I did. We shared some of the same pains, and life's experiences.

My mother, Nivea Alona Rice—who gave me her first and middle names as my own middle name—loved the trappings of being a hood-rich trophy wife than she did for me. She gave birth to me. Then, three months later—after she met some big-time drug dealer who wanted to *wife* her up, she dropped me off on my father's doorstep and never looked back. Years later, she was found murdered in the trunk of her Porsche with two bullets to the head. I was twenty.

Felecia's mother had more love for drugs than she did for her. Cocaine was her first love, then later on, crack. Felecia didn't know her father. However, I knew mine. But he was more invested in the streets than he was in raising a daughter. Ralphie Allen, aka The Boogey Man, loved me. But he was a hood nigga with a vicious rep who loved the streets and shaking niggas up more.

As a result, we both lost our parents to the streets, and the drug game. My father—a drug dealer himself—was murdered when I was eleven. And Felecia's mother, my father's sister, died from a drug overdose a few years later.

Sadly, we were both orphans long before either of our parents ever hit the ground and the dirt got tossed on them. Luckily, we had a grandmother who loved us. She not only opened her home to us, she raised us as if we were her own.

So the thought of Felecia betraying me hurts. That bitch cut me deep. I never wanted to think my own blood would snake me the way she has. Didn't want to believe the shit Mona used to tell me. That she was jealous of me. Still, I couldn't put my finger on it. However, there was always something that didn't sit well with me when it came to Felecia. Maybe it was the way I'd often catch her cutting her eyes at me on the sly. Or how she always brought up Jasper's name. Or the way she'd be looking at him before he got locked up, then after he was released. Or how I would always catch her whispering with Stax anytime he came by the salon. Something wasn't right. But my love for that conniving bitch blinded me. I slept on her ass. And instead of distancing myself from her like I should have, I ignored the nagging feeling in the pit of my soul.

And that shit cost me.

The night I was attacked in front of my house—after being out sucking dick, she was the only person I had to call, but something deep inside of me told me not to. I should have listened. But I didn't. I wanted, needed, to trust her. But, now thinking back, that bitch sat up in my kitchen consoling me and judging me at the same time. That bitch is the one who probably told Jasper about my attack. He *claimed* it was my old neighbor, Clint. But I never believed it. From what I'd seen of him, Clint seemed to stay to himself. He minded his own business. And, prior to the attack, he and I barely spoke when we'd see each other coming or leaving our homes. So, he'd have no reason to tell Jasper shit. Why would he? He and Jasper didn't know each other that I knew of. And he didn't know shit about me. That scheming-ass bitch, on the other hand, is a whole other story.

My cell rings bringing me out of my thoughts. I reach over into the passenger seat and fish it out of my bag, glancing at the screen. Speaking of that fucking bitch, it's her calling me now. I hit IGNORE.

I haven't spoken to her in almost two weeks. The day I reached over the receptionist's counter at the salon and tried to slap her face off, then told her to pack her shit and get the fuck out of my shop. She was fired.

Truth be told, I don't think I would have really fired Felecia had it not been for Booty, I mean Cassandra, coming down to the salon with her messy-ass putting Felecia on blast in front of everyone like she did. But she did. And I had to set that bitch straight and take it to her face. Then I told Booty, I mean Cassandra, that I thought it was best that she didn't bring her ass up in my shop again. She keeps too much shit going. I can tell I had hurt her feelings. *"Bitch, boom! You ain't said nothing but a word. I ain't ever gotta come back up in this trap."*

Sadly, drama or not, Cassandra has always been one of my most loyal customers. And I know in her crazy-ass head she was only trying to look out for me. But the drama with her is waaaaay too much for me. And the thing is, I really like Cassandra. She's probably as real as it gets. Sometimes, maybe a little too real, if that's even possible. Still, drama follows her wherever she goes. And, as far as I am concerned, her and Felecia going at in front of the clients was the last straw for me. The whole thing was unreal, but couldn't be overlooked.

"Oh, no, honey boo," Cassandra said to Felecia in front of everyone. "The only one 'bout to get tossed is you. I've been waitin' to do you, any-goddamn-way. So how 'bout you be a real bitch and tell Pasha how you told me Jasper whoops her ass and she's scared of him, huh, bitch? How 'bout you let her know how you done fucked him, too."

My eyes popped open in shock. Not that she had called Felecia out on it like that because she had already told me over the telephone a few weeks prior what Felecia had told her, so that was of no surprise to me. The shit that rattled my nerves was that she did it in front of all those nosey, gossiping-ass stylists of mine. She could have waited to confront Felecia when it was only the three of us around instead of in front of prying eyes. That shit was messy. But I knew her ass wasn't lying. Cassandra Simms might be called many things, but she's never been one for lying. If she says it happened, you can almost guarantee it did.

And even though Jasper and Felecia both denied fucking, I didn't believe one word from either of them, then. And I don't now. Jasper is a pathological liar and chronic cheater so nothing that comes out of his mouth is believable. Besides, I've caught him in enough lies when it comes to fucking other bitches to know not to believe shit he says when it comes to pussy, and other bitches. And Felecia, well, I can't trust shit that bitch says anymore; especially after finding out she'd been talking about me behind my back.

Like Cassandra had warned me a week or so prior to that incident down at the salon, "Pasha, boo. The only thing Miss FeFe is tryna have is your man, trust me. And if she don't want Jasper, you can trust and believe she damn sure wanna be up on his big-ass dingdong…that's how them messy bitches do it.…Fish that bitch…I ain't been tryna feature Miss FeFe every since she told me that shit about you. This bitch really thinks you mighta been out there suckin' all kinda dicks behind Jasper's back. I'm tellin' you, Miss Pasha, girl. That bitch is scandalous, boo..."

Well, I couldn't exactly confess to Cassandra that Felecia was right. That I *was* spinning a bunch of niggas' tops behind his back. Still, whether it was true or not, that bitch, Felecia, still had no goddamn business talking to Booty, I mean Cassandra, about it. No. The bitch should have come to me. We're the ones who were *supposed* to have been so close, like *sisters*.

I don't know why bitches stay thinking I'm some silly little bitch who won't handle or check them because I'm not one of them loud-mouth ghetto bitches always looking to get it in. Felecia, of all people, *should* know better. She *knows* how I *used* to be. How I'd fight bitches with no hesitation. How I sliced a bitch with a blade freshman year from ear to ear for talking shit. She *knows* the old me better than anyone else. That side of me I've tried to keep tucked away, hidden. That bitch with the quick temper and quick hands who'd fight *her* battles *and* mine. Before I grew the fuck up. Before I realized I had a whole lot more to lose than most of them dumb-ass hoes, including her two-faced ass. But trust and believe. That face slap was nothing compared to what she has coming to her. *When she least expects it!*

I should probably call to check in on Jaylen. I reach for my cell and decide to call Sophia, my live-in nanny, who also travels along with me—an older Brazilian woman who I hired a few months ago—to help me care for Jaylen. Sophia answers on the fourth ring in her thick Spanish accent. I let her know that I am on my way back to the condo. She tells me Jaylen's still asleep. That he woke up in the middle of the night looking for me. I ask her if she wants anything while I'm out. She says no. She asks if I want her to prepare breakfast for me. I thank her. Tell her no. A few moments more of conversation, I end the call.

Five

A bitch has to free herself of the present in order to let go of the past…

As I'm merging onto CA-110 North, my cell rings. I glance at the screen, ready to send it straight to voicemail if it's Felecia again, or Jasper. It's neither. It's Mona, Jasper's cousin and my closest friend. In fact, she's the reason I ended up with Jasper in the first place had she not introduced us.

Mmmph.

Twelve-and-a-half years ago. Time flies too damn fast, sometimes.

I'll never forget that night. Friday, October 6, 2000. She had been stressing me for weeks to go to some birthday party at a nightclub for one of her relatives. But I wasn't interested. She had this bright idea that while I was there, she'd introduce me to one of her male cousins who had recently moved to Jersey from Connecticut. "And he's your type," she had said.

"And what's my type, Miss Know It All?" I had asked.

She snickered. "Dark, chiseled, and hood…and you're exactly what he's lookin' for." Then she stated he specifically requested a *fine, fly bitch with a fat ass* who wanted something more out of life than running the streets.

Mona and I were cordial to one another in high school, but we never really hung out. She always seemed a little strange to me back then, like withdrawn. When she went MIA in the middle of the school year for like four months, then returned the following fall, the gossip was that she got put away for trying to kill herself. Mmmph. I never asked her about it. And I never cared to know. Not even after we ended up going to the same college and sharing a dorm room together. We clicked. Then over time became very good friends. So it didn't matter. It still doesn't.

Anyway, Mona knew I had a weakness for hood niggas with extra swag. And Jasper was it. But what she failed to mention is that the nigga was a chronic cheater and that I would have to slash tires, fight him, and beat up a bunch of his sidepiece-hoes almost every other month.

Big dick and all, Jasper was fucking trouble from the word *go*. And instead of cutting him off like I did with every other nigga I had been with, I kept fucking with him until his ass had me just as dick-dumb and dizzy as the rest of them bitches he'd been fucking. But the one thing I had that *none* of them other bitches ever got was his love. Get a hood nigga to fall for your ass, and see what you get. Borderline damn stalker, okay! Anyway, I knew I had his ass hooked, even if he was fucking other bitches. Those retarded-ass hoes were getting his hard dick, but I had his heart. At the time, that's all that really mattered to me. Now, if I could rewind the clock, I would have left his ass on that dance floor that night at the party and *never* looked back.

Oh well…

"Hey, girl," I say, taking the Fourth Street ramp toward Downtown L.A. "How's everything?"

"Pasha, girl, please tell me you're back from L.A.," she says, sounding distressed.

"I'm still out here, girl. I'll be home tomorrow around five, your time. Why, is everything okay?"

"N-no." Her voice cracks. "Some shit hit the fan Thursday and I think…no, I *know*, it's about to get real ugly. Ohgod, Pasha. I don't know what the fuck I've gotten myself into."

My heart jumps. "Ohmygod, Mona, what in the world are you talking about? What happened? Is everything okay with Mario?" Mario's her sixteen-year-old son who stays in some kind of trouble over these young hoes because he can't keep his dick in his pants. Like father, like son. And if he's anything like his father, I know he's slinging one big-ass dick. Not that I've fucked Avery, Mona's husband. But I have seen it before. And believe you me. It's one big, juicy sausage! Mmmph.

I guess you want to know how I know this. Well, um, let's say—without going into too many details—that he was prowling around up on Nastyfreaks4u looking for a little sidepiece head and sent an attachment of his hard dick to my Deep Throat Diva email. For some reason, his email stays stuck in the back of my memory.

Hey Deep Throat Diva, I'm 5'11 black 195lbs with a nice 8.5 thick, fat cock for your mouth and throat. Private, very discreet. Married with family here. Cool laidback guy…

Unfortunately, I didn't know it was *his* dick or that *he* was the man behind the email or screen name READY2NUTINU until I got to Mountainside Park, stepped out of my car and he rolled down the driver's side window of his tinted-out black SUV. Talk about shocked! My face cracked. And so did his.

I was fucking sick to my stomach. And to think of all the email exchanges, IM-ing and cyber-sexing he and I had done in the wee hours of the morning—with Jasper asleep in the other room; and probably the same for Mona. How he loved his wife, but was bored in bed with her. How he loved head, but his wife didn't like sucking dick. How, when she did, it was half-assed. How I called his wife whack for not keeping his dick wet. How I told him how

I couldn't wait to taste his fat dick, how I couldn't wait to make love to it with my mouth, lips, tongue and hands; how I loved to deep throat; how I was going to suck his dick in a way that his wife never had, never could, never would. How I was fantasizing about being on my knees and worshipping his cock and swallowing his creamy load.

I told Mona's husband all of this.

And, then…even after Avery realized it was me, the nigga still pulled his dick out and wanted, practically begged, me to wet it. And, yes, I got the shakes. And my mouth watered. I'm not going to lie. But I refused to go there. However, um, I did reach into his truck and stroke it a few good times, gripped that thick-ass sausage with its big fat cockhead with my paraffin-soft hands and jacked him off until my conscience got the best of me. Then I let it go, shaking.

As bad as I wanted to click on the whore-switch and hop in the passenger seat of his truck, lean into his lap and cock-wash the skin off that shit, I couldn't do it. Not after finding out whose husband he was. I couldn't do that to Mona. And I couldn't bring myself to do it to myself. I already felt guilty for doing what I was doing behind Jasper's back. I didn't need to add Mona to the list. No matter how messy I was being. And, yeah I know I was fucked up for even touching his dick. I should have spun on my heel and sped off in my car. But I didn't.

Sadly, every time I look at Mona, knowing she's a lazy dick sucker, I hear him saying, "She *half-sucks* my dick."

I wish I would have never gotten in my car that morning to sneak off to suck another nigga's dick when I should have listened to the nagging voice that was in my head warning me to leave well enough alone. But I didn't listen. I lied to Jasper, telling him

I was on my way to the gym. Then found myself face-to-face with my best friend's husband.

Now when I see Avery, which is rarely, there's an awkward tension between us. Every time I look at him, the only thing I see is his beautiful eight-and-a-half-inch dick. The only thing I'm sure he sees is what he almost had. These soft, pretty lips wrapped around his hard dick.

"Pasha, *that* I could deal with," Mona says, bringing my attention back to our phone conversation. "But this shit right here…" She pauses, pushing out a heavy breath. "This is some serious shit, Pasha." She sighs. "I think I've gotten myself into some shit way over my head."

"Mona, what in the world is going on? Tell me something. You're talking in riddles."

"I can't go into it over the phone. But the *minute* you get home we have got to talk—in person. First thing. And whatever you do, Pasha. You have to promise me that you'll keep this shit quiet. You can't repeat this to *anyone*."

"Mona, you know me better than that. I don't flap my gums like most bitches."

"I know. But after you hear what I have to tell you…"

"Mona! What the fuck is going on? You can't call me with this, then leave me hanging like this. You need to tell me something, girl. Does it have anything to do with Avery?"

"No, no; not at all. Avery does what he does, but you know I keep his ass on a short leash. I'll tell you when I see you—*every*-thing. Anyway, have you talked to Jasper?"

I frown. "Yeah, earlier but I hung up on his ass. Why, does this have something to do with him? If so, I'm not interested in hearing anything about him caught up with some other bitch."

"Girl, no worries. You know I stopped calling you about dumb shit like that years ago. This is on some other shit—more *serious* shit. But, like I said, we can't have this conversation over the phone. The minute you get home, you *have* to call me."

"I will. But I don't know how you expect me to go another day and not know what the hell is going on. What can be so bad that you can't tell me over the phone? You said it's not about any of Jasper's bitches. And, obviously his ass isn't locked up since I spoke to him earlier. Is it about Stax or your brother Sparks?"

"No. Stax and Sparks are fine, girl. No one's locked up. *Yet*, anyway."

I catch the yet part, knowingly. All them niggas riding Jasper's nut sac are caught up in the game one way or another. His whole street team is mostly the niggas in his family. It's like them niggas were all born into it. And it's only a matter of time before someone gets knocked, again. I wonder if Stax would take the weight for Jasper's ass if they got popped. I hope he wouldn't. But I don't ever see him snitching either. Then again, who knows what a nigga looking at football numbers will do.

Anyway, Stax is another one of Jasper's cousins. He's also Jasper's right-hand man. You see one; you're bound to see the other, partners in crime. They say birds of a feather flock together. But, unlike Jasper's messy, cheating-ass, I've never heard Stax getting caught up in any female drama, even when he was with his baby's mother, Mariah. If Stax is out there doing dirt, you'd never know it. Obviously, he knows how to move. Something Jasper's sloppy-ass needs to do better at. Jasper would fuck a bitch right up in our bed—if he hasn't already—then try to lie his way out of it once he got caught pulling his dick out of her.

But, whatever! Back to Stax. Although I've never looked at his chiseled six-foot-six, fine, milk-chocolate-ass sexually, there's some-thing about the way he looks at me with those beautiful sparkling brown eyes of his that unnerves me.

I've never been one to get caught up in gossip. However, word among the nut-hungry hoes is that he has a big-ass dick and a set of big, juicy, plum-size balls hanging real low with it. And, shame-fully, over the years of knowing Stax, I've occasionally had to fight myself to keep from sneaking peeks at his crotch, especially when he wears sweats. And, well, the few times I've slipped, I always caught a glimpse of a thick, long lump in his pants. So I believe the rumors are true.

But that's neither here nor there, since I don't want him. Every time I see him, knowing that he's Jasper's right-hand nigga, I can't stop thinking, wondering, if somehow he was one of the niggas who was down in the basement with me, shoving his dick down in my throat. Although none of them that I can recall had his gym-ripped body, or a tattoo of their daughter on their forearm. Still, I wonder.

And the fact that Stax does his best to avoid me, and only comes around me when he's with Japser, makes him suspect. Makes me wonder how much of what went down with my kidnapping he played a hand in. I know he knows all about the dick-sucking rampage I was on. Jasper tells him everything.

Still, regardless of what he knows or whether or not he was down in that basement, he's never treated me indifferently or looked at me with disgust in his eyes. Nevertheless, I search my brain, re-playing the horrible scenes in my head over and over, trying to see if any of those eyes peering through the slits of those black ski masks belonged to him.

I always come up blank.

Six

The way to perdition requires traveling a long, dirty, ruthless road...

"Yo, Pasha, real shit," Jasper says, grabbing me by the arm as I'm walking out of Jaylen's bedroom. I've finished giving him his bath and finally gotten him to fall asleep. And now all I want to do is get out of these clothes, get in the shower, then crawl into my plush bed. My flight out of LAX was delayed due to heavy rains and air traffic congestion, or some shit. So we ended up landing in Newark almost four hours behind schedule. I'm exhausted and want to be left the hell alone. But, noooo, this nigga has other plans. He wants to be all up in my damn face, reeking of alcohol and weed.

Stay focused. Stay on script. His day is coming.

I snatch my arm back. "Why don't you take your drunk ass back downstairs with your company, and get out of my face? I'm not in the mood for your shit tonight, Jasper. I'm fucking tired." I brush by him, heading toward the master suite. Of course the nigga's hot on my heels.

I've been home less than two hours and he's been on his bullshit from the moment I stepped through the door. The minute I drove through the electronic gates and pulled around the circular drive-way and saw his car along with Stax's and three other niggas' cars,

I braced myself, knowing this nigga was going to be turned all the way up.

And he is.

"Yo, fuck them niggas. They know what it is. I ain't seen my muhfuckin' wife 'n' son in almost a week. I missed my family, yo."

I roll my eyes. "Yeah, right. And how many other bitches did you fuck while your so-called *family* was gone?" I ask, not that I give a fuck. Because truth is, this nigga can stick his dick in whatever lonely hole he wants. Shit, that's what his ass was doing any-damn-way throughout most of our relationship when I did care. So the only thing that's changed now is me not giving a fuck. Shit, I welcome another bitch to take his ass. I'll gladly help her pack his shit.

He huffs. "Aye, yo. Here you got wit' ya bullshit, Pash. Fuck them other hoes, yo." He grabs the bulge in the front of his sweats. "You already know what it is. This dick is all yours."

I roll my eyes, walking into our bedroom with him hot on my trail. He follows me into the master bathroom. "You stay talkin' slick at the mouth, yo. I'm tryna keep shit a hunnid wit' you 'n' you wanna be on some ole other shit, yo. Seems like you ain't satisfied until I'm puttin' my fist in ya jaw. What you want, Pasha, huh? Me to have that shit wired for you, is that it, yo? You want a muhfucka to put his hands on you, don't you?"

I glare at him.

This nigga drains me, emotionally. Looking at him disgusts me. Staying with him after what he did to me is one thing. Sometimes it's like I'm having an out of body experience, like I'm aimlessly floating in time watching my life roll in slow motion. The sound-track of lies and deceit and resentment plays over and over in my head. *I* did this to me. *He* did this to me. But the fact that I still married his ass screams crazy. And the truth is, I *am* fucking crazy!

Crazed for vengeance.

Crazed for his suffering.

Crazed with wanting to know who every last one of those niggas were he had violate me. It's all I think about. It's all I ever pray for.

Answers.

Retribution.

Opportunity.

Yet, nothing seems to come. Jasper refuses to tell me how he found out, or who told him, about what I was doing. The last time I asked him who told him, he told me not to worry about it. That it didn't matter. "All you need to know is that I have eyes 'n' ears e'erywhere, yo. I'm watchin' you even when you think I ain't, Pasha. So you ain't ever gonna be slicker than me, yo. I love you, baby, real shit. But you fucked me over. And you hurt my heart, yo. But check this. I promise you, if you *ever* play me again, I'ma cut ya muthafuckin' pussy out 'n' fuck ya pretty face up, baby, 'n' make sure no one else ever wants to fuck wit' yo' ass again. Ya heard? Real shit. Let me find out you got another nigga's dick in ya throat 'n' it'll be da last dick you swallow. I'ma break e'ery muthafuckin' bone in ya face, then have ya fuckin' neck cut out."

I blinked. Tears rolled down my face as this nigga leaned in and stared me dead in the eyes and told me this shit. "Now stop all this cryin', yo. Shit's over." He started kissin' my tears. Then gave me another icy stare. "And, Pash, if you open ya muthafuckin' mouth 'n' tell anyone 'bout this shit," he rubbed my pregnant belly, "I'ma get at da ones you love da most, yo; startin' wit' Nana. Then anyone else." He kissed my stomach. "I'll take e'erything from you. Cheat on me again, yo."

I gasped, grabbing my stomach. My heart sank. The idle warning to harm my baby was there. The threat to hurt Nana was real. He knew how much Nana meant to me. How much she still means to me. And as bad as I didn't want to believe him, there was something in the way he said it and in the way that he looked at me that made me believe his every word. Besides, after what he had done to me, why would I not take him seriously?

"Fuck wit' me if you want, Pash. And you gonna learn." He sealed it with a kiss on my lips, then said, "Now get some rest."

Rest? How the fuck was I supposed to rest after he made those kinds of threats? Would he kill my baby? Nana? Would he beat my baby out of me? Would he beat Nana the way he'd beaten me?

I couldn't risk either.

Jasper knows I'd never call the police on him. Snitching isn't what we do. But sometimes I wish I had told the detectives what happened to me. That *he* had me kidnapped. That *he* orchestrated having me sexually violated. *He* did that shit to me. Maybe his black ass would be behind bars, rotting.

But that wouldn't do shit for me. I still wouldn't know what I needed, wanted, to know.

Truth is, ratting on his ass and seeing him go to prison would have been too easy. I want this nigga to pay, my way…on *my* terms. And he will. Not tonight though.

"Oh, so you gonna fuckin' ig a muhfucka now, right?"

I push out a heavy, aggravated breath. "Jasper, do whatever you feel; how's that for an answer?"

I turn my back on him. Start humming in my head, turning on the double showerheads in the glass-encased shower. I feel Jasper staring at me, hard, as I go about pretending he's invisible. I'm not arguing with this nigga, especially not when he's been drinking. My son is not going to be subjected to his craziness. Not tonight.

He yanks me by the arm, pressing me up against the wall. My

heart starts racing. He grabs at my belt buckle. "Take these mutha-fuckin' pants off, yo. I know you been fuckin' some other nigga while ya ass was out there in Cali, yo."

The crazed look in his eyes tells me he is not going to get out of my face anytime soon unless I give into him.

"Nigga, you're crazy. You know that, right?"

"Yeah, yo. I'm crazy for yo' dumb ass. You got my dick crazy for this pussy. Now take these muthafuckin' shits off." He yanks at my belt. "What you want, yo. A muhfucka to take this shit, huh?"

"So you're going to rape me, is that it, nigga?"

He scowls. "Go 'head wit' that dumb shit, yo. What da fuck I look like, rapin' my own wife? Fuck outta here. I'ma take what's mine. This pussy's mine, yo. Don't get it fucked up."

I give him a disgusted look. "What, you wanna smell my pussy? Is that it, Jasper? You wanna sniff to see if another nigga's dick has been in me?"

His jaw tightens. He gives me a look that says he'll snap my neck right now. "I'm tellin' you, Pasha. Don't fuck wit' me, yo. Fuck another nigga, and see what I'ma do to you." He presses himself into me. His thick dick is hard. I attempt to push him off of me. But he's pressed to fuck. I tell him no. Tell him to get off of me. But he's not hearing it.

"Yo, fuck outta here. You haven't given me this pussy in weeks. We fuckin', yo. Tonight. Right now. Ya heard?" He shoves a hand between my thighs and starts massaging my crotch over my jeans. The friction causes an unexpected jolt to shoot through my clit. Electricity heats my pussy. "I'm puttin' my dick up in this shit, yo. This my shit. Tell me this pussy ain't wet for this hard dick." He grinds himself deeper into me, his dick pressing against my inner thigh.

I roll my eyes up in my head, reminding myself to stay on script.

To keep playing my position until it's the right time to strike. Jasper starts kissing on my neck, nibbling on my ear. My body starts to heat.

But fucking this nigga clouds my judgment. It blurs my perspective. I push him back. He stumbles a bit. I storm out of the bathroom with my jeans undone, trying to distance myself from him, trying to exhaust the flames slowly burning inside of me.

"You my muthafuckin' wife, yo." He snatches my arm again, swinging me around to face him. The nigga's switch flips. The veins in his neck swell, and I can literally see them pulsing. "Pasha, I done tol' you I own dis shit, ya heard? Don't have me punch ya muthafuckin' lights out, Pasha. What you want, a muhfucka to beg? Is that it?"

He pushes me back on the bed, gets on top of me, pinning me down with his weight. I don't put up a fight. Again, I let him think he's won. He holds both of my wrists up over my head with one hand, then uses his other hand to rip open my blouse. Yes, I know I could scream. I can also fight this nigga off of me—if I really wanted to. But I don't. And I won't. Jasper knows this. But what he doesn't know is, it's all an act. I want him to keep thinking I'm still helpless and weak. He'll learn soon enough. They'll all learn.

Besides, knowing his goons are here, the last thing I want is for this nigga to flip and decide he wants to invite them all in up here, pinning me down and each of them taking turns running up inside of me. I don't trust any of them niggas he has up in here. Well, maybe Stax. But I can't be so sure about his ass, either.

"Ya muhfuckin' ass been holdin' out on dis good shit for weeks and a nigga been lettin' you get that off, yo. I'ma fuck the shit outta this pussy tonight, yo. I know you been fuckin' some other nigga, yo. Keep shit a hunnid, yo." He glares at me. His nose flares. "Who da fuck was you out there fuckin', yo? And *don't* lie to me, Pasha."

I don't blink. Don't flinch. "Nigga, you're crazy."

He grabs me by the throat. "Tell me who da fuck you been fuckin', yo. Is it one of them Internet muhfuckas, huh? Let me find out ya ass still fuckin' wit' dat online shit, Pash, 'n' I'ma bust yo' ass. Is you back on ya bullshit, yo?" He starts shaking and choking me. I'm gasping. My eyes start bulging. "Answer me, yo?"

This is the shit I have to go through. What *I've* allowed myself to go through—Jasper's erratic bouts of rage and jealousy, his obsessive need to control me.

He doesn't respect me. Doesn't trust me. How could he? After all the dick sucking I'd done behind his back.

Still, I don't respect his ass, either.

Yet…here I am. No trust, and no real love for this nigga.

Deception is the one thing I've mastered. Pretending. Smiling at the right time. Saying the right things. Lying by omission. Telling this crazy nigga whatever it is he wants to hear. Knowing when to give the illusion of defeat for a greater good. I've learned this shit—all of it—from this dirty nigga.

He loosens his grip on my neck, and the lie pushes its way out. "N-nooo."

He glowers at me. Searches my eyes for any hint of deceit. There is none. Still, I can tell he's scrambling to believe me. Fighting to trust I've learned my lesson. His nose flares. He doesn't.

"Take these muthafuckin' drawers off, yo."

I stare at him, narrowing my eyes to tiny slits. I lift my hips and pull my jeans down over them. He yanks my pants off, angrily throwing them across the room. "Real shit, you gonna have me fuck you up, Pasha."

I blink back tears.

Tears of hurt.

Tears of guilt.

Tears of frustration.

Tears of blame.

Yes, I blame myself for this crazy-ass mess I'm in. I had no business being on an Internet site posting sex ads up. I knew it then. And I know it now. Cheating is cheating no matter the extent, no matter how I tried to justify it or redefine it. At the end of the day, *I* did this shit. And I got caught. All Jasper did is find out. Then fuck me over in more ways imaginable.

And this is my hell.

Nevertheless, I still can't wrap my mind around what kind of monster this nigga really is? That's the question I've been asking myself over and over. I struggle for the answer.

So far, there is none.

"I'll fuckin' kill you and my muthafuckin' seed you carryin', yo, if you even think about leavin' me..."

"It's over wit', baby...all that shit you was doin'..." he paused, let his words hover over me, then reached for my hand and kissed it. "The only way you gettin' away from me is in a body bag, Pasha; real shit."

So what was I supposed to do?

I went down the aisle with this nigga, that's what *I* chose to do. Still said, "I do." Yes, I already know. Only a crazy, sick bitch would go through with marrying a nigga like this. And what scares me the most is, I'm realizing that I'm no different from him. We're both fucked up. And, *maybe*...we deserve each other. *Maybe* staying with Jasper is my punishment for my own sins.

I spread my thighs, inviting the devil inside.

Seven

Good dick isn't always attached to a good nigga.
A smart bitch knows the difference...

I pull my pussy lips open for him. Jasper forces my legs open wider, presses his face into my crotch and sniffs. My pulse quickens. A knot forms in the back of my throat as he slides his middle finger into his mouth, then pushes it into my pussy.

I grunt, mindful to clench my pussy muscles.

His finger pumps in and out of me. Against my will a moan slips out. He's stirring my pussy. My mind is screaming one thing. But my body is crying out something else.

I shut my eyes. Try to imagine Thick Seven's fingers inside of me instead. "You mine, yo. This shit belongs to me."

I feel the weight of his body shift as he goes down my body. His thick fingers digging into my hips as he buries his face between my thighs. His lips find my clit.

Oh, God, no! Mmmm...

I try to fight the sensation. But it is becoming too overwhelming. I spread my legs wider. In my head, I'm over this nigga. But my body...right at this very moment...has a mind of its own. It is still connected to him. Jasper's fingers light a slow building fire. My anger toward this nigga is the accelerant that causes wet flames to shoot through. "Aaah. Uhhhh..."

"This is my pretty pussy, yo," Jasper says, breathlessly against my pussy lips as he licks them. I don't want this. Not from him. But the feeling...oh God...it's overpowering me, clouding my judgment. He parts my slick lips, licking the center of my pussy, then sucks on my clit.

Nasty motherfucker!

I hate this nigga!

I know this is about Jasper's need to feel as if he still has power over me. Truth is, he does; only because *I* let him. But not for long I keep reminding myself.

I let out another moan as he buries his face deeper, his tongue slinking further into my wetness. Inside, the fearless me is smirking, hoping Jasper can taste the lingering remnants of Thick Seven's nut. But the cautious me, prays he doesn't. I hold my breath, hoping he can't detect another nigga's scent on me—or in me, knowing all too well the feeling of his wrath if he does.

Still, I live on the edge.

Bitch, you keep playing with fire! Your ass is going to get burned!

I'm so fucked up in my head, in my thinking. Jasper's done this to me. Has me confused. I've done this to me. I hate him for making me feel like this. I hate myself for feeling like this. Torn and confused and angry and turned on.

I groan.

He continues exploring my pussy with his fingers and tongue, searching for what's been left on the sheets back in Santa Monica, and long rinsed out in L.A. There are no signs of my indiscretion still lingering.

He lifts my hips up, then places my legs over his broad shoulders, pressing the head of his swollen dick up against my slit. He grinds himself into me, his thick veiny dick sliding up and down between my lips, coating his shaft with pussy juices oozing out of me.

I moan.

Against my will, another wave of heat sweeps through me. I want him to hurry up and fuck me. I want him to fuck me fast and deep and hard and dirty so he can be done with it. I want him to fuck me like the dirty bitch he thinks I am. Like the dirty bitch I've been. Then I can wash him *and* my guilt off of me. But this nigga wants to take his slow sweet time. I remind him that he has company downstairs. Remind him of the running shower.

He grunts. "Yo, fuck them niggas. Fuck that water. Let the shit run, yo. You mine, Pasha. I tol' you, ain't shit changed. But you stay wantin' to be on ya bullshit. All you gotta do is act right, baby. And shit's gonna be aiight. All that slick shit you be poppin', it's deaded, yo...."

Think what you want, nigga. Ain't shit over with!

"We gonna die in this shit, yo. So whatever lil beefs you got goin' on in ya pretty lil head, let that shit go, baby. It's you and me, ya heard?"

I blink.

He doesn't wait for me to say anything. There's not shit for me to say. He plunges his dick in me—deep, so very deep and hard. I gasp. Surprised at how wet I am.

"Yeah, this wet-ass pussy," he says as he starts stroking my insides. "This good-ass pussy, yo." He grunts, thrusting deeper inside of me. Before long, I'm grabbing his muscular ass, digging my nails in and pulling him further into me.

I can't lie. The dick is pounding into my wall of resistance.

I hate this nigga!

Hate this dick for being so damn good!

Oh, God, yes...

"Don't have me kill no one over this shit, yo."

He stretches me with his thickness, knocks the bottom of my

pussy with his length. His nine-inch dick is so much bigger than Thick Seven's. It's not better, just bigger. And heavier.

Oooh…

Oh God!

Jasper rapidly pounds and grinds into me, then slows his pace, churning my insides with each stroke. This nigga has my head spinning, has my insides spurting juices, like an erupting volcano, violent and angry. I can pretend with everything else. But not this. My wet pussy defies what's in my heart. The lusty moans, bordering on growls, seeping out from the back of my throat, disregard what's in my head.

This is what I struggle with. This is what I fight to avoid. As long as I don't let him put his dick in me, I'm good. I'm focused. As long as I deny him this pussy, I can stick to the script. But the minute I let him in, allow him to force himself in, the second his dick pushes past my resistance, I'm done. I become weak all over again. The devil keeps fucking me over and over. And I keep bending over and letting him.

Because the dick is so good!

Ooooh, yes…uhhh…

I hate this fucking nigga! I repeat in my head. *Hate this good-ass dick!* I want this shit over with.

I clutch his dick with my pussy, milk him, and start talking real nasty hoping it will speed things up. Talking a bunch of shit usually helps Jasper nut faster.

"Ohhh, God, yessss! Fuck my pussy, nigga…uhhh…Yeah, nigga…mmmph…oooh, yes…give it to me. Fuck me deep, daddy…"

"Yeah, yo…that's what the fuck I'm talkin' 'bout. Talk that nasty shit, yo…you like it when I beat them insides up, don't you? You love daddy's big dick. Yeah, give ya daddy that pussy…"

"Yesssss…ooooh, fuck me…mmmm…"

He quickly pulls out, flipping me over onto my stomach, then smacking my ass, causing it to jiggle and sting. My pussy starts to pop. "Get on your muthafuckin' knees, yo. You got this dick harder than a muhfucka, yo."

There was a time I loved everything this nigga stood for. Loved his roughness. Loved his hood swag. Loved every thuggish, aggressive bone in his buffed, dark-chocolate body. So much has changed between us.

He's reckless.

I'm reckless.

He can't be trusted.

I can't be trusted.

I hate him for doing this to me.

I'm sure he hates me for doing the same to him.

We are both trapped in our own craziness.

For now, I remind myself.

I lift up on all fours, give the nigga what he wants as he man-handles me. He rams his dick in, yanking my head back. "Yeah, you like it when a muhfucka beats this shit, huh? You like this big-ass dick guttin' ya ass up, don't you, yo? Wet-ass, muthafuckin' pussy." He slaps my ass.

I fight back a scream, bucking my ass back on his dick. I am coming. My orgasm fueled by hate and lust.

My pussy is clutching and milking his horny dick. "Aaaah, shit, yo…yeah fuck…I'm 'bout to spit this nut…uhh, yeah. Throw that hot-ass pussy up on this dick…fuckin' bitch…gotta muhfucka beggin' for this good shit…"

He slaps my ass again. Left cheek, then right cheek; each strike, louder and harder than the one before—his big hand heating my

ass, causes my pussy to get wetter. A moan is lodged in the back
of my throat. I am pushing against the waves rising and splashing
around inside of me. I am about to scream out, glancing over my
shoulder. And then...

"Awww, shit, damn," I hear in back of us. "My bad, yo."

I jump, trying to cover myself while my ass is still up in the air.
Jasper looks over toward the open door, seemingly unfazed, his
dick still pounding away. It's Stax! And he's standing in the doorway. He shifts his stare from me to Jasper. The look in his eyes
telling me he's seen more than he should have. Jasper doesn't
jump. Doesn't even attempt to stop fucking me.

"Yo, what the fuck?! Don't you see me gettin' it in wit' my wife,
yo? I'll be finished in a sec. Goddamn, muhfucka!"

"Yo, word is bond, fam. No disrespect. But we gotta situation
on our hands that can't wait." Stax glances over at me, then back
at Jasper. Jasper sucks his teeth, pulling his wet, sticky dick out of
me, then climbing out of the bed.

I quickly snatch the throw from off the bed and cover myself,
trying to avoid Stax as he quickly shifts his eyes from me as I race
for the bathroom. JT's another one of his cousins and dirty nigga
on his team. I shut the door, pressing my ear up against it.

"Perfect timin', muhfucka," I hear Jasper say. "I'm in here tryna
get some pussy, nigga, 'n' you come up in here 'n' fuck that all up."

"Yo, nigga, chill. You know I wouldn't be up in ya space wit' no
bullshit, yo. Besides, muhfucka, you shoulda had the door closed.
Buh, uh, check it. Something's popped off wit' Jaheem, yo. His
wife been blowin' up my shit, stressin' like crazy. Said she ain't
seen or heard from that nigga in almost a week, yo. And da nigga's
voicemail is full."

"Yo, what da fuck you mean sumthin' done popped off wit' JT?
When's the last time you talked to that nigga?"

"Just what I said, fam. That nigga's missin', yo. I haven't talked to his ass since last Wednesday. You know how that nigga stay missin' in action, feel me?"

"Yeah, true. Muhfucka prolly somewhere knee-deep in some bitch; still that muhfucka usually answers his shit."

"Yeah, true shit. But he ain't been answering his shit in like four days. And his wife can't track his shit 'cause he only fuck wit' them pre-paid joints."

Mmmph. Jaheem and Jasper, although they're first cousins, can actually pass for brothers. Their resemblance, their body builds, is uncanny. I don't know who's worse, him or Jasper. They both cheat. They both lie. They both put their hands on their women. And they're both dirty motherfuckers caught up in the drug game.

"Shit, this nigga. I hope his dumb ass ain't caught up in no dumb shit, yo. I keep tellin' that muhfucka to stop fuckin' 'round wit' all these crazy-ass bitches." I hear moving around the room. He's probably putting his clothes back on, I think. I frown at the thought of him stuffing his wet, sticky dick back into his boxers. There was a time when I would have eagerly sucked it clean for him. *Nasty nigga!*

I quickly hop in the shower in case he decides to use the bathroom. Luckily, right on time too.

"Yo, Pash," he calls out, swinging the bathroom door open. "I'm out, yo. I'll be back later tonight to finish bustin' that ass. Make sure you take ya ass to bed 'n' get some rest 'cause you gonna need it, yo."

I roll my eyes, turning my back to him.

Nigga, please! Tonight *is the last night you run your dick up in me.*

Eight

A two-faced bitch will never see the error of her ways
'til you knock her sockets out.

"Good morning, Nappy No More. Pasha speaking." No one says anything. "Hello?" I glance at the caller ID. It comes up UNKNOWN NUMBER. "Hello? Nappy No More, how can I help you?"

There's still no response. I hang up, eyeing the crystal clock up on the wall. It's 8:01 A.M. My first appointment is scheduled for 8:15. I flip through the schedule book and see that I'm booked back-to-back up until four o'clock. I smile when I see my ten o'clock is with my cousin Persia, an identical triplet. I haven't seen her or her sisters since my wedding over the summer. I've spoken to Paris a few times since she and I have always been the closest out of the three of them. And I ran into Porsha and her fiancé, Emerson, a few weeks ago at the mall. So it'll be nice to see Persia and get caught up with her.

Last I heard, through Felecia's gossiping ass, that she and her sisters had pretty much stopped sharing—or should I say, *fucking*—the same men. For awhile the three of them scandalous divas had been the talk of the family with their man-swapping shenanigans.

My ringing cell pulls me from my thoughts. *Shit*, I think, when I see that it's Mona calling. *I forgot to call her last night.* "Hey, girl."

"Ummm, why didn't you call me yesterday? I told you to call me the minute you got back in town." I apologize. Tell her I got in later than I planned. That I honestly got sidetracked with Jasper literally riding my ass and nerves from the time I stepped through the door. I let her know I'm down at the salon and that I have a break in between my appointments at one if she wants to talk then. "Okay, good. But we need to talk somewhere private."

"I can't leave the shop. So how about we just meet here after the shop closes, when everyone's gone? Looks like the last appointment scheduled today is at seven. So come through around nine. Everyone should be gone by then."

"Okay. See you then."

"Oh, wait," I quickly say before she hangs up. "Have you heard about JT? I overheard Stax telling Jasper last night that no one's seen or heard from him since last week."

Silence.

"Hello? Mona?"

"Pasha,"—her voice cracks—"I gotta get off this line. I'll talk to you tonight."

"Oh, okay I'll—"

The line goes dead.

Mmmph. That's strange. I shrug it off. "Oh well," I say, picking up the salon's phone on the third ring. "Good morning, Nappy No More. This is Pasha speaking."

"Pasha," the voice on the other end says, sounding depressed and pitiful. I roll my eyes, staring down at the caller ID. It's Felecia. She's calling from a number I'm not familiar with. "Pasha, the least you could do is accept my calls. I can't believe you'd believe some ghetto-trash bitch over *me*. That's so fucked up. You're my flesh and blood."

I frown. "Bitch, you must be on that shit, or have you forgotten that it was *flesh* and *blood* that fucking kicked my back in. So, ho, please. Save that shit for the next bitch. Now what do you want, Felecia?"

"We need to talk."

"Really? You think?"

"Yes. About you firing *me*. About you letting Cassandra's messy-ass come between us. You know that bitch loves to keep drama going. I would never kick your back in the way that lying bitch says I did."

I laugh sarcastically. "Oh, please. Save it. Cassandra's messy. But she has never been one to *lie* or make up shit on anyone. She knew a whole lot more than she should have known and it's shit that she could have only gotten from you."

"But how you gonna think *I'm* the one who told her that shit? Anyone who worked at the salon could have told her all that shit. And you know it. It coulda been Shuwanda or Alicia for all you know. Them bitches stayed talking about you behind your back."

"Bitch, lies. It was you. Admit it."

"Pasha, you're going to think what you want no matter what I say, so go ahead and think it. All I want to know is, why you denied my unemployment?"

"Excuse you? *You* talk shit about *me* behind my fucking back—at, and outside of, the salon, then *think* I'm going to sponsor you sitting home on your ass at my expense. Bitch, suck a dick! I don't think so! I financed you long enough. So yeah, I shut your claim down. Appeal the shit."

"I thought we were better than this, Pasha."

"Really? Is that what you thought? *Before* or *after* you told Cassandra that Jasper beats my ass? Or was it before you told her that I was probably out sucking a bunch of niggas' dicks. That is what *you* said to her, isn't it?"

"But you haven't even given me a chance to explain my—"

I go off, shutting her ass down. "Whore, you can't explain shit to me, you fucking trifling-ass backstabbing bitch. If you had been a loyal bitch from the rip, we wouldn't be having this conversation. Your messy ass would still be here working and we'd still be family. But, nooooo. You out and about running your motherfucking mouth, putting my business out in the streets, then grinning all up in my motherfucking face. So fuck you. I'm going to keep fighting your unemployment claim. Let Andre sponsor your ass, bitch."

"That's fucked up, Pasha."

"No, hun. You being a backstabbing bitch is what's fucked up. Now, if you don't mind, I have work to do. Don't call my numbers again, Felecia. And if you even think about showing your two-faced ass anywhere near my salon, I'm going to beat the skin off your face." I hang up on her ass just as my first appointment walks through the door.

I can already tell it's going to be one long-ass day.

Nine

The past is who I was. The present is who I've never wanted to be…

At five minutes to ten, Persia saunters through the door with a delicious-looking mocha-colored man with spinning waves in tow. I blink. They're holding hands. But what really makes my knees buckle is when I see this fine specimen of a man lean in and kiss her on the lips before taking a seat in one of the leather chairs out in the waiting area.

In all the years I've known Persia, she's never been one to show any kind of public display of affection with anyone other than her sisters. And even that is a rarity. Persia has always come off as emotionless. Detached. So seeing her waltzing in smiling and holding the hand of a man definitely takes me by surprise. Then, again, it's been years since I've seen her with a man; let alone one of her own.

"Hey, Cuz," I say, smiling and opening my arms as she makes her way toward me. We embrace, faces pressed cheek to cheek, tossing air kisses. I step back, taking her in. She's wearing a pair of Roberto Cavalli jeans, a cute white form-fitting blouse and a pair of gray Gucci animalier heels. Her plush hobo bag is hanging in the crook of her arm. "You look fabulous."

"Thanks. So do you. Hell, you always look good, girl. And them diamond boulders you have in your ears are gorgeous. All that bling can blind a blind man, girl." She takes a seat in my chair, placing her bag up in her lap.

"It's about time you got in here to let me handle this hair, girl," I say, as I snap the cape around her neck, purposefully not acknowledging the four-carat diamond studs she's referring to. They're one of Jasper's most recent guilt gifts after I told him to pack his shit and be out of my house by the time I got home from the salon the day Booty made her public announcement that he and Felecia fucked.

"Girl, I know. It's been a long while since I've been here." I ask her what she wants done. Her dark brown hair hangs past her shoulders. She tells me she wants a change; that she's ready for a new look. "Give it to me short and sassy, girl. I want it all cut off."

"Say what? Are you serious, girl?" I run my hands through her luxurious hair, massaging her scalp. "You know I've been dying to lay this hair out."

She chuckles. "Well, today's your lucky day. I'm looking for a change."

I lean in and whisper, "Would this change have anything to do with that fine man sitting out there in the waiting area?"

She grins. "Wellll, uh, I'm not going to say he has *every*thing to do with it. But he definitely plays a part in it."

"Good for you, cuz. It's about time you settled down." *And got yourself a man of your own.* "I'm happy for you."

"Thanks. Pasha, I'm telling you. If someone would have told me two years ago that I would be involved with a man eleven years younger than me, I would have laughed in their face." I ask her how old he is. "He'll be twenty-five in three months."

I turn her chair around facing the mirrors. "And what's his name? And when am I going to be officially introduced to him?"

"His name is Royce." She pulls her phone out of her bag and sends him a text to come to the back. A few minutes later, I see him as he walks toward my station. All eyes are on his tall, lean frame. He's dressed in a pair of loose-fitting designer jeans that hang slightly off his narrow waist, but not enough to show his underwear. A Gucci belt keeps them from falling around his knees. "Baby, I want you to meet my cousin, Pasha. Pasha, this is my boo, Royce."

The shit the three of them had going on in the sheets is all too messy and confusing to keep up with. I'm sure she thinks I don't know that she and her sisters fucked him together. Or that the three of them had been fucking Porsha's fiancé for months until he decided he no longer wanted to dick the three of them down because he'd caught feelings for Porsha, and wanted to spend his time exclusively with her. Felecia told me about their sexapade with Royce. But it was Jasper who told me about them fucking Porsha's man, too—news he'd gotten from Desmond whom Paris had shared the information with. I tell you niggas gossip worse than bitches.

Royce extends his hand. I glance at his long slender fingers, then into his almond-shaped eyes. "Nice to meet you," he says, revealing straight white teeth as he smiles. There's a hint of a Caribbean accent in his tone.

"Likewise," I say to him. "You must be one special kind of man to keep my cousin's attention."

Persia waves me on. "Girl, please. Not a word. This man has my undivided attention, trust. Baby, why don't you come back and pick me up in like an hour. I don't want any of them young hoes sitting out in that waiting area trying to entice you."

He laughs. "You know I only got eyes for you, baby." He leans over and kisses her on the lips, making it clear to every bitch in the room that he's off-limits. I grin.

Persia's face lights up. "Good answer. I'll see you when you get back." We all watch as he swaggers out. The whole back area is quiet until he walks out the door.

Then it's on. They all go in...

"Giiiiiirl, he's fine as hell," one customer sitting in my stylist Kendra's chair says. Kendra was hired a few weeks after I fired Alicia's ass. Alicia could do the hell out of some hair. But, after her man, Chauncey, coming up in here and beating her ass down in my office, she had to go. He beat her ass so bad I thought he was going to kill her. She got carried up out of here on a stretcher and his ass got hauled off in handcuffs. That whole scene was out of control.

"Oooh, yes lawd," another one chimes in. "No harm, girl, but he looks like he beats it up in the bedroom."

Persia lips slip into a sly grin. "Not a word. A woman never kisses and tells."

"Mmmmph. Girl, you don't have to say a thing. I saw how he was walking. I can spot a little-dick nigga a mile away. And there ain't nothing little about him."

"How old did you say he was?" someone else asks.

"He'll be twenty-five."

"And how old are you?" another client wants to know.

"Thirty-six."

"Girl, do you," Rhodeshia, another one of my newest stylists, says, butting into the conversation like she always does. I don't know why bitches feel the need to always be in the middle of someone else's business. "Ain't nothing like getting it in with a young stud. I'm twenty-six and I like all of my boyfriends under twenty-one. My baby's father's ass is nineteen. Well, he was seventeen when we first got together. I thought he was a lil older though.

But, mmmph. The nigga rocked in them sheets like he was a grown-ass man. I love 'em young."

I blink. I had no clue this bitch was a cradle robber. Then again, why should I be surprised?

"Oooh, girl," the client in her chair says, waving her hand in the air. "I can't with you. Your ass tryna do a bid."

A few people laugh. I shake my head. I hired Rhodeshia about a week after I fired Shuwanda's grimy-ass. That's another two-faced bitch I'd like to stomp a hole in if I thought I could get away with it. She was right along with Felecia talking shit about me behind my back. But how she fucked up is, she was running her mouth to a few of her clients. Problem is, she didn't think any of them would ever come back and tell me the shit the bitch used to say.

"Girl, you ain't heard this from me," one of her clients said to me, walking into my office one night. "But you better watch Shuwanda's ass. Between you and me, she's one messy bitch. That bitch is calling you a dick-sucking freak behind your back. Saying some guy walked up in your salon and wanted you to suck his dick and you didn't do shit, but stand there and let him disrespect you, girl. Now I don't know if what she's saying is true or not. All I know is, it isn't right. Then she said she believed him when he said you sucked one of his boys off in his car while he was driving. I know she does the hell out of my hair, but I don't like the shit's she's been saying. I thought you should know what kind of people you have in your space."

My heart leapt into my throat. However, I learned a long time ago to not immediately respond to shit people tell you. Truth is, I had sucked plenty of niggas off in their cars at one time or another. But I *never* did that shit while they were driving. That's the shit I'd only done with Jasper. Not that *that* makes it any better.

Then she added, "I'm not one to gossip. But I like you. And all I'm saying to you is, watch her. Don't let her know you got this from me. But, word on the street is, she's also skimming money from you. And I can't stand a thieving-ass bitch…"

I thanked her for the 4-1-1. Then the next day, I confronted Shuwanda's ass. And the bitch said with a bunch of attitude, "Yeah, I said it. And what?"

"Bitch, you're fired! Pack your shit and get the fuck out of my salon." I didn't even bother asking her about the money she was supposedly stealing from me. It didn't matter. She talked shit the whole way out the door. Called me every name in the book. But the bitch kept it moving. Lucky for her she didn't try to bring it to me. Otherwise I would have rolled up my sleeves and introduced her to the old me, then dropped her jaw.

Exactly what I'm gonna do to Felecia's dumb ass.

Anyway…Rhodesia can do the hell out of some hair. And she can slay the shit out of braids, too. Girlfriend stays booked. And she keeps that paper flowing in real heavy. So, at the end of the day, I don't care who she's fucking. As long as she keeps my cash register lined and keeps any drama she might have at home, we're good.

I lean in and whisper into Persia's ear, "Are you and your sisters still man swapping?"

She coughs, almost choking on the piece of candy in her mouth. "Girl, no; especially not after all that mess that went down with me and Paris."

She's referring to the shit that happened at my wedding reception with her sister finding out that she had been fucking the guy she was digging. The same guy who just happened to also be in my wedding party because he's another one of Jasper's first cousins.

Desmond. I didn't see how it all went down that night since I was too busy pretending to be the happy bride in the midst of over a hundred guests. But from what gossiping-ass Felecia had told me and from what I heard from other family members, it got real messy. Apparently, Paris had met Desmond when he came into her boutique, Paradise, to pick up a handbag for his mother. A few days later, she fucked him and hadn't told her sisters about him because she didn't want to share him with them since that was their MO—you fuck one of them, you fuck all three of them.

The three of them really took sharing men to a whole other level. But who am I to judge? I have my own indiscretions.

Anyway, the condensed version of the story is, while Paris was off raw dogging Desmond behind her sisters' backs, she ended up getting pregnant. But, Desmond somehow stopped calling or coming down to her boutique where they would fuck. So she thought he had simply moved on to the next or dropped off the face of the earth.

But, baby, the shit hit the fan—right there at my reception, when Paris found out that the reason she hadn't heard any more from him was because he was too busy being sexed down by Persia's messy ass pretending to be her. And because they're identical triplets he couldn't tell them apart. But, from what Jasper told me, Desmond backed off when, whom he thought was Paris, wanted him to fuck her rough, choke her up, slap her titties up, spit in her asshole and fuck her in it, and call her all kinds of slutty names. He told Jasper he wasn't with that extra shit. Not on a regular, anyway.

Of course when Desmond found out that he'd been fucking Persia all them weeks and not Paris, he was all fucked up behind it. I had overheard him telling Jasper that he loved Paris and wanted to raise his son with her. But I also overheard him telling

Jasper how Persia still looks at him like she wants some more of the dick. I wouldn't put it past her ass, either.

Talk about scandalous!

Persia shakes her head, scrolling through her phone. "So, no, girl, there's no more man swapping going on. Porsha is all in love with Emerson. She's busy planning their wedding…"

"*Wedding?* Get out! I had no clue. That's fabulous. Have they set a date?"

"No, not yet. But I know she wants it to be in either the spring or early fall of next year. They recently closed on a house out in Fort Lee."

"Oooh, I really like that area. Good for them."

"Yes. I'm happy for her."

"And how's Paris and the baby doing?"

"Oh, they're doing great. Lil Desmond is so adorable. And spoiled rotten."

"I'm sure he is." I ask her how she and Paris are making out, if they've been able to work through their differences, and repair their relationship.

"Things with us have gotten much better. That whole mess really shook our relationship."

I shake my head, placing Persia's head under the water. "I'm sure it did. It became the talk for most of the night at my reception. You know that kept the family's gossip mill going for weeks after that."

She waves her hand dismissively. "Girl, don't remind me. I apologize about that. I really wish things would have turned out differently that night."

Mmmph. Then you shouldn't have done what you did. Of course, I'm not really in a position to say much so I keep my thoughts to myself.

Seems like messy runs in our family.

Ten

A quiet bitch can turn out to be the most treacherous bitch…

"Girl, I've been dying to ask since I walked up in here," Persia says as I'm putting the final touches on her new do. "What happened between you and Felecia? You know Aunt Lucky burned a hole in my mother's ear about you slapping her face and firing her. Tell me it ain't so, girl."

"Mmmph, I don't even want to get into it. But whatever you heard, it's true. That bitch no longer works here. And I don't want that two-faced ass anywhere around me."

"Pasha, but she's still family."

I blink, tilting my head. "Oh, like you and Zena, right?" Zena is another cousin of ours. The two of them have hated each other since childhood. Well, it got worse in high school, when Persia, once again, fucked this boy Zena liked. But in Persia's mind he was fair game since he didn't know Zena had a thing for him. Persia didn't really want him but since Zena told her to stay away from him, Persia chose to do the opposite. She fucked him instead. Even though Zena ended up marrying him—well, they're in the process of a divorce now for some messy shit she did—she never got over what Persia did.

Persia shrugs. "Well, that's different. You and Felecia were practically raised like sisters."

"We *were* like sisters. And the bitch turned on me. And from what I'm hearing she fucked Jasper at some point as well." *And your messy ass knows all about fucking someone else's man.*

"How do you know this?" I tell her I got it from a reliable source. She eyes me through the mirror. "And you *believe* this *source?*"

I nod. "I sure do. The person who told me has no reason to make the shit up. And, to be honest with you, the more I think about how Felecia was always eyeing Jasper, I believe the shit's true. She either fucked him, had his dick stuffed in her throat, or both."

"Ooh, that bitch is scandalous. I don't want to even think she'd be damn dirty to do some shit like that to you. Gossiping, yes. Fucking your man, let's hope not. "

Girl, please. You have some nerve!

"Did you at least ask her? I mean, did she admit to it?"

I frown. "I *know* that bitch did it. My gut says she did. And even if she didn't, she was still doing shit behind my back that she had no business doing. So, let's leave it at that."

"Girl, I didn't mean to get you going. I had no idea." I wave her on. Tell her that it is what it is. I spin her around in the chair, then finish tapering her neck with the clippers. "I hear you. Well, between you and me, you know Paris is still kinda pissed at her ass for gossiping about us to that chick she was with at your wedding."

"Which chick? Cassandra?"

"I don't know what her name is. But she was the chick with the real big ass. The one who wore that fly-ass white dress and had almost every woman at the reception ready to poke their man's eyes out for struggling to keep them off her ass."

I chuckle. "Oh, you're talking about Big Booty. Uh, I mean Cassandra."

"You had it right the first time. *Big Booty.* Yeah, her. That chick knows she has an ass on her. Mmmph. Well, anyway, she ran into Paris and Desmond at Short Hills a couple of weeks ago and told Paris that she and Felecia had been talking about how messy I was for fucking her man. Then that ghetto-trick told Paris that she had better watch *me* around Desmond because I was a messy bitch, or something like that. Can you believe that shit? Who the fuck is she? The nerve of that bitch! All I know is, Paris was hot. And that shit didn't sit well with me, either."

Well, shit. It's the truth. And, yeah, I can believe it. After that stunt you pulled, Paris should be watching your sneaky-ass like a damn hawk.

I decide to keep this to myself. "Well, Felecia had no business running her mouth to Cass about that. But that's what that bitch does. Runs her goddamn mouth. Listen. I don't want to waste any more air space talking about that bitch. She's dead to me. And I mean that."

"Girl, that's fine by me. She deserves whatever she gets."

I purse my lips. Nothing more needs to be said on the matter. Persia and I move on to other things like work, her plans for the future, business down at the boutique she owns with her sisters, etc. Forty-five minutes later, her new look is complete.

"Girrrl, you laid this hair out," she says, looking in the hand-held mirror, then handing it back to me. "I feel naked without all my hair. But I am loving my new look."

I smile. Tell her I'm glad she likes it. Then I walk her up front to the register so that she can pay for my services. She hands me a twenty-dollar tip. We hug. Promise to do better staying in touch, which is something we always say, but never follow through with.

"Well, now that you have this sexy little cut, you'll need to maintain it at least every two weeks to keep it looking fresh and sassy."

She laughs. "And we know how sassy I am. So I guess I'll see you in two weeks then." We hug again. Then she's out the door. I watch as her boy-toy hops out of the car, grinning from ear to ear. He says something to her as he opens her door for her. She smiles, then I see her grab at his dick on the sly as she slides into the passenger seat. He shuts the door for her, then hops back in his big-body BMW, taking off. I keep watching until his rear tag ROYCE disappears from my view.

I smile, truly happy for her. *Looks like Persia got herself a keeper,* I think as I head back to my workstation with my next client following behind me. *Let's hope she doesn't fuck him over.*

The rest of the morning flies by without incident. But the afternoon heats up real quick. The salon is packed, the way I love it. Every stylist's chair is full; the manicurists and pedicurists are all booked solid.

By the time we close the shop's doors at eight o'clock, I'm exhausted. And the only thing I want to do is take my ass home. But I know Mona is on her way over. So I'm sitting at my desk with my heels off, feet propped up on the desk, waiting.

Jasper's called me three times already, talking shit about me coming straight home so he can run the streets, talking about he has some business to handle. Fuck him. I told him I had a late appointment, and couldn't change it. Whether the nigga believed me or not is not my concern. Knowing his ass, he probably has one of his goons eyeing the salon, and trailing me. Ever since my kidnapping, I'm extra cautious. I'm always looking over my shoulder, always double-checking locks, and I never leave home without my weapon tucked in my purse. I also keep one here in my office locked in my top drawer.

The good thing is, I have three security guards, standing over six feet and stacked with rock-hard muscle working here. And they are all armed. And one is always here with me at night to make sure I get to my car safely. Then for extra safety measures, after someone bust out the front window of my salon last year, I had security cameras installed out in front of the salon and in the parking lot area. Shit, I wish I had all this security before I started getting all those harassing phone calls, and…the fliers.

I try to swallow back the memory, but it comes rushing up like hot lava. FOR THE BEST HEAD IN TOWN, PASHA ALLEN'S GOT THE DICK SUCKING GAME ON LOCK…FOR THAT 24 HOUR DICK WASH, COME THRU NAPPY NO MORE…

Hundreds of fliers with all kinds of disrespectful shit about my dick sucking were literally plastered all over the outside of the salon's windows and door. The nigga behind it was scorned because I didn't want to give him another round of head when he hit my email up asking for some more of this throat.

The nigga would have never found out who I really was if I hadn't participated in Nana's Missionary Day program and let the press snap photos of me. My face was plastered all over the COMMUNITY SECTION of the paper. That started the beginning of my troubles. First the phone calls to the salon, then the harassing letters, then some nigga walking up into my salon calling me out in front of all of my clients. All that because of some lunatic-ass nigga being pissed that I wouldn't spin his top again.

"…I'm gonna keep fucking with you until you do…" he warned, before hanging up on me.

Three hours later, someone tossed a metal pipe through the front window of the salon, smashing glass everywhere. Of course, no one was able to give a description of the nigga who did the shit, other than he was short and dark-skinned, wearing a hoodie.

Then, miraculously—out of nowhere, Jasper and Stax show up

here. *No, that shit wasn't coincidence. And it wasn't a damn miracle. That shit was planned.* The nigga was toying with me. *It had to be Jasper behind it.* After everything that has happened, I can't put it past him. I slept on that nigga once, but not again.

And, *now*...I got his ass sleeping on *me*.

Eleven

Karma is that cold bitch that'll make sure a dirty nigga gets what he gets...

"Hey, Pasha," Lamar says, knocking on the door to my office as he pops his head in. I take in his six-foot-four frame, his smooth dark-chocolate skin tone, broad nose, and thick lips. His dreads are pulled back with a leather band, the tips dyed blond. He's definitely eye candy for the women who come into the salon. "Do you still want me to hang around until you're finished up?" He steps back to let Mona by. She's fifteen minutes late.

"Hey, girl," she says, taking a seat on the leather sofa. She sits back, crossing her legs. She looks stressed out. Her eyes are red and puffy as if she's been crying. Something is clearly weighing heavy on her mind.

"Hey, you," I say, glancing at her, then back at Lamar. "Yes, please, if you don't mind. I'll have a little something extra for you when I'm done."

He smiles. "I got you."

I smile back, wait for him to shut the door, then get up and walk over to where Mona is sitting and sit beside her. "Girl, what is going on? You've had me on pins and needles ever since you called me Saturday."

I give her a hug.

She immediately bursts into tears. "Pasha, JT's dead! And I helped get him killed!"

My eyes pop open in shock. *"Whaaaat?* Girl, what do you mean 'JT's *dead*' and *you* helped get him killed?" *Ohmygod, so that's why Jasper's running around acting all nutty. But he didn't say anything about JT being dead. Only missing. Wait. Maybe he doesn't know.* "Was it some kind of set-up or something?"

She shakes her head, clutching her chest, crying. It takes her almost five minutes to pull herself together before she's finally able to speak. "No. It wasn't a set-up. I mean it was sort of. But not like a robbery kind of set-up, or anything crazy like that." More tears start rolling down her face. "But I got him killed, Pasha. *I* got my cousin killed." She covers her face in her hands, sobbing.

"Mona, what the hell is going on? You need to pull yourself together and tell me what the hell you're talking about."

She looks over at me, swiping tears from her face. "Pasha, you have to *swear* to me you won't repeat this shit to anyone.." I stare at her. There's a glint of desperation in her tone, and in the way she's looking at me.

"You have my word. Now, *please,* tell me what the heck you're talking about."

"It…" She shakes her head, wiping more tears as they fall from her eyes. "It wasn't supposed to go down like this."

"Like what, Mona? What wasn't supposed to go down?"

Her hunched shoulders shake. I get up and grab the box of tissues from off my desk, then walk back over and hand them to her. She takes a few, then starts blowing her nose. She takes a few more, wiping her face. I wait for her to finish. She shakes her head, shutting her eyes tight. I sit back down beside her. And wait for her to start talking.

She takes a deep breath. Grabs more tissues and blows her nose again. "Okay. A few months back I ran into Cassandra at the Prudential Center after the Trey Songz concert and she gave me her number and told me she had something to talk to me about. Now, you know she and I have never been cool like that, but she said it was important. And that what she had to say I needed to keep it under wraps."

"Okay. And?"

"When I finally decided to call her, she wanted to talk to me about *you*."

I blink. Inch up in my seat, plop my hand up on my hip. Tilt my head. "Me? About what?"

"About everything. What happened with you when you were kidnapped, that shit with some nigga coming here to the salon and disrespecting you, then you being attacked in your yard—I didn't even know about that. I knew about the front window and your car window getting smashed. But the shit Cassandra was telling me was news to me. She told me she was going to track down the niggas behind it. She wanted them to get handled for what they'd done to you because you didn't seem too pressed to handle it."

I frown. I had told that bitch to let it go when she had asked me if I wanted her to track his ass down and get her goon squad on him. I told her no, to leave it alone. And she assured me she would.

Now I hear this shit.

Mona blows her nose again. "Cassandra told me that you told her to drop it. But you know how she stays in the streets, and in drama. She said a few niggas were talking about some chick sucking niggas' dicks behind her man's back and got her ass beat after he set her up when he found out. Then Felecia got up in her ear telling her shit about you, lies or not."

I blink.

I keep my tone even. "And did she find out who it was."

"Well, not at first. But she said she thought Jasper was behind it. And that Felecia also had something to do with it. But you know how extra Cassandra can be. I thought the bitch was reaching. Then she came up with this bright idea to start fishing JT. She knew he was digging her and since he was always in her face tryna fuck her, she thought she could reel him in real good and fish him for info on the sly while running his pockets."

"*Wait!* Cassandra and JT were fucking?" She nods. "How in the hell did I miss that?" I ask her how long it had been going on. She tells me for about seven or eight months, maybe longer. "Wow. She definitely kept that quiet. I had no idea. Then again, she's so sly with her shit, you never know who she's fucking unless she putting the nigga on blast."

"Exactly. That was the whole idea. To keep it real quiet. JT didn't want anyone to know he was creeping with her, either. Besides, you know how crazy Leticia is. If she had caught wind of it, all hell would have broke loose. And you already know how sneaky JT's ass is."

Mmmph. Leticia and JT had been together since she was sixteen. And he'd put her through the wringer with all of his sidepiece bitches and street antics. Yet, she stood by his side through it all, fighting other women, throwing him out, then taking him back, him beating on her, bringing her home—not *one*, not *two*, but *three*—STD's. And she still stayed with his trifling ass.

Not that I'm tossing shit on her after all the craziness Jasper's done to me, and put me through, over the years. The only thing he *hasn't* done is, give me a damn disease. Anyway, Leticia's thing has always been, "It comes with the territory. So you buckle up and stay ready to fuck a bitch up."

I guess—no I *know*—I used to be stuck in that thinking, too, at one time. But, shit, she's thirty-three years old now. It's time to let that crazy shit go.

"Okay, so JT and Booty were fucking. How does this add up to him getting killed?"

"She told me his ass started getting possessive, acting like he owned her. You know his ass has always been two screws from nutty."

I nod knowingly. JT's ass is crazier than Jasper. So I can only imagine what he tried to do to Cassandra with all that mouth she has.

Mona tells me how he popped up at her house last Thursday and snatched her by the throat and started beating her ass. I shake my head, not surprised at that. But I am surprised that he went over there and didn't get jumped on by all Cass's crazy-ass kids.

"None of her kids were home. They were still in school. Cassandra was on her phone with her oldest son when she opened the door and he started blackin' on her." She repeats what Cassandra had told her. That he was going to gut her insides out and kill her for always running her mouth. "He pulled his gun out and put it to her head. Then he tried to rape her."

I gasp, grabbing my chest. Hearing this hits painfully close to home for me, confirming what I've felt in the pit of my soul. That JT was definitely one of the niggas Jasper let violate me. "Ohmygod!" I cover my mouth, feeling myself getting sick. I lean forward, clutching my stomach. All of sudden images of the six masked niggas who ravaged me start popping up in my head. My mind starts reeling. I start rewinding the imageries. There was the tall thick nigga with the jeans; the first one to violate me—the one who snatched me by the neck and started choking me when I refused to suck his dick.

"Bitch, don't you know I will snap your muthafuckin' neck? You either suck my dick or you gonna die tonight, ho...."

I didn't want to die. So I sucked him as if my life depended on it. And it did. Then bit into his huge, hairy balls and tried to chew them off, causing him to let out a blood-curdling scream as he tried to punch me off of his shit. I chewed his balls until I drew blood. I remember someone had to run down the stairs to help pry my mouth open. But I didn't let go of his balls until the nigga's knees buckled and I had blood seeping out of my mouth.

No, that wasn't JT.

I blink another nigga into view. The one with long, muscular legs in the Duke Basketball shorts. I kept referring to him as Calm One because out of all the others he wasn't aggressive or disrespectful to me. In fact, he tried to keep them from hurting me—too bad.

His voice drifts through my memory. "...If you wanna get out of here alive, then you gotta do what they tell you, understand me?"

Something in his eyes told me I knew him from somewhere—the way he walked, his body build, was familiar to me. But I wasn't able to put my finger on it. I still can't. At the time, I was too frightened to try to figure it out. I only wanted to come out of that shit alive. But now...now, I'm certain, I *know* him.

But that wasn't JT, either.

Wait...there were more than six niggas that night. The nigga I bit, Quiet One, then the six rowdy motherfuckers, all liquored up, who came stomping down the stairs—one after the other, faces masked, wearing different colored basketball shorts. JT had to be one of them...

I blink the memory away. Swallow back the rising anger swelling in the pit of my stomach. I turn my attention to Mona. "Then what happened?" She continues. Tells me that Booty was able to find one of the knives she keeps stuffed down in her sofa cushions and stabbed him in his stomach with it.

She swipes tears from her face as she's telling me this. "None of this shit would have ever happened if JT hadn't been so busy tryna fuck that whore-ass, gold-digging bitch. It wasn't supposed to go down like that, Pasha. You know I would have never gotten involved in no shit like this. All that bitch was supposed to do is fish around for info, maybe catch him slipping during one of their fuck sessions.

"Then she was going to come to you so she could help you get them niggas back. But you know her ass is money-hungry so she started running JT's wallet, making him one of her sponsors. And you already know how JT is about his money, and the side bitches he fucks. Anyway, he attacked her because of how she turned up at the shop that day, calling Felecia out in front of everyone and putting Jasper on blast. Pasha, I swear I think Jasper knew he was creeping with her and told him to check her ass on her mouth. Why else would he go storming over there like a maniac?"

"Oh, I'm sure Jasper knew they were fucking. And he probably did tell him to check her. But to *kill* her?" I shake my head. "That makes no sense."

She gives me a grave look. "Pasha, there's never any rhyme or reason for nothing JT does. He's unpredictable. He probably went over there thinking he was gonna snatch her up for running her mouth, and she went in on him, which only set him off more; who knows. All I know is, he's dead."

Mmmmph. Good for his ass. Dirty bastard!

Payback is a motherfucker isn't it, nigga?!

"Pasha, that crazy bitch didn't have to do all that. She stabbed him, for God's sakes. Then she turns around and bashes him in his head with a baseball bat."

I take a deep, painful breath. "Mona, listen. I know you're upset, and rightfully so. But there's something you need to know. I think JT was one of the niggas who sexually assaulted me the night I was taken."

Her eyes widen. "Ohmygod, *nooo*. Are you sure?" I tell her I'm almost ninety-nine-point-nine-nine percent certain of it. "And Jasper?"

I blink back my own tears. "*He's* the one who set it all up. Then turned around and almost beat me to death."

Mona covers her face in her hands and sobs. In all the years I've known her, I've never seen her this emotional. I reach over and pull her into my embrace. She's crying so hard until she's hiccup-ping. Snot and tears all running down her face. I rub her back and rock her, doing my best to help calm her.

I get up and open the door, calling out for Lamar. I tell him that this might take longer than I thought. That he can leave. He tells me he's good. Then stops midway as he turns to leave and says, "Pasha, listen. I got your back, for *whatever*." I wonder where this is coming from. The way he looks at me when he says this, I know he's serious. "I'm not clocking out until you clock out. So, do you. I'ma be right here."

I smile. Thank him. Make a mental note to give him a nice bo-nus for his loyalty. Then shut and lock the door, bringing my at-tention back to Mona.

I sit beside her. "Mona, I know you're hurting. But, in all hon-esty, JT got what he deserved for trying to *rape* her. I'm sure she did what she felt she had to do in that moment."

The tears continue streaming down her face. "My cousin is dead, Pasha! Because of *me!* Now everyone thinks he's missing. And I *know* he's not only missing. He's *dead*, Pasha! And I can't say *anything* to *anyone* in my family about it because *I* helped Cassandra do him in. I knew I should have avoided that bitch and never let her drag me into her shit."

"Mona, listen to me," I try to reason, grabbing her hand. "*You* didn't tell JT to go over to Cassandra's house. And *you* didn't tell him to beat her or try to *rape* her. He got himself killed. So stop blaming yourself."

"I *can't* help it. It's tearing me up inside knowing that he's dead somewhere. And now you're telling me that Jasper's the one who had you kidnapped and beaten. And that JT was somehow involved as well. You've never wanted to talk about it, none of it. And I never pressed you." She shakes her head, taking a deep breath, then exhaling. "What the fuck is wrong with them niggas? Why would he do that shit to you?"

She starts wailing again. And I let her get it all out. The whole time I'm trying to console her, trying to get her to see it's not her fault, my mind is racing with questions: How much does Cassandra really know?

Does she know who else was in on it?

Why hasn't she called me? No, she has been calling me, but I've been ignoring her phone calls. Maybe this is what she was calling me about. It has to be.

Even though I've heard everything Mona's said, something isn't adding up. I hop up from my seat. "I need to call Cassandra." I grab my cell from off the desk. "There's no way I can let this shit wait. I need answers, *now.*" I scroll through my call log, then dial.

"That bitch is *ruthless*, Pasha," Mona hisses, her tears falling unchecked.

Mmm. Sounds like we all have some confessions to make.

Twelve

The truth may set you free,
but payback makes a bitch feel a whole lot better!

"It's 'bout time you got ya mind right, Miss Pasha, girl," Cassandra says as she struts into my office, shutting the door behind her. "You been tryna do me, goddammit. A bitch ain't had her head done since you tossed me up outta ya shop. And you know I need my damn wig did on the regular. Can't a bitch lay fingers through my hair but you, Miss Pasha, girl. And I ain't had my hair done in two weeks. I need my shit did, boo. You got me walkin' the streets lookin' like Miss *Beeeeyaaawncé* with this tore-up weave. I'm doin' head wraps 'n' you know I ain't no damn head wrap bitch. Get your mind right, goddammit. I need my wig fixed."

I blink, shaking my head at this heifer. She hasn't even gotten in the door good and her ass is already talking shit. But she's the kind of crazy bitch you can't even get—or stay—mad at 'cause she says some of the funniest shit. Still, she's a fucking mess. And right now isn't the time.

Still, as always, she's hood-fabulous in a pair of distressed jeans that look like they've been poured on and molded over her hips and ass. Her white blouse is tucked in. And there's a Louis Vuitton belt cinched around her tiny waist. I glance at the oversized handbag dangling from the crook of her arm. My eyes flutter down to her feet. She has the nerve to be wearing the pink Balenciaga Revers pump I'd been eyeing. If this visit were under different circumstances, I'd tell her she was serving me for filth. But she's not here for a fashion commentary. And I'm not interested in giving one.

She keeps rattling on, "You tried to do me, Miss Pasha, girl. Tossing me up outta here when all I was tryna do is put you on notice about how messy Miss FeFe was. I tol' that bitch so what if you was suckin' a buncha dicks. That shit was none of her messy-ass business. I'm tellin' you, Miss Pasha, girl, if you wasn't my sugah-boo, I'd tell you to eat the insides of my ass for that shit you pulled."

I frown. Cassandra is delusional. And she's never going to see just how damn messy she is. But, she's real. And you never have to second-guess when it comes to her. The bitch has no filter. She says whatever the fuck she wants.

When I called her to let her know that Mona was here at the salon and that the three of us needed to talk, she said, "Miss Pasha, girl, don't do me. Why you think I've been calling ya high-class ass the last week? But you been tryna be messy, iggin' my calls. Oooh, you been bein' real shitty, Miss Pasha, girl. Yes, we need to talk, goddammit."

"Can you come down to the shop now?" I had asked, not allowing myself to get wrapped up in her extras. I've learned to let Cassandra be Cassandra—messy and loud, without getting sucked in. But, it's not always easy.

"Sugah-boo, I'm on my way down to the Crack House to get my snap 'n' tap on. You know usually I turn it up on Thursday nights on Thug Night, Miss Pasha, girl. Monday nights usually ain't shit ever jumpin' off down at the club, but they doin' a male revue tonight. And a bitch like me likes to be pressed up at the bar, *early*, watchin' all the dick swing in."

The Crack House is one of the local hot spots for every hood star, wannabe gangster, and ghetto-fab bitch in the Tri-State area, known for their infamous drinks named with sexual connotations.

I rolled my eyes. "Cassandra, under the circumstances, this is urgent. We need to talk, *now*."

"Mmmph. Let me call Dickalina to let her know I'ma be late. Lucky for you, I'm three blocks away. I'll be there in a few." She hung up.

And now…here she is—live and direct, and in full effect.

She glances over at Mona, sucking her teeth. "Oh, here we go with the waterworks. Sugah-boo, *boom!* I know you not still cryin' over JT's coon-ass after that nigga tried to do me. That nigga-coon got what he deserved. So you need to pull it together, boo."

Mona glares at her. Clenches her teeth. "*Bitch*, are you serious right now? That is still my cousin."

"Correction, sweetness," Cassandra snaps, tossing her handbag up on my desk, "that nigga *was* your cousin. What he is *now* is shark bait. And *what?* The nigga-bitch got what he got 'cause he had it comin'. Period. So, don't do me. He told me that before he gutted my face, he was gonna fuck me in my ass, then scrape my insides out. Oh, no sweet thang, that nigga-coon got what he got for that shit. And, yes, I stabbed that nigga up real goddamn good for it."

I blink. There's not one ounce of remorse or guilt…nothing, in her voice as she says this. And, the scary thing is, something inside of me shifts. A part of me wishes I had been the one stabbing him up. I can't say this to Mona, but…I'm glad the nigga's dead. That motherfucker shoved his dick down in my throat, and didn't have an ounce of regret for me. So motherfuck him!

Mona bursts into tears again. "I-I t-t-thought I c-c-could handle this, b-b-but I can't. T-t-this is too much. How can I look in my family's face, in Leticia's face, in his mother's face, *knowing* I know what really happened to him?"

"Bitch," Cassandra huffs, stamping her foot and slamming a hand up on her hip. "The same way you *been* lookin' in they faces— with a goddamn smile. See. I knew ya ass wasn't built for this life. You knew it was gonna get messy. You knew that nigga-bitch was crazy. You warned me about his ass. Bitch, I don't do drama. And I don't do murders. But guess what? I did what I had to do to save me. And I'd do it all over again. I didn't wanna kill that nigga, but, *bitch*, ain't no way I wanted that nigga tryna kill me, either. So you can eat the insides of my ass with that shit. That nigga-coon tried to steal my pussy. Mmmph. No thank you, sugah-boo. That nigga-bitch had to go."

"Look, you two," I say, trying to diffuse the situation before it gets out of hand. "Bickering isn't going to change what's already happened. We all have to try to stay calm. And figure something out."

"Mmmph," Cassandra grunts, pursing her lips. "Oh, I'm very calm. So save that shit for that coon sittin' over there 'cause she's the one actin' like she needs a Day Stay on the psych ward."

Mona jumps up from her seat. "Bitch, where is my cousin's body? You still haven't said shit about that."

I watch as Cassandra yanks open her bag and snatches out a can of Mace. "Booga-coon, *boom-boom*, goddammit! Make my day. I won't beat ya ass down too bad 'cause you one'a them prissy bitches. And I can't stand tryna whoop up on no prissy bitch. But I will mace ya ass down real good up in this bitch tonight, then split your face if you even think it. I mean it, Miss Mona. So you better have several seats *waaaay* in the back, goddammit, before it gets messy up in here."

It takes me several minutes to get Mona to calm down. She's hysterical again. I rub her back, scowling at Cassandra. "Really, Cass? You're going to pull out a can of Mace when Mona's grieving over her cousin?"

"Sugah-boo, *boom!* I'm grieving, too, goddammit!" She tosses the can back into her bag. "I loss me a good goddamn sponsor behind that shit. So don't do me. That nigga-coon tried to slice out my cootie-coo." She replays pretty much everything Mona said. I ask her why JT would get pissed at her for putting Jasper on blast about Felecia.

She raises an arched brow.

"'Cause that nigga-coon was crazy; that's why. And the bitch thought he owned me and could run me. He ain't like me hippin' you to Jasper's no-good nigga-ass. But JT knew he could eat the inside of my ass. *Big Booty* don't dance to no-goddamn-body else's drumbeat but her own. And ain't no coon-ass nigga *ever* gonna run shit over here.

"Obviously, that nigga-bitch didn't get the memo—don't. *Fuck.* With. *Me.* So he got himself a nice shiny blade plunged into his stomach, then a bat to his skull." She snaps her neck over at Mona. "So, Miss Mona, you can sit there wringin' ya goddamn hands if you want, but you just as guilty as I am. And know this, Miss Thingaling, if I *ever* go down, I'm takin' ya punk-ass wit' me."

Mona gasps. "*Bitch!* You can't be serious?! I'm not the one who stabbed him, or beat him with a bat. Or tossed his body God knows where!"

"No, sugah-boo, you didn't stab that coon-nigga-bitch. *I* did. And *what?* Don't do me, booga-coon. 'Cause you were down with it, too, tryna fish Sparks to see what that coon-nigga knew. And you damn sure didn't have a goddamn problem takin' any of the money I was sharin' with ya greedy ass, with ya ole frigid ass. Now did you…?"

I shoot a confused look over at Mona. She avoids my stare.

"So, booga-coon, *boom-boom!* From where I'm sittin' that makes you a co-conspirator, goddammit. *You* took blood money, sugah-boo. Don't do me. We'll both be doin' them football numbers over at Clinton State Prison. And you better hope like hell when ya ass gets released, you don't come out lookin' like one of them He-Man clit-lickin' bitches."

"Cassandra, fuck you! You ain't shit! Yeah, I took the money, so the fuck what?! But I didn't sign up for you killing my fucking cousin, okay, bitch. And you *still* haven't said shit about where his body is."

"And I ain't sayin' shit, either. Report his ass missin' 'n' let the motherfuckin' pigs do they jobs. Isn't that what y'all workin'-class bitches pay ya taxes for?"

"Okay, look," I say, getting up from my seat. "Both of you need to lower your voices, please. Yelling and screaming"—I eye Booty—"or threatening—"*isn't* going to change what's already done." I look over at Mona. "Mona, why were *you* taking money from Cassandra, anyway? I know you and Avery aren't pressed for money like that."

She shrugs. "It was something the two of us agreed on."

I tilt my head. "That's still not telling me much, or making any sense." I want to know *why*. "There's something more to this shit." Mona shifts her eyes. Booty toots her lips, cutting an eye over at Mona. "As far as I'm concerned, neither of you had any right trying to meddle in my business."

Mona wipes more tears from her face. "I know, I know. But I felt bad. It was like you were hiding something, or trying to protect someone. And you looked so broken. It hurt me, Pasha. You're like a sister to me. And you know I'd do almost anything for you. So when this crazy bitch approached me about her idea to pump JT for info, I went along with it. I let her ass drag me into this shit."

Clap, clap, clap! Booty stands up, her diamond bangles clacking as she claps her hands. "And the Oscar goes to…bitch, *boom!* You better pop you a molly 'n' spark you a goddamn blunt 'n' get yo' mind right. What's done is done."

I lean forward, covering my face in my hands. Then look at the two of them. "This shit is crazy. Booty, how in the hell did you even get caught up with JT in the first place? And please don't sit there and tell me you were doing this *all* for me. You saw an opportunity and you ran with it."

Booty blinks her long lashes. "Now, wait a minute, Miss Pasha, girl. Sounds like you tryna do me, sugah-boo. I wasn't thinkin' 'bout that coon-ass nigga. But the nigga stayed in my face, okay. And yeah, I saw me an opportunity. And *what?* A bitch like me is always lookin' to come-up. I stay lookin' to get to the next level of hood fabulousness, okay. But that's besides the point."

I huff. "Well then. How about you get to the *point*."

She says JT had been pressing her for a minute, but that she kept igging him. Until, one night when he, Jasper, and Stax were down at the Crack House, and he tried to get at her, again.

"After a few drinks, it was on. I was droppin' this ass up on him on the dance floor, then next thing I know, he's tellin' me how he wants me to be his. I told the nigga to show me the money 'cause Booty wasn't fuckin' no nigga for free, especially no crazy-ass nigga like him. And you already know I love me a nigga with long ding-dong and long dollars. I knew that coon-bitch had both. And I wanted me a lil taste.

"Like I said, I saw it as a way to run the nigga's pockets. Shit, a bitch gotta keep her heels and handbags up. So yeah, I wanted to line my purse with his paper. Still, I thought it was gonna be a one-time fuck. But the dick was good, and the nigga's pockets were plentiful. Once I put this booty heat up on that nigga, he started talkin' that talk, tellin' me he wanted to keep me on-call. It costs to keep Booty, okay. And you know on-call means you tryna keep my purse lined with that greenery, ohhhkaaay. And I don't mean weed. So I decided to make the nigga one of my sponsors since he said he wanted to keep gettin' all this crack-crack. I got the nigga-coon sprung on this booty heat."

I sit up on the edge of my desk. "Again, *you* saw it as an opportunity for *you*. So why did *you* feel the need to get information out of him, or anyone else about *me*, especially *after* I told you to leave it alone?"

She cuts her eyes at me. "Now wait a minute, Miss Pasha, girl. Don't you start showin' ya ass, sugah-boo. Somebody needed to get shit poppin' 'cause ya ass actin' all sugary 'n' sweet like you scared to get them hands dirty. I know you ain't no pussy-soft bitch, Miss Pasha, girl." She cuts her eyes over at Mona. "Unlike some bitches, you got street bitch in ya blood, sugah-boo. But you actin' like you all scared to pull her outta the closet. No, Miss Pasha, girl, it's time you pull that bitch out 'n' turn up the gas on them niggas, goddammit. I know you said stay outta it. Sugah-boo, *boom!* Booty do what the fuck she want.

"And ain't no goddamn way I wasn't gonna stay outta shit when I ain't like how niggas was tryna do you. Don't no-goddamn-body shit on you. And I ain't like how that nigga-coon came up in here tellin' you to suck his dingaling. Why you think I told you I was gonna have my goonies be on alert when that Hill Harper-lookin' nigga came up in your shop 'n' tried to do you? 'Cause the streets were talkin', sugah-boo. And what they was sayin' wasn't cute. And neither was the shit Miss FeFe was tossin' up on you. So, like it or not, I did it 'cause you my damn boo, Miss Pasha, girl. Unlike some bitches, I'ma *loyal* bitch to the bone."

"And if Miss Messy FeFe's messy ass wasn't poppin' her shit eaters 'bout you, maybe I woulda took it down a pinch. But that bitch couldn't wait to drag you e'ery which way. She did you filthy, sugah-boo. Tol' me all 'bout someone draggin' you for raunch in ya yard 'n' tried to snatch ya breath. And how you ain't wanna get the police involved. That's when the lights started goin' off in my head, like you musta knew who tried to do you.

"And I was gonna let it go like you said until Messy FeFe told me about the strange phone calls you were gettin' from some nigga 'n' how he kept callin' back to back…"

I blink. Fighting to keep my anger in check as she continues telling me how that bitch Felecia told her—instead of me—that one time when the nigga called back he demanded to let him speak to "that cum-suckin' bitch, Pasha."

"That *bitch*," I hiss, balling my fists.

"Unh-huh," Booty says all animated. "Miss FeFe was doin' you, boo. And she tol' me how she thought you really were out there fuckin' other niggas behind Jasper's back. Then when you went missin' for three days, shit didn't make no sense. Something smelled real messy 'bout the whole situation. And you know I *know* messy when I see it."

You should when it's staring you in the mirror every-damn-day.

"And speakin' of messy, I found out who the nigga is who came up in here and tried to do you."

My heart starts pounding in my chest. That day flashes through my head and I immediately feel a headache coming on. I see the nigga's face clearly. He was thuggish and young, like early twenties. And he had dreads and big round, brown eyes. "Yes, can I help you?" I asked, looking up from Booty's head. She was in my chair and I was removing her weave when he stepped to me at my workstation.

I remember how the nigga was eyeing me and licking his lips when he said, "Yeah, my man said if I came through, you'd hit me off with one of ya deep throat specials."

At that moment it felt like everything froze in the salon. I could hear gasps and air being sucked in around me. All eyes were on me. I felt lightheaded. What the nigga said was true. I was known for giving out deep throat specials by those who had the pleasure of experiencing the warm, wet sensations my dick sucking skills delivered, which is why my AOL account stayed flooded with horny men asking for repeat service. But I couldn't admit that shit. And I couldn't stand there and let that nigga pull my card in front of everyone like that. So I did what any self-righteous diva in my position would do. I went the hell off. Told him to get the fuck out of my salon. Told him to go back and get his facts straight because he had the wrong one. Oh, yes…when all else fails, go off!

He backed his way out of the salon when Felecia came at him with a bat. But that didn't stop the nigga from grabbing his crotch and telling me to suck his dick, before running out of the salon. I ran to the door, yelling and cursing him as he ran down the street.

That motherfucker had pulled my ho-card and rattled my nerves. Had my stomach in knots. Then I had to walk back into *my* salon with my head held high, trying like hell to ignore the questioning glances and the nerve-wrecking silence as I sashayed back over to my workstation to finish up Cassandra's hair.

I take a deep breath, flicking the memory out of my head, glancing at Booty. "How? When?" She tells me she met him through some-one else down at the Crack House one night while she was out having drinks.

"I ain't know who the coon-nigga was at first. But I knew I had seen him somewhere before. One thing I don't ever do is, forget a face. Once I figured out who he was, *boom-boom*, goddammit! I knew I hit the jackpot. We tossed back a few drinks, then I had the bitch-ass coon pull out his dingdong…"

Ugh! I roll my eyes, shaking my head.

Mona shifts in her seat, frowning.

"Now, wait one minute. I know you bitches ain't tryna do me, goddammit. Shit, you know it ain't no shame in my game. I love me some dingdong. And the nigga was talkin' like it was all this 'n' that, so I tol' him to show 'n' prove. Ole stumpy-thick dick nigga-bitch. But I started fishin' him 'n' he gave it to me good. Yes, gawd…"

"Cassandra!" I snap. "Will you just move this along, *please*. Just tell me who the hell nigga is."

She shoots me a dirty look. "Unh-uh, Miss Pasha, girl. Don't. Do. It. 'Cause you know I ain't one of them messy bitches. But you tryna take me there. So how 'bout *you* tell us if you'se a cum whore or not, like Miss FeFe and this nigga said you was since you ain't never really say if the shit was true or not. And *then* I'ma tell you who the nigga is. But know this, sugah-boo, when I tol' the nigga that you was a real dirty bitch for that shit and that you shoulda had yo' ass whooped for that…"

I blink.

"You wanna know what that coon-nigga said? He said, and I quote, 'Real shit, she did. She got fucked up real good.'"

Everything inside of me cracks. I feel myself becoming fucking undone. "Booty, who the fuck is he? I'm not in the mood for all your long drawn-out theatrics."

Of course she's not fazed by what I've said. The bitch ignores me, sliding a fingernail through her front tooth, then flicking something to the floor from beneath her nail.

I let out a frustrated sigh, *"Welllll."*

She reaches for her bag on the desk and pulls out a pack of gum. I swear I don't know how much more of this shit I can take with her and her dramatics. I don't know how much longer I can hold on before the tears come bursting from my own eyes.

"Booty, stop dragging this shit out. Tell me who this nigga is."

I eye her as she rolls the stick of gum in her mouth. "Sugah-boo, his name is AJ. And the nigga's on ya dirty-ass husband's payroll." She chomps on her gum. "Now was *you* suckin' dingaling or not?"

Thirteen

Secrets can chain a bitch's soul to her own misery...

"Yes," I say, my voice dropping to a guilty whisper, admitting my dick-sucking sins to her and Mona. This is the first time I've confessed to anyone.

Mona gives me a surprised look. "Oh, God, no. Why, girl?"

Cassandra sucks her teeth, then dramatically rolls her eyes. "Obviously, she loves suckin' dick. Oooh, I ain't wanna believe the shit was true, Miss Pasha, girl. But I knew you wasn't no Miss Goodie-Two Shoes. Yesssss, goddammit! You ole sneaky whore." She glances at her timepiece, plopping down on the sofa next to Mona. "Ooooh, I need me a drank 'n' a blunt on this one."

I can feel tension coiling through my body. I run my hands through my hair, then along my neck as I try to explain it to Mona in a way that doesn't sound too crazy. "I got caught out there. I loved Jasper. And I jailed with him the best I could. It was hard. And unless you've done a bid with a nigga, you won't really be able to understand. It got lonely. My hormones got the best of me. I just needed, wanted, something to take the edge off until he got home.

"I knew what I was doing was wrong. I rationalized it in my head. Deluded myself into thinking that sucking dick wasn't really cheating as long as I didn't let any of those niggas fuck me. I justified it by reminding myself of all the times Jasper had crept out on me and had his dick stuffed down in some bitch's throat, and he'd tell me getting his dick sucked wasn't *really* cheating."

Mona frowns. "And you believed that dumb shit?"

"Of course I didn't. But I tried—"

"Miss Pasha, girl, fuck the *whys*, sugah-boo. All I wanna know is, did you swallow? Or was you wastin' good nut, boo?"

Mona lets out a disgusted sigh. "Ugh! What the fuck?! Who the hell cares whether or not she swallowed. The fact is that she was out there sucking dick and *cheating* on Jasper." She cuts her eyes over at me. "Did you even know any of these niggas?"

Avery's dick pops into my mind. "*She half-sucks my dick.*" I shake my head. "No."

"Booga-coon, *boom!*" Cassandra snaps, cutting her eyes over at Mona. "You sound like you tryna judge her. So what, she was guzzlin' up dick. And *what?* Jasper's coon-ass is the same nigga who stayed cheatin' on her. Get it right, sweetness. That nigga-coon been slingin' his dingaling all around Jersey for years. All Miss Pasha did was finally go out 'n' get her a lil taste. So what if she was suckin' dick down like steamed oysters? Please. His black cheatin' ass was behind the wall, any-damn-way. A locked-up dick can't do shit for a wet, horny cootie-coo. And who got time to be acceptin' collect calls for some phone fuck. Booga-coon, *boom!*

"You good, Miss Pasha, girl, 'cause I woulda gave that nigga his papers 'n' tol' him to come see me when his ass hit the bricks. Ain't no way Booty puttin' no pussy on hold for no nigga. Not the way I like to ride down on some dingdong. But anyway…this ain't 'bout me, sugah-boo. This is 'bout you and ya cum-guzzlin' ways. Oooh, I knew you was real gutter with it. A real live cum-whore, yessss, goddammit!"

I ignore her theatrics. "I admit that what I did was wrong. But what Jasper had done to me as his way of *teaching* me a *lesson* is something I'd never wish on my fucking enemy. I see and hear and feel everything that happened to me. The shit is etched into my memory. And every time I look at Jasper, I see what that nigga did to me."

I don't tell them this. But there are times when I see my reflection in the mirror and I don't even recognize the bitch staring back at me. The sparkle in my hazel eyes is gone. All I see is dimness. Darkness. A shell of a woman.

I blink back hot tears, closing my eyes, trying to shut back the well of emotions as I regurgitate every last dirty little detail.

There's a nigga standing in front of me with his face inches from mine. And I can tell he is a fucking, certified, raving lunatic. That's what's running through my head. He's not the one from earlier. Or the nigga whose balls I bit. Or the two who kidnapped me. But, whoever he is, this motherfucker is a fucking loose cannon. He's yelling and spitting in my face, practically foaming at the mouth. I can smell weed and alcohol on his breath. I want to scream, but I am unable to. My throat is dry and raw. My neck is aching. And I have pissed all over myself. I glance around the basement. A sliver of light seeps through the small window along the wall. That's the only way I know it's daylight—a new day. And I'm still alive.

"You dirty, cock-suckin', cum slut! You stink, you pissy bitch! I should beat the shit outta you. You like feelin' a hard dick in your throat, whore? I heard you suck a mean dick. You like makin' a muhfucka's toes curl, don't you? Like teasin' him 'til he can't take it anymore, then tossin' a muhfucka to the side when you have no more use for him, don't you, bitch? Answer ME!"

I rapidly shake my head. "N-no, that's not what I like to do. I—"

"Liar!" he yells, pulling out a box-cutter from his back pocket. He presses its blade to my neck. "I will cut out your muthafuckin' tongue and stuff it down in your goddamn, rotted-ass throat. You stupid, lying bitch!"

"Please," I whimper, forcing myself to fight back tears. "Don't hurt me. If you want money, I can get it for you."

He swings his arm back, then slaps me with a force that rattles my jaw, makes my face throb. My ears ring. "Bitch, I don't want your fuckin' money. I want your lips on my dick. I want you drinkin' my nuts. Swallowin' my babies, you filthy, whore-ass bitch! And, if you suck my dick like the good, little cunt you are, I might let you live to suck another dick. But if you don't, I'm gonna slice ya muthafuckin' throat. Then set ya pretty ass on fire. You understand me, bitch?"

I stare him down. The nigga is a pyscho. I'm fucking exhausted, frightened out of my damn mind and dying of thirst. Yeah, I keep punking out and begging for any of these niggas not to hurt me because—truth be told, I want to get the fuck out of here alive. But, right now I am so damn tired and hungry and goddamned agitated that I am not thinking when I decide to give this nigga a piece of my mind. Whatever he plans to do to me is what he plans on doing, regardless. I've already sucked two niggas' dicks, and that shit's got me nowhere. So, I decide to test him. There's a part of me that needs to push the envelope far enough to see exactly how much of a walking bomb this nigga really is. Is he all bluff and fluff or is he the type of nigga who's really about getting it in?

"Do you hear me, you nasty, slutty-ass, dick-suckin' bitch?!"

He has his face inches from mine, again, hurling insults at me, his hot, funky breath beating me in my face. "Fuck you, nigga!" I snap. Then without any thought, I spit at him. My saliva clings to the front of his mask.

He punches me in the head. "Bitch, you fuckin' just spit on me! I should break ya damn jaw."

"Fuck you," I snap again. "Break it, nigga."

"Oh, I'ma break it aiight, bitch. After you suck down my dick and I nut in ya slutty-ass mouth."

"Fuck you!" I yell again. "Just kill me and get it the fuck over with, you weak-ass motherfucker. Ugh, hiding behind a mask! You bitch-ass, limp-dick nigga! You ain't no real nigga, pussy! The only bitch in the room is you."

What I've said must have struck a nerve. The nigga charges me, grabbing me by the neck and throwing me to the ground. "Bitch, I've been tryna be nice to your ho-ass, but you wanna play me. I will snap ya fuckin' neck..." He tightens his grip around my neck.

OhmyGod, he's really going to kill me, I think, feeling the life being choked out of me. I try to search the room for an escape, a weapon, or both. But my goddamn hands and feet are tied. I am fucking helpless! My eyes grow wide, pleading. The only thing I can think about is getting out of here alive. Hoping someone finds me. Hoping this nut will show some pity on me, and let me go. However, at this very moment, it's obvious I've not only pushed the envelope to the edge, I've sent this maniac into a fit of fury. In his eyes I see death—mine!

"You wanna die, bitch?"

"N-n-nooooo," I manage to push out, gasping for air.

Somebody from upstairs opens the door and yells down. "Yo, nigga, I told you the bitch is pregnant, so chill the fuck out down there. Get ya nut, and bring ya dumb-ass back upstairs."

"Fuck!" he snaps, glaring at me. Finally, he loosens his grip. I cough and gag, and try to suck in air. "You gonna act like you got some fuckin' sense, and do what the fuck I say?"

I'm convinced if I want any chance of making it out of here in one piece, then I had better put on an Academy Award performance and act as if my life depended on it. And in this case, at this very moment…it really does!

I blink back tears, nodding my head. "Yes," I say in a whisper. "Anything you want, baby."

He keeps me pinned under him, his hands loosely around my neck. "I don't wanna hurt you, but I will. You understand me?"

"Yes."

"You want me to hurt you?"

I rapidly shake my head. "No."

"You gonna suck this dick the way you did my man, right?"

I nod. "Yes. I'll suck your dick all night for you. Any way you want it. Just don't hurt me…please."

"If you bite my shit like you did my nigga, I'ma shoot ya brain outta ya skull, you hear?"

I nod. "Yes."

He lets go of my neck, wraps his hand over my mouth and face, squeezes. His thumb presses into my left cheek while the rest of his fingers dig into my other cheek. Stares me in the eyes. "I'm a nice guy, yo. But I promise you. Any slick shit and I'm gonna bring it to ya fuckin' head, you dig?"

I nod.

"Good," he says, letting go of my face, then lifting himself up off of me. "Don't diss me; don't talk slick; don't have me split ya shit." He sets the chair up, then roughly pulls me up off the floor and sits me on it.

With one hand, he pulls his dick out of the slit of his boxers while holding the barrel of his piece to the side of my head, then presses his dick up against my lips. It's bigger than the last one I sucked. It looks to be almost eleven, maybe twelve, inches. And it's about as thick as a can.

"Lick that shit," he orders. I do. In slow, wet strokes I slather his dick with my spit until he is as hard as a gold brick. "That's right, wet that shit up…now open ya mouth and suck on that shit." I do what I am told. My lips stretch over the head of his dick, my jaws unlocking to adjust to the width. I serve up the head nice and wet and sloppy. I slurp and suck and stroke his dick with my lips, mouth, and throat for what feels like forever. But in my head, I am counting the number of slurps; I am counting the rhythmic number of times my head bobs back and forth on his cock; the number of times he pulls back from me 'cause the shit's getting too good to him. "Aaah, fuck…goddamn, bitch, your throat game is…aaah, fuck…"

The final count in my head is a hundred and forty-seven thrusts before his body shudders. He lets out a loud moan, then shoots his load, emptying himself into my mouth as if it is a septic tank. It's hot and slimy and has a strong odor that is making me gag. He cocks his gun. "Spit my shit out and I'ma blow a hole in ya skull." I clamp my mouth shut, hold his waste in my mouth, hoping he hurries up back upstairs so I can spit this nasty shit out. As if he's read my thoughts, he walks over to the pool table, tears off a piece of duct tape and walks back over to me with his wet, sticky cock still dangling out of his boxers.

He covers my mouth with the tape. "Just in case you think you gonna be slick and spit my nut out." I gag. "Hurry up and swallow that shit, so I can take that tape off. Otherwise I'ma leave it on." I take a deep breath, frown, then swallow it down. "That's a good bitch," he says, grinning. He yanks the tape from my mouth.

"Why?" I ask, hoping I can get this nigga to open up, maybe

get him to have a change of heart and let me go. But the nigga dashes any hopes of that happening when he slaps the duct tape back over my mouth.

"Yo, you ain't here to be muthafuckin' friends, so don't be askin' a buncha muthafuckin' questions." He starts walking toward the stairs, but turns around. "You need to use the bathroom?" I nod. "Piss on ya'self," he snaps, walking off. "You smelly bitch!" I watch him take the stairs two at a time, then shut the door at the top of the stairs, locking it.

Mona's crying snaps me out of my reverie. My own face is now wet from tears. This time it is Mona who is up on her feet, rubbing my back, trying to comfort me. "Them fucking bastards! Oh, Pasha, I'm so sorry you had to go through all that." She wraps her arms around me. "And Jasper fucking did this to you?" I nod, wiping my tears. Rage sweeps through me like never before. More determined to make that nigga pay for what he did to me. "He ain't shit for doing this!" Mona snaps.

"He's a no-good, grimy nigga, that's what the fuck he is," Cassandra hisses. *Click, clack, click-clack.* "Now you see why them niggas gotta go down. And JT's ass was right in on the shit, too, like I knew. Ole big-dick, dirty nigga. That's why I sliced his thick juicy dingaling clean off the goddamn bone. But, my gawd, he could fuck. Shame the nigga had to be put down, like the rabid dog he was." She pops her gum again. "All that big, thick dick gone to waste. Mmmph."

Mona and I both stare her crazy-ass down. I think we're both too stunned to say shit. It's not every day you hear some chick talking a matter-of-factly about how she sliced a nigga's dick off right after she stabs him up. A part of me wants to know what she did with his dick. The other part of me knows enough to know that some things are better left alone. *I wonder how many other niggas' dicks she's sliced off.*

Mona's right. This bitch is ruthless.

"Now, Miss Pasha, girl, I need to know if any of them niggas slipped up at any time 'n' said anyone's name."

I shake my head, shutting my eyes while flipping through the snapshots of my kidnapping. "No. I don't think so."

"Think, long 'n' hard, sugah-boo."

I rewind the memory disc in my head. And then a voice comes to me. *"Yo, she bit the shit outta L. Tried to take that nigga's balls off, yo…"* I quickly blink open my eyes. "I remember one of the niggas referring to the nigga whose balls I tried to bite off as *L.*"

"L?" She blinks. "What did he look like?" I take a deep breath. Tell her he was taller and thicker than the two niggas who snatched me up in the parking garage. He was more menacing, too. I can still see everything the nigga had on. Faded blue jeans, a gray wife beater and a pair of green, white, and gray AirMaxes. He was dark-skinned and had a real deep voice. And there was something in his eyes that made me think he was two screws from crazy.

"That's all I can remember. His face was covered. I keep playing over in my head how that nigga told me he wasn't the kind of nigga to take no for an answer. That he takes what the fuck he wants."

"Ooooh, nooooo, goddammit. He sounds *exactly* like this crazy nigga I had met down at the club a few weeks back. And his name was L. No, it was something else, but he introduced himself to me as L. I know I had got my throat real wet that night, but I know my shit wasn't *that* drenched. I think that's the same nigga who tried to do me at the bar, Miss Pasha, girl. That dirty nigga told me he wanted to fuck me deep in my fat ass. And although my cootie-coo did get kinda moist when he said that shit, there was somethin' in his eyes that told me he'd punch a ho's sockets in and use her titties as a punchin' bag. The nigga practically told me he took what he wanted, the same shit he tol' you. Ooh, that nigga-coon told me that he wanted to take me outside and fuck me inside out."

"Cassandra, please," Mona says dismissively. "That could have been anyone."

"Sugah-coon, *boom!*" Cassandra snaps. "You stay tryna test my patience. Don't do me with that it coulda been anybody shit. I wasn't just anybody. You wanna know why? Because a week or so later, Dickalina told me that her nigga Knutz wanted to introduce me to some nigga fresh outta jail. And she called him *L*. And then she told me that he didn't like anyone playin' with his balls 'cause some bitch had tried to bite his shit off so he don't like anyone tryna lickin' on 'em.

"Now tell me, sugah-boo. How many niggas *you* know who got niggas callin' them *L*, and he done had his balls almost bit off? No, that's the same nigga. Oooh, yes, gawd! That's that nigga-bitch. I knew there was somethin' real messy about his ass. I'm so glad I ain't give that dirty nigga none of this booty heat."

I feel my jaws tighten. I can still hear him screaming, mercilessly, for help as I bite into his balls.

Mona blows her nose, then says, "All of this shit is fucking crazy. I can't believe what I've gotten myself into. Pasha, I know you said earlier you were almost certain JT was there, too. But now I need to know if you're absolutely sure."

After hearing all that I've heard tonight, I'm one hundred-percent for sure. That nigga was there.

I nod.

"Oh God!" she gasps. "What about Stax? You think he was there, too?"

I shut my eyes one last time, bringing the memory back into focus. Stax has his daughter's face tattooed on his right forearm. Most of them wore long-sleeved tees. The ones who wore short-sleeves, I don't remembering having tattoos. Maybe he wasn't one of the niggas down in the basement ramming his dick down my throat. Maybe, he was upstairs the whole time. I open my eyes, fighting back more tears.

"I honestly don't know."

Cassandra stands, stretches, then walks over to my desk, digging through her handbag. "Then there's only one way to find out." She pulls out her cell and a folded piece of paper. She glances at the phone screen, grunting.

I raise a brow. "How's that?"

"You're gonna have'ta fish the nigga. And before you start babblin' 'bout what you can't do, don't think I ain't peep how that sexy motherfucka be peepin' you on the low, Miss Pasha, girl. Stax's fine ass wanna do you, sugah-boo. So, use that shit to ya advantage. You need to do what you do best. Give that nigga one of ya deep throat specials 'n' suck the info outta that nigga's big-ass dick. The streets stay talkin' 'bout that dingaling being big 'n' juicy. But I still ain't run up on a bitch, yet, who can confirm if it's tree trunk thick or not. And if it is, that nigga's real stingy with it. I know who can get it though." She tosses her head, giving me a raised eyebrow. "You, Miss Pasha, girl."

"Bitch, your ass is crazy and trifling to the highest degree," Mona snaps, getting up from her seat. She tosses all the balled-up tissue she's had in her hand in the trashcan. "Pasha isn't gonna stoop that low and do no nasty shit like that."

Cassandra plants a hand up on her hip. "Mmmph. I don't know

why not. It ain't like she wasn't already out there suckin' dingdong anyway. Shit. And that ain't no rumor, sugah-boo. That came straight out of the cum-guzzler's mouth. She loves to suck that wee-wee."

I shoot her a nasty look.

"*What?* What I say that you ain't already say? Shit, you know it ain't no secret. Booty loves takin' it in the ass. And *whaaat?* So what if you love takin' it to the back of the throat? Suckin' dick is good for the soul, Miss Pasha, girl. Do what you love, sugah-boo. But this time, don't be no fool about it. Suck that shit for a cause."

Mona rolls her eyes. "Stax is Jasper's cousin. Or have you forgotten that?"

"Booga-coon, *boom!* And the nigga wants to fuck *his* wife, who likes takin' dingdong to the back of her throat. And *whaaat?* Ain't nobody forget shit. But obviously *you* have. Now I ain't one to be messy. And I ain't about to spill no family secrets, so don't do me. But *you* know all 'bout how messy them nigga-coons are; especially JT's no-good, child-molestin' ass."

What in the hell is Booty's crazy-ass talking about now? I cut my eyes over at Mona. The color in her face starts to drain. She blinks. Whatever family secret Booty is referring to has clearly shaken Mona. But she holds it together.

Of course Cassandra isn't the least bit concerned by Mona's reaction to her comment. "Miss Pasha, girl, do what you gotta do to get them pussy-niggas who tried to do you *got*. Throat that nigga, sugah-boo. And trust me. If you swallow his nut real good, you'll have that nigga in the palm of ya messy-ass hands. Oooh, I wanna watch, goddammit." She hoists her bag up over her shoulder. "Look, I gotta get down to the club before I miss all the dingaling swingin'. I need my throat wet." She slides me the folded paper in her hand. "Don't open this 'til you get in your car. Then call me.

Mona ain't ready for this shit we 'bout to do. But you know I love me a good goddamn fight."

She swings open the office door, then glances over at Mona who is sitting stone still, almost in a trance. "So you might as well keep your trap shut 'n' have several seats *alllllll* the way on the back of the bus 'cause you ain't ready for the front row, sweetness. And you definitely ain't built for this life. I can't stand me no pussy-ass bitches."

The face hidden behind a mask isn't always a pretty one...

"Good morning, Nappy No More. Pasha speaking."

"Miss Pasha, girl, you still ain't said shit 'bout me comin' through to get my hair did, goddammit. You saw me wearin' that ole nasty head wrap last night. After I left y'all asses last night, I got to the club just in time to see me thirty minutes of them ole oily ding-dongs swingin', then I tore the dance floor up. Chunky Monkey did me right, goddammit. Oooh, yes, sugah-boo. I dropped it down so low I done sweated this ole nasty mop out."

I shake my head, baffled by how over-the-top Cassandra is; yet, so unfazed by the fact that she has a dead body on her hands. I'm still in shock that she actually *killed* JT. And I'm even more stunned—and silently awed—at how she can keep it moving, doing her, acting like what she did is no big deal.

I shudder.

Somehow, although Cassandra didn't kill him on my behalf, I feel as if I owe her for doing what she did. That nigga *deserved* to die. And hearing the news of her killing JT—after he beat her and tried to rape her, for some reason, liberated me. It confirmed my pain. It authenticated my burning desire for vengeance. Now he's one less nigga I gotta do in. Still, a part of me feels like she stole my moment, wishing I could have been there to see his demise. I would have loved to look in that nigga's eyes before he took his last breath. I would have loved to be the last face that nigga saw before she snatched his breath away. Oh well.

I fight a yawn back. *I'm exhausted.*

After Booty left up out of here, Mona broke down again. And it scared me. I thought she was having a nervous breakdown the way she screamed and cried, saying how she felt so guilty for secretly wanting JT dead. How at first she was relieved that someone had finally did him in. She kept talking in riddles. Kept alluding to him fucking her life up. Then in the next breath, she was saying how much she loved him. How much her heart ached that he was gone. She had me confused. I literally held her in my arms until she was finally able to calm down. Then I asked her what family secret Booty was talking about. And why it had her looking as if she was about to pass out.

She covered her face in her hands, quietly sobbing. We sat in my office for almost ten minutes before she finally blurted out, "Jaheim molested me when I was eleven years old."

My eyes widened in shock, disgust, and then filled with sadness for her. *That fucking savage!* I asked her if she had ever told anyone. She said no. Said she was afraid to.

"Oh, Mona, I'm so sorry to hear this. Was it only once?"

She shook her head. Told me no. That he had been going on for almost three years. At first it was only kissing and touching. Then feeling on her chest to sucking on her nipples, then rubbing between her legs. Then over time it went from licking her pussy to him wanting her to touch his dick, then kiss his dick, then suck on it. Then it went to him finger-fucking her. Then full-fledged fucking by the time she was twelve.

I gasped, feeling tears well up in my own eyes.

From what I remember about his delinquent ass through Jasper, he was sent to live with Mona and her family when he was like ten. Before that he had been living with his mother in Connecticut where they are all from. But he was constantly in and out of trouble, always fighting and hanging out with the wrong crowd all hours of the night. He had even been arrested a few times for breaking into cars with a group of older boys. JT was the one that no one's parents ever wanted their kids to play with because he was so thuggish and grown for his age.

"When did it finally stop?" I asked, clasping her hands into mine. She told me when she turned fourteen. Right after he got sent to juvie for a gun charge.

She started sobbing again. "I swore I'd never talk about this after he left. I wanted to forget it. I knew what he was doing was wrong. But after awhile, it felt good. I looked forward to him sneaking into my room and spending that time with him. I looked forward to him *fucking* me." I cringed hearing her admitting that. "When he got arrested and sent away for that gun charge, a part of me was relieved. And I was angry. But, there was that other part of me who secretly missed him. I cried."

And then I almost hit the floor when she told me freshman year in high school she was pregnant with his baby. And how she wanted to keep it. That by the time she finally told her parents, she was almost four months' pregnant.

I blink.

"Pasha, they demanded to know who the father was. I couldn't tell them it was JT's. So I lied. I told them I didn't know. I'd rather they thought I was out there being a fast-ass, than for them to know the truth. I couldn't tell them what he'd being doing to me. I felt like I had to protect him. To protect our secret."

She started crying again. "Him getting locked was the best thing that could have happened to me. Then when he got released and went back to Connecticut, I knew I'd be okay. By that time he was messing with Leticia. I didn't see him much after that, except maybe holidays or a family function. And when we did see one another, we pretty much avoided each other. Then I graduated and went off to college. And then I met Avery, who was the first man I felt like I could be with. I've only had sex with two men in my life. Avery. And JT.

"Pasha, I'm so ashamed to admit this. But I can't fucking believe I was jealous of Leticia. I hated her. I mean, I really felt like she had stolen JT from me." She shook her head, wiping tears. "That's how fucked up in the head he had me." She paused, shutting her eyes, then opening them. "I shouldn't even say this. But sometimes I don't even like having sex with my husband. Sometimes when he wants me to give him head, I can't. It's like after all these years, sometimes I still see JT's dick being shoved in my mouth."

Ohmygod…no wonder she has issues with dick sucking, I thought as I consoled her. I was tempted to tell her she should tell Avery about it, but decided against it. So I suggested she should get counseling. But how hypocritical was that? There I was telling her she should probably see someone to help her heal. Yet, I had refused to see someone when it was offered to me at the hospital. Then recommended once I was released.

No. I didn't need some shrink to try to get up in my head to help me figure out shit, then. And I damn sure don't need one now. I already know what I need to do. Moving on for me, healing for me, comes is bringing Jasper down and making them niggas pay for what they did to me. Retribution. That's all the counseling I need.

Between murder, attempted, molestation, then add my shit to

the mix, and the three of us were bitches who had been affected by JT's slimy ass in one way or another. Thinking about it makes me sick to my damn stomach.

Booty grunts, bringing me back to the conversation. "And I ain't even get me no dingaling last night. Them tired-ass niggas last night wasn't ready for none of this booty heat. But I do have me a new sponsor now."

"I'm not surprised. I know you stay in recruit mode."

"You got that right. Shit, I got kids to feed. And I likes to keep myself did up right, goddammit. So you know these niggas gotta do Booty right, sugah-boo. But anyway, this new nigga is a gorilla in the face, but he got one'a them big ole king-size anaconda dingalings; the kind that'll rip ya insides out if you ain't no skilled dick rider. Thank gawd. All I gotta do is let him sniff my panties 'n' I got him peelin' off stacks. Ain't no tellin' what Gorilla Face gonna do once I put this heat up on them balls, Miss Pasha, girl. But that ain't neither here nor there. I need my hair done today. And you better not even try to do me, goddammit."

I shake my head, flipping through the appointment book. My schedule is rather light today, which is a good thing since I want to get home a little earlier. I tell her if she can get here in the next ten minutes, I can fit her in.

"Sugah-boo, *boom!* I'm already outside. I'll be in a sec."

I chuckle to myself. "Ohmygod. I can't with you. I'll see you when you get inside." We hang up as my cell phone starts ringing. I pull it out of my pocket, glancing at the screen. It's Thick Seven. "Hello."

"Hey, beautiful. My dick misses you."

I smile. "Oh, is that so? Well, we'll have to try to do something about that."

"Soon I hope," he says all low and raspy. "You know I'm hooked, right?"

"If you say so."

"Nah, I know so, baby. You already know what it is; don't front. You keep my dick hard. You the only woman who has ever made my balls tingle while gettin' head. I wake up with a hard-ass dick, thinking about you. Real shit, baby, you'll fuck around and have me giving you my whole paycheck."

I laugh. "Well, lucky for you I don't need it."

"Yeah, lucky me. I got kids to feed. Listen, though. I got a hard dick and I want some of that throat work."

I grin. "Is that all you want?"

He lowers his voice. "What you think?"

I see Booty heading toward the door. She stops, her hand on the door, when some tall, young guy who looks to be in his early twenties says something to her. He's grinning and licking his lips as he talks to her. But judging by the way Booty is rolling her neck, the conversation must not have gone well. I hear her say, "Niggah-coon, boom! Eat the inside of my ass," as she walks through the door.

"Oooh, these young niggas stay tryna get me turnt up early in the morning." She's wearing another fly-ass pair of heels. This time chocolate brown peep-toes. Her designer jeans wrap around every curve of her body. She walks by the counter as I'm on the phone, tossing a hand up at me. I cut my eyes over at her backside, then shift them back to the appointment book.

"So when you think we're gonna be able to link up again?" Thick Seven wants to know. I tell him I'm not sure, that my next appointment's here and I'll call him later. "Aiight, bet. I gotta bounce anyway." We disconnect.

"Come on, Cass, girl," I say, slipping my phone back into my pocket, heading back toward my workstation. "Let's see how much of a mess your hair is."

She grunts, taking a seat in my chair. "Mmmph. Don't do me, Miss Pasha, girl. You know this wig's a damn mess." She plants her Louis bag up in her lap, then unwraps her head wrap. "Now do me right, goddammit."

The way she's carrying on, I expected to see her tracks tore up from the roots, but they're not. She's actually taken good care of them.

Rhodeshia laughs. "Girl, you're hilarious."

Booty grunts. "And you're too goddam nosey. You still runnin' ya dick lappers with Miss FeFe?"

"Uh-unh, Cassandra. Don't have me toss you up out of here. Today's your first day back up in here. Don't start."

She laughs, waving me on. "Miss Pasha, girl, *boom*. You know I'ma keep it classy. But, still…that *bit*—I mean, chick—*is* nosey. And I think she's messy. And you know I don't do messy."

Rhodeshia shakes her head. "Well, I'm sorry you feel that way. But that's so not me."

Booty shoots her a dirty look. "Mmmph. You talk to Miss FeFe?"

Rhodeshia gives her a confused look. "Who?"

"See, there you go playin' retarded. Miss Messy-Ass *Felecia*, that's who. Do you talk to her?"

"Yeah, sometimes. Why?"

Cassandra looks at me through the mirror, giving me one of those "see-I-told-you-that-bitch-is-messy" looks. I sigh, already knowing what I'm going to have to do if I ever catch her wrong. Fire her!

"Mmmph, well, tell that messy bitch the next time you talk to her that she got an ass-whoopin' on layaway waitin' on her."

Rhodeshia frowns. "Um, no thank you, boo. I don't play messenger."

"Nigga-coon, *boom!*" Cassandra snaps, shooting an imaginary gun at her. "The first chance you get, you're gonna be on the phone with her yappin' your cum box. Miss Pasha, girl, you know I don't do messy. But I know messy a mile away."

I shake my head, leaning her head back into the sink. "I know you do, girl." I cut my eye over at Rhodeshia, making a mental note to keep my eye on her.

"Miss Pasha, girl, watch that ho." She lowers her voice. "Did you get a chance to look at that note I slid you last night?" I tell her I forgot all about it. She smacks her lips together. "Ain't gonna say much right now 'cause you know you got nosey-ass bitches lurkin' 'round here. But, anyway, I had me a good damn time down at The Crack House last night."

"Ohmygod," Kendra shrieks as she turns her client around in her chair facing the mirrors. She's finished her client's micro-braids and is now curling her ends. "I love the nights Chunky Monkey deejays, with his fine self."

Her client chimes in. "Girl, I heard he's good in bed, too."

"Mmmph," Cassandra says low enough for only me to hear. "What I tell you? A buncha nosey-ass bitches, lurkin'. Anyway, that fine-ass nigga is all balls, sugah-boo. But you ain't hear that from me 'cause you know I can't stand a gossipin'-ass ho."

I shake my head, chuckling at that. *Sweetie, you're the messiest of 'em all.* She's so thick in denial that it's almost hilarious. "Cass, you're a mess."

"Uh-huh. But you know I ain't ever messy." Her cell phone rings as I'm wrapping a towel around her head. I raise her up from the sink. Then start combing conditioner through her hair. She answers her phone. "What is it, Day'Asia? No you can't stay the night over Clitina's...what you tryna do, suck dick in the stairwell tonight? Yeah, right. I know how you do. And I know that whore-ass Clitina, too.

"Bring yo' ass in the house right after school, Day'Asia. Matter of fact, I want that nasty-ass bedroom cleaned by the time I get home. And I better not find no bloody draws stuffed under ya mattress, either..."

I cringe. *Ugh!*

"No, goddammit...what the fuck I say, Day'Asia...? No, she can't stay the night, either. Look, *don't* do me...Bitch, I'm tryna keep it classy, but you tryna have me take it to the ghetto with ya ass. Now keep it up...What the fuck did I just finish tellin' ya black, crusty ass? See...no, bitch, you tryna make me flip on the ghetto-switch 'n' turn it up on ya goddamn skull. Don't have me fuck you up."

She disconnects the call. "Goddamn kids stay tryna do me," she mutters, tossing her phone into her bag. "Miss Pasha, girl, be glad you ain't have you no hot-in-the-ass girl. I swear I don't know where the hell she get that shit from."

I blink. I don't say a word. But, in my head, I'm thinking, "She's exactly like your ass, *sugah-boo.*"

The only difference is, Day'Asia isn't pregnant. Booty's hot ass been fucking and sucking since she was twelve, and was knocked up by the time she was thirteen, or fourteen. I can't remember. All I know is, she was pregnant almost every year after that, popping babies out like damn rabbits. And here she is, ten kids and eight baby daddies later.

"Miss Pasha, girl, I'll be glad when her ass turns eighteen. She's gettin' the fuck outta my house. Ooh, she works my last damn nerve."

I chuckle.

A few clients chime in, sharing their woes with having daughters.

I don't say much. Shit, if I had a daughter, I'd be worried her ass would be another Day'Asia, sucking dick in stairwells and shit. Hopefully, the only thing I'll have to be concerned with when Jaylen becomes a teenager is, him getting caught with his dick down in some girl's throat at school. And, hopefully, not getting some hot-ass girl pregnant.

I shudder at the thought, relieved that I have a long way before I have to worry about any of that. I glance up at the wall clock. 10:15.

I'll be glad when this day is over!

Fifteen

There's a calm before every storm. And then the aftermath...

"Yessss, goddammit!" Cassandra says, looking in the mirror admiring her new do when I'm finally done. She turns her head from side to side. "You shitted your drawz with this right here, Miss Pasha, girl." I removed the weave I had put in several weeks ago, then washed and conditioned her hair. Then I cut it into a short sassy style and gave her a sweeping bang over her right eye that drops to her jawline. I added some weave to give it more body, although she has—well, had—a head full of hair and doesn't need weaves. Anyway, the back is tapered real close with asymmetric points along the nape. She swings her hair. "Oooh, you did me right, goddammit!"

I can't help but laugh at her ass as I unsnap the cape from around her neck. "Thanks, girl." I glance up at the clock. It's only eleven o'clock and I'm already exhausted.

Booty stands, fixing her self in the wall mirror, handing me back the handheld mirror. "Ooooh, I'ma tear the club up tonight. Mmmph. Miss Pasha, girl, can't a bitch do me like you do, sugah-boo. Ooh, wait. I need you to bring down the back a taste. I wanna keep these edges real tight." She runs her hand along the nape of her neck. "Yesss, goddammit, you did that. You need to come on down to the club tonight. You ain't gotta stay long, sugah-boo. But it's time you get out 'n' sweep it to the floor a taste. Let ya wig down, sugah-boo. And you ain't gotta worry 'bout no kinda hood drama kickin' up tonight; they real classy ghetto on Tuesday and Thursday nights. The coon-boogas 'n' nigga-trolls don't come out 'til Friday and Saturday nights."

I shake my head, knitting my brows together. "Booty, you know I'm not gonna be caught dead up in there. That's not even my type of club."

She raises her eyebrow, eyeing through the mirror. "What you tryna say, Miss Pasha, girl? That you too good for the Crack House? You standin' here soundin' like you tryna say only a buncha hood-rat 'n' ghetto hooker-boos hang out down at the club. And I know I ain't neither one of them kinda bitches. I always keep it real hood-classy when I step out. Well, unless a coon tryna do me, then I gotta flip up the ghetto switch a taste. But I don't ever keep it turnt all the way up. I go out to have me a good goddamn time. Something you need to learn to do. You too uptight, Miss Pasha, girl; what you need'a do is come out 'n' make that cootie-coo pop a taste. Swirl them hips 'n' dip it down low."

As I'm about to open my mouth to say something, Jasper and Stax walk toward my station. I didn't hear the door open with all the chatter and commotion going on back here.

"Yo, let me holla at you for a minute," Jasper says, walking up on me. I can already tell his ass is still tight with me for getting home well after midnight last night. Yet, that nigga left up out of the house and still hadn't gotten home by the time I left to drop Jaylen at daycare this morning.

But whatever!

I step back from him. Booty eyes me, then sits back down in my chair. I snap the cape back around her neck, turning on the clippers. "I'm still doing Cassandra's hair."

He looks Booty up and down. "Her shit looks done to me. What's good, Cass?"

She igs him.

Stax and I exchange uneasy glances. I shift my eyes from his.

"What's good, Pash. How you?"

"I'm good." I catch him eyeing me through the mirror.

"That's wassup." He speaks to Booty. She speaks back.

"Oh, that's the only muhfucka you see?" Jasper says to her. "You can't speak, yo? That's how you doin' it now?"

"Nigga-coon, *boom!*" she finally says, rolling her eyes at him. "Ya ass is invisible, darkie; with ya ole lyin'-ass self. You trick-niggas kill me. Annnnywaaay, Stax. When you gonna stop all these games, boo, 'n' let me put this booty heat up on you?"

He laughs. Tells her she's shot out. I shake my head, chuckling.

Jasper mutters something under his breath, then asks her when was the last time she'd seen JT around. And that sets her switch off. She goes from zero to a hundred. The whole shop gets quiet listening to her snap.

"What the fuck you askin' me 'bout *that* nigga-coon for? Do I look like his goddamn secretary to you? I don't keep up with that pussy-bitch. You should be askin' his dumb-ass wife that shit, with her non-dick sucking ass 'n' dry-ass pussy. I ain't on goddamn coon patrol. Askin' me some shit 'bout his black-ass. When's the last time you fucked that lil Indian-lookin' bitch, huh? Since you wanna ask questions 'n' shit."

I blink. *She must be talking about Chanel.* Chanel's a chick from Brooklyn who'd come into my salon a few times to get her hair done. But the last time she was here, Cassandra caught Jasper winking at her, and Miss Lady giving him the "you-can-get-it-on-the-sly" eyes. And of course, Booty put them both on blast.

Jasper glares at her. I can see the muscles in his jaws tightening. Booty has definitely hit a nerve. She slides a hand down in her bag. "Nigga, I wish you'd even think it."

"This fuckin' bitch," he mumbles. "Let me get the fuck away from her triflin' ass before I do some crazy shit. Yo, Pash, let me holla at you." He walks off toward my office, leaving Booty cranked all the way up on high.

"Nigga-bitch, get crazy. Do me, nigga. And do me right, god-dammit! You *know* I got your motherfuckin' card, nigga. And that shit's 'bout to get punched real quick, bitch."

I shoot Booty a look to get her to shut her fucking mouth. She has the whole shop on pause, catching an ear-and-eyeful.

"Damn, Cass, relax, baby," Stax says, walking behind her. He starts massaging her shoulders. "Why you spazz out like that, yo?"

"You know I can't stand Jasper's goddamn ass. And that nigga stays tryna do me. Oooh, that feels so good, sugah-boo. Oooh, yes, thug daddy, do me right, goddammit. Now *you* on the other hand, boo-thang, can do me all night. Oooh, you so goddamn fiiine, Stax. You make my cootie-coo whistle e'ery time I see you, boo. I don't know why you bein' stingy with the dingdong. All I want is me a lil taste, boo. I'm not tryna keep it."

He laughs, stopping his mini-massage and walking away from in back of the chair, quickly cutting his eyes over at me. "Yo, Cass, chill, ma. You shot out, yo."

"Mmmph. Shot out hell. I only wanna shot of that cum juice, boo. I ain't ever been one to sip on the slut-juice, but I'll toss a bucket of it back for you for some of that love cream, boo. Yess, *FahverGawd*, I sure will."

Stax is cracking up. "Yo, Cass, I ain't fuckin' wit' you, ma. You wild as hell, yo."

"I ain't playin', Stax. You need to let me drop down on that dingaling one good time. Put this heat all up on them balls."

I shake my head amazed at how she can go from one extreme to the next in the blink of an eye. She has practically everyone in tears laughing at her antics.

"Cass, I can't with you, girl."

"Pasha, what the fuck, yo!" Jasper yells out.

I frown. *Oh this nigga has really lost his mind!* I take a deep breath, keep my focus on finishing up Booty's neck. I shut the clippers off when I'm done, setting them down. "Give me a sec to go see what this crazy nigga wants," I say in a hushed tone.

"Mmmph. You good, sugah-boo. I'd make that no-good nigga wait, comin' up in here like he runnin' thangs. Booga-coon, *boom-boom!* You ain't it."

Sixteen

Some bitches are born crazy. Others just snap…

I walk into my office and find Jasper sitting on the edge of my desk, looking extra tight. His legs are stretched out, arms folded tight across his chest. I shut the door.

I swear this nigga's bipolar.

I take a deep breath. "Okay, Jasper, what do you need to say that couldn't wait?"

"Yo, why the fuck is Cass's ass sittin' up in this muhfucka? You know that bitch likes to keep shit stirred up, yo. That trouble-makin' bitch stays runnin' her muthafuckin' trap, yo. She ain't gonna be satisfied 'til a muhfucka knocks her lights out."

Yeah, like you did to me! And like JT's ass tried to do to her! Only difference, his black ass is dead.

"Look, Jasper. Don't start. Cassandra is a good customer, a loyal one at that. And she pays top dollar for my services, so don't come up in here disrespecting her or tryna mess with my money."

"Fuck outta here wit' that dumb shit, yo. I asked that bitch one simple question 'n' she come outta her fuckin' neck at me all sideways."

"Well, why in the world would you be asking *her* of all people about JT?" I ask, feigning ignorance. "You still haven't heard anything?"

He sneers. "Yo, why the fuck you think I asked her dumb-ass? If I heard from the nigga, do you think I woulda asked that bitch? That bitch disrespected me, and ya dumb-ass ain't even check her on it."

Let me hurry up and get this motherfucker up out of here before I go off!

I bite down on my bottom lip. Count to ten in my head. He stuffs his hand down into his front pocket, pulling out a wad of bills. He peels off three Benjamins, flicking them at me like I'm some stripper bitch.

"Here's ya top dollar for ya services, yo. Tell that ghetto-ass bitch this is her last time up in this muhfucka. 'Cause the next time I come up in this muhfucka 'n' that bitch comes at me crazy, I'ma have her fuckin' neck snapped."

I slam my hand up on my hip. I've had enough! "Nigga, you must be on that shit. Don't come up in here making those kinds of threats. You better go back outside and read the sign. It's *Nappy No More*, nigga. Not *Jasper's*. So don't come at me like it's your name up on the sign. You might *think* you run shit at home. But you *don't* run shit up in here."

"Yeah, aiight, yo. I'ma take it to ya mouth real quick, yo. I'm tellin' you, yo. I'm not in the mood for ya shit. You 'bout to catch it, Pasha. Keep poppin' shit, ya heard?"

I tilt my head. "Jasper, you know what? I'm done with your threats. Do what you gonna do and be done with it. You can't do no more to me than what you've already done, nigga. Now what do you need to *holla* at me about? This is my place of business and I have clients to tend to."

He stands, walking over to me. "Yeah, aiight, whatever, yo. Take them drawers off, yo. I want some pussy."

I give him a disgusted look. "Nigga, I don't think so. I'm not your fucking whore. Those days are over. I *let* you fuck me when I got back from California. But this pussy is no longer on the menu for you. And I mean that."

I turn to walk toward the door, but he snatches me by the arm.

"You *let* me? Fuck outta here. Yo real shit, Pasha, don't let that crazy bitch out there put a battery pack up on ya back 'n' get you fucked up, yo. "

I yank my arm back. "Oh really? Why, because she put you and Felecia's asses on blast? Or is it because she called you out when she caught you making googly eyes with that Chanel bitch while her ass was sitting in my chair? You come up in my shop and disrespect me, flirting with some other bitch."

"Yo, you still on that shit? Fuck outta here, yo. Wasn't nobody makin' googly eyes or flirtin' wit' that stuck-up bitch. And ain't nobody ever fuck Felecia's dirty ass. But you wanna listen to some hoodrat bitch. I'm tellin' you, yo. Go 'head 'n' keep listenin' to that hood roach if you want. That bitch gonna get your jaw dropped."

"You know what. I'm doing this with you. Get the fuck out of my shop. I'm sick of you—"

Before I can get the rest of my words out, this nigga smacks the shit out of me. I stumble back, grabbing the side of my face. Stunned.

"I'm sick of ya muthafuckin' mouth, yo. You stay poppin' that dumb shit, Pasha." He hits me again. And I swear it feels like he's knocked me three feet backward. "I don't know why you make me have'ta put my fuckin' hands on you, yo. You must really like it when I fuck you up. Is that it, yo?"

I'm literally in shock. Jasper has put his hands on me six times too many. And he's always done it behind closed doors—at home! This is the first time that this nigga's put his fucking hands on me *here*…in my goddamn salon. I touch my lip, then look at the blood on my fingers.

I charge him, punching and slapping him all upside his head. My nails dig into his face, his neck, slicing open his dark skin. He tries to restrain me. I elbow him in his ribs. I use every technique I've learned in my self-defense training over the last year. And give it to him.

"Yo, what the fuck, yo? Don't have me fuck you up, Pasha. Chill."

"*Chill*, hell, motherfucker! I'm sick of you putting your god-damn hands on me." I dig my nails into his neck, clawing him up. Bite him in his chest. He swings me around. Wraps his thick arms around me in a bear hug, trying to squeeze the air out of me. I dig my nails into his arm, bite into his flesh. Clamp down so tight until I break skin, until this nigga starts to howl. He lets go, then wrestles me down to the floor.

"Fuck, yo!" He slaps the shit out of me. His hand feels like lead. And I swear I hear my jaw shatter. A part of me is relieved that my office is all the way in the back of my salon and door is shut so no one can hear us in here tossing shit up. But another part of me wishes someone would barge in and catch this nigga on top of me, my arms pinned up over my head. Screaming would be a moot point since I had my office soundproofed over the summer.

I clench my teeth. "Get the fuck off of me, Jasper."

"Hell, naw. Not until you calm the fuck down, yo. You outta pocket, yo."

I spit at him, a mixture of my blood and his. "No, nigga. *You're* the one who's outta pocket for thinking you can keep putting your goddamn, motherfucking hands on *me*. Get. The. Fuck. Off. Me!" I try to wriggle myself from under him, but he has all of his weight on me.

"What the fuck's wrong wit' you, yo, huh? You want ya ass beat, is that it, Pash?" Something comes over me and I stop wriggling around. I lie there on the floor, staring him down. My nose flares. This is *finally* it for me. I'm fucking *done* with this crazy nigga always talking shit. I'm done with his goddamn threats. I'm done with him *thinking* I'm his personal punching bag. I'm done with dragging out what I should have already done. Handled this nigga, once and for all.

This motherfucker has the nerve to start grinding his dick into me. "You stay on ya bullshit, Pasha. I want some pussy, yo. You got my shit hard as fuck. I wanna fuck you, right here. Let me get up in them muthafuckin' drawz. You gonna have a muhfucka kill yo' ass if you don't chill the fuck out."

I hear Booty's voice in my head saying, *"Do him right, goddammit!"*

A sly grin eases over my face. I flip the script on his ass. "I know, Jasper. You make me so fucking crazy; that's all. You know you the only nigga for me." He eases his grip off my hand. "You keep my pussy wet, Jasper."

He groans. "Then act like it, yo. And stop playin' all these muthafuckin' games, yo." He lets my wrists go, moving one hand along the side of my body; his other hand grabs at my breasts. "Let me get up in this pussy, yo."

My arms and wrists are bruised from where he's grabbed them. My jaw aches. I can feel the side of my face swelling. My bottom lip is swollen and throbbing. I take a deep breath.

"I wanna suck your dick, first. Can I have daddy's big thick dick, huh, baby?"

He hops the fuck up off of me real quick at the thought of getting some of this neck-pussy. Nigga acts like nothing ever happened. That he didn't just have me pinned down on the floor, or slapped me up.

I eye him as he hastily unfastens his belt, unzips the fly of his True

Religions, then fishes his semi-hard dick out of his underwear. I ease up on my knees, licking my lips. I kiss the head of his dick. "Oooh, look at that big dick…"

I yank his jeans and boxers down to his knees.

"I'ma give it to you real good, Jasper," I say all low and sweet. "All this big, beautiful, black dick," I whisper, taking it in my hands, looking up at him. I kiss over and under and along the shaft. "All this good dick."

"Yeah, that's right. 'Bout time you handle ya man right. Put ya mouth up on that dick, yo."

I slowly lick around the head. Then wrap my lips around it, suckling it. His dick thickens and stretches as I suck it into my mouth, inch by inch, until it hits the back of my throat. I throat it nice and slow, long neck it, short neck it. Bring it back up to the head, then gulp it right back down to the base. The deeper his dick goes down into my neck, the wetter my mouth gets. I suck this nigga's dick like it's the last supper. My tongue, my lips, my throat all working in sync, giving it to him in a way he'll never forget.

"Aaah, shit, yeah, yo. Fuck, Pasha! You gonna have me kill a muh-fucka over you, yo. Fuck! Aaah, shiiit, yeah…"

I cup his heavy balls. Lightly tug at them. Graze them with my fingernails. I pull his spit-coated dick from out of my neck, glide my hand over its slippery head, then slowly jack him off, while licking around his balls.

"Aaah, shit, yeah…lick them balls…Yeah, jack that dick, yo…"

I glance up at him, his balls deep in my mouth, the back of my throat humming, grinning. His head is tossed back. His bottom lip is pulled in. He has both hands up on his hips, rocking at the knees. I wet his balls up real good, rapidly stroking his dick. He grunts and groans. Tells me he's about to nut.

And, then…

I lock my jaws around his ball sac and bite into his balls with everything in me. I chew and grind. I use all thirty-two of my teeth to tear into his flesh. Jasper lets out a bloodcurdling scream. He tries to punch me off of his shit, but the pain is too intense. The more he tries to fight me off of him, the harder I bite. I gnaw into his balls until the nigga's knees buckle and he hits the floor. And I don't let go until my mouth fills with blood. Until tears spring from this nigga's eyes, until he breaks out in a sweat, and he nearly passes out.

"Arrrrrrrrrgh, fuuuuuuck!!" He cups his balls, rolling back and forth, legs balled up to his chest. "Aarrrrrrgh…! I'ma…uggggggggh! Fuuuuck…!"

I calmly pull myself up off the floor. Walk over to my desk, pull out the key to my top drawer, then unlock it as he's groaning and rolling around in pain, making all kinds of threats toward me for chewing his balls up. I yank open the drawer.

"I'ma…fuckin'…arrrgh…kill…arrrgh…!"

The metallic taste of his blood is coated on my tongue. I clench my teeth, snatching out my Clock then calmly walking back over to him as he attempts to get up, bringing the butt of my gun across his face.

"Aaaaaah! Fuck! Aarrrrrgh…!"

"Motherfucker! This is the last time you'll *ever* put your hands on me, threaten me, or get your dick wet by me." I hit him across the face again, causing a deep gash over his eye. "I'm fucking done with you! Now get the fuck up!"

I can tell I got the nigga dazed. But he isn't going down. He struggles to get up. There's blood trickling down his leg. He leans over, cupping his groan. When he glances at the blood on his fingertips, looks as if he's about to pass out.

"Ugh shit! What the fuck...?!" Blood streaks down his face. He keeps his eyes on me as he tries to pull up his pants, groaning. He drops back down on his knees. "Uggh! You fucked...my balls up...shiiiit...uhhhh...!"

"I want you the fuck out of my life, nigga!" I screw on the silencer. His eyes pop open. "You should have killed me when you had the chance, nigga." I aim the gun at his head. His eyes pop open.

For the first time in a long time, holding this gun in my hand, it pointed at Jasper's goddamn head, seeing his eyes pop open, makes me feel powerful. Like I'm the bitch in charge—*finally*. I could really kill his ass, right here, right now. And feel nothing.

He throws one hand up, his other still holding his bleeding ball sac. "Whoa, whoa...Uggggh, fuck...Pasha, what the fuck is...shit, yo you doin'..."

I cock the gun back, and shoot over his head. I purposefully miss, hitting the wall in back of him with a heavy *thud*. But it gets his ass shook. The nigga didn't think I had it in me. Didn't think I'd ever pull a gun out on his ass.

"I'm goddamn done. You come *any*where near me, Jasper, and I *will* put a fucking bullet in your motherfucking face, nigga. I want you the *fuck* outta my salon, nigga. And I want you outta *my* mother*fucking* house by the time I get home tonight."

He frowns, wiping the blood from his face with the end of his shirt. "That's my shit, too, yo...ugggh, fuck..." he hunches over, clutching his balls again. "Uhhh, fuuuuck...! I think you fucked up my balls! Aaaah fuck, yo...!"

"Nigga, count your blessings. The next time you step to me for any of this neck or pussy, I'm going to finish the job."

"Fuck, yo! You got my muthafuckin' balls bleedin', bitch!"

"Jasper...hurry up...and get. The. Fuck. Out. Or I will blow your fucking skull in." He keeps his eyes on me as he slowly backs up toward the door. The nigga can barely stand. I swing open the office door, call for Stax to come get this nigga.

A look of shock covers Stax's face the minute he steps through the door and sees Jasper on his knees bent over, his jeans and underwear hanging off his ass—showing his whole ass, groaning. "Oh, shit! What the fuck?" Stacks snaps, taking Jasper's bloody appearance in, then glancing at me. "What the fuck happen, yo?" Stax looks from him to me. He stares at Jasper's clawed-up neck, the gash over his eye, the bleeding teeth marks in his arm, the blood on his hands.

"The nigga put his goddamn hands on me and I clawed his ass up."

"Uuuh, fuck. Uhh, this bitch bit my balls, yo…uhhhh…"

"Get him the fuck up outta my motherfucking salon. And make sure you take his black ass to the house to get his shit. *All* of it! I want him out of *my* house by the time I get there, or I promise both of you he won't be the only motherfucker miss…" I catch myself before it all slips out.

Jasper pulls himself up, his pants drop around his hips, he quickly grabs them, trying to pull them up. He tries to walk but the nigga almost falls. Stax catches him, helping him limp his way to the door. His pants are falling off his ass. "Fuck! Uggggh! Bitch tried to bite my muthafuckin' shit off…get me the fuck up outta here, yo…I'ma fuckin' kill her…uggh, shiiit! Fuckin' bitch…ugggh!"

Stax helps walk him out of my office, groaning his way through the salon and out the fucking door with me following behind. Talking shit.

The whole shop is quiet. All eyes are on me. I have literally turned the place out, airing my personal business for all to see. And every jaw is dropped. Even Cassandra is deadpan.

It isn't until I look down that I finally realize what everyone is staring at.

I am still holding the gun in my hand.

And there's blood all around my mouth.

Seventeen

Sometimes you need to know how to fall back,
in order to plan an attack...

"Ooooooh, yes, goddammit, Miss Pasha, girl. You bent over 'n' showed yo' *assssss*, sugah-boo. You put the hood in classy 'n' turnt it all the way up to goddamn gutter. Yes, *FahverGawd!* You clawed that nigga-coon's neck up real good 'n' goddamn gooey, sweetness. Then you chomped into his balls! Came out with your mouth all bloody. Yessss, *FahverGawd!* Miss Pasha, girl, I ain't think you was gonna ever crank up the ghetto-switch, goddamn you! But you did me right, goddammit! I ain't even gonna lie, sweetness. My cootie-coo got a lil juicy when I looked down 'n' saw you had a gun in ya hand. And then to hear you done tried to eat his balls off. Oooh, yes, *FahverGawd*, you gave them messy bitches down at the salon some shit to gag on. And it wasn't no dingaling. Yessss, sugah-boo..."

With a blank expression and an icepack up to my face, I stare at Booty as she flaps her mouth a mile a minute, trying to figure out how in the hell I *ever* let her ass talk me into leaving the salon with her. But she did. And somehow I let her.

"Sugah-boo, that greasy-coon tried to do you," she stated, standing in the doorframe of my bathroom as I washed blood from my face, trying to convince her to take a break and get out of the office. "You need to get out 'n' get you some fresh air to get ya mind right."

"Oh, trust. My mind is more right than it's been in a long time."

She tooted her lips. "Mmmph. All'a bitch is tryna do is get you outta the buildin' for a taste so you ain't gotta be locked up in ya office, wonderin' what these messy bitches up front sayin' 'bout ya ass. But if you wanna sit up in here with ya face all lumped up and that nigga-coon's dingaling hairs all between ya teeth, starin' at the walls, then do you, sugah-boo."

I blinked, blinked again.

She continued, "After the way that nigga-coon tried to do your face, it's time you stop draggin' ya heels 'n' turn it up on his ass."

"Oh, I'm ready. I'm fucking done with his black ass. And the sooner I shut his ass down, the better."

"Allllright now, goddammit. You talkin' my talk, sugah-boo. Now, get ya handbag, sweetness, 'n' let's get the hell outta here so we can come up with a plan to do that nigga-bitch up right."

"Booty, I can't. I have another client coming in."

"Oh, no goddammit. *Boom-boom*, sugah-boo. See. You standin' here tryna do me with lies, Miss Pasha, girl. I done already swept my eyes across the schedule book up front before I came back here to talk to you. So don't do me, Miss Pasha, girl."

I couldn't help but laugh. I was busted. *This bitch has no boundaries*, I thought as I gathered my things, then locked up my office.

Five minutes later I was walking out of the salon, climbing up into the buttery soft seat of Booty's Range Rover and letting her drag me out.

And here I am...

In the heart of the hood.

At her house!

Sitting in her living room, on a plush leather sofa flanked by gorgeous marble end tables. A Bose home entertainment system is connected to a sixty-five-inch Sony television on the wall in front of us. There's a one-hundred-and-forty-gallon fish tank built into the wall on the right side of me with gorgeous tropical fish and coral reef inserts. And all of her kids' rooms—with the exception of her daughter's, which is a hot sloppy mess—is piped out with flat-screens, Apple PC's, and every latest game system out. I'm speechless!

"And this is how Day'Asia's filthy-ass is livin'," she stated as she opened the door to her room. "I ain't buyin' this nasty bitch shit 'til she learn how'ta keep her room clean. She lucky I broke down 'n' bought her that mattress 'n' box spring, but you see she ain't got no bedframe. She wanna be ghetto, then that bitch gonna sleep on the floor on them hard-ass K-mart sheets I bought her ass."

This is my first time ever seeing how Booty lives. Not only is it clean—the shit's laid out, like something out of a damn magazine. And as I'm sitting here listening to her rattle on, I can't help but keep thinking, "this bitch's driving a Range Rover, gets Section-8, almost nine-hundred dollars in food stamps, and has tens of thousands of dollars' worth of high-end shit in a home she rents and there are people who really need services and can't get them." *Something's seriously wrong with this picture.*

"Miss Pasha, girl, I had everything redone after that nigga-coon came up in here and tried to do me. My tables 'n' shit were all busted up from gettin' tossed up fuckin' wit' his ole crazy dead ass. I had them do me that fish tank in the wall over there, too. It was time to upgrade any-damn-way."

Who the hell cuts a hole into a wall of a home they're only renting to put a fish tank in it?

Anyway, it's not my concern.

"Oooh, I wish you woulda took it to the nigga-coon's skull," Booty says, causing me to look at her. "That coon-bitch nigga shoulda went rollin' out on a stretcher for doin' ya face up 'n' tryna snatch that cootie-coo, sweetness."

"Next time he will," I assure her.

"So how you wanna do these nigga-bitches, Miss Pasha, girl? 'Cause I'm ready to get messy, goddammit. And you know I don't do messy. But, them kinda niggas gotta get it real messy."

I push out a heavy sigh. "I…"

She hops up from the sofa. "Oooh, wait, sugah-boo. Hol' that thought. Let me go get my head right so I can relax my mind. I don't like to talk messy unless I'm in the right frame of mind." Her round ass bounces and shakes as she walk-runs down the hall. "We got three hours before the twins get home from school so we got plenty of time to chop it up real right, Sugah-boo," she calls out from down the hall. A few minutes later, she comes walking back with a bottle of Hennessy in one hand, two shot glasses and a fat blunt in the other.

I put a hand up to stop her from pouring me a drink. It's twelve-thirty in the afternoon. And I have to get back down to the salon soon. "Oh, no, girl, I'm good. You go on ahead and do you. But don't get your ass too tossed. I need you to get me back to the salon in one piece."

"Ooooh, nooo, sweetness. You tryna do me. Booty can drink a bar out 'n' still handle her business. I ain't ever gonna get so sauced I can't drive. I ain't tearin' up my shit." She fills both shot glasses. "Now, c'mon." She offers me a shot glass. "One taste ain't even gonna hurt you, Miss Pasha, girl."

"No, really." I glance at my watch. "I'm gonna have to get back to the salon soon."

Her brows furrow. "Don't do me, Miss Pasha, girl. You don't have another appointment 'til five o'clock. You ain't ever been to my home and you mean to say you can't relax your heels for a few. And I know you can use you a lil taste to numb that face, sugah-boo. I know that nigga-coon got ya face on fire. So don't even get cute. Step off that high horse 'n' c'mon down wit' the real bitches. You can have you one drank with me. As much coins I done spent in your salon, Miss Pasha, girl. And this how you gonna do me?"

Oh this bitch is really tryna guilt me. I give her an incredulous look, reluctantly taking the glass. "Booty, you're a damn mess, you do know that, right?"

"But I ain't ever messy. Now bottoms up, sugah-boo." She tosses her drink back. I follow right behind her, shaking my head as the elixir slides down into my chest, burning.

Three shot glasses later, I'm feeling more relaxed than I antici-pated. My heels are kicked off and my left foot his curled up under my right leg. I have my left arm draped over the top of the sofa. My body slightly shifted toward Booty. She's tossed back her fifth shot. And has smoked her blunt practically down to a roach.

"Miss Pasha, girl. I don't even know why I like your high-class ass. But I do, sugah-boo," she says, blowing a thick cloud of smoke up into the air. "You a real classy bitch. But you a sneaky bitch, too...."

I blink.

"Well, it's true, sweetness. You know Booty ain't one for lies 'n' games. I keep shit a hunnid, sugah-boo. But, anyway, you a mess, Miss Pasha, girl. Then I find out you is a cock 'n' cum freak, on top of that. Yes, *FahverGawd.* You are a mess. You better be glad I ain't no nigga 'cause I'd have my dingaling all down in ya gullet.

Yes, gawd, I'd fuck ya throat raw, Miss Pasha, girl. Ooh, you so lucky I ain't got me no real dingdong hanging over this cootie-coo. I'd give you what you like, goddammit. Do that throat up right...."

Mygod...this bitch has no limits!

"And here's two things I know for sure when it comes to you: a bitch bet' not ever say some sideways shit 'bout you to me or they gonna get a bottle to they heads. And when it comes to keepin' this hair did, can't a bitch do me like you do. But, mmmph, when we was in sixth grade I wanted to be your friend, but you wasn't beat for a bitch like me."

"That's not true," I lie. Truth is, I did my best to avoid her. She was loud, obnoxious, and extremely wild back then. Mmmph. Even now...not much's changed.

But here I sit.

She rolls her eyes, waving me on. "Oh, please. You was one'a them real uppity light-skin bitches with them pretty cat eyes. Ole spooky-lookin' bitch. But you was real cute. A lil too cute for ya own good, Miss Pasha, girl. All them street niggas stayed tryna suck the liner out ya drawz back then. And now you tryna suck the nut out theirs."

I feign insult. "Ohmygod, I can't believe you'd say some mess like that. That's so not true. We were just from two different worlds; that's all. You were a little too fast and wild for me, girl. All that fighting you did."

"Oooh, yess. I did have to drag a few bitches through the play-ground. I had to let them hatin' hoes know." She laughs. "And you know this big booty kept them lil horny niggas givin' up them lunch tickets 'n' milk money. But don't you even do me, Miss Pasha, girl, 'cause you *know* I know you used to do a lil slicin' 'n' dicin' ya'self. And I saw you drag plenty'a bitches ya'self, sugah-boo. And didn't you get dragged off in handcuffs a few times, too? Ooooh, yes, goddammit! You done got soft as cotton, Miss Pasha, girl. You need to pull that street bitch back out 'n' get it turnt up, goddammit!"

I shift in my seat. "Girl, that was then. This is now. People change, or at least try to. So let's fast-forward." I give her a serious look, wanting to change the subject. I let her know I really appreciate her wanting to have my back.

She twists her lips. "Sugah-boo, we gonna slay them niggas real right. And I mean that shit. Speakin' of which, you still ain't said shit 'bout that lil note I gave you the other night. Did you even look at it?"

I'd honestly forgotten about it. Without going into a bunch of details, I tell her I've had so much other shit going on that it keeps slipping my mind. I rummage through my handbag. But then it dawns on me when I can't find it that I've changed bags. "Cassandra, girl, I don't know what I did with it so you might as well tell me what it was."

She grunts. "Mmmmph…see you playin' games, Miss Pasha, girl. A real bitch is out here in the trenches for you, sugah-boo, 'n' the least you can do is be on top of shit I give you…"

I frown. "Ummm, wait one minute, Cass. Don't get it confused. *I* didn't ask *you* to jump down in the trenches to do shit, okay. You did that shit because you wanted to. Because you *like* being in the middle of shit that really has nothing to do with you. So whatever dirt you got up caked up under your fingernails is by your own doing. So let's get that straight right now."

"Hol' up, wait a minute, goddammit, Miss Pasha, girl. See you tryna be messy. I ain't gotta damn thang confused, sweetness. The confused one is *you* for marryin' Jasper's crazy-ass, but I ain't tryna get messy wit' you, sugah-boo, 'cause that's not how I do mine. But you tryna take me there. So don't do me. I *know* you ain't ask me to get down 'n' dirty for you. I did it 'cause you my goddamn boo. And I'm not lettin' no goddamn nigga-coon do my boo 'n' they think they gonna get away with it. No, goddammit. Not to-day, sugah-boo.

"So you can sit up on your messy-ass high horse 'n' toss shit down on me if you want, Miss Pasha, girl. But know this: Ain't another bitch out here gonna set it off like me. And you know I don't do messy, but I'm ready to get messy with you, sugah-boo. And can't a bitch bring it like I do. Not even Mona's scary ass. Where's that bitch at now? Somewhere rockin' 'n' wringin' her goddamn hands. So get yo' mind together. Get yo' life, goddammit! And let's do these nigga-coons in."

This bitch doesn't care what she says. But she's right. It's time for action. It's time to bring them niggas down. But I'd rather not be involved in any of Booty's shenanigans. Her ass is too reckless.

Maybe reckless is what I need to finally get this shit over with once and for all.

"Now, is you ready to set it off on these coon-niggas or what? One thing about Booty, baby, I do *whatever* I gotta do to get the job done, goddammit. A nigga-bitch tries to fuck me over, I'ma fuck 'em first. And, trust, sugah-boo. I'ma tear they asshole out the frame. It's gonna be rough 'n' goddamn dirty. And that's how we need'a bring it to them coon-niggas. Now to answer ya ques-tion 'bout what was on that paper I gave you. You know, the piece of paper you ain't even look at…"

I sigh. "Booty, will you tell me what was on it, please."

She smacks her lips. "I gave you that nigga-coon AJ's address."

"Suck my dick, bitch!"

My pulse quickens. "His address? How'd you get it?"

"I have my ways, sweetness. Now you wanna go there tonight 'n' kick in his door. Let's take it to his head, goddammit."

I shake my head. "No, no. Everything that happens needs to happen quietly. I don't want a bunch of unnecessary attention drawn to us. I wanna catch every last one of them when they least expect it. I don't want anyone to ever be able to link shit back to me, or you."

"Oh, no, sugah-boo. Booty knows how'ta move. I can reel his ass in for you. All I gotta do is tell him I'm ready to put this booty heat up on that stumpy dick 'n' he'll come runnin'."

"That's definitely something to consider. Oh, before I forget. Do you know anyone who has a tow truck?" She tells me she does. Scrolls through her contacts, then texts the number to my phone. "Thanks."

Something comes over me and I make a quick call to Sophia to find out if Jasper went to the house. She tells me no. I let out a sigh of relief. I don't trust him. *That motherfucker might try to take my son.* I tell her I want her to pack some things for Jaylen and have the car service drive them up here. That I'll meet them at the townhouse, then disconnect the call.

Booty eyes me. "Ooh, you real fancy, sugah-boo. I ain't even know you still had your place up here. I let her know I never sold it; that I've kept it empty since moving out of it. "Ooh, Miss Pasha, girl, you coulda rented that out. Got you a Section-8 tenant, 'n' boom, sugah-boo, you coulda been makin' you some nice greenery." I give her a confused look. "Money, sweetness. Get with the program, sugah-boo. Anyway, let me get somethin' to write with." She walks into the kitchen and returns with a pen and notepad. She starts writing. "Okay, let's see…"

She starts going through the names we have so far. "We'll put Miss Messy FeFe first since she's the one who did you the messiest. I mean them niggas did, too. But that bitch is family 'n' she side-swiped you, sugah-boo. And a bitch like her gotta get it good 'n' goddamn dirty! We can scratch that nigga-coon, JT off the list since he's already dropped. So Felecia's first. Then the nigga-coon, AJ, then I guess we should work on fishin' out that nigga-coon L. I still can't think of what he said his real name is, but whatever. I can call Dickalina 'n' get her to give him my number, then I'll make a date to give him some pussy. You know good pussy is a nigga's kryptonite, okay, sugah-boo. Plus, I wanna see what that dingaling look like. And I wanna see what them balls lookin' like after you done chewed 'em up."

I reach for the bottle and pour myself another shot. Talking these niggas up is starting to shake my nerves. She eyes me, smirk-ing as I toss my drink back. "Yes, goddammit. Wet that throat, Miss Pasha, girl, with ya ole long-necked self."

My cell phone starts ringing. I pull it out of my back. It's Jasper. I press IGNORE.

"Okay, so we now have four names, with one already down," I say, going over everything we've discussed. "So that leaves us with three. Hopefully we can get one, or all three of 'em to tell us who else was in on it." She asks about Stax. If I'm going to put him on the list or give him a pass. I tell her I don't know, yet.

"But you *are* gonna do what you do best 'n' suck him sideways, ain't you, sweetness? Oooh, yesss, *FahverGawd*. I know your messy ass gonna suck his dingaling 'n' lick all 'round them balls. Do him right, goddammit."

I shake my head. Tell her I'm not sure. That it's a possibility—only if I really have to. I let her know I prefer to twist, squeeze, slice and poke whatever information I can out of one of the niggas already on the list.

"One of them niggas," I say, sitting up and slipping my feet back into my heels, "has to know something. And if they don't..." I pause not really sure what happens next if they don't rat out the rest of them niggas. Or what happens to them after they do. Letting them niggas go might not be an option. Then what?

"Then we shut they motherfuckin' lights out!" Booty finishes excitedly, slapping the back of her right hand into her left palm. Her glassy eyes narrow to slits as she says this. She doesn't even bat a lash. "We make them niggas breathe they last breaths, god-dammit!"

I open my mouth to speak, but she is so amped up talking about slaying niggas and slicing throats and breaking bones and chopping off hands that I don't get a chance to tell her that I'm not signing up for murdering anyone.

She's on a roll...

"Motherfuck 'em, goddammit! After what them coon-nigga bitches did to you, Miss Pasha, girl, they gotta get served to the sewer rats. And Jasper's no-good ass gotta get it the worst. I'ma help you lure these other niggas in real right. But, *you*, Miss Pasha, girl, gonna have to handle Jasper's coon-ass. And I. Do mean... *handle.*"

She shoots me a look for effect as she reaches for the bottle of Henny, pours us both another shot, then hands me a glass. "And the last bitch we gonna make sure they asses see before we seal they coffins, is *you*, sugah-boo."

She raises her glass. "Here's to takin' it to they fuckin' skulls, goddammit!"

Reluctantly, I raise my glass. "To payback."

"And good goddamn dingalang," Booty adds, tossing her drink back.

I shake my head, silently chuckling inside. *Booty is all over the place.* The conversation gets serious when it shifts to trying to come up with a discreet location, somewhere off the beaten path, where it'll be hard for us to get caught, a place where we can light these motherfuckers up without any unexpected interruptions. Booty says she might know someone, one of her sponsors, who might be able to help with that. We spend another twenty minutes devising a plan. Then discuss all of the supplies we'll need. I dig in my wallet. Peel out eight Ben Franklins and hand them to her. Tell her she'll need to handle getting our supplies. She hands me the money back.

"Oh, no, Miss Pasha, girl. This is my treat, goddammit! I'ma have everything ready to go. We 'bout to light they fires, goddammit!"

"Umm, Booty…speaking of lighting fires and taking it to skulls and whatnot, exactly what *did* you do with JT's body? And *who* helped you dump it?"

She bucks her eyes. "See, now, sugah-boo. You tryna know too much. Shit, I don't even know where his dead ass ended up. And I ain't ask, either. Don't ask, don't tell, goddammit. All I know that nigga-coon got his bloody ass rolled on up outta here in'a rug. And where he landed, I don't wanna know. But I do have a lil souvenir, I'm keeping on ice."

She gets up and walks into the kitchen. I can hear her shuffling things around. "Oh, nooo, goddammit, I know one of these lil motherfuckers ain't come in here 'n' fuck with my shit, goddammit. I packed it right down in the bottom of this motherfuckin' freezer. Oh, *FahverGawd*, say it ain't so. I know these greedy niggah-coons ain't…oh, yes, goddammit. I was 'bout to go off."

After a few more seconds of fumbling around her freezer, she comes back out holding a freezer Ziploc bag. "That nigga-bitch came up in here"—she opens up the bag and pulls out the Tupperware bowl—"tryna do me, and got did up real right." She pulls up the lid. "Coon, boom-boom!" She hands me the bowl. "I got me a breakfast treat."

My eyes almost pop out of my head. My mouth drops open.

It's JT's dick.

Frozen and thick.

Eighteen

Don't ever ignore the elephant in the room—
hop on that big bitch and ride it...

It's exactly four P.M., when Booty finally drops me off back at the salon. "Miss Pasha, girl," she says as I open the door, swinging one leg out of her truck, "You a real special bitch 'cause I don't let a lotta bitches up in my home. I usually entertain they asses outside on the porch or in the backyard on the patio. Shit, Dickalina ain't even been allowed to sit 'n' kick her heels up inside my house like you. And me and her been friends for years. Then again, I know the bitch got roaches so I only let her ass stand when she comes through 'cause I don't want her leavin' none'a her lil friends behind. I always tell that bitch to make sure she takes her pets with her when she leaves. I ain't even tryna house none'a them nasty fuckers."

I shake my head, laughing. "Cassandra, your ass is a hilarious mess. You do know that, right?"

"Uh-huh. But I ain't ever been messy."

"Cass, I can't with you. Listen. Thanks for dragging me out of here today. Whether I wanted it or not, I needed it. Talking everything out really helped put things in perspective."

"It sure did, sugah-boo." She tilts her head, pursing her lips. "We gonna turn them motherfuckas *out*. You got the list, right?"

I nod, double-checking inside my handbag. "Yeah. I got it."

"Yesss, *FahverGawd*, they not gonna know what hit they asses." She reaches in the backseat and grabs a large black plastic shopping bag, then hands it to me. "This is for you, Miss Pasha, girl."

I give her a quizzical look, peeking inside the bag. "What is it?"

"It's a lil treat to get this party started right."

I pull out the box. It's a black Double Trouble Stun Gun.

"We gonna do 'em up right, goddammit. We gonna zap they asses 'til they drop, 'n' by the time they come through we gonna have they asses hog-tied how they had you. And I ain't tryna hear nothin' else 'bout you draggin' ya heels, either, Miss Pasha, girl. Ya lumped-up face should be enough to keep the fire lit up under ya ass. And I hope you gonna do what I tol' you 'n' suck Stax's ball sac inside out. We need to know what he knows. And the only bitch he gonna tell shit to is *you*."

I sigh. "Like I told you earlier, I'm not sure I really want to go there."

Her neck snaps back. *"What?* You're not sure you wanna go there? Sugah-boo, *boom-boom!* You better put them lips to use 'n' be the best cum-guzzler you can be 'n' guzzle us out some Intel. Get ya mind right, Miss Pasha, girl! Do that sexy motherfucka. And if he ain't got shit worth sayin', at least you got to get you a mouthful of that Mandingaling 'n' a taste of that hot cock sauce."

I blink. The only thing I can do is smile and I let what she says go over my head. At the end of the day, I know without a doubt, Booty means well. "Again, thanks." I reach over and grab her hand. "It means a lot to me to know you have my back."

"I sure do, goddammit. And I enjoyed havin' you over, Miss Pasha, girl. Next time you gonna have'ta stay for a bite to eat. Now get on up outta my truck. You know Booty ain't for none'a this sentimental shit."

I chuckle. "Get home safe, girl." I shut the door and watch her peel off down the street, running through a red light.

I look over at my salon, wincing as I touch the side of my face. It's tender and sore. But the swelling isn't as bad as it could have been. *Fuck you, Jasper! Putting your motherfucking hands on me at my place of business! You really helped seal your goddamn fate, nigga!*

My personal life may be all fucked up. But a bitch can't say shit about my professional life. I've put a lot of sweat and tears and heartache into this shop, my shop. The long grueling hours and exceptional services offered over the years have truly paid off. Despite all the personality clashes, cutthroat cattiness and back-biting that often goes along with owning a salon, my shop remains a thriving, extremely successful hair, nail and body salon. Our clientele list continues to grow, and loyal patrons from around the Tri-State continue to pack us to the seams.

I glance up at the NAPPY NO MORE sign hanging vertically over the shop's window and grimace in an attempt to smile. I place a hand up to the side of my face. *This is my shit,* I muse, walking toward the building. *And in a couple more weeks, it should be official. I'll be the proud of owner of Nappy No More II out in Beverly Hills. I can't wait to get the fuck away from here for a while. I only hope this shit with Jasper is over before then. Booty's right. It's time.*

Through the shop's window, which I had bullet-proofed thanks to the nigga who smashed it out last year, I see there isn't anyone manning the receptionist desk and there are about ten clients sitting in the waiting area. I step through the door, immediately greeted with the sound of laughter and lively chatter over the sounds of…playing through the speakers. I speak to everyone sitting in the waiting area, then make my way toward the work-station area, catching the tail end of Rhodeshia running her mouth about…*me!*

She's so busy talking sideways that she doesn't even notice me standing here, leaning up against the side of the partition.

She's parting and spraying her client's scalp. "Girl, I don't know what popped off in her office earlier today, but I heard he been whoopin' that ass every since he got home from prison and found out she was sucking other niggas' dicks...."

Her client chimes in, "Mmmph. Depending on how long he was locked up, I probably woulda did me a little dick sucking on the side, too. Shit. It's hard jailing with a nigga, especially when he doing more than two years. We got needs, too. Shit."

Rhodeshia grunts. "Chile, please. I know jailin' ain't easy. So go out and get you a lil boo on the side. Not a whole neighborhood of niggas like Pasha was doing...I heard she suck'a mean dick, too."

I hear Lamar's voice coming from over the railing upstairs in the loft that overlooks the workstation area where manis-and-pedis are given. "Yo, ma, chill wit' that; you really outta pocket. How you gonna stand there and kick Pasha's back in like that in front of all these peeps, yo. You bein' mad reckless at the mouth right now."

She sucks her teeth. "Nigga, please. Why you care? What you gonna do, run back and tell her?"

"Nah, that's not what I do."

"Then how about you just *do* what you're paid to do and mind your business."

"Aiight, ma, you know what. Do you. That shit still ain't cool."

She waves him on. "Whatever. Like I said, mind yours and leave mine alone."

Even two of my pedicurists, Trish and Anna, confront her to shut it down, but this bitch still keeps on going. I bite my tongue.

You wanna know what a bitch really thinks about you? Listen to what she says about you behind your back.

I stand here taking it all in. A few clients' eyes open in surprise when they spot me with my finger up to my lips for them to keep quiet. A few eyes light up in anticipation for a lil juicy shop drama. Looks like today is one of those days.

Kenyatta, another one of my newest stylists, tries to clear her throat, motioning with her head over in my direction, nodding to Rhodesia on the sly that I'm standing here. But Rhodeshia's ass is too stuck on messy to pick up on it. The patrons in the chairs watch on in amazement, watching me watch her as she continues flapping her gums about me.

"...I like Pasha and all, but she a damn fool. She got her a fine-ass nigga who's paid out the ass and she too busy out trickin' instead of stayin' posted up at home playin' her position, waitin' for her man to come home. I swear. Chicks don't know how'ta ride a bid out with a nigga. And that's exactly why she probably got her ass beat in her office today. If you ask me..." Her mouth drops open when she sees me through the mirror.

I wave at her. "Hi. Don't stop now. You were on a roll, bitch. So go on. Finish what you were about to say. If we asked you *what?*"

"Oh, um, I-I...girl, I was only talking shit."

"Yeah, about *me* in *my* salon, bitch!"

The salon goes quiet.

Yeah, center stage, all eyes on me now—*again*.

I stalk over toward her with a hand up on my hip, tossing my handbag in my chair. I don't know if I have a contact high from the two blunts Booty smoked while I was with her, or if it's the effects of the five shots I ended up tossing back. But whatever the reason, I light her ass up in front of all to see. Something I've never been known to do—with the exception when I slapped Felecia in front of everyone. Besides that, I've always tried to handle things behind closed doors, in the privacy of my office, away from prying eyes, professionally.

But after the shit with Felecia kicking my back in, I'm done with keeping shit professional. If these bitches want to see the ghetto side of me, then so be it. Obviously that's the only language most of these hoes respond to any-damn-way.

"Bitch, the one thing you must not know is that I don't do two-faced bitches."

"Pasha, girl, I-I—"

"Don't 'Pasha, girl' me, bitch. You can finish up your client's hair, but when you're done putting them braids in, you can get the fuck out of my salon. Pack your shit and bounce. You wanna talk shit, then let's talk shit. Yeah, I was sucking dick behind my husband's back while he was locked up. What the fuck you care for? The nigga did five years, okay? And, yeah, he came home and beat the shit out of me. So the moral of the story is, don't suck another nigga's dick behind your man's back. Or if you're gonna do the shit, don't get your ass caught with it stuck down in your throat."

She opens her mouth to speak, but quickly shuts it when I put a hand up in her face.

"Bitch," I sneer contemptuously, "*instead* of talking shit about me behind my back, you shoulda been coming to me for some dick-sucking tips 'cause from what I hear, your *baby father* stays up in the strip clubs getting his private party on in the back rooms with whatever whore he can trick the rent money up on. And he's always somewhere tryna get his dick sucked 'cause the bitch he has at home ain't sucking it." Then I use one of Booty's classic lines, "Don't do me, goddammit!"

A few patrons gasp. Some start laughing. Others cling to every word, waiting to see who's going to swing fists first. Right now as fired up as I am, it'll be me taking it to this bitch's head.

I hear a few saying shit like, "I heard that, girl."

"Shit. I know that's right. Let me stop in your office later, girl, for some throat tips."

"Girl, don't you know if you ain't suckin' your man's dick, another bitch will?"

I ignore the comments, narrowing my eyes at Rhodeshia who is now looking like she's ready to crawl up under her sink. She starts apologizing, saying how wrong she was for disrespecting me. How she got caught up in the gossip. Blah, blah, blah…

"Bitch, gossip or not, don't ever apologize for shit you meant to say, or for shit you feel. Be a woman about your shit; that's all. Fact is I walked up on ya ass throwing shit on me, now you wanna backpedal. Don't. I can respect a bitch who says 'yeah I said it' instead of some phony-bitch tryna apologize her way out of it. So *if* there's something any of you wanna say to me, or *about* me, be woman enough to say it to my face. If you're going to work for me, I expect loyalty—from *everyone*. I don't talk about anyone behind their backs. And I expect the same goddamn courtesy to be extended to *me*. If not, pack your shit and get the fuck up outta my salon. Period.

"And another thing, since we clearing the air." I point to my face. "You see this bruise right here." I turn around in the middle of the floor. "I want all of you to get a good look at it. My husband did that this, okay. *Jasper* came up in here earlier and smacked me the fuck up in my office. Why? Because I wouldn't give the nigga some pussy, okay. And I clawed his neck, then tried to bite his goddamn balls off. So, yeah, he was beating my ass. But know this: *Today* was the nigga's *last* time he'll ever lay his hands on me and get to walk."

I shoot my glare back over at Rhodeshia as she continues corn-rowing her client's head. "From now on, *bitch*, if you wanna talk, make sure you have all your facts." I stare her down. She looks up from her client's head, nervously shifting her eyes. "Bitch, you lucky I don't punch you in your goddamn sockets."

She snaps her head back, raising a brow. "Now wait a minute, Pa—"

I put both hands up on my hips. "What, you wanna leap? No, *bitch*, you wait a minute." I lower my voice, punctuating every other word. *"If you ever…*talk *slick…*about *me*. Behind. *My*. Back *again…*I'm going to personally *slice* your *motherfucking…throat*."

Her eyes widen in shock. She's never seen this side of me. None of them have. Well, guess what? It's a new goddamn bitch in town! And her name is Pasha Nivea-Alona Allen. And they gonna learn today!

I glance around the salon. "Now. Is there anything else any of *you* want to know or say before my five o'clock gets here?"

"Yeah, girl," this attractive brown-skinned chick says. I've never seen her here before. "I wanna know where I can sign up for those dick sucking lessons?"

"LaQuandra, girl…I can't with you," Kenyatta says, chuckling as she spins her around in her chair. "You're a hot mess."

She grunts. "I'm serious. I need to learn how to suck that trifling-ass baby mother of his up out of his system. He can't seem to shake that crazy bitch."

The salon explodes with laughter.

Nineteen

Behind every nightmare there's a thin silver lining...

"**W**ake the fuck up, bitch!" someone screams, scaring the shit out of me while snatching the blanket off me. "I want my dick sucked." When my eyes focus, I realize it's the lunatic who choked me. He has on the same clothes, which tells me he hasn't washed his funky-ass balls yet. "Get ya nasty-ass up out this muthafuckin' bed."

"Yo, nigga, chill," another voice says. It's the nigga who fed me and watched me shower. Calm One. He's wearing a pair of dark-blue Hampton University basketball shorts and a white wife beater. I glance at the tattoo of a panther across his shoulder. For some reason, I am relieved to see him. He seems to be able to keep this other nigga from going too far.

"Yo, fuck that. I want this bitch to clean my dick and balls."

"Nigga, fuck!" Calm One snaps. "You got all day to get ya dick sucked. Let's stick to the script, nigga. Let me feed her, first. Then when the rest of these niggas get here, ya'll can do what the fuck you want."

Lunatic sucks his teeth. "Fuck feedin' her ass. The only thing this bitch needs to eat is this nut."

I feel myself about to scream on this nigga. I count to twenty in my head. I don't like nothing this motherfucker stands for. I stare him down, counting backward. My mind is made up; these niggas can do what they want, but this motherfucker right here will not get shit sucked by me. Before I can stop myself, I tell him so.

*"Bitch, what the fuck you just say?" he snaps, charging toward me. I
don't flinch. Calm One grabs him by the arm.*

"Yo, chill, nigga. Damn."

He sneers at me. "Yo, fuck this bitch."

*"No, fuck you," I snap. I've had enough. "I'm tired; I'm hungry; I'm
sick; I wanna go the fuck home; and I don't give a fuck! So fuck you and
your raggedy-ass dick 'cause newsflash, motherfucker, I'm not sucking
shit attached to you, bitch!"*

*He yanks his arm away from Calm One. Then in one swinging open-
hand, he smacks the shit out of me and mushes me in the face. I stumble
back onto the sofa.*

*"Is that all you got, nigga? You like slapping up on females? Nigga,
you ain't shit."*

*Calm One grabs him before he hits me again. "Nigga, what the fuck?!
You buggin', for real, son. You know what the order was. You really comin'
outta pocket, son."*

*Lunatic snatches his arm back, storming off. "Fuck that dick-sucking
bitch!"*

*"Yeah, nigga, I suck dick. But I won't be sucking yours. I put that on my
life, bitch!"*

*Calm One helps me up, shaking his head. "Yo, ma, you really got ya'self
in some serious shit."*

I jerk up in bed, sweating and shaking, looking around the massive
bedroom. I glance at the clock. 12:07 A.M. I turn on the lamp and
climb out of bed, slipping into my robe to check on Jaylen. An
eerie chill slivers its way up my spine. I shiver, wrapping my arms
around me as I make my way to my son's room. I stop in my
tracks, turning back around and walking back into my bedroom
to retrieve my gun from out of the top drawer of my dresser.

Don't ever get caught without it. I unlock the dresser drawer, then slip the gun down into one of the front pockets of my robe.

The house is exceptionally quiet. I check all the security panels to make sure everything is secured. It is. The lights from the motion sensors blink red, the alarm green. I breathe a sigh of relief. Then head down the hall. I open Jaylen's bedroom door, and peek in. His room aglow from the wall nightlight, he's sleeping soundly. I walk over to his bed, then lean in and kiss him on the side of his head. *Mommy loves you so much.* I gently rub his head.

I stare at him. Torn. I don't want Jaylen to grow up without a father in his life. I see the way he lights up, his smile wide, every time he sees Jasper. Sadly, he's too young, too innocent, to know, to understand, that his father is a fucking brutal savage. A nigga I'm going to do in. I want him to die a slow, torturous death. A quick death would be too easy. I want that nigga to live and suffer. I want his motherfucking ass to beg for his life, then finally beg for me to end it. I want to violate him. The way that he violated me.

I never imagined I'd ever feel this level of contempt toward anyone, let alone Jasper's ass. But I do. I want him fucking...*dead!* Slow and torturous! And the frightening thing is, I can feel my pussy getting wet thinking about emptying a clip into his mother-fucking head. My only hope is, Jaylen never learns the truth. If I can help it, he never will. I'll take my transgressions to the grave with me.

Taking a deep breath, then slowly exhaling, I sit in Nana's rocking chair—the one she'd rock my father in when he was Jaylen's age—and rock in silence, listening to the *Blues Clues* clock on the wall tick off the seconds and minutes—feeling my heart hardening, becoming thicker, with each pulsing second, a deeper hatred for Jasper coursing through every artery in my body.

The aching in my chest is so profound I can hardly breathe as I think back on what *I've* allowed Jasper to get away with. Images of that night flood my brain, flashing and swirling—slow and steady, like strobe lights. Masked faces, lust-filled eyes, stiff dicks stabbing the back of my throat, menacing voices, dirty and gruff— all taunting me, ripping into my spirit, fucking and grunting deep into my mouth. In a flash, I became a rough, dirty train ride; being ridden fast and hard. The evidence of each nigga's fare coated on my lips, stuck in the back of my throat.

Tick-tock, tick-tock...

The clock ticking in my head, the telling sign that time waits for no one, I wonder if it truly does heal wounds; maybe, hopefully, some of them, at least. Hot tears spill from my eyes, everything in me drowning all over again. What's left of my spirit breaking open, shattering into a-million-and-one tiny painful pieces; remnants of a haunting memory. I put my face in my hands, and in the ticking silence, I start to sob uncontrollably for what seems like forever. I let it all out. Then, just like that, as quickly as my tears had fallen—my emotional well dries, and they stop.

You've screwed me raw long enough, Jasper. Now it's time I screw you!

I wipe the remainder of my tears with the back of my hand, finally getting up. I stare at my beautiful son a few minutes more, then lean down and pick him up and hold him in my arms. "Mommy's little man is getting so big," I whisper, rocking him in my arms. He doesn't stir. He's a hard sleeper like...his father.

"I love you so, so much, sweetheart." I pull him close to my chest, holding him tightly; inhaling him, breathing in his innocence, wanting to believe with everything that's in me that he was conceived out of love. But with all that has happened, I am no longer certain. I lie him back in his bed, pulling the blanket up over him. Then lean in and give him another kiss on his head before walking out and closing his door, leaving it ajar.

Nigga, your fate is about to be forever sealed!

My gait back to the master suite is swift, purposeful—my feet sinking deep into the carpet with each step. I snatch open Jasper's enormous walk-in closet and start yanking all of his shit off wooden hangers. I go downstairs to the kitchen, grab a box of sixty-count, thirty-gallon Hefty CinchSak trash bags—no this nigga isn't worthy of luggage; not good luggage, that's for sure—then race back up the stairs, two at a time. I toss all of his shit—designer button-ups, polos, pullovers, hoodies, jeans, dress pants, suits, tons of shit still with tags on it—into bags, stuffing each one to capacity.

Next, I sweep his vast collection of sneakers, boots, and hard bottoms into trash bags. When I am done—thirty-six trash bags later, I start pulling open his dresser drawers and dumping his underwear, T-shirts, socks, and everything else, inside another bag.

I'm done with you, nigga!

I race into the bathroom, reach for the trashcan and sweep all of his colognes, electric shavers, clippers, and other manly cosmetics into it. Then I drag, kick, swing everything down the stairs, then drag it into the foyer, setting all of his belongings along the wall near the door.

I am exhausted from all the dragging and pulling and lifting, but I am too wired to sleep. I walk back into the kitchen, deciding to fix a cup of white tea. I fill the kettle with spring water and set it on the stove, turning the eye on.

I stand in the middle of my gourmet kitchen with its enameled lava stone countertops, marble flooring, Swarovski lighting, and Viking appliances, sweeping my eyes around the luxurious space. It's all fucking full of pretense! The whole house—way out here in fucking No Man's Land, with all of its trappings of wealth—is nothing but glitz and show and tell.

Like my life, nothing about it feels right.

Yeah, it was Jasper's drug money that paid for this gated-hell-hole. But it was my impeccable credit that sealed the deal. It was my sweat and labor that turned this—fifteen-thousand-square-foot, two-and-a-half story, ten-room, five-bedroom and six-bathroom—estate into a damn home, or a facsimile of one. Be it an unhappy one, or not. So, Jasper has no claims to shit, except for the third-floor rec room, his man cave, which he had designed and decorated specifically for him.

I sigh, making a mental note to contact my realtor in the morning as I open a cabinet and pull down a large mug. I open another cabinet for the tea canister, then drop a teabag into my mug and wait for the water to boil.

Walking over to the floor-to-ceiling window, I glance over at the digital clock on the stove. 2:37 A.M.

No sense in going back to bed now.

Part of playing your position is always knowing when to play stupid and to keep your mouth shut and your eyes and ears wide open. Always acting disinterested in the street hustle. And over the years, I've done exactly that. I've overheard the phone calls. I've deciphered the broken code words Jasper's used to whomever was on the other end of his hushed calls. And I've memorized everything that has ever come out of his mouth.

By the time I'm done with Jasper, he's going to wish I would have simply turned over state's evidence on his black ass. He'll regret not beating me to death that night down in that basement. I'm going to fuck this nigga in his pockets—for all of my pain and suffering, first. Then I'm going to finish him off nice and slow.

As I'm staring out of the window, overlooking the three acres of manicured backyard property—waiting for the kettle to whistle, a switch clicks on in my head. *The safes.*

I hurriedly shut off the stove, then climb the stairs up to my bedroom, swinging open Jasper's now-empty closet. I feel along the edges of his cherrywood shelves until I find what I'm searching for. The button. *Yes, here it is!* I press it twice and watch as the side wall panel slowly slides open. I glance up at the hidden cameras I had secretly installed in his closet a few months back, smiling.

Yeah, nigga, you never know who's watching you!

I step inside the small hidden room, which contains a large safe, and feel along the wall for the light switch, flicking it on. It takes me three attempts to figure out the two six-digit pass codes. It's his birthday—month, date and year, then year, date and month: 11-07-76.

Stupid-ass!

It clicks. I grab the lever and pull down on it. The heavy door opens. And I am instantly greeted with rows of neatly stacked money. I'm immediately blown away. Breathlessly, I quickly step out of the space, race out into the bedroom and into my own walk-in and grab a large black four-wheeled Tumi travel case. I hurry back into the space and start stuffing everything inside, emptying it out. I shut the chrome door, spin the dial, shut off the light, then press the button underneath the shelf twice, watching the wall slowly close shut. *You won't be getting your hands on any of this!*

I grab another four-wheeled suitcase out of my closet. Then slip out into the darkness, beneath a full moon, gripping my gun in one sweaty hand and briskly rolling the suitcase with the other, heading toward the pool house—my heart frantically pounding loudly in my chest with each step.

Forty minutes later, everything is secure. I am back in the house. My mug of hot tea with lemon in my hand, I head upstairs to my room, climbing back in bed, then turning on the fifty-five-inch

TV, and surf through the channels. After about two minutes of scrolling through channels, I settle on last week's episode of *Scandal*, then fluff two pillows in back of me, sipping on my tea.

Fifteen minutes into the show, a sly smile finally inches its way over my lips as sleep finally finds me.

I may not be a bitch from the streets, but it's in me. It's been all around me. Underestimating me is Jasper's *worst* mistake. I may not hustle and game niggas, but I know all too well how to bait a nigga. I know the game. Play or get played. Plot or get plotted on. I've sat back and watched long and hard. It takes a sly bitch to outwit a ruthless street nigga. *Now*...the rules are about to change.

And Jasper's black ass is about to get beaten at his own damn game!

Twenty

Deception and lies come easy to the cunning...

Eight-thirty A.M., the minute the doors open, I am strutting through the doors of the bank on Prospect Avenue in West Orange, stylishly dressed in a black Diane von Furstenberg wrap dress that hangs four inches above my knee—still sexy, yet conservative, and six-inch pumps. My hair is pulled back in a sleek, shiny ponytail, my long bang swept in one big curl along my jaw. A pair of black Chanels cover my lashed eyes. My earrings, choker, and tennis bracelet are flooded in diamonds. The five-carat rare red diamond solitaire on my left ring finger perfectly matches the red lipstick coating my lips. Matches the fire burning in my blood, symbolizing the war being waged against Jasper, and the dangers soon to follow once the nigga learns I've cleaned out his safes.

Two six-foot-seven, three-hundred-plus-pound bodyguards—compliments of my newly appointed security team Lamar put together—follow me through the bank's glass doors, rolling behind them the fruits of Jasper's drug dealing.

It's not every day a beautiful black woman struts into a bank with two handsomely strapped, suited-up men, wheeling in two suitcases packed with money. I had to dress the part. Look the part. Be the part.

A fly bitch on the move.

Immediately, the branch manager greets me, a wide smile pressed over her glossed lips. I state my business, hand her my safety-deposit box key, then follow her down the red-carpeted aisle to a shiny-chrome elevator. She slides her key-card in, the door opens and we step in. A few seconds later, we're down in the basement walking a long corridor to the vaults.

She greets two security guards as we walk by. One of them walks behind us. The huge concrete and reinforced steel-cladded vault door is already open. She punches in a few codes, then slides back the thick steel gate. The officer with us, stands guard.

I watch as she takes my key and inserts it into a lock and turns it simultaneously with a key—among many others, on a large ring. On the outside, I am cool and calm, the epitome of sophistication. But everything on the inside of me shakes. I am a nervous wreck. From the second I slid behind the wheel of my Benz and rode through my gates—with these muscled men trailing behind me, I've been on high alert, practically bordering paranoia. The only thing I kept thinking during the entire ride here is, I'm being followed. I'm going to be ambushed, robbed, and killed.

And even now, in spite of being flanked by two beefy, hard-bodied bodyguards, Jasper's fucking ass has me on edge!

My buzzing cell phone causes me to blink. I dig it out of my purse, glancing at the screen. I roll my eyes. It's him. I press DECLINE.

The bank employee glances over her shoulder. "If you need to you use your phone, don't even bother trying. We have horrible reception down here."

I pull my shades up over my head. "There's absolutely no one I need to speak to at the moment. So no worries."

Within moments, she pulls out the large, long metal box, then tells me to follow her to a private room. She smiles. I take the huge box from her and walk it to one of the tables. "Take as much time as you need."

I smile back. "Thank you." I walk back out and grab the luggage from my protectors, wheeling them into the room and closing the door behind me. I sit my purse beside the heavy box on the table, then open the safety box hinge. I take a few deep breaths, then quickly empty out the contents of each suitcase, neatly lining the thick stacks of money inside the metal box.

I haven't even bothered counting any of it. It doesn't matter. I already know it's more than enough to have Jasper lose his mind over it. But the one thing I'm sure of, he won't try to kill me without knowing where his money is first.

But the nigga's crazy enough to…*Ohmygod! Jaylen! He'd try to do something to our son in order to get to me, and his money.* I gasp, the realization causing my chest to tighten. *I can't let anything happen to my son. I have to keep Jaylen safe and out of that crazy nigga's reach.*

I run my hands along the rows of money, one last time, grabbing two stacks, then dropping them inside my purse. I close the safety box. Once it's safely secured back in its compartment, we head back up to the main lobby. I step out of the bank with a new purpose. But my first—and most important—mission before anything else is, keeping my son safe.

The minute I slide behind the wheel of my car and lock the doors, I call Anna, one of my nail technicians, on her cell to let her know I won't be in today and to please cancel the three appointments I have and to reschedule them for tomorrow afternoon. Next, I call Sophia and leave her specific instructions. Then I make three more calls—one to my realtor, the other to my travel agent. My last call is to my saving grace.

Four hours later, I am on a last-minute flight with Jaylen, Sophia, and, Greta—the only person I *think*, hope, I can entrust Jaylen to until this shit with Jasper is over. Greta is not only another longtime client; she's someone I also consider a friend, whose hair I've been doing since high school. She's a single, social butterfly with no kids whose only addiction—that I know of—is hard dick. We don't talk often. And I've never had to call on her for anything. But when I called her this morning, knowing she's been unemployed for the last three months, and propositioned her to look after Jaylen for a few weeks or so, she didn't hesitate.

I'm not sure if it's because she heard the urgency in my voice; or if it's the promise of getting two thousand dollars a week, in cash, that made it easy for her to say yes. And it doesn't matter. All I care is that my son is going to be out of Jersey, and three thousand miles away from Jasper's scheming ass.

The fact that Jasper is afraid of flying, has always refused to step foot on a plane, and has no knowledge where my L.A. condo is— let alone that I own one out there, offers me some relief. Still, I *know*, if I am going to snare Jasper and the rest of them niggas, I have to set more than one trap and stay three steps ahead. And I can't, don't want to, be worrying about Jaylen's safety.

While Greta and I play catchup since the last time I'd seen her—about six weeks ago, I fill her in, giving her the condensed version—and, of course, leaving out specific details she doesn't need to know—of what's been going on in my life, leaving her to believe I'm a helpless victim who's been caught in a vicious cycle.

"Girrrrl, no," she hisses, her green-colored eyes narrowing to slits. I take in her flawless caramel skin. Long gone are the days of thick glasses, a thick lopsided-afro and gapped teeth. Thanks to expensive orthodontic work, Lasik surgery, personal trainers, and devoted years of patronage at Nappy No More, that ugly duckling has been transformed into the graceful, beautiful diva before me. "That dirty motherfucker! I had no idea you've been going through that *hell* all this time. I can't believe he's been putting his hands on you. Then the bastard has the nerve to force himself on you whenever he feels the urge to get his rocks off." She grunts her disgust, shaking her head. "That nigga was *raping* you. Your own damn husband."

Mmmph. You have no idea!

I sip my champagne. "Believe it. He's out of control. I knew what I was getting myself into when I married his ass over the summer. So it's not like I'm surprised. Jasper had shown me *exactly* who he was"—*in more than one way*—"long before I said I do. Still, I thought I could deal with it. But I can't. And I'm not going to. It's gotten progressively worse over the last two months. It's too much."

"Mygod! And the two of you have only been married since... what, August?"

All for show and tell, an elusive illusion of happiness. I cringe. "Girl, please. Don't remind me. Three months and a hundred-thousand-damn-dollars later, I'm done. I've decided to put the house on the market the first chance I get, and start fresh—away from his ass."

She reaches over, grabs my hand. "Good for you. You don't deserve that shit." She glances around the cabin, leaning in closer. "You know I'm not ever a fan of violence. But there are always exceptions. And a man putting his hands on a woman, or trying to rape her, are two of them. You should have sliced his damn dick off, then shot him in his head."

"Oh, trust me. The next time, if there ever is one, I will." We share knowing glances. "Right down to the base."

"And Felecia." She snorts, shaking her head. "That chick is a mess. But she's always been like that. So I'm not the least bit surprised to hear what she's done." She takes a liberal sip of her drink, then sets her glass down. "She's always been two-faced. I'm only surprised she didn't get caught out there sooner. You know I used to warn you about her when we were in high school."

I nod pensively. Streaks of bright natural light, streaming in from the opened window shade, bounce off the thick tennis bracelet on my wrist, causing the sparkling diamonds to dance about the plane's cabin.

I blink.

"Yeah, you, Mona, and everyone else who saw her for who she really was. I was the only one blind to it. But I *see* her for all she is, now. Felecia bit off the hand that has fed her and fought her battles for most of her life."

"Pasha, girl, and this," she pauses, tossing her honey-blonde tresses over her shoulder, "is another one of those exceptions I was talking about. *That* bitch needs to be handled."

My body goes cold as a chill slices up the center of my back. I toss my head in Greta's direction and say in an icy tone, "Oh, I'm going to handle her real good. When I'm done with her ass, she'll *never* part her lips to let my name roll off her tongue again."

I'm going to bust that bitch's fucking face in!

She lifts her flute to mine; our glasses clink.

We both take slow, deliberate sips. Silence meets us. And I use it as an opportunity to think. Things were moving fast, maybe a little too fast, with very little time to plan, to think things through, to wrap my mind around the turn of events. But I have to keep up. Yet, not move in haste. There's too much riding on it. One miscalculated move, one poorly executed attack, can blow up in my face. No. I have to think smart, move smart, be smart. I have to take them down, one at a time. I can't allow myself to be outsmarted. Not this time. There are too many things at stake, my life, my freedom…and Jaylen.

Feeling Greta's probing eyes on me, I purposefully turn my head ever so slight, bite the inside of my lip, and start fidgeting with the huge rock on my finger. I summon up an unhappy memory, allow pang of sadness to claim me. Then methodically dab at the corners of my eye.

Greta gently touches my hand. "Are you okay?"

I sigh. Slowly turn to face her. My bottom lip quivers.

A look of alarm paints her face, the tone of her voice layered with concern. "Pasha, what is it? Talk to me."

I drop my wet gaze down to my hands, nervously twisting my ring. In a hushed whisper, I finally say, "If anything…happens to me"—I look up, allowing my eyes to meet her searching gaze—"please promise me you'll look after Jaylen for me. That you'll raise him and love him as your own."

"Ohmygod, Pasha, I'd be honored. Of course I would. But… *why?* What makes you think *something* might happen to you?"

I lean in to her. Stare her dead in the eyes. "Greta, Jasper is *ruthless.*"

Her eyes widen. "You don't think he'd…*kill* you?"

My eyes never leave hers. I don't blink. "I *know* he will."

She falls back in her seat. The look of horror plastered all over her face. "Mygod!" She reaches for her drink. Takes two long gulps, then leans over in her seat and waves over the flight attendant. She orders another round, for the both of us. She waits for the attendant to saunter off. "Pasha, whatever you do, just *try* to be careful."

The flight attendant returns with a chilled bottle of champagne, refills our glasses, then whisks off.

Nothing else is said. We both settle back in the comfort of first-class, sinking into the leather seats. I smile inwardly. The notion of being killed by Jasper now etched in Greta's mind. The worried look still carved into her face as she guzzles down her drink.

I glance over at Sophia, seated in the row across from me. She has Jaylen in her arms. My heart melts for him. There's nothing I'm not willing to do to keep him safe. To keep him from ever growing up and becoming anything like Jasper—a coldhearted, dangerous nigga!

I peer out of the window, dazing into the puff of white clouds hovering around. My head starts reeling as I try to absorb everything that has happened in the last few days since my return from L.A. on Sunday. In less than three days, my whole life has been drastically shaken up and is about to change. For the better, I hope. Still, it'll have to get worse before that happens. And it will.

Desperation changes a lot of things. So does hurt. Betrayal. And hatred. There's a big difference in screwing and being screwed. Getting fucked is dirty and vile. Its strokes are rough and jagged. And it's not always done with a hard damn dick. No. It's done when you least expect it—by the ones you least expect, right in your damn face with a smile. Felecia screwed me. That bitch fucked me, deep.

I lift my flute to my lips, taking a very careful sip of my drink as I give thought to what Felecia's looming fate will be. This is war. It's going to get messy. There's going to be casualties. And that bitch is going to be the first to go down.

Twenty-One

Forgiveness and second chances are forfeited
the first time you fuck a bitch over...

The next morning, Rihanna's "Diamonds" is blaring through the speakers as I step through the salon's doors at eleven A.M., and the first thing I'm greeted by is Booty's ass bouncing and shaking, fingers popping, knees dipping, hair swinging. "Yesssss, goddammmit! Diamonds 'n' dingaling on my mind... Oooh, Miss Rih-Rih tore her drawz..."

The salon is packed to the seams. And all the seats in the lounge area are full and this bitch is flouncing around, giving everyone a show, like she's about to turn my shop into a damn strip club and ride down on a pole. I scan the room and spot Janelle—my eleven o'clock, twisted in her seat, eyeing Booty as she literally performs.

"...Yes, *gawd*...feel the warmth between these thighs"—she winds her hips, then pops her shoulders—"...shine bright like a diamond...yes, *gawd*...Rih-Rih soaked my drawz with this right here..."

This bitch has no shame!

Of course her back is turned so she doesn't hear or *see* me when I saunter in, taking a deep breath. I walk around to the receptionist's counter, grab the stereo's remote, lowering the volume and shutting her one-woman party down.

"Cassandra, what in the world do you think you're doing?" I ask, hand on hip, head tilted. "Seems to me you're at the wrong address. If I'm not mistaken, The Coochie Cutter is ten blocks over." The Coochie Cutter is one of the local strip clubs in town where most of the hand-to-hand drug dealers and wannabe ballers and ratchet and makeshift divas frequent. I've even heard that in the past, a few of their dancers/strippers had bullet holes and razor cuts on them.

"Ooooh, no, Miss Pasha, girl," she says, walking over to the counter as she's dabbing her forehead with a napkin, "don't do me, sugah-boo. I had to take me a lil break."

"A break? A break from *what?"*

"From"—she reaches over the counter and hands me a stack of messages written on pink Post-it notes—"this. I done handled all these messages for you. I've been here since nine o'clock waitin' on you, sugah-boo. And Booty's exhausted. You know I ain't used to doin' no kinda work unless it's in the streets or in the sheets."

I blink. "Umm, Cass, why were *you* taking messages for *me?"*

She gives me a one-eyed stare as if I've asked her the most ridiculous question. "Sugah-boo, it's been packed in here since the doors opened. These nigga-coons have been carryin' on tryna get they hands 'n' feet done." She must notice the puzzled look on my face. Today's Wednesday, the salon is usually not this packed on a Wednesday morning. "Mmmph. You act like you ain't runnin' a special today. You know anytime you run them thangs, these booga-coons come scramblin' up in here like you givin' away free eggs 'n' cheese…"

Shit! I'm so wrapped up in my personal drama that I completely forgot all about the ad I ran for two weeks advertising for the "Nappy on the Go" special, running Wednesday through Friday of this week.

"Ohhhhkay. But that *still* doesn't tell me *why* you are answering the phones?"

She sucks her teeth. "'Cause ain't nobody else around to do it. The phone been ringin' crazy all mornin'. You still ain't got you no counter help. You're two stylists down 'cause they don't know how'ta keep they dick suckas shut. And *you* just now struttin' in, like *you* ain't got clients to see. Your eleven o'clock is already here. And I done put me in for right after her. Twelve, sharp."

I stare blankly at her. The phone starts ringing. I go to grab it, and this bitch slaps my hand away. I catch Janelle's eye, holding a finger up for her to give me a minute. I hold my breath as Cassandra answers the call. "Nappy No More...yes, yes...we sure do, ma'am... Excuse you? Oh, no, sugah-boo. Rho-Ho don't work here no more... sweetness, that ho got fired...ooh, see you tryna be nosey..."

I quickly snatch the phone out of her hand. "Hello, good morning. This is Pasha. How can I help you?"

"Yes," the woman on the phone says, sounding frantic. "I was just told by someone that Rhodeshia no longer works there. Is that so?" I tell her it is, as of two days ago. She groans. "For the love of God. Do you know what shop she's at now?" I tell her no. But what I really want to tell her is, "the bitch won't be working in any shops around this area."

She's another bitch I've blackballed from working in any black-owned hair salon in this county. I eye Cassandra as she rolls a stick of gum in her mouth. The woman on the phone sighs. "Oh, I see. Well, listen. I'm in a crisis. I have this retirement party to go to tonight and I need my hair done. Is there any way I can get an appointment for today? The sooner the better." I reach for the appointment book, flip through today's appointments. Tell her I can fit her in at twelve. Cassandra gives me a dirty look, snapping her fingers in my face.

"Not today you won't, sugah-boo. You tryna tear ya drawz. Don't do me, Miss Pasha, girl. I'm a good-payin' customer and you *know* I been good to you. That ho ain't tippin' you like I do. You better drop that booga down to the next slot. Or I'ma be standin' outside to greet her at the door 'n' it ain't gonna be as no Welcome Committee."

"Wait," I say, raising a brow at Booty. "I already have someone for twelve. But you can see Kendra at that time instead. May I have your name, please?"

"*Queenie*—spelled K-w-e-e-n-i-e—Starbright," she says. I blink. Ask her to repeat herself, not certain if I misunderstood her. She repeats herself. "Okay, *Queenie* with a *Kay*. I'll let Kendra know to expect you." She thanks me, then hangs up.

Booty rolls her eyes. "I know one thing; that better not be the Queenie with a *Kay* I know. That old rusty, thievin' bitch owes me a refund for clothes I had her boost for me eight years ago, but I ain't seen her 'cause her ass went to prison for slicin' two Macy's security guards."

I open my mouth to say something and she immediately shuts me down as the phone rings.

"Not now, Miss Pasha, girl...Nappy No More"—she pops her gum into the phone, causing me to cringe—"Sugah-boo, before you start flappin' them gums, hol' on'a minute..." She places her hand over the mouthpiece. "Umm, why is you down in my throat, Miss Pasha, girl? The last I knew you did hair, not dental work and you"—she points over toward the waiting area—"have someone waitin' to get hers did."

I lean in, then say in a sharp whisper, "Cass, *don't*. Do. It. If you're going to sit here *and* answer the phones, then *don't* crack your gum into the phone, *don't* refer to anyone as a goddamn coon, and save all that pussy popping and booty bouncing for the Crack House. *Understand?*"

She eyes me, popping her gum. "Don't do me, Miss Pasha, girl. You know I know how to keep it classy." She puts the phone back to her ear, dismissing me with a flick of her hand. "Sugah-boo, I'm back…now what you say you needed again, them hoofs done…? Oh, no, sugah-boo. We ain't doin' no bunion 'n' corn work over here at Nappy No More…ooh, see you tryna be messy…now I'm tryna keep it classy…don't do me…uh-huh…and I'm *tellin'* you we *ain't* touchin' them hoofs. Sounds like you need you a miracle. Or some new damn feet…"

She hangs up.

"Miss Pasha, girl. Mmph. Some'a these hoes callin' up in here need some phone manners. But they gonna learn today." The phone rings again. "Nappy No More. *What?* This is *Booty.* Now who is you? And how can I help you…?"

I clutch my chest and grit my teeth. *Please, God!* I walk off, hoping like hell this bitch doesn't have me put out of business by the time I get her ass in my chair, and the hell out of my salon. I glance up at the clock. 11:10 A.M.

I walk over and give Janelle a hug, then quickly usher her to my station. I look over at Kendra, who's engrossed in a conversation with her client about cheating men, and let her know I scheduled her a twelve o'clock.

"Okay, cool," she says, looking up from her client's head. She goes back to curling her client's hair, waving the iron in the air every so often as they go in on dumb-ass women who always want to blame the jump-offs and mistresses, like they're the problem, when the real problem is lying up in bed with her.

I tune the conversation out. "Janelle, girl, how you been?"

"Fine. You know me; work, work, work."

"I hear that."

Chris Brown's "Don't Judge Me" floats through the speakers. I start humming along as I snap the cape around Janelle's neck. All of a sudden the volume goes up and I see Booty jump up, a hand waves in the air, then she starts swaying. She yells over the music, "Yessssss, goddammit…don't judge me…'cause things can get ugly…gonna have me take it to ya face…!"

I blink. Swallow hard.

A few people laugh, shaking their heads.

"Janelle, hold on one minute." I quickly pop my hips back out to the front, tell Booty to lower the volume and to stop all that cussing and dancing up in here. She gives me a blank look, then turns her attention to the ringing phone.

"Girl, when'd you hire that one?" Janelle wants to know when I return to my station.

"I didn't. She decided she wanted to help out."

Janelle chuckles. "Looks like you're going to have your hands full. How long is she going to be *helping* out?"

"If that's what you want to call it—*not* long. Only for the next"— I glance up at the clock—"forty-five minutes. Trust me. I was caught by surprise, girl, when I walked up in here and saw her carrying on."

She shakes her head. "She's a piece of work; quite entertaining that's for sure."

I swallow, feeling my stomach tightening. "Yeah, to say the least." I'm thankful Janelle is only here for a wash and set. I can quickly whip her up and get her under the dryer, then get Cassandra's ass in this chair. *Who the hell told her to take it upon herself to answer my goddamn phones?* I fling the chair back, almost banging Janelle's head on the edge of the sink.

She jumps.

"Oooh, girl, forgive me. Something must be wrong with this chair." Janelle gives me the eye. I smile. Every time the phone rings, I cringe inwardly and my stomach knots. I try not to focus on what kind of irrevocable damage Booty's up front causing to my business, how many potential clients she's chased away, the hundreds—maybe *thousands*—of dollars I might lose in the next forty-two minutes and counting if I don't hurry up and get Janelle out of this goddamn chair.

Janelle grunts and winces. "Ugh...Oooh, ooh. Mmmph...ugh... ohmygod, Pasha..."

I blink, apologizing profusely for digging and clawing my nails into her scalp and swinging and jerking her head under the spigot, getting water and shampoo all in her eyes.

Goddamn you, Cassandra!

"Girl, what's going on with you today? I like it a little rough and I don't mind a little hair pulling. But in the sheets, behind closed doors. *Not* in my stylist's chair."

"Janelle, I'm so sorry, girl. Forgive me. This one'll be on me." I quickly rinse the shampoo out, then run conditioner through her hair. "My mind is all over the place today."

She chuckles. "Girl, no worries. You know I'm only messing with you. But you do seem a little distracted."

"Chile, I am."

I glance out toward the front area of the salon as the door opens. A brown-skinned guy sticks his head inside the door. I can't see his face clearly since he has the brim of a blue Yankees-fitted pulled down low over his eyes. But I see when Booty hops up and plants a hand up over her hip, then she storms over toward the door. *My God! Please don't let her get to cussing and fighting up in here!*

I quickly summon one of my security guards over, then quietly tell him to stay posted up in the front. And to toss Cassandra's ass out if she even sneezes, blinks, or looks wrong.

"You know what, girl," Janelle says as I start combing through her hair, "I think I want you to give me a trim and add a little color to my hair."

I blink.

Bitch, you have got to be kidding me?!

I glance up at the clock. 11:30 A.M.

I can already tell. This is going to be a long goddamn day!

Twenty-Two

The unveiling of truths can become a nigga's salvation
or the key to his demise…

"I see you got that triflin' bitch answerin' the muthafuckin' phones over there now. Why the fuck you ain't answerin' ya shit when I call you, yo…?"

I glance up at the clock on my office wall. It's a little after two in the afternoon. And this nigga's been blowing up my phone all day, calling back to back, sending me crazy-ass text messages. When I landed in Newark this morning from my flight out of L.A., and turned on my phone, I almost screamed when I saw that I had over a hundred and thirty text messages from this nigga.

Inhale.

Exhale.

Inhale.

Exhale.

Don't let this nigga get under your skin.

I haven't seen or spoken to this motherfucker since I chewed his balls up two days ago. And why I'm even wasting my time talking to him now is beyond me. But, what I do know is, Jasper's going to learn you don't *ever* fuck with (or fuck over) a bitch who knows all of your dirty little secrets. And Jasper's hands are real fucking dirty. He doesn't think I know where most of his stash houses are. But I do. I just haven't said anything.

Anyway, his fists, Booty's theatrics, and multiple shots of Hennessy on Tuesday, were all the motivation I needed to march back up in here—*after* I lit into Rhodeshia's gossiping ass—and place a call to Bianca, one of my salon clients and good friend. I called her to speak with her fiancé, Garrett, who's a state trooper and who also happens to be related to my cousins Persia, Paris and Porsha on their father's side.

I hadn't seen Garrett in ages. But I'm always kept abreast of his life either through Bianca whenever she comes into the salon. Or Paris, whenever we talk. So seeing him at my wedding with Bianca was a sight for sore eyes.

At the reception, while Garrett and I were sharing a dance, he pulled me into his arms and whispered, "I truly hope you know what you've gotten yourself into, Pasha. He's a real slick one."

I nodded knowingly. The DEA, the FEDs, they all want a piece of Jasper. But Jasper has always been able to slip under their radar.

"Who you love or who you marry is none of my business," Garrett had said to me as we danced to Miguel's "Adorn," "but you and I go way back, Pasha. We're like family. If there's anything—and I mean, *any*thing—you ever need, you call me."

And with that said, he kissed me on the cheek, then stepped aside to allow Jasper—who had been eyeing us the whole time we were on the floor dancing—to cut in.

So when Garrett called me twenty minutes after I hung up with Bianca, I told him what happened, but made it clear I didn't want Jasper arrested; just to stay the fuck away from me. He said he'd make a few calls, and get back to me. Ten minutes later, he called back and told me everything was taken care of. All I had to do was stop down to the precinct in my town when I left the salon. So I did.

Of course, before he hung up with me, he tried to persuade me to file criminal charges. But my mind was made up. Charges and a potential arrest were not an option. No. I wanted Jasper's black ass to know playtime was over. I wanted his ass to be served those papers before the sun went down.

And he was.

I sigh heavily into the phone. "What do you want, Jasper?"

"What the fuck you mean what I want? You fucked my balls up, yo. Got my shit fuckin' swollen 'n' shit. A muhfucka still can't fuckin' walk 'cause you wanna be on some funny shit. Word is bond, yo. That was some foul shit you pulled, Pasha. But I'ma see you, yo."

I grunt. "Oh well, nigga. You had no business putting your hands on me. Next time, I will make sure I rip them motherfuckers off. Now come *see* about that."

"Real shit, Pasha. I'ma bust ya ass for that shit. Then you stuff all my shit in trash bags 'n' dump 'em out in front of Stax's yard. What the fuck, yo?! Got muhfuckin' bum-ass niggas rummagin' all through my shit. Then, on top of that shit, you hit me wit' a fuckin' restrainin' order, yo. What the fuck is you doin', yo?"

"Something I should have done a long time ago."

"I see you wanna be grimy, right? Is this how you wanna do it, yo? Huh, Pasha? You bite my shit up 'n' pull a fuckin' burner out on *me!* Then have me put outta my shit. You really feelin' ya'self, yo. You let that bitch get ya ass all gassed for some shit you ain't ready for, yo. But it's all good, baby. I'ma bust ya muthafuckin' ass; believe that."

"Jasper, do what you feel you need to do. But know this, I'm done with you, nigga. And I mean that."

"Fuck outta here. You pulled some real savage shit. But I'ma see you."

"I know, Jasper. You already said that. Now what?"

"Oh, you wanna be a smart-ass, right? Keep talkin' slick, Pasha, aiight? I know that ghetto-ass bitch, Cassandra, got you doin' all this dumb shit…"

I pull my cell away from my ear, looking at it incredulously.

"Cassandra didn't put me up to do shit. *You* did. You put your hands on me one time too many. And I've had enough. I'm done with you and your jealous ass, nigga. Period. The *only* savage is *you*. You staged having me kidnapped and sexually assaulted, then practically beat me to death, *knowing* I was pregnant with *your* son and you're calling *me* a savage. Nigga, *please!* Drop dead! You're fucking delusional. And the only motherfucking thing you're going to *see* is the lid of a coffin if you come anywhere near me."

"Yo, what the fuck is you back on that shit for, huh? I tol' ya ass it was over wit'. What happened; happened. It is what it is. You took ya lumps for what the fuck you did to me. And I forgave ya ass. Now let the shit go. Move the fuck on. I tol' ya ass what it was if I ever caught ya ass playin' me, yo. So what the fuck is you still on this shit for, huh? Ya whore-ass was the one out here suckin' muhfuckas off while I was on lock! Got me sittin' in that muh- fucka stressin' 'n' lookin' like a fuckin' fool, yo!"

"Like I've said a million and one times, I know what I did was fucked up, Jasper. I accept that. I've owned it. But, *you*, nigga…you took the shit too far. What *you* did to me was *brutal* and fucking *repulsive! I* don't *forgive* you for that shit! And I'm *not* over it."

He starts yelling like a maniac. In my mind's eye, I see him foaming at the mouth like the rabid savage he is. I think to hang up on him, but decide to hear him out. Nothing he can say or do at this point will stop what's already in motion from happening. But I want to hear what he has to say. And I want answers.

"Yo, what the fuck?! And you don't think what the fuck ya cum-guzzlin' ass was out here doin' wasn't repulsive, huh? Fuck outta here! *You* fuckin' humiliated me, yo! Got muhfukas talkin' all sideways 'bout what the fuck you was out here doin'! And I'm checkin' muhfuckas, 'like nah, you got the wrong one, yo. My girl ain't on no shit like that.' And, come to find out, ya trick-ass was! How the fuck you think that made a muhfucka feel, huh?! Like a muthafuckin' joke! A fuckin' pussy, yo. *You* did that shit! *You* had my muthafuckin' heart 'n' you shitted on me…!"

For the first time since all of this shit happened, this is the first time I really hear the hurt in his voice. I swallow back what's left of my own hurt, and guilt, knowing I caused this. Still, it doesn't change shit!

It's too late.

"So yeah, muhfucka, since you love suckin' random muhfuckas off 'n' shit, I had muhfuckas bang up ya throat. I tol' ya ass you don't know who I know, or who the fuck I got watchin' shit! And I tol' ya ass what I was gonna do if ya ass was outta pocket! I kept fuckin' warnin' ya ass, Pasha! I gave ya ass fair warnin', yo, And enough muthafuckin' time to stop doin' whatever the fuck you was out there doin' before I touched down! But ya slut-ass still kept doin' grimy shit! Now all of a sudden, ya muthafuckin' ass wanna act like you traumatized. Bitch, ya ass wasn't all that concerned when you was takin' muhfuckas to the back of the throat! Get ya ass into counselin', yo, 'n' work that shit out. Stop fuckin' around, Pasha! Go drop that fuckin' restrainin' order! And get them fuckin' robo cops up off'a my muthafuckin' property so I can get the fuck back home, yo!"

"You're not getting back into shit. You did what *you* felt you had to do. Now, I'm getting ready to do what needs to be done. I'm not dropping *shit*. The locks have been changed. All of the security codes to the house and garages are changed. And, *yes*, since obviously you tried going over to the house, I now have a security team on the property, in addition to all the security cameras that *you* made sure we had. So, if you come anywhere near *my* property, you will be arrested for trespassing—if a bullet isn't put in your head, first. All of your clothes and other shit are in those trash bags. Anything else you want out of *my* house, you had better come with a police escort and a court order because that is the *only* way you're ever getting inside to get shit else."

"Yo, how the fuck you gonna keep me outta my own motherfuckin' house, huh? Fuck outta here! That's my muthafuckin' paper up in that muhfucka! I paid for that shit, yo! I'll have that muthafucka burned to the muthafuckin' ground 'fore I let you move another muhfucka up in shit I fuckin' paid for! You hear me, yo?! I'll burn that bitch down wit' *you* in it. Don't fuck wit' me, yo! Ya heard?!"

My heart catches in my throat, but I don't let him hear it in my voice. "Oh, well, nigga. Do what you gotta do. It's in *my* name, free and clear. Isn't it? So, you don't have claims to shit. Not over on Canterbury Lane you don't. "

"Say what, yo?! You wanna play dirty, huh, Pasha?! Is that how you really fuckin' doin' it, now?! You wanna be on some bitch shit 'n' fuckin' snake me after all the shit I've done for ya stupid ass? After e'ery muthafuckin' thing we've been through, yo. Fuck you, man! You ain't shit, Pasha. Real shit, yo! I want all the paper in them safes, yo."

"*Safes?*" I say, feigning ignorance. "I only know about *one* safe. Where's this other one at?"

"Fuck outta here! Don't worry 'bout all that. Let me come get my shit. And I want my shit outta your muthafuckin' bank accounts, too. You hear me? I want my shit by tomorrow, Pasha! All of it! E'ery muthafuckin' dime!"

I sigh. I hear Booty's voice in my head. *"Fish this nigga, goddammit!"*

"Okay, Jasper, you want your money? Fine. You want to come back into the house? Then it's going to cost you. I want answers, nigga. First, I want to know: *did* you fuck Felecia? And don't fucking lie, nigga."

He sucks his teeth. "Fuck, yo! You really wanna do this shit? Just drop it, aiight."

"Nigga, I'm not dropping shit. And I'm not giving you *shit*— not one fucking dime—*unless* you tell me what I wanna know."

"Are you fuckin' serious, yo?"

"Nigga, you got five seconds to start talking before you get the dial tone."

He blows a heavy breath into the phone. "You bein' a real fuckin' bitch, yo. You know that, right?"

"Oh well. Buckle up, nigga, 'cause you haven't seen shit, *yet*. Now *did* you fuck that bitch or not?"

"Hell, no, I ain't fuck her bird-ass. That bitch is a snitch. What I look like fuckin' wit' a weak-ass bitch like that? All that bitch ever did was *suck* my dick, lick on these balls, and eat these nuts out. And the bitch couldn't even make a nigga's toes curl. Bitch can't even hold a dick down in her throat. All she did was swallow my nuts 'n' I hit her ass wit' some product 'n' paper for keepin' tabs on ya ass. Bitch wanna be *you* so fuckin' bad."

I blink.

"That bitch didn't give a fuck about you, yo. Desperate bitch wanted ya spot like crazy. She came at me wit' the shit, aiight. I ain't tryna dry-snitch the bitch out but it is what it is. She shot me a kite while I was behind the wall 'n' put me on to you, yo. She wanted me to put her on my visitin' list 'n' I did."

I feel myself about to choke on my anger as he tells me how she'd drive down to Southwoods Prison to see him, then tell him all this shit about me. Eventually he started letting her suck his dick. That fucking dirty bitch was sucking him in the goddamn visiting room! As I listen, I'm squeezing the phone so tight that it starts cutting off the circulation in my hand.

"I ain't want you to know. But fuck it! You tryna fuck wit' my paper. I want my shit, yo. So it is what it is."

I take a deep breath. Steady my nerves. "Well, since you're *finally* telling the truth about something, if that *is* the truth. Tell me this: were *you* behind having the windows smashed out of my salon and car?" He says he wasn't. Says he didn't know shit about it popping off until Felecia texted him. I ask him if he was the nigga who had me attacked that night in the yard. He tells me no. Tells me he heard that shit from Felecia, too.

I feel sick to my stomach.

That dirty bitch! If I thought I could get away with it, I'd fucking kill her!

"Ya own fuckin' fam snaked you, aiight. You satisfied? Now let me get my shit, yo!"

I swallow the thick lump in my throat. I fight to keep my anger from getting the best of me. "Give me the names of the niggas who you had kidnap and attack me and you can have every dime of your money back. And I'll even sign over the house to you."

"Yo, you fuckin' buggin' now. Fuck that. What the fuck I look like puttin' them niggas out like that?! Fuck outta here, yo! You already know it was me behind it 'n' shit. So that's all you need to know, period. You don't need to know shit else."

I take another deep breath. I knew this nigga wasn't going to make it easy. "Then suit yourself. But understand this, Jasper: I'm not giving you a motherfucking thing. Whatever's in those *safes* you speak of you *won't* ever get your hands on if I can help it. And the money in my money market accounts, chalk it up as a loss, nigga. I *know* you. And you *know* I know what kind of weight you're pushing out there. You're far from broke. And you and I *both* know you have shit stashed all over the fucking place. So I'm not giving *you* shit unless I get those names—*all* of them. And I mean it. Otherwise, you better go hit up one of the stash houses you have scattered all over the place, and reup your stacks. Bottom line, I'm done, nigga. And I'm done with *you*."

He snaps. "Yo, fuck outta here wit' that shit! Ain't shit done, bitch, 'less I say it is, ya heard?! You must really wanna be out there whorin' again, is that it?! You stay showin' ya ass, yo! Let me find out who the muhfucka is you creepin' wit'! I'ma dead that shit, yo! Real shit, Pasha! You don't know *who* the fuck you fuckin' wit', yo! Shit ain't sweet! I *thought* I taught ya whore-ass a lesson the last time you crossed me! What I gotta do this time, huh?!"

I fight to keep calm. I refuse to get into a screaming match with this nigga. "Do whatever you want, Jasper. You're right. There isn't shit sweet about what's about to go down, nigga. So don't get it twisted. I *know* exactly whom I'm *fucking* with. You're the nigga who had me tied up down in some basement, sucking a string of niggas' dicks. You're the nigga who then came down and beat the shit out of me. Then had your goons toss my body in a park. You left me for dead, nigga.

"So yeah, I know *exactly* who you are. You're the same crazy nigga who married this *whore*. And you wanna know why *you* still married a bitch who *you knew* was sucking a buncha niggas' dicks behind your goddamn back while you were in prison? I'ma tell you, nigga. Because ya ass is crazy for this deep throat. This throat pussy is like crack, and you know it, nigga. And this hot, wet pussy between my legs is deep and tight. That's why you still married this *slut-ass whore*, nigga! Your ass is strung out and crazy for this good shit. Always have been, always will be."

I can practically feel the fire shooting out of his nostrils. Can see him balling his fists. "Yo, you think this shit's funny, huh, Pasha?! Fuckin' bitch! You think I can't get at you, huh, Pasha?! Is that it, yo?! You think some fuckin' piece of paper is gonna keep me away from you?! Fuck outta here, yo! The only reason ya ass is still breathin' is 'cause I want you to! And don't think I won't be stoppin' by *Nana's* as soon as my shit gets right 'n' I can walk to have a lil talk wit' her! *Don't* fuck wit' me, Pasha!"

My heart drops. "Jasper, stay the fuck away from her! Do you hear me, motherfucker?! I mean it! Stay the *fuck* away from my grandmother! I swear to you! If something *ever* happens to her, I will personally unload a clip in your motherfucking head!"

I hang up on his ass. But the nigga calls back. Then calls the salon's line when I don't pick up my cell. "*Whaaat*, Jasper?! *Stop* fucking calling me, or I will call the police and have you arrested for fucking harassing me!"

"Real shit, Pasha," he says calmly, "you gonna fuck 'round 'n' have me put a bullet in ya shit."

The line goes dead.

Twenty-Three

*There's no repentance for being a snitch,
only having your tongue cut out...*

"**Y**ou gonna fuck 'round 'n' have me put a bullet in ya shit." I fall
back in my seat. It isn't until I remove the phone from my
ear, clutching it in my hand, that I realize that I'm shaking.
My cell buzzes in my hand causing me to jump. *This nigga has my
fucking nerves rattled.* I glance at the caller ID, breathing out a
sigh of relief, quickly answering the call.

"Hi, Nana," I say, happy to hear her voice. I close my eyes.

"Hey, baby." Hearing my seventy-two-year-old grandmother's
warm, soothing voice warms causes a tear to roll down my cheek.
I quickly wipe it away. I ask her how she is. "The good Lord woke
me up this morning, and spared me another day. I am truly blessed."

"You sure are. That's a blessing." I blink back tears.

"It sure is. *My* God is truly in the blessing business. He's an awe-
some God. Amen. And He's been mighty good to you, Pasha."

Oh, no. Please. Not today, Nana. "I know He has, Nana."

"Uh-huh. Then why have you forsaken Him?" Inhale. All it takes
is a pregnant pause for her to start up. "Seems like you're too
busy tryna keep up with the devil these days. You need to get right
with God. Put Him first. And stop letting the devil have his way."

Exhale. "Nana, I'm a work in progress. God knows my heart."

"Uh-huh. We're in the last days, Pasha. When the pearly gates finally open…"

I cut her off. "Nana, I love you very much."

"And I love you. But you *need* to love the Lord more."

I sigh. "Nana, as much as I'd love to stay on the phone and fellowship with you, I have to make this real quick." I tell her my reason for calling. "If Jasper happens to stop over, please do me a favor and do *not* let *him* or *anyone* else who comes to the door that doesn't look familiar to you inside. Don't even open the door for them. I want you to immediately call the police."

She wants to know why. I tell her I've put him out; that I have a restraining order against him—and she's listed as someone Jasper's to have no contact with; that I'm worried about her being in that house all by herself. I try to convince her to let me send her on a vacation for a few weeks. Try to encourage her to visit her niece, Penny—my cousin Persia and her sisters' aunt—and her family out in Arizona. But Nana isn't hearing it.

"Chile, hush. I'm not going anywhere. When you live by faith, you aren't moved by fear. You know I stay armed and ready. I'm covered in the blood of Jesus. The Lord's armor will protect me from any wickedness. In the name of Jesus. In the name of Jesus. In the *name*…of Jesus. Amen."

"Nana, please," I plead. "If you don't want to go for a few weeks, then go for a week."

"Baby, I walk through the valley of the shadow of death…I fear no…"

I see she's not budging, see there's no convincing her. I let it go. "I know you do, Nana. Anyway, I'm going to let you go, okay? I only wanted to let you know what's going on with me and to check on you."

"Thanks, baby. I'm glad to hear you're finally letting that husband of yours go. You know I've never fancied Jasper. But I'm a good Christian woman with an open and loving heart. So I have loved him best I can." She grunts. "You and Felecia have always been stubborn when it comes to them street thugs. Just like your mothers. You girls love them heathen men; especially you, Pasha."

I sigh. *I knew this shit was coming.* "Nana, please. Let's not go there. I'm *nothing* like her, or my mother."

"Mmmph. I'm leaving it all up on the altar. I don't know what happened to you while you were missing. But you haven't been right since, Pasha. Whatever them filthy heathens did to my sweet baby has changed you. I wish you'd give it to God. Your spirit is heavy. And them beautiful eyes don't have that sparkle in 'em like they used to, baby. I wish you'd come to church. Let me have Pastor lay hands on you. Let him shake the devil and his serpents out of your life. You need to get right with God, Pasha. Let Him heal your spirit before it's too late. Please, baby. Do it for your Nana, and that precious baby of yours."

I feel myself starting to tear up. "I will, Nana, soon."

"Uh-huh. Soon it'll be too late, baby. I know I can't tell you what to do 'cause you grown. But I'm telling you this, baby. Jasper's spirit isn't right. It's never been right. And he's gotta hold on you."

You have no idea.

"I'll fuckin' kill you, yo…to teach you a lesson…don't have me fuck you up, yo…you stay wantin' me to beat ya ass, yo…" Jasper's voice plays over and over in my head, his threats churning a hole into my memory.

I feel myself getting sick. I dab at my eyes to keep the tears from falling.

"Anyway, baby. Felecia was here this morning and told me you and her had a big falling-out and you done fired her from the salon. She's all broken up behind that. Now I hear you're fighting her unemployment. Tell me this isn't so? You know my heart can't stand hearing none of this mess."

I grit my teeth. *That bitch!* "Yes, it's true, Nana. I fired her." She wants to know why. I tell her that I'd rather not talk about it; that it's between her and me.

"Well, I pray the two of you work it out. All you have is each other." I roll my eyes in my head. *Psst. Please. After what I've just heard, I'm over that bitch!* "You know I raised you and Felecia better than to turn on each other. The two of you have always been like sisters."

"Well, that's changed Nana. Felecia and I stopped being like *sisters* the day she stopped being loyal. Did she tell you that?"

"No, she didn't. But that doesn't matter. What matters is that *you* do right by her. You know better, Pasha. Felecia has always been a troubled girl. And she's always needed a little extra care. You know she had it hard not knowing her father and then her mother—God rest her soul—being strung out on that stuff. I'm telling you the devil stays busy."

Yeah, Nana. The devil was busy sucking Jasper's dick behind my fucking back!

"It's not right what you doing to that poor child, Pasha. You know she's never been too right in the head after all the things she seen her mother do growing up."

"*Ohmygod, Nana!*" I shriek in disbelief. All my life Nana has taken up for Felecia's miserable-ass and has made excuses for her. There's always been some kind of justification or rationalization for that bitch! She's sad. She's misunderstood. She just needs to be loved. She needs more attention. Mmmph. Blah, blah, blah...

And what the fuck about me?

"Are you serious right now? Felecia's a grown-as"—I catch myself before I finish the rest—"woman. She's not some little girl who doesn't know what she says or does. I know she had it hard. I had it hard, too, Nana."

"Your mother wasn't a drug addict, Pasha. And you had your father in your life. Felecia didn't."

I frown. "Nana, please. You don't think I had it hard having a mother who wanted to be the next kingpin's trophy instead of a mother to me. Or a father who'd rather sling dope and rob people on the streets instead of raising his daughter. Okay, so he bought me nice things and made sure I had whatever I wanted and needed. Still, *he* wasn't raising me. *You* were. They left me, Nana. I was abandoned, too. But you don't see me making excuses for what I do as an adult. Nana, Felecia's choices have nothing to do with what she's been through as a child. And if they do, shame on her. Because at the end of the day, she is still responsible for what she says and does as I am. And like it or not, she *will* be held accountable; period."

"Is this how I raised you, Pasha? To be spiteful and talk fresh to me? Is this what being high-and-mighty, living out there in that mansion, has done to you? Have you turn your back on your family and disrespect *me?* I put a roof over your head and fed and clothed you and made sure you had braces to fix them raggedy teeth so you could have that beautiful smile and *this* is how you speak to me. *My* God is a mighty good God and He leads me in a path of righteousness so *before* I let the devil take my tongue, I'm going to lift you up in prayer. I know the God I serve is a merciful God. And the devil is a hot *dang* lie. Oooh, I'm hotter than grits with you right now, Pasha. You got me cussing."

I'm going to stomp Felecia's ass!

"Nana, I'm sorry if I spoke to you disrespectfully. You know I love you and would never intentionally be disrespectful to you, or get you to *cussing*." I shake my head. If I weren't so pissed right now, I'd actually be laughing at Nana for thinking saying *dang* is *cussing*. "Nana, I'm just sick of Felecia always playing the victim. She created this mess between us. And quite frankly she's going to need a whole lot more than prayer to get out of it."

"Mmmph. You almost made me take it to you, Pasha. I thank God *every day* for keeping me anchored in His word. I almost went back to my old heathen ways on you, baby. Don't speak to me in that fashion again, Pasha. I *know* I raised you better than that."

In an instant, I feel like a child again being scolded. "Yes, Nana, you did. And I apologize. I love you."

"Mmmph. Sister Peterson is outside blowing the horn for me. I love you, too. And remember to always keep God first. He's the *only* one who can't help see you through it."

We talk a few more seconds, then end the call. I set my cell on my desk. *I can't believe that fucking bitch Felecia! Anytime shit goes wrong in her life, that bitch is always the victim. She can't ever take responsibility for her shit.*

I take a few deep breaths to steady my nerves, picking up my cell and scrolling through my call log. I force myself to keep the edge out of my voice when she answers. *Reel this bitch in!*

"Hello?"

"Felecia? Hey. It's me. Pasha. It's time we clear the air."

"Yes it is," she says, letting out a loud sigh. "I'm glad you're finally ready to talk so I can explain my side to you and we can put this crazy mess behind us."

I bite down on my lip. Keep from calling her every *bitch* in the book. "Don't get excited. I'm still not fucking with you. But, if nothing else, I don't want to spend my life harboring grudges, especially toward you."

Yeah, right!

"Me either, Pasha. I know I might have done and said a few things I—"

I cut her ass off. "Look, I didn't call to get into all that. If we're going to talk, we need to do it face to face."

"I agree. When would you like to meet? Today?" I tell her ass no. Tell her I'll meet her Sunday night. Nine P.M.

Here at the salon.

Just her and me.

Alone.

I disconnect on her ass, then hop up from my desk and race into the bathroom, tossing my guts up into the sink. I start dry-heaving. *Fucking dirty, backstabbing bitch!*

Twenty-Four

In the still of the night clarity comes. And revelations become reality…

One, one-thousand…two, one-thousand…three, one-thousand… four, one-thousand…

Counting in my head is how I can guesstimate how long it takes for Calm One to come back. It takes almost ten minutes before the door opens and he comes down carrying a bag of things. He drops the bag to the ground, then squats down in front of me so that he's at eye level with me. He narrows his eyes. I've seen those eyes somewhere. I blink, take in their intensity. Where do I know this nigga from?

"I'm gonna untie ya feet, first. Then ya hands. If you try any dumb shit, the goons are gonna be down here to handle you, if I don't empty this lead in you, first. You understand?"

I nod. But I am also smart enough to know that right now, killing me is far from the plan. Maiming me, perhaps, but definitely not putting me in a body bag. My only saving grace is that whomever is behind this, wants me alive.

"Aiight, cool." He pulls out a knife and slices through the tape around my ankles. I stretch and open my legs out. He walks in back of me, releasing my hands. I wince when I attempt to move my arms. They ache from being behind my back for so long. I can't believe I have been sitting in a puddle of my own piss. I feel sick to my stomach. A ton of questions are running through my head. I think if I can keep him talking that *somehow I'll be able to pick up on his voice and figure out who he is. My gut tells me these niggas are all familiar with me in some kind of way. He tells me to hold my hands out in front of me. I do. Then he snatches my freedom away by placing a set of handcuffs on me.*

He tells me to stand up. But my legs are too wobbly to hold my own weight. I stumble. He grabs me and walks me toward the bathroom. There's a small sink, toilet and glass-encased shower stall. He tells me to take off my clothes. I stare at him.

"Yo, take them shits off. What, you think I haven't seen a buncha ass and titties before?"

"That's not it," I say, lifting my arms, showing him the obvious. "I'm cuffed so taking my shirt and bra off will pose a problem."

He shakes his head. "Yeah, you got a point." He walks over, pulling out his knife. It's a dagger of sorts. He slides the handle of it between his lips, using his mouth to hold it while he unbuttons my jeans. He smells me—pissy, and shitty, but he doesn't flinch. He pulls my pants down over my hips, then my soiled panties. I am so relieved to have them shitty drawers off that I don't give any thought to the fact that this nigga is undressing me. He takes my soiled garments and puts them in a garbage bag. Then he removes the blade from his mouth. "Stand still," he says as he slices through my four hundred-dollar designer blouse. He cuts my bra straps, then slices through the front of it. My titties sway freely. And he locks his eyes on them. Subconsciously, he licks his lips.

I am standing in front of him naked, wearing only a pair of handcuffs around my wrists. I glance over at the toilet. Tell him I need to use it. He stands there, waiting.

"Well," I say, hoping he'd get the hint and step out.

"Well, what?" he asks. "If you need to use the toilet, then do it." Noticing he doesn't intend on giving me any privacy, I squat over the bowl and take a piss. I reach for the toilet paper and attempt to wipe my

privates. The idea of wiping my pussy from the back to the front makes me sick. So I pat dry my box, instead. He tells me to turn on the shower, then walks over and hands me a washcloth and bar of Dial soap. I look at him.

"How do you expect me to wash myself clean with my hands cuffed?"

"Either I wash you, or you figure out how to wash ya'self. Those are you only two options," he tells me, leaning up against the door. He can't seem to keep his eyes from roaming my body. When the shower starts to steam, I pull open the glass door, then step in. The hot water feels good against my body. He watches me struggle to wash between my legs. He walks over, opens the shower door, and tells me to hold out my arms. I do. He unlocks one cuff, releasing my hands.

"Thank you," I say, quickly turning back to face the water. I can feel him soaking in my nakedness. I lean my head back, close my eyes and let the steamy stream of water beat against my neck and chest. I lather up and scrub and scrub and scrub until my skin feels raw and the hot water burns. I am grateful he allows me all the time I need.

When I am finished, he hands me a towel. I dry off, wrap it around my body, then step out. He keeps his eyes on me, handing me a bottle of Tease scented body lotion by Victoria's Secret. When he hands me a Victoria's Secret white, lacy cut-out halter teddy, I frown. "Why are you giving me this to put on?" I ask.

"Yo, ma," he says, sighing. "You either put the shit on, or go naked; your choice."

I drop my towel and shimmy my way into it. I'm surprised it's a perfect fit. The nigga is having a hard time keeping his eyes off my curves. Despite my baby bump, my body can still stop traffic. "What time is it?"

"Time for you to hurry up," he huffs, tearing his eyes away from my titties.

"How would you feel if someone had your sister or niece or daughter

tied up somewhere and she was being sexually assaulted? Would you want someone to have enough heart to let her go?"

He turns his head for a moment, then brings his attention back to me. *"Hold out your hand."* I do. And he re-cuffs it. *"Come on."* He leads me out of the bathroom, then walks me over to the other side of the basement. *There's a small room with a black leather sofa bed and small flat-screen TV. There's a set of sheets and a blanket sitting on a chair.* *"Make ya bed,"* he tells me. *"If you wanna get outta here, tomorrow's gonna be ya big day to shine. You perform well, you get ya wish."*

"And if I don't?"

"Then you stay until you get it right."

"And what is it ya'll gonna have me do?"

He laughs. *"Don't play stupid, ma. Do what you do best—suck dick. What else?"*

I am too fucking exhausted to respond. I take the sheets and make up the sofa, then lie on it, pulling the blanket up over me. As bad as I want to stay awake, as scared as I am that someone might try to rape me while I'm sleeping, I am having a hard time keeping my eyes open. I lift my head and see the same nigga sitting in a chair blocking the door. He must sense my worry.

"It's all good, ma. No one's gonna fuck wit' you tonight. Get ya rest, baby. You're gonna need it."

My eyes pop open as pieces of my dream that awoke me start to surface. The tattoo! Why hadn't I remembered it before now?

The sleek panther tatted on Calm One's shoulder!

Where have I seen that tattoo? I know I've seen it before. But where? I won't be able to rest until I find out who you are, Calm One.

It's almost midnight. My heart is pounding in my chest. I am coated in a film of sweat. I think I hear something. A noise. Even though I have a security system—with infrared cameras, motion detectors, window sensors, and vault doors that look like regular doors that prevent anyone from kicking in my doors—being in this big-ass house alone has my nerves on edge.

I feel for the Baretta I sleep with under my pillow and grab it, then sit up, placing my feet on the floor, then turning on the light on the nightstand. I grip the gun and sit quietly, listening, waiting. For what, I have no idea.

This shit is crazy! I take several deep breaths to steady my nerves. Then stand, removing my damp nightgown. I take a quick shower, towel off, oil my body, then walk over to my dresser, rummaging through a drawer filled with an array of negligees, teddies, flyaways, before finally settling on a pair of pink lace boy shorts and a matching tee.

After checking the security panel and monitor, I pick up the house phone and call out to the security booth to speak with the guard on duty. He assures me everything is fine, that I have no cause for alarm. I breathe out a sigh of relief, hanging up.

I climb back in bed and reach my cell off the nightstand. I have eight missed calls, four text messages. I press the prompts to retrieve my voice messages. There are seven of them.

First message: Today, four-thirteen P.M. It's Mona sounding frazzled and desperate and at her wits' end. "Pasha, it's me, Mona. I need you to call me as soon as you get this message. I don't know how much longer I can keep this in. Leticia has filed a missing person's report. Girl, call me."

It sounds as if she's been crying. I shake my head. *I know she's going through it right now. But I'm really going to need her to pull it together, or she's going to end up getting us all jammed up in some shit.*

I know JT's her cousin. And I'm sure his wife, Leticia, and his mother are stressed out with worry. But fuck that dirty nigga. She has to remember what the fuck that nigga did to her. *Fucking molester!* She can't be falling apart like this over his ass. Not after what he put her through. I glance at the television, wondering how many other girls he did that shit to, or tried to rape.

Maybe Booty's right, Mona's ass isn't built for this shit. I wonder if the police will find his body. And if they do, will they be able to trace it back to Booty?

Second message: Today, five-forty P.M. As soon as I hear his voice, I cringe. This nigga is fucking crazy! "Pasha, what the fuck, yo. That was some real bullshit you pulled, yo. You bein' a real bitch, yo. Keep lettin' that fuckin' bitch, Cassandra, gas ya ass up, aiight? Why is you puttin' me through a buncha fuckin' changes, yo? I'm tryna give you ya space, yo. But you really testin' me. Drop that fuckin' restrainin' order, yo. I wanna see my fuckin' son, bitch! And I want my muthafuckin' paper!"

I frown, saving the message. *Fuck you, nigga! I'm so over you and your bullshit!* I glance at the television screen getting caught up in the taped episode of Olivia's romp in the sheets with Fitz. *You go, girl. Get your sloppy seconds!* She's the only jump-off I know who gets main bitch treatment. And the wife gets treated like she's the real trick in the room.

Third message: Today, six-eighteen P.M. "Yo, Pash. It's me, Stax... hit me up." Fuck you, too, Stax! I delete the message.

Fourth message: Today, seven-thirty P.M. "Miss Pasha, girl. I'm tryna keep it classy, and you know I don't do messy. But I'ma split-second from bangin' Mona in her goddamn head. Help that coon-bitch get her goddamn mind right. That bitch is all over the place."

I roll my eyes. "I can't with these bitches," I say, deleting the message.

Fifth message: Today, nine-eleven P.M. "Yo, Pasha. It's me. Lamar. I got you on the brain, ma. Just wanna make sure you got to the crib safe and you aiight. I'm still kinda hot 'bout that shit you told me. Hit me up so I know you got in okay. I'ma be up pretty late."

Sixth message: Today, ten-thirty P.M. "Pasha, it's me again. Lamar. Yo, don't have me drive down to ya crib to make sure shit's aiight wit' you. Call me. If I don't hear back within the next hour, I'ma be at ya gate."

I smile. I don't bother listening to the last message. I scroll through my contacts, then call his cell. He picks up on the first ring. "Damn, I'm relieved to hear your voice, Pasha. You had a muhfucka over here stressin', real shit."

I smile. "I appreciate that. I'm okay."

"Shit, I was 'bout ready to send out the troops to make sure you were safe…"

A light bulb goes off in my head as I'm sitting up in bed listening to him. *Shit's about to get real messy in a minute. This nigga's someone I need on my team.*

I replay the conversation we had earlier in this evening in my head. He had expressed concern for me, wanting to know if everything was okay with me. After several moments of him prodding, I finally decided to tell him about my phone call with Jasper earlier in the day.

His jaws tightened. "Say what? Fuck that! Pasha, I might be a part of ya security team here, but this lil gig ain't what I do. There's a whole other side of me you don't know, ma. I gotta crew that'll shut shit down. And, real shit, I'll light that nigga up." His nose flared. I could see the veins in his neck bulging. "That muhfucka's gonna have to come through *me* if he even tries to get at you. That's my word. I'm still hot about that pussy muhfucka puttin' his hands on you the other day in ya office. Pussy-ass niggas do that dumb shit. And now he talkin' about tryna put a bullet in you. Nah, not happenin'; not on my watch it's not. You need to let me have that nigga's shit pushed in for you."

I'd never seen Lamar like that. He's always so laid back and easy-going. But I'm not going to lie and say that seeing his aggressive, protective side hadn't flattered me, or turned me on. Because it damn sure did.

"As tempting as that is, I have to let it ride, for *now*. I don't want you getting yourself in any kind of trouble on my account."

"Nah, there's def no trouble to get in. I move swift. The circle of niggas I roll with know how'ta move. We skilled at what we do. That nigga'll never see it coming."

"Trust me. Jasper's going to get his." I wasn't about to elaborate. But I let him know that his protectiveness of me didn't go unnoticed and was greatly appreciated. He helped me gather my things, then followed me out of my office and waited for me to set the alarm, then lock up.

"Thanks, again," I said, walking alongside of him as he walked me to my car. "I'm really glad I have you working here."

"No doubt. I'ma ride or die for *you*, Pasha. I know you're my employer 'n' all, but you cool-ass peeps…" He held open my door for me, waited for me to slide in, then added, "And you sexy as fuck, no disrespect. But I've been wantin' to say that for a while now." He licked his lips as his hungry eyes roamed over my body.

I blushed, shifting my eyes from his hot gaze, instantly feeling a throbbing in my clit. I've never, ever, been one to mix business with pleasure. I've always maintained a "no fraternizing, no fucking the staff" policy at the salon.

Until now…

I blink back the memory of Lamar's brown gaze locked on mine, deciding to test him. Dare him. To see how far he'll really go—*for me*.

The reality is this: After being slapped by Jasper, then being threatened by the motherfucker earlier today, I'm more anxious than ever before to shut his ass down. And the truth is, I'm desperate to come out of whatever happens unscathed. So to ensure that, I am willing to do *whatever* I have to do, including fucking *and* sucking—like Cassandra put it—for a cause. And that's exactly what I intend for this to be—a good fuck for a greater cause.

I press my thighs together. "I know it's late. But, what are you doing right now?"

"Kicked back. Why, what's good?"

"Tell me, Lamar," I coo into the phone. "Did you *really* mean what you said when you told me *anything* I need from you, you got me?"

"No doubt, ma. I'm a real-ass nigga. I stand by my word. I meant that on my life. *Any*thing, yo. I got you. It's whatever, Pasha. And don't worry, I'm mad discreet wit' my shit. So whatever jumps, jumps on the low. Why, you got somethin' you need me to handle?"

I sly smile eases across my lips. "Yeah. Come eat my pussy."

Twenty-Five

A possessed pussy can fuck a nigga's demons loose…

"Yes, oooh, yesss. That's it," I murmur as Lamar licks the tip of my clit, his wet tongue exploring every angle of its distended flesh before trailing along the slit of my pussy. His tongue darts in, deep. "Oooh, yes, eat my pussy…"

I shiver as his strong hands ease over my hips. He inches up on his elbows and slides his palms under me, grabbing and squeezing my ass cheeks. His warm mouth blankets my pussy, his tongue swirling around my clit every so often, causing soft moans to float around the room.

Lying here naked with my hands tangled in Lamar's locks while his face is pressed in between my thighs—knees bent up toward my chest—and his mouth and tongue feast on my pussy is not what I had planned for tonight.

No. Lamar isn't supposed to be here, in my bed, between my legs. But he is. Mmmph…his tongue, his mouth, his fingers aren't supposed to be causing heat to flare through my pussy.

But they are.

The wet smacking sounds his mouth makes as it slurps and gulps in my juices becomes a seductive melody to my ears. "Damn, baby," he whispers against my pussy, "you taste good as fuck…mmmm…"

None of this should be happening. But it is.

Because *I* want it to. Because Lamar wants it to.

He's offered himself to me, in any way needed. He's, unexpectedly, become a window, an opened door, of opportunity. And I'm taking it.

So here he is.

Here I am. Thrusting my hips up, grinding my pussy into his mouth, fucking into his face, clutching his tongue as he pushes it deep inside of me.

"Mmmmhmm, there you go…get all up in that pussy."

I play with my breasts, lifting my head and pushing them together, sucking and licking, my tongue twirling over and around my large brown areolas. My nipples are swollen and stiff and extremely sensitive as he circles his tongue around my wet pussy, shamelessly begging to feel his dick inside.

I've not seen his dick, yet. Have not even felt it. He's still in his clothes. Eating my pussy is what I requested, but now I want more. I want him naked. Stretched out. His legs spread, his cock and balls on display. I want to throat his dick, wet it with a bunch of spit, then fuck it deep down into my neck, stroking my tonsils.

God, I hope this nigga doesn't have a little-ass dick!

The size of his dick shouldn't matter. I'm not trying to fall in love with his ass. I'm trying to get whatever it is he has to offer me. I know this. Still, sucking a small dick is not only going to be disappointing, it'll be a fucking bore!

He grunts, his mouth full with pussy.

I moan, my body full of lust and fire.

"Oooh, yes, nibble all up on that pussy…mmm…"

I can't front, can't even pretend, that he's not on top of his tongue game. His pussy-eating skills are heavenly. His lips and tongue feverishly devour my pussy lips in long, deep, wet strokes. "Ooooh, yes, motherfucker, yessss…"

He looks up at me. His lips are shiny, glazed, with my juices. Holding my gaze, he removes one hand from underneath me, licking his index and middle fingers. He slips them between my thick pussy lips, then thrusts them into my wetness, drawing a gasp from deep inside me. His fingers jam in deep, stirring and twisting, brushing up against my G-spot. "Yessss, get it, Daaadddy, yesss…"

Lamar finger-fucks my guts causing my whole body to quiver. I lift my legs and hook my arms in back of my knees, pulling them up over my shoulders, opening my pussy wider for him as he pumps his fingers inside of me in a steady rhythm.

Mmmm. As delicious as this feels, I'm ready for some dick. I want to feel him inside of me, fucking inside of me—my pussy, my mouth—deep and fast. I want to taste him. Suck him. Swallow all of him. But his only focus is devouring my pussy, its sweet, tangy juices coating his lips and his tongue and fingers.

He finally comes up for air, licking his cum-coated fingers, then lips. "Daaayumn, ma, your pussy's so sweet. I wanna keep fuckin' you wit' my tongue 'n' these fingers until you nut so hard 'n' so much, baby, that your pussy juice soaks my hand, my lips, my tongue. Then I'ma push this hard-ass dick all the way up in you. Fuck you real good, Pasha. I'ma scrape ya insides up with this dick. That's what you want, ma? Me to beat this gushy shit up for you?"

He says all this as he's pressing on my clit with two fingertips, moving them in a circular motion. I grind my hips in anticipation. "Oooh, yessss. I want you to fuck my pussy. Gut my pussy. Uhh-hh…I'm getting ready to cum…put your tongue back in me…"

His head lowers back into the space between my thighs, his tongue back into my throbbing wet pussy.

I gasp, growling low in my throat, tightening my fingers in his thick locks, while pushing him into my pussy. My thighs clamp around his ears. Goose bumps dot my skin as his head moves rapidly up and down, then side to side, his tongue in sync as his fingers hold my swollen cream-slick lips apart.

My hips buck.

"Yessss…get it, get it…oh, yes…eat my pussy…"

I moan. Allow myself to luxuriate in a few extra minutes of his lavish tongue-swab over my clit and pussy before loosening my thighs from around his head and reaching for him. "Get up," I say breathlessly. "I wanna suck your dick."

He hops up and begins stripping out of his clothes. His shirt hits the floor first, followed by his wife beater. I take in his dark muscular torso. His bulging biceps, his chiseled triceps and broad shoulders are the result of long hours spent in the gym. I lean up on my forearms, eye his dark-pebbled nipples. I have the urge to lick them. My gaze travels along the fine black trail of hair that leads from under his belly button down into the waist of his jeans.

I hold my breath as he unbuckles his belt, unzips his pants, then drops them. I tell him to keep his red and black striped boxers on. I can see the imprint of his cock. It is swollen, but not brick hard—not, *yet*. I scoot down off the bed and kneel down in front of him. My knees sinking into the carpet as I lean in and kiss the outline of his shaft. Then lick it. Then slowly suck the tip of his hanging dick over his underwear.

I tease him. Nibbling all over the steady-growing dick, then abandoning it, trailing my tongue up the inside of his leg, around his knee, then up his thigh, my wet tongue streaking his skin along the way back up to his crotch.

He moans. "Aaaaah, shit, yo…mmmm…what the fuck…?"

I take a deep breath, reach for the waistband of his boxers and yank them down. I exhale, relieved and pleasantly surprised as my gaze measures the length of his smooth dark dick. It's thick and curved. Nestled in a thick patch of black pubic hair.

I reach for it. Hold it in my hand. Marvel at how hot it is. How heavy it is. I inhale the mixture of soap and his man scent that clings in his pubic hair and wafts from underneath his medium-size balls. They're about the size of golf balls. I cup them. Massage them, then slip them into my mouth, slathering them with a bunch of saliva while wrapping my soft hand over the head of his dick, stroking it, taunting it.

"Aaaah, shiiiit…"

"Does your girl tease your cock with her tongue?" I ask, tracing my tongue along his piss slit, then around the head, slowly sliding it down along each side of his thick shaft. I allow my tongue to lightly flick around his balls, then slide back up the backside of his dick.

He moans.

My lashes flutter as I glance up at him. "Or does she suck you fast and hard and nasty?"

Before he can respond, I plunge his dick all the way into the back of my mouth. It's luxuriously wet with excitement as the head of his dick pushes past my tonsils, the warmth of my throat heating his cock. There aren't too many bitches hungry for the dick the way I am, who can hold a dick in their throat the way I can, for as long as I can. And the niggas who experience a taste of this deep throat usually can't hold out long.

He'll be no exception.

He's already trembling.

Already bucking.

It becomes a game to me. To see how fast I can make a nigga nut.

I grip the back of his thighs as he finally grabs me by the back of my head and bangs his hips hard against my face, his balls rapidly slapping my chin.

I grunt, reach between my thighs, slip two fingers inside my cum-soaked pussy, then pull out and glide them over my swollen clit. I pinch it.

Lamar pulls his dick out and slams it back into my throat over and over again. His balls tighten. I grab his ass. Dig my nails into his flesh, then glide a finger along the center of his crack. He plunges in and out of my neck tunnel.

It's only a matter of time, seconds, before he explodes into my neck.

His legs shake. One knee loses balance and he almost topples over, reaching for the bed to brace himself. He is grunting and growling and clutching the carpet beneath his feet with his toes.

Yes, you horny motherfucker, I think, sucking him hard. His hand stays clamped around the back of my head. *Give me that hot nut!*

He groans, his hips rotating to the pulsing rhythm of my mouth. The way he's grunting and fucking into my mouth, I know it isn't going to take much longer before he is filling my mouth with his hot, creamy seeds.

And he doesn't.

"Uh, uh, uh, uh…aah, aaah, aaah…"

I spin his top in less than eight minutes. Pleased.

He staggers, then collapses onto the bed. He turns to face me. His eyes, glossy and dazed. "Goddamn, that shit was good."

Of course it was. I grin. Tell him to turn over on his back. "I'm not done with you," I say crawling on top of him. I position my pussy over his dick, then slide its length along my sopping slit, bathing it in a fresh batch of my pussy juice. I lean into his ear. "I'm going to suck the life out of you tonight, nigga. By the time I'm finished with you, you're going to forget your own name."

"Oh, word?"

I shift my body around into the sixty-nine position, taking his dick back into my mouth. I suck him hands free, lowering my pussy onto his mouth. His tongue slinks its way back into my slit. My hands curl in the sheets, clutching them as I ride his tongue.

No, I don't want this nigga. He's simply a pawn, a means to a very dangerous end. But for now, I suck him for everything he is.

And give into the sensations. Ride the wave of pleasure and cum, filling his mouth with everything I am.

A bitch tossed in the middle of a shootout will either drop,
or come out a gunslinger...

"Motherfucker!" I scream into the phone, pacing around my office, my body shaking from the inside out. "You just tried to have me fucking *killed*, you dirty, mother-fucking sonofabitch!"

My nerves are wrecked! My heart is pounding. Seven-thirty A.M., I pulled up in front of the salon and the *last* thing I expected—as I stepped out of my car and shut the door and started walking around toward the salon—was to be greeted by fucking gunfire!

But I was!

I had spotted the black GMC with tinted windows up at the corner when I initially pulled up this morning. But I didn't pay it any mind. I shut off the engine and sat in the car for a few minutes, listening to the radio before flipping down my visor and gliding a coat of MAC Russian Red Tinted Lipglass over my lips. After-ward, I fussed with my bang a bit, slid in my diamond hoops, then finally grabbed my handbag and stepped out of the car, setting the alarm.

Out of the corner of my eye, I saw the SUV slowly start driving in my direction. But, again, it didn't cause pause for alarm. So I dismissed it. I figured someone had gotten lost and pulled over to get directions or take a call. But then something didn't feel right. Ever since my kidnapping, I've been much more alert of my surroundings, canvassing the area around me, taking in every detail. Yet—this morning, for some reason, as I stepped out of my car, my mind rushed back to my night with Lamar. I chuckled to myself thinking about the expression on his face when I told him that I wanted him to fuck my pussy deep, then quickly stopped him when he positioned himself between my legs, gripping the base of his rock-hard dick, attempting to slide it into my slit. "Yo, why you stop me?" he asked, giving me a confused look. "I thought you wanted me to beat this wet pussy up, ma."

I smirked. "I do. But I'm not talking about *that* pussy."

I quickly shifted my body, hanging my head over the edge of the bed. I met his gaze upside down and said, "I'm talking about the one down in my neck." I opened my mouth, extended my tongue out, then welcomed his chocolate dick down in my warm, wet, and waiting throat, reaching my arms up over my head as he straddled my face. I grabbed him by the ass, urging him to pound my neck out. And he did. And that's where my mind was. Stuck on his hard damn dick!

So as I walked toward the salon with lustful thoughts of Lamar's hot creamy nut coating the back of my throat, something told me to glance over my shoulder. It was then that I noticed the truck slowly moving in my direction, and realized that I didn't have the salon's keys in my hand. Usually, I'd already have the keys out and in my hand, but this morning I'd forgotten to take them out of my bag before getting out of the car. It's a blessing in disguise that I hadn't already had them in my hands; otherwise, I might not be standing here.

As soon as I stopped in the middle of the sidewalk to dig down into my bag, I caught a glimpse of the SUV's rear driver's side window slowly rolling down and the tip of a shiny barrel being aimed at me. I don't know if it was instinct or reflex, but I dropped down a split-second before the nigga holding the other end of the gun opened fire, letting out six shots in my direction, missing me completely. But hitting the front of the building. I didn't see his face; all I saw were his eyes.

Everything happened so quickly. I saw the gun. I dropped down low. I heard gunfire. All I saw was my life flashing before my eyes. And I reacted without thinking clearly, pulling out my gun and—in my skirt and stilettos—started chasing the SUV as it sped off, firing back. I shot three rounds, shattering the rear window before the truck turned off down the next block.

Those grimy niggas had *me* running in my fucking heels shooting back at them, like I was on the set of a damn gangster movie. It wasn't until they disappeared that I started shaking and felt something warm trickling down the inner part of my legs.

I had pissed and shitted on myself.

Luckily, I always keep a change of clothes and toiletries here at the salon; otherwise, I would have been fucked.

I kick off my heels. "Really, nigga?!" I yell into the phone, walking into my private bathroom and removing my clothes. "You'd really have dumb-ass motherfuckers doing drive-bys for you, huh, motherfucker? I can't believe this shit! Then again, *yes* I can. You ain't shit, motherfucker!"

This nigga is calm and cool, like he's been smoking blunts all morning. "You tried to bite my muthafuckin' nuts off, yo. My shit's still fucked up. You got a muhfuckin' restrainin' order on me 'n' you tryna fuck me outta my paper. I tol' you, Pasha, I'ma see you. I got eyes and ears e'erywhere, yo. That's all you need to know, baby. I want my muthafuckin' money, Pasha. I ain't fuckin' 'round wit' you, yo. Pull that shit outta the bank 'n' let me get into them safes at the crib—"

"Nigga, you had me *shot* at!" I yell at the top of my lungs. "I'm not giving you a motherfucking thing! You hear me, nigga?! Not a mother…*fucking*…thing! You want it, come take it. I got a bullet waiting for your black ass when you get here! I know your lil puppets told you what I did to the back of that fucking truck! Don't *fuck* with me, Jasper!"

He laughs. "Oh, you really wanna be on some gangsta shit now, huh, Pasha? You done got you a lil firearm 'n' some range time 'n' now you think you ready to rock wit' the big dogs. But check it, yo. You a lightweight, baby. You started this shit, yo. Tryna bite my muthafuckin' shit off, then pullin' heat out on a muhfucka, like that shit's gravy. Then you cracked my shit open wit' it. I had'a get stitches fuckin' wit' ya dumb ass."

"Good, nigga! Next time you'll get a toe-tag!"

"Yeah, aiight, Pasha. Keep poppin' shit. I got some shit for ya ass; real shit. Now all of a sudden you wanna get a spine. Fuck outta here, yo. Give me my shit, Pasha, 'n' we can part. It's obvious you got all this hate for a muhfucka, like you still holdin' on to shit."

"I've *always* had a spine, motherfucker. But know this: even the *spineless* have a breaking point. You coming up in here putting your hands on me was probably the best thing you did. You pushed me to the fucking limit, Jasper. Now I'ma show you what kind of *spine* I have, motherfucker!"

"Pasha, I ain't tryna take it to ya skull on the strength of my son 'cause I want him to have his moms, but you…"

"Your *son?*" I screech, stopping in the middle of the floor, placing a hand on my hip. "Motherfucker! You have got to be fucking *kidding* me! You're motherfucking crazy! You don't give a *fuck* about *my* son! He is the same son you almost *beat* out of me, or have you forgotten that little known fact?"

"Okay, here you go wit' this shit, again. Fuck outta here, yo. I ain't tryna hear that shit. Is ya ass dead, yo? Is my son dead, huh? *No.* If I wanted either one'a ya asses boxed, that's what the fuck woulda happened, yo. So fall back from that bullshit, Pasha. I wanna see my son."

"Oh, now you want to see *your* son. Nigga, please! All you been talking about is *your* money. Now all of a sudden you talking about you want to see *your* son. Motherfucker, if you wanna see Jaylen, then take me to court because that's the *only* way you're going to ever see him."

"Yo, Pasha, real shit. I'm tellin' you, yo. Don't fuckin' play wit' me. I ain't tryna have you touched. But you keep pressin' it, yo. We can peace this shit up now, ya heard me? Let me see my son 'n' run me my shit—*all* of it—'n' we good. Real shit, Pasha. I'm tryna be nice to ya dumb ass. But you really fuckin' pushin' it, yo."

"Fucking bastard! I'ma show *you* who can get *touched*, motherfucker! You got eyes on me?! Well, guess, what, motherfucker?! *Now* I got eyes on you. So instead of watching me, you had *better* start watching yourself, motherfucker!"

My hands are shaking.

I still can't believe this shit! Me in a fucking shootout! Me! Running in motherfucking heels, ducking and dodging bullets, chasing behind a fucking truck shooting and screaming like a madwoman!

"Nigga, you're lucky I don't call the police on your black ass right now and have them lock your fucking ass up for violating the restraining order!"

"Oh, word? It's like that? You dry-snitchin' on muhfuckas now, like your whore-ass cousin did you, right?"

I *tsk*. "Oh, now she's a *whore-ass*. But it was all good when she was all up in your ear and down on her fucking knees telling you shit about me. Nigga, don't compare me to her. I'm nothing like that two-faced bitch who *you* were fucking and letting suck your dick. So don't go there."

He pushes out a sarcastic laugh. "Yeah, right. Maybe you not a dry-snitch, baby, but both of you fuckin' dick suckers, yo. And the only difference wit' that is, ya head game on top. That's what the fuck got ya ass fucked up in the first place, Pasha! *You* did this shit to us, yo! Cum-suckin' ass! *You* really fucked up what we had on ya bullshit! All this hard-ass dick you had comin' home to you 'n' you couldn't hold out for a muhfucka. You had to be out there throat-fuckin' muhfuckas. And I *still* took ya dumb-ass back. Yo, real shit. Don't have me fuck you up again, Pasha. Them bullets today *missed* ya ass 'cause *I* wanted them, too. Ain't shit happenin' to you unless *I* say it is. Next time what you think's gonna happen, huh? I'ma…"

"Motherfucker, then you had better get me *before* I get *you!* You got me once, but motherfuck *you* if you think I'm gonna be silly enough to let you get me twice! Nigga, I'm gonna shut your shit down! *Watch* what happens next, Jasper!"

I hang up on his ass.

Never in my life have I ever been shot at…until this morning. And never would I have imagined that I would *ever* have to pull out a gun and start shooting at niggas in broad daylight. But I did…*today!* Thanks to Jasper's motherfucking ass!

Fuck!

I didn't sign up for this shit!

I'm reeling, feeling dizzy from the turn of events that have transpired over the last four fucking days. From finding out Cassandra killed JT, Mona being molested by him to Felecia secretly visiting Jasper in prison and fucking him to me biting his balls and pulling a gun out on him to getting a restraining order, and now this shit—getting shot at!

And it's only going to get worse.

Being a vicious bitch isn't who I've ever been. And it's not who I *want* to be. But, that crazy motherfucker has crossed enough lines. And I'll be damned if I let *him* violate me ever again, or do anything else to me without giving him, or his clown-ass goons, a run for their goddamn lives.

I scroll through my call log, then dial the number I'm looking for. "Yo, what's good? You aiight?"

"No, I'm not. But I will be. I'm ready to take you up on that offer." I give Lamar the rundown of what happened earlier this morning.

"Whaaat?!" he snaps. "Yo, what the fuck, yo. Are you hurt, ma?" I tell him no. He lets out a sigh of relief. "See, ma. I told you this mornin' before I bounced to start lettin' muhfuckas drive you where you gotta go. Me, or any of the other cats you got on ya security squad should be wit' you at all times. That's what you pay us for, to keep you safe, feel me?"

"I don't want a bodyguard or someone escorting me around everywhere I go; every time I have to be somewhere. Besides, Mel was going to meet me here at eight, but I happened to get here a little earlier."

"Yeah. And look what happened? You coulda been bodied, ma, feel me. Then what?"

"I know. But I wasn't. I'm not hurt. I'm shaken up a bit but that's it."

"I feel you, Pasha. But right now it ain't about what you don't want. It's about what you *need*. Shit's gettin' real, yo. And right now you *need* a strong team of gully muhfuckas who are gonna hold it down for you. That nigga takin' shit to a whole other level; got muhfuckas comin' at you wit' burners now. Word is bond, ma. That nigga's way outta pocket, yo. He gotta get handled—*today*."

I walk into my bathroom, pull open the glass shower door, then turn on the water, allowing steam to fill the space. I glance into the mirror, quickly touching the side of my face where Jasper slapped me. The bruise is still slightly visible.

Sonofabitch!

I step back out into my office, glancing up at the security monitor. Mel's six-seven, two-hundred-and-seventy-five-pound frame comes into view. He's at the front door. I watch him as he slips his key in, then enters the salon. Every time I look at him, with his golden-brown skin, thick neck and bulging biceps, he reminds me of the wrestler-turned-actor, The Rock—with his fine, sexy self.

I quickly shut my office door.

"He does," I say to Lamar as I unlock my closet and pull out the skirt and blouse I have hanging up, "need to be handled. And he will be. Not today, though. I have something else in mind for his ass. By the way, Mel's here now."

"Oh, aiight; cool. I shot him a text 'n' tol' him he needed to get there ASAP."

I smile. His concern for my well-being and safety is refreshing. "What time are you scheduled to come in today?"

"Not until two. But I'm hoppin' in the shower now. I'll be there in like twenty minutes. And don't go nowhere unless you have one of us wit' you, aiight?"

"Yes. I hear you. I'll talk to you when you get here. I don't have any appointments until eleven-thirty."

"Aiight, bet. See you then."

I end the call. Then walk over and lock my office door. I head for the bathroom. I quickly brush my teeth, then hop in the shower, scrubbing and washing off the grime from the events of this morning. *Shooting at me? I can't believe this shit! You forced my mother-fucking hand, Jasper! Now it's lights out, nigga! I'm coming for you!*

I shut off the water, reach for my towel, drying myself off. As I'm applying body oil to my skin, slipping into my panties, snapping on my bra, then dressing, I can't get the black SUV, the the barrel of the gun aimed at me, out of my head. Can't shake the thought of a bullet having my name on it. Or the frightening possibility of ending up...

Dead.

Twenty-Seven

There's an erotic lure to the danger of plotting a nigga's demise...

Twenty-five minutes later, Lamar steps into my office, carrying a small duffel bag and shutting the door behind him. He hands it to me. Tells me from now on I am not to fire any of my own weapons unless I absolutely have to. Inside the bag are three guns, a Glock, a .40 caliber, and a .45. He tells me the latter two are better for protection. That the .40 caliber has less recoil, whatever that means. There are two boxes—50 rounds in each box—of Speer Gold Dot hollow point bullets. He tells me none of the weapons will be traced to me if/when I have to use them. There are also two new disposable phones. He tells me to use these from now on. Once finished with them, to remove the SIM cards, then destroy the phones.

I don't ask him where he's gotten any of this stuff. And I don't care. The only thing on my mind at this moment is giving Jasper's ass a taste of what he's forced me to become. A small sampling of what I'm *really* capable of.

Lamar sits in one of the chairs across from me. His legs spread open, his masculine scent mixed with soap and cologne, oozing from his pores, wafts through the air. I breathe him in. Strain not to eye his crotch. Subconsciously, I lick my lips, wondering if he can smell my thick juices slowly simmering.

A sweet delicious tension roils up from my clit, bubbles up into the pit of my pulsing pussy and hitches in the back of my throat as flashes of his hard, thick dick swirl around in my head. As the memory of his long tongue, dipping and curling in and out of my dripping slit flashes through my mind. As the lingering memory of the heat from his mouth melting against my pussy as he sucked in my clit, my cunt cream spurting out and coating his chocolate lips, causes my nipples to swell and ache for his wet mouth.

I see his lips moving, see his brown eyes gazing back at me, but in a matter of seconds I've become swept up in desire, and want. An urging need to fuck him—suck him, into my mouth, then into my throbbing pussy, takes me by surprise.

I clear my throat, pressing my thighs together, pushing back the salacious memory along with the rising well of wetness threatening to spurt of my throbbing pussy. "Um. What did you say?"

"I said I'm glad you aiight; real shit, yo. Now what you got planned for that punk-ass nigga, ma. I'm ready to put that work in."

I lean forward, resting my forearms on my desk. I slip out of my four-inch Manolos, crossing my feet at the ankles. "I want Jasper hit fast and hard."

He nods his head, rubbing his chin. "I got you, ma. All you gotta do is tell me how you want it."

I open my center desk drawer, pull out a small pad and pen, then write down three addresses in the South, East, and North Ward sections of Newark. I tear the sheet of paper off the notepad and slide it over to him. The tips of our fingers touch. "Here are addresses to three of his stash houses. They'll be heavily manned with lots of gunpower, I'm sure. I don't know how much work and money there is at the first two addresses, but I *know* for sure there's plenty of both at the one on Fourteenth Street."

Through listening, overhearing, and ear-hustling over the last year, I know Jasper is not only pushing coke out on the streets, but he's also distributing that molly shit now—a controlled substance considered to be the purest form of a chemical used in that party drug, Ecstasy—in crystal and powder form. And I *know* the nigga is racking in money hand over fist as a result.

"Aiight, aiight. Cool. So you want me to do surveillance?"

"*Surveillance?*" I quickly shake my head. "No, no. I want them both *shut. Down.* Whatever money you come up with, I want. You can do what you want with whatever else you find. Then I want them both *burned* down to the ground. And whatever bodies get dropped, go up in flames along with 'em." I eye him, tilting my head. "Is *this* the kind of *anything* you can handle for me?"

He locks his eyes on mine, leans forward, slowly rubbing the palms of his hands together. His tone is even as he slowly and clearly says, "Ma, when I said *anything*, that's what I meant. *What*-ever kinda work you need handled, it's handled; period." He doesn't blink when he says this. There is no room for misunderstanding. He means what he says. "Them motherfuckers won't know what hit 'em."

I smile, slowly running the tip of my pink tongue along the bottom of my bright copper-painted lips. A moan catches in the back of my throat. Just the mere thought of burning down two of Jasper's stash houses, fucking with his money, lights a flame of lust between my thighs. My pussy slowly heats. My lush mouth becomes moist. I am instantly turned on. The thrill of finally turning the tables on Jasper's ruthless ass becomes an aphrodisiac.

"Mmm, I love the sound of the that." It comes out in almost a seductive purr. I can feel my simmering juices stirring in the well of my slit.

Lamar eyes me, then allows his gaze to slowly drop to the swell of my nipples, the way my breasts raise and fall beneath my draped silk blouse. He licks his own lips, shifting in his seat

I bet his dick is hard as brick…

Lamar's eyes meet mine. "Is there *any*thing else I can do for you?" It's a loaded question; one filled with endless possibilities.

He opens, then closes his legs.

I lick my lips.

He fans them open again, then shuts them.

I glance at the time. I have another forty minutes before my first appointment arrives. I get up from my desk, walk over to the door and lock it, then saunter back over to Lamar, positioning myself in front of him. "Before I start my day," I say, dropping to my knees as my fingers skillfully unbuckle his belt, "I want to swallow this thick dick down in my throat."

His eyes drop half-mast, instantly filling with lust as he licks his lips. "Damn. I tol' you, ma…*any*thing you need, I got you."

I unzip his pants. Stick my tongue into his navel. Allow my fingers to roam along the tufts of hair that disappear down into his boxers. Then slip my hand down into the elastic of his boxers. His dick springs forward when I pull the waistband down.

It's hot and heavy. And throbs in my hand. I stroke it.

"Mmmm…looks like someone's already excited to see me," I tease, flicking the tip of my tongue over the clear, sticky nectar already seeping out of his piss slit. I lick up and down and around his shaft, coating it with spit. The hot juices in my mouth start to flood my throat as I slowly suction him in until his dick pushes past my tonsils.

His eyes roll in the back of his head. "Aaah, fuuuck…oooh, shiiiiiiiiit…"

Without a word said, he lifts up and I yank his pants down over his hips, pushing them down to his ankles. He wants me to suck all of him, his dick, his balls. I slowly bob my head up and down, soaking him, wetting his balls. I gulp him down in long deep strokes, cupping his heavy sac and flicking my tongue at his balls on every down stroke.

"Uhhh, aaaah, fuck…mmmm…word is bond your dick game is fire…aaaah…"

I make rhythmic suck-sounds as he fucks himself into my mouth, thrusting deep until my lips are pressed at the base of his thick shaft, then drawing back until his dick almost slips from between my lips. My mouth becomes a vacuum, suctioning him tightly. He grips the back of my neck and grunts as I suck him. I can feel his body trembling and I'm certain his knees would surely buckle if he were standing. I grin inwardly at the thought of him dropping to his knees, his hard dick shooting out his nut, spraying me in the face.

"Aaah shiiiiit…ya mouth…uhhh…is sooo fuckin' good, yo… mmmm…A muhfucka could get use to this neck work, yo…uh, uh…oooh, shiiit…"

I glance up at him. His head is tossed back. The lids of his eyes have become thin slits. His eyes are rolled in the back of his head, evident by the sliver of his whites I see. Yes, I have this nigga caught up in the rapture, lost in the sweet heat and suck-fuck sounds of my lush mouth and long throat.

I slip a hand up my skirt, slip two fingers in between the elastic of my panties, then slide my fingers into my horny pussy, matching the thrust of my fingers to the bobbing of my neck. Lamar's thighs shake. He grabs my head and bounces it all the way down into his lap, grunting and grinding and fucking himself into my throat.

I dig my nails into his hips. He grunts again. Thrusts harder. Faster. He shakes and cums, *hard*, emitting a low howl from somewhere in the back of his throat as his hot creamy nut coats my tonsils and slides down my neck. He shudders. And I keep sucking him, siphoning out every last drop, until his dick goes limp.

I stand up, licking my lips, then my fingers. Lamar doesn't move. He's slumped to the side. His eyes are shut. And for a second I think he's not breathing, wonder if I need to do a pulse check; that perhaps I've literally sucked him to death—until he lets out a hard breath, shaking his head and his eye lids flutter open.

He looks dazed.

I tilt my head, smoothing the wrinkles out of the front of my skirt. "Ummm, are you okay?"

He blinks, focuses to keep his line of vision glued to my probing eyes. He blinks again. "Yeah. I'm good. You got'a muhfucka zonin' 'n' shit, that's all. On some real, I've had mad head in my life, but, on everything, you the first chick that has *ever* had my head spinnin' 'n' had me seein' stars as I'm bustin' off."

I keep from smiling.

Sucking dick for a cause is a delicious mess, but it has to be done. I'm on a mission. So it might as well be done by a bitch like me who loves the thrill of having a nigga's dick down in her neck.

I eye Lamar as he bends over, grabbing his pants and standing up. I glance at his shiny dick—compliments of spit and cum, watching it disappear beneath black boxers and black slacks as he zips, fastens, then buckles his belt.

I watch as he heads for the door, admiring the view. *My, God, he has a nice ass. And that dick…mmmph! Yes, God! That young hard dick is exactly what I need to get the job done.* I place a hand up to my neck, grazing my fingers along my collarbone.

Lamar reaches for the door, his hand on the doorknob. He turns slightly, glancing at me over his broad shoulder. "I'ma have that situation handled *tonight*."

Our eyes meet, one last time. No words are needed. We are both keenly aware of our roles—his, to serve and protect—by any means necessary. Mine, to suck and serve.

Twenty-Eight

*The sweetest, most delicious part of revenge is
watching from the sidelines...*

Eight a.m., Saturday morning, and Booty's ass is one of the
first ones walking through the door bright and early, along
with two other clients, one for Kendra; and the other for
one of the estheticians. She says her name is Tasty. Tasty Evans. I
welcome her to the salon. Thank her for her patronage, then ask
her who her appointment is with since she's not in the appointment
book. She says she called a few days ago, spoke to someone who
kept popping her gum in her ear.

I shoot a dirty look over at Booty, wondering how many other
appointments this bitch done fucked up. She rolls her eyes, turning her back to me. I bring my attention back to Tasty. She's here
for a lip, chin, and chest wax and a back facial. I strain to not stare
at her thick mustache and whiskers as she's talking. *Mmm, looks
like you can also use a good waxing on those hairy-ass knuckles,* I think
glancing at her hands. Then back up at her. *Ooh, no, girl! And them
bushy eyebrows are a wild mess.*

I blink. Tell her to have a seat. That Nina, another one of my
newest estheticians, should be in shortly. Mel, who's sitting on a
stool in the corner, looks up from a magazine he's reading to eye

her, then Booty—who I know is only here first thing in the morning so she can flounce her ass in front of him.

I stand up and walk around the receptionist's desk to turn on the flat-screen in the waiting area. I watch Booty eyeing the Tasty chick—who's wearing a short denim skirt with a pair of peep-toe pumps. Both of her big toes, with their long toenails, are peeping out of her shoes—as she takes a seat.

Booty grunts, slinging a brown snakeskin Bottega Veneta bag off her shoulder, swinging it into one of the waiting room chairs. "See, this is why I ain't schedule this booga-coo—"

"Cassandra," I warn.

"Miss Pasha, girl. You know I'ma keep it classy. Don't do me."

Oh, God, no, please. Not today! And definitely not this early in the morning!

"Now, sugah-boo," Booty starts, placing a hand up on her hip, "what you say your name is again?"

"Tasty, why?" she asks with attitude.

"Oh, no, sweetness, don't do me. Take down that *stank* in your tone a pinch. I ain't messy, okaaay? I heard you over there tellin' Miss Pasha, girl, that you was here for a waxin'. But sounds like…"

"Cassandra, girl," I quickly say, knowing she's about to crank it up, "c'mon to my station so I can hurry and get you up out of here."

She shoots me a look. "See, Miss Pasha, girl, you tryna do me. All I was gonna say is, that it sounds to me like Miss Tasty over here needs the works. Not just some wax." She turns her attention back to Tasty. "Now, sugah-boo. I been comin' here for years, okay. And can't a bitch in the Tri-State area do me, like Nappy No More, okay."

The Tasty chick seems to relax a bit. "Girl, I heard that. One of my good girlfriends told me about this spot. That's why I made me an appointment, that *somehow* didn't get put in the book."

I hold my breath. Mel lowers his eyes, shaking his head.

"Girl, *boom!* You here, ain't you?"

I race over, snatching up Booty's bag and grabbing her by the arm, ushering her toward my station. "Miss Evans, don't mind this one here. She's on meds."

She shrugs, waving me on, shifting in her seat.

Booty starts talking sideways, telling me I'm trying to be messy; that I stay trying to *do* her. That all she was doing was trying to get me more business. "Don't do me," she hisses. "You ain't see that booga-beast's hoofs, Miss Pasha, girl? Mmmph. You know I ain't ever been messy." She lowers her voice. "But that booga-beast right there needs to be in a cage somewhere. Ain't nothin' *tasty* 'bout that hairy bitch."

"Cassandra, stop," I say, turning on the water on and adjusting the temperature. "You need to really learn when to keep your mouth shut. You can't go around saying whatever you want to people."

I snap the cape around her neck.

"Miss Pasha, girl, *boom!* I don't know why not. I ain't even tryna hear you right now. It's too early in the mornin' for you to be tryna do me. You stay tryna say I'm bein' messy when I'm *only* bein' me."

Yeah, messy!

I wave her on dismissively. "Cass, stop. Now what are you in here for *today?* You were *just* in here a few days ago getting your hair done."

She eyes me. "See. There you go, again. Tryna do me. You know I likes to keep them ole stank cooter-boos down at the club on they toes. You know it stays crackin' down down at the Crack House on Saturday nights. And Booty gots to be laid like no other, okaaay, sugah-boo. I wanna keep my bang, though, Miss Pasha, girl, 'cause you did that. But I want you to toss me a lil blonde through it. And I'ma need me a lil silky yak swooped down over

my left shoulder. You can keep it shorter on the right side. And"—
she runs her hands along the back of her neck—"lay this kitchen
down real flat, sugah-boo. I want it tighter than a baby's crack."

I chuckle, leaning her back in her chair. "I got you, girl." I hear
the door open. It's Nina walking in. She greets Tasty, then throws
a hand up in a wave at me as they make their way to one of the
waxing rooms.

"Oooh, Miss Pasha, girl. You know that nigga-boo over there in
the corner is some kinda fine. Mmmph. Too bad he ain't shakin'
in no real paper, though. My cootie-coo ain't friendly to no broke
dingaling."

I shake my head, laughing. "Cass, how you know he's broke?
And his name's Mel."

"Mmmph. 'Cause my cootie-coo don't ever get juicy when I look
at him." I tell her it's not always about money. That he's a really
nice guy. "Mmmph. Then how 'bout you give 'im a lil taste, if you
ain't already swallowed him down in ya neck, 'n' tell me how it is."

I splash water in her face. "Don't have me drown you, Cass."

"Sugah-boo, *boom!*" I tell her I'm loving her bag, changing the
subject. Compliments sidetrack her ass real quick. "Miss Pasha,
girl, you know how I do, sugah-boo. Heels 'n' handbags stay turnt
all the way up." I shake my head. Ask her what else she's passionate
about besides heels and handbags. Ask her if she has any goals.
"Miss Pasha, girl, don't do me, boo. You know I'm passionate 'bout
good damn dingaling, keepin' my handbag lined with greenery—
that good *get right* 'n' them Benjamins—'n' takin' care of my kids."
I rinse out the conditioner, then turn off the water, wrapping a
towel around her head and lifting up her seat. "And of course I
got me some goals. Makin' sure all'a my kids graduate from high
school without bringin' me home no grandbabies or goin' to jail,
then makin' sure they hurry up 'n' get the fuck outta my house…"

I blink. "Okay, those are definitely some goals. But what about goals for yourself?"

Every so often I glance up at one of the flat-screens situated on the walls back here as I wash Booty's hair. The morning news is on.

I turn her toward the wall mirror. She eyes me as she talks. "You know my goal is to get to the next level of hood-fabulousness, Miss Pasha, girl. I'm always tryna keep me two or three sponsors on deck at all times."

I blink again. "Okay, that's definitely another goal. But I was thinking more along the lines of professional goals, like maybe going to school, taking up a trade. Wouldn't you like to work somewhere one day, maybe have a job with benefits? Wouldn't you like to own a home of your own one day?"

She huffs. "See. Here you go tryna be messy again. Who gonna hire me, huh? And don't even think I'ma be ridin' up 'n' down on no poles, either. Been there, done that. The only pole I'm ridin' down on now is a long damn dingdong. This cootie-coo 'n' good juicy booty is my moneymaker, okaaaay. And, sugah-boo, I got me good benefits with my Medicaid card. And I'm already doin' it big in the house I got with my Section-8. What I need'a buy me a house for when the government done already laid me out right? Don't even get cute."

I blink. *It's too early in the morning to have this conversation.* I reach for the remote to the television when I see the caption: THREE RAGING FIRES IN NEWARK scroll across the screen and the lead anchorwoman for Channel Two News is standing in front of an insert of a roaring fire in the background.

"...In other breaking news...Tragedy strikes in the city of Newark as firefighters in the city's North, East, and South Wards were called onto the scene of three separate fires early this morning, blazing through three homes, claiming the lives of at least ten unidentified victims. The first fire in the city's East Ward section was called in at two-fifteen a.m., by a neighboring resident who reported flames coming out of the windows and front door of a home believed to be known for drug dealing. An unidentified man was seen running out of the house yelling and screaming engulfed in flames. Fire fighters arrived minutes before the flames swallowed the entire house. The unidentified man was rushed to University Hospital where he remains in critical condition…"

My pulse quickens. I quickly swallow a sliver of guilt as it slices its way up to the back of my throat.

For God's sakes! Get a hold of yourself. No sense in feeling guilty now. The damage is already done. You knew there'd be casualties. Some more innocent than others. It's collateral damage. Oh well.

"…The second call came into fire fighters in the South Ward section of the city at two forty-eight this morning. Officials indicate the five-alarm fire was so intense that fire fighters were unable to get inside. One unidentified man engulfed in flames jumped from a second-story window seconds before the center of the home collapsed. He was rushed to Beth Israel Hospital…"

"My *gawd!*" Cassandra exclaims, shaking her head. "We in the last damn days, Miss Pasha, girl. How much you wanna bet them fires ain't no accident. I bet you it was some of them crazy-ass nigga-coons fightin' 'n' tryna take over blocks. You know there ain't nothin' but drugs 'n' gang wars over in Newark, sugah…"

"Cassandra, please," I hiss, gesturing with a hand for her to shut the fuck up so I can hear the rest of the news correspondent's report.

"Oooh, no-no, Miss Pasha, girl. You tryna be messy." I roll my eyes, turning the television up louder. She grunts. "Don't do me. I want my damn wig did. You better catch the midday news 'n' get them fingers up in this scalp." She pulls out her cell, when she hears it vibrating in her bag. She starts texting back and forth with whoever it is.

Good! That should keep her ass quiet.

"...the third fire swept through a home in the city's North Ward section of Newark and quickly began to swallow up the building as fire firefighters arrived on the scene. A source in the investigation indicates all three houses were known for illegal activities and had been under federal investigation. The known causes of the fires are still under investigation by the Fire Marshal..."

I lower the volume. *Come see me now, motherfucker!* I think, running a comb through Booty's hair while drying it with the blow drier. In my mind's eye, I see Jasper blacking out, stressing about the loss of three of his operations. *Oooh, I'm going to fuck the shit out of Lamar's ass first chance I get.*

I work my magic, weaving and styling Booty's hair, humming. She remains surprisingly entertained on her phone, texting, up until the last ten minutes, then shoves her cell back into her bag. "Mmmph. So, you ready to act right, Miss Pasha, girl? 'Cause you stay showin' ya ass, goddammit."

I laugh, giving her a dismissive wave. "Cass, hush."

"Ooooh, you better be glad you my sugah-boo 'n' I need you to keep me lookin' right; otherwise...mmmmph. Ooh, I'd do you right, goddammit. So when you seein' that ole messy bitch, Miss FeFe?"

"We're supposed to meet sometime this weekend," I say, purposefully not mentioning our meeting tomorrow night.

She *tsks* in the back of her throat. "You better do her up right, Miss Pasha, girl. Betrayal ain't cute. And it ain't acceptable. A bitch turn her back on you 'n' try to do you for filth, you do her one better—good 'n' goddamn dirty."

I agree, saying no more than necessary as I hand her the mirror, spinning her around so she can see the back of her hair. "Yessssss, goddammit! You stay doin' me, right, goddammit. And I got me a date tonight, too. Mmmph. That ole big-dick gorilla ain't gonna know what to do with all this fine booty heat when I step up in the restaurant." I ask her where her dates taking her. She tells me into the city to an Indian restaurant in Tribeca.

I remove the cape from around her neck. "Oh, that should be nice."

She grunts. "Sugah-boo, *boom!* What the hell I wanna be in some Tribeca—wherever the hell that is, eatin' some goddamn curry shit for? I tol' that gorilla he better do me right 'n' find me one'a them fancy soul food spots. I want me a slab'a damn ribs 'n' some buttery biscuits."

I laugh, shaking my head. She follows me up to the front, paying her bill, then handing me a hundred-dollar tip. "Thanks, girl. And try to behave yourself tonight. It's nice to have a man to want to take you out on a date sometime."

"Miss Pasha, girl, *boom!* All that freaky, big-dick gorilla wanna do is sniff my cootie-coo-scented drawz. And I don't mind lettin' him, either, since he pays me good. But he ain't gotta take me over to no damn New York to do it. All I know is, he better have me back 'cross the water before the club closes tonight."

I chuckle. "Cass, I can't, girl."

"Uh-huh, and you won't, sugah-boo." She puts a hand up on her hip. "But you better hurry up 'n' get ya mind right, Miss Pasha, girl, 'cause come Monday I ain't gonna be playin' no games with ya ole uppity-ass. I see I'ma have'ta strike a match up under them ole fluffy booty cheeks of yours to get the fire started."

I smirk, raising a brow. "Girl, please. The fire's already been lit. *Trust.*"

She grunts, tossing me a hand wave in the air, handbag in the crook of her arm, ass bouncin' every which way as she struts out the door. A few minutes later, my next client walks through the door, followed by Kendra and two other appointments, looking fabulous as always.

Kendra and I say our good mornings as I stand. "Heeeeey, diva," I say, walking around the counter to give Bianca a hug. We embrace. I step back and take her in. She has her hair pulled back in a ponytail. Her smooth chestnut-brown skin is absolutely glowing. "Bianca, girl, you look *great!* What in the world are you doing with yourself?"

She smiles. "Girl, besides finally planning for this wedding, which I *know* you had better be at, not a thing."

"Girl, *please*. You know I'll be there front and center, with bells on. I wouldn't miss it for the world." She follows me to the back, then takes a seat in my chair. "How's that handsome baby of yours?"

"Which one?" She chuckles. "Oh, you mean Cairo." Bianca spent a month vacation over in North Africa and fell in love with Egypt, so she named her son after its capital. Her face lights up. "Girl, I am *so* in love with that child." She opens her handbag, pulling out her phone, then showing me several pictures of him. And all I can say is, he's a gorgeous little boy.

"Ohmygod, he's so adorable," I say, snapping the cape around her. "He needs to be doing print ads or commercials."

She playfully swats at me. "Oh, no, girl. I'm not even trying to become one of *those* mothers. He can do all of that when he's grown and on his own."

I chuckle. "So when's the big day?" She tells me in June. "Girl, you don't have much time. That's in like…"

She gives me a dramatic sigh. "Seven months. Don't remind me.

Between my mother and Garrett, I don't know who's going to drive me crazy first. My mother is already talking about flying in from San Diego to stay until the wedding." I ask her whom she'd be staying with. "Girl, please. Not me. *Maybe* for a week or two, but that's about it. The way me and Garrett stay locked in our bedroom." We laugh. "And, *don't* even get me started on him. All he wants to do is rush down to City Hall."

I smile, truly happy for her. If this were three years ago, Bianca and I would be having another kind of conversation since she was— as she used to say, "allergic to relationshps" and against love. But, Garrett—who was initially one of her many man toys, chipped away at that wall and finally broke her resolve. She opened her heart and took a chance on him and love. And it's paid off. She seems and looks so happy. She is one of the fortunate ones. She has herself one of the good men out here.

She waves me on. "Please. Garrett swooped in, snatched me up, knocked me up, and got me strung the hell out, girl. And I ain't too proud to beg, okay. That man *knows* I'm not going anywhere. And he better not, either; especially now that I'm four months' pregnant with baby number two."

"Girl, shut your mouth," I say, spinning her around in my chair staring at her through the mirror. "Congrats! How many more do you think you'll have?"

She smiles wide. "Girl, one more, and that's it. But Garrett would have me pregnant every year if I'd let him. He's wants at least six kids. And I want to keep my shape, okay? So we compromised. I told him I'd give him three babies. But that's it. And even three is one too many if you ask me; especially the way this economy is."

"Tell me about it."

She lowers her voice. "Now enough about me. How are things

with you?" I tell her all is as good as it can be, considering the circumstances. I don't mention to her about the shootout. "Garrett told me to tell you if you need anything to make sure you call him. He doesn't care what time of the day or night it is."

I smile, glancing over toward the door as Lamar walks in. He walks over to Mel, giving him dap. "I appreciate that. Believe it or not, the light at the end of the tunnel is getting brighter by the day."

"Good. I really thought things would work out for the two of you."

"Girl, it is what it is. Nothing in this life is promised to us, or guaranteed. Jasper and I shared what we've shared. And now it's time to move on. I'm so done."

She smiles. "Good for you. And how's little Jaylen doing?"

Now it's my turn to beam. "He's fine. That little boy gives me life, girl."

She nods knowingly. "Hopefully you and Jasper will be able to work through your differences for his sake. Lamar and I lock eyes briefly as he says "good morning" to everyone, heading toward the back.

"Time will tell," I say, glancing up at the television. Kendra's client starts talking about the fires.

"Girl, that's some shit," she says. "They said mad bodies got *burnt* up, too."

Kendra keeps her eyes glued to her client's head, her fingers fast at work putting in her weave. "I heard there was some kinda shootout, first. Some Rambo niggas kicked in the doors, then started snuffin' niggas out left 'n' right before they torched them spots up."

"Girl, that's the same shit I heard," her client says. "All I know is, whoever kicked in them doors 'n' set them fires wasn't playin'. They asses meant business. And they *shut*. Shit. *Down*."

You got that right! And I'm not through!

My heartbeat quickens. The suspense of not knowing, not *ever* knowing—per Lamar and my "don't ask" agreement—what really went down this morning is a sweet torture that has me on the edge of an orgasm. I don't need, want, to know details, anyway. All I care is that the deed is done.

Seven more to go. And each week I'm going to keep burning them all down until Jasper's ass is left with *nothing.* Then I'm going to finish his ass off—for good.

"Garrett and I were watching it all on the news this morning," Bianca says, shaking her head. "It's tragic what happened."

I turn her chair back around, hiding a look of satisfaction. "Girl, *yes*, it is. A real damn tragedy."

Twenty-Nine

A smart bitch never lets a nigga know her next move...

I turn the cold water on, then splash some on my face. I glance up into the mirror, staring at my reflection. I'm exhausted. By the time I finished up with Bianca's hair this morning, the salon all of a sudden got packed, which is always a blessing given the way the economy is. Still I had hoped to leave early today. However, as you can see, that didn't happen.

I got hit with three walk-ins. One was a wash and curl, which wasn't a problem. Another wanted a perm and cut. Then there was a baldhead chick with double E breasts that wanted a sew-in weave, but didn't want anything done with her unibrow. Whatever. I had never seen her before, but she asked specifically for me. So, I took her. But it took me almost an hour and forty-five minutes to remove the raggedy shit she had glued up on her scalp. Fucking with her ass put me behind schedule. And the one thing I don't like to do is keep any of my clients waiting any longer than they have to.

I swear, I don't know what the hell these chicks are thinking when they let some makeshift beautician slap glue all up in their shit, especially a chick who doesn't have much hair to begin with.

Anyway, I love what I do. Wouldn't change anything about it. But some days I just don't have it in me to be on my feet all damn day, listening to a bunch of cackling, gossiping-ass bitches. But then I see the finished product, the fruits of my creativity and labor, and the smiles on my clients' faces as they strut their new looks out the door, and it's all worth it—throbbing feet and all. Anyway, my last client walked up out of here thirty minutes ago. And Kendra finished her last appointent ten minutes after mine left.

Now the only two people still here in the shop are Mel and me. And all I want to do is lock up and get home so I can take off these clothes and curl up in my bed with a chilled bottle of chardonnay.

I splash more water on my face, replaying this morning's new over in my head. All day, the fires were the hot topic of the day. They appeared on every news channel and it's all clients talked about.

I bet Jasper's black ass is *sick* right about now! Stash houses down, street soldiers down. *Everything around you is going to crumble, nigga!*

I reach for a towel and pat my face. Then brush my teeth and gargle. Finally I dig through the emergency make-up kit I keep under the sink and pull out an applicator of concealer to smooth out the puffiness under my eyes. When I am satisfied, I apply a coat of cherry wine lipstick over my lips, then a coat of lip gloss to make them pop. No matter how I might be feeling on the inside, I'll *never* let myself step out looking any kind of way.

I open the door, flicking off the light and stepping back out into my office. I jump. *"Ohmygod!* You scared the shit out of me. What are *you* doing here?"

Stax gets up from the sofa, removing his Brooklyn Nets fitted from his head. "My bad. Didn't mean to startle you, Pash. I wanted to come through to check on you. To make sure you're aiight."

I rush over to my desk; an uneasiness in my stride, making a mental note to give Mel holy fucking hell when Stax leaves for sending people to my office without alerting me first. *Mmmph. If Lamar were here, his ass wouldn't have gotten back here.*

I raise my brow, eyeing him. He's wearing a long-sleeved True Religion T-shirt and a pair of loose-fitting jeans. I glance down at his Timb-clad feet, then back up at him.

"Do I *look* all right to you, Montgomery?"

He cringes. "Oh, wow…that's how you really doin' it, Pash?" No one in his personal space ever refers to him by his birth name. They either call him Monty or Stax—his street name. He rubs his chin, nodding. "I know you're goin' through it right now—"

I narrow my eyes to slits, cutting him off. "You don't know what the hell I'm going through." I jab a finger in the air at him. "So don't stand there and try to patronize me. Now, if you'll excuse me, I need to finish up in here."

His brown eyes search mine. There's a brief pause. And suddenly I'm feeling flustered. "Damn, it's like that, Pash? What's up with all the 'tude? I thought we were bigger than that, yo."

I shift my eyes from his stare. "I thought so, too. But I guess I was wrong. Now do me a favor. Go run along to your puppet master. And be sure to let him know that the *next* time I pull my gun out on his ass, it *will* be to blow a hole in his face." I stare him down for effect. He keeps his eyes locked on my glare. "Now, if you don't mind. You can see yourself out."

He raises his voice slightly. "Puppet master? *Don't* get it twisted, Pash. Just because I ain't on no rah-rah type shit like the rest of the niggas in my circle, doesn't mean I'm some soft-ass cat. I'm not *anyone's* puppet. Believe that."

I glance over toward the door. It's Mel standing in the doorway. Seven minutes too damn late. "You good, Pasha? I thought I heard yelling." He cuts his eye over at Stax. "We cool in here?"

Stax doesn't acknowledge him. He keeps his eyes trained on me. I tell Mel everything's fine. Assure him I'm okay. Then tell him he can leave for the night. He tells me he's good. That he leaves when I leave. I smile, knowingly, then ask him to shut the door and make sure no one else *ever* gets back here to see me without him clearing it with me, *first*. He picks up on my stern warning, ensuring it won't happen again. I wait for him to shut the door, then bring my attention back to Stax.

"So you're telling me that Jasper didn't send you here to play gofer?"

"C'mon, Pash. I don't have to stand here 'n' bullshit you."

"Then why are *you* really here? To finish what them niggas tried to do to me yesterday? *Kill* me? Is that it? Were you one of the niggas in the truck that shot at me yesterday, huh, *Monty?*" I ease open my top drawer, the glint of my gun catches my gaze for a moment and I rest my hand on it. "Maybe it was *you* who pulled the trigger."

His eyes widen. His jaw drops. A look of—what appears to be genuine—shock etches his face. He actually looks worried. But I can't be too sure with any of these niggas. Maybe it's all an act. "Say, *whaaat? Kill* you? Niggas shot at you, when?"

I glare at him. "Yesterday, early in the motherfucking morning! Right outside here, in front of my salon. The very next day after Jasper *threatened* to have a bullet put in my goddamn head!" I'm now shaking with anger. "The motherfucker pretty much said it was a warning. That the next time, they won't miss. Well, guess what, *Monty?* Jasper and his goons had better go back to the lab and try again because I got something for his ass! So my advice to *you* is, if you don't want to go down with him, stay the fuck out of the crossfire!"

The omninous threat lingers between us. We stare at each other. He's looking at me as if he's pondering the implications of my threat, wondering what exactly I'm threatening. I'm eyeing him, considering his role in all of this shit. A part of me thinks, wants, to warn him to stay away from those stash houses, but I quickly dismiss the notion. Besides, he and Jasper never go to any of the drug spots. There's someone else responsible for that.

I don't break my stare from his serious eyes.

After several moments, Stax holds his head, then slowly runs his thick hands along the ripples of his deep, spinning waves. He mutters, mostly to himself, "This nigga. What the fuck is wrong wit' him?"

I snort, finally removing my hand out of my drawer, away from the gun. I shut it. "The nigga's crazy, that's *what* the fuck's wrong with him. You know it. And I know it. So don't try to act surprised. I don't need your fake-ass concern, *Monty*. So save it. I'm not looking for a Superhero to come save the goddamn day, or to save *me* because when I needed a nigga in a cape to come for me, he was too goddamn busy somewhere plotting on me."

Stax bristles at the harshness of my words. He shifts his probing eyes and exhales a slow, pained breath. "I wasn't a part of any of that. This shit between you and Jasp is gettin' fuckin' crazy."

I lean slightly, opening my bottom desk drawer and pulling out my handbag. I close and lock the drawer, removing the key from its lock. I look up at him, letting out a sarcastic laugh. "Oh, really? *Getting crazy?* You *think?* How about shit's been crazy between us since the day we fucking met. And it's gotten crazier ever since the nigga came home from prison and had me fucking kidnapped, then beat the shit out of me *after* letting a string of niggas ram their fucking dicks down in my throat..."

He winces, seemingly uncomfortable hearing this. I narrow my eyes at him. "And you want to know the *craziest* part of this sick, twisted saga, *Monty?* I *still* married his crazy ass! Then crazy-ass me let the nigga disrespect and put his hands on me whenever he got into one of his jealous fits, taking it as my just due because silly me *thought* I fucking deserved it for sucking a bunch of niggas' dicks behind his back. *After* all the goddamn cheating he's done on me, I really thought I deserved what the fuck he did to me. But guess what? The last straw was Tuesday when the nigga came up in *here*, in *my* goddamn salon, and put his motherfucking hands on me, then tried to bum-rush him some pussy. But *you* already know all of this, don't *you?* Like you *know* everything else."

He frowns. "What's that s'posed to mean?"

I suck my teeth, rolling my eyes. "Don't stand here and play stupid with me." I feel my blood starting to boil. This is the first time that I've had a chance to confront him—by himself. Alone.

I defiantly fold my arms across my chest. There's an awkward silence building between us. Booty's voice flits through my head. "*...You're gonna have'ta fish the nigga...Miss Pasha, girl, do what you gotta do to get these niggas who tried to do you got. Throat that nigga, sugah-boo. And trust me. If you swallow his nut real good, you'll have that nigga in the palm of ya messy-ass hands.*"

"Answer me this, *Monty*: Where the fuck were *you* when Jasper and his goons had me down in that basement tied up like a fucking animal? Was making sure I ate, and used the bathroom, and showered so them savage motherfuckers could face-fuck and disrespect me a part of your show of concern for me? Was it *you* who fucking stood by and let them niggas force me to suck their dicks? You stood there and watched them humiliate me. And *you* did nothing to stop them....." I feel myself getting choked up.

He flinches. Gives me a pained look. "Yo, Pash, I'm bein' dead-ass. I had nothin' to do with that shit."

My lips tremble. Either Stax's a good fucking liar. Or what he's saying is true. "Fuck you! I was there, *Monty*. I know what I saw. You were there." Truth is, like I already stated, I really don't know if he was there or not. I need to know. So I pretend, like I've done with so many other things. A part of me is hoping he really wasn't there.

"You don't have to lie. Admit it. You were there, Monty." I fight back tears. *"You* were the *Calm One*. The one who came down to check on me, the one who fed me, and cleaned up my piss and shit; you were the only nigga there who didn't force me to suck his dick."

He shifts his weight. "Real shit, Pash. I don't know nothin' 'bout no *Calm One*. I'm tellin' you, I wasn't there."

The tears start falling.

I feel myself becoming undone.

Then who was he?

His saddened gaze on me is unsettling. "Yo, c'mon, Pash…don't." He steps toward me and reaches out to me. I step back. Tell him to stay the fuck where he is. "On my life, Pash. I wasn't there."

I want to believe him.

"You want me to believe you weren't there. Well, I *don't* believe you, Stax! Wherever Jasper is, you are. So don't fucking lie to me."

He holds his hands up, palms out. "On e'erything I love, Pash. I wasn't there when that shit went down. I didn't want any part of that foul shit. I tried to talk Jasp outta that shit, but he wasn't hearin' it. He was on some other type shit. And I wasn't down wit' it. I tol' him point blank I wasn't gettin' caught up in none'a that crazy shit. On e'erything, Pash, I wanted to tell you to watch ya steps, but…" He shakes his head, his voice trailing off. "I couldn't. I gave Jasp my word."

"Fish this nigga, sugah-boo."

"Them no-good dirty niggas gotta get got, Miss Pasha, girl…"

I swallow. "I get it, *Monty*. Blood over Bitches, right? Your loyalty is to Jasper. And we both know how that nigga is all about loyalty. Well, fuck *him* and his motherfucking loyalty." I remind him of something he said to me once when he showed up here a few days after that nigga smashed out the salon's window with the pipe. "You told me if I *ever* needed you that you got me. You remember that shit?"

He nods. "I—"

I cut him off, pointing a finger at him. "I'm not fucking done. You *fucking* stood right here"—I jab a finger at the spot where he was that day—"and looked me in the eyes and told me *I* was your peoples so if someone was fucking with *me*, then they were fucking with *you*. Do you remember that shit, *Monty?* Or was that a bunch of bullshit you felt like feeding me that day?"

He shakes his head, giving me an agonizing stare. "Nah, I meant that shit, Pash. I never wanted to see anything happen to you, ma. When I heard what really went down, that shit fucked me up." He walks toward me again, reaches out to touch me. But I push him away.

My lips curl into a contemptuous sneer. "Yeah, right! Get the fuck away from me!"

He steps back. It takes everything in me not to take my six-inch heel off and stab him in his throat, his eyes, his motherfucking head. I glare at him, nostrils flaring, chest heaving. I want to hurt him the way Jasper hurt me. Want him to feel a sliver of what that nigga put me through.

"You knew all along that Jasper suspected me of cheating on him and *you* didn't say shit to me. You could have warned me! But didn't! You smiled in my fucking face all the while knowing what Jasper had planned for me!" I hear myself, sounding like the wounded soul, playing victim, when I'm the one who put myself in that situation in the first place.

He steps toward me again. "Pash, I wanted to, yo; real shit. I was torn." He pauses, letting out a sigh. "I mean, fuck. Jasp and I are blood, period, feel me? But I got mad love for you, too, Pash; real shit. Not bein' able to say shit fucked me up. It still fucks me up, yo. I don't know how to take it all back. Why you think I only come around you when I'm with Jasp, huh? I do that shit because e'ery time I see you, it fuckin' reminds me of how I fucked up, Pash. Jasp's my fam, yo. But, you..." He averts his eyes from glare.

"What about *me*, Monty?"

"C'mon, Pash. Don't act like you don't know."

I stare at him, my eyes filled with hurt and confusion. "Don't *act* like I don't know what, *Montgomery?*"

"That I care about you. You've always had a special place in my—"

I gnash my teeth, giving him an incredulous look. "Fuck you, Monty! You don't get to come up in here and *now* wanna have a Hallmark moment. No, nigga! *Motherfuck* you! If I was *sooo* fucking special to you, *where* the fuck were you when I was being kidnapped, huh?"

I feel the tears swelling, pushing past the rims of my eyes, but I fight to keep them in check. I feel my anger pushing up against the pit of my stomach. My chest tightens.

He tries to apologize. But I'm not having it.

"Save your goddamn apology for some other bitch!" I snap, advancing on him. I'm on him, fast, reaching up and slapping his face. But it's not his face I see. It's Jasper's. It's not his voice I hear. It's Jasper's. And, in that very second, I lose it. The dam breaks, and my emotions come flooding out of me. Everything I've held in, everything I've pretended didn't exist, explodes out of me.

"I fucking hate you!" I slap and punch him. He stands there, taking blow for blow without flinching. My fists hit against hard flesh. I bang my fists into his chest, crying. "Fuck you, nigga! You let that nigga lure me into a trap! And *you* did *nothing!* I hate you!"

I bang and bang and bang, and slap and punch him until I am exhausted. He lets me have my moment, my breakdown. Lets me get it all out. And then he does the unthinkable: he grabs me in his muscular arms and holds me tight. And I fall into his strong embrace.

"I know that shit got you all fucked up. I fucked up, aiight. Shit got outta hand, ma." He rubs my back. "I swear to you, Pash. I'm sorry that shit happened to you. You didn't deserve that shit. If I could take that shit back, I would."

I cry into his chest. He tightens his arms around me. I am emotionally out of control. He lets me rant, cursing and screaming. Lets me have my meltdown, rubbing my back. He lowers his voice to almost a whisper. Tells me, again, how sorry he is. Apologizes over and over. His voice and big hands are gentle and calming.

After awhile, I am no longer sobbing. I am whimpering. Hic-cupping. Trying to steady my breathing. Moments pass. There's nothing but my hiccups and choppy breathing between us. He lifts my chin with his finger, takes all of my emotions in. My eyes a drowing pool of pain and humiliation, my face streaked with tears. He kisses me on the forehead.

I look him dead in the eyes and see something in them I've never seen before. Or maybe it was always there, but I was too wrapped up in Jasper and my own mess to really see it. I thought lust was what I always saw in this nigga's eyes. I thought the tension was sexually charged. But no...the desire I see in his eyes goes much deeper than him wanting to fuck me.

Booty's voice pops into my head. *"Miss Pasha, girl, fish that nigga. Do what you gotta do to get what you gotta get to get them niggas, good."*

My life, my freedom, my sanity, is all on the line. I need something to hold on to. Need something to turn to. Stax is that something. I rise up on the balls of my feet and pull him into me. I kiss him, a quick peck on the lips at first. My actions catch me—as well as him, off-guard. He's staring into my eyes, burning a hole into my empty soul. But when he doesn't pull back, I kiss him again; this time more urgent.

I am surprised when he kisses me back. His tongue finding its way between the slit of soft, full lips. My tongue pushes against his as I press my body up against him. I can feel the bulge in his pants rising, thickening. His hands slide along my back to my ass, cupping it. He pulls me further into him. His hard dick pressing against my stomach causes my pussy to pulsate.

No, I've never been sexually attracted to Monty. I've never given him any thought. He's always been off-limits. Until now...

He pulls back. "Fuck, Pash!" He runs his hands over his face, then along his thick neck. I can see the swell of his hefty dick through his jeans. I shift my eyes, swallowing back a mouthful of drool. "This shit's wrong, ma. Fuck!"

"I know, I know." I cup my face in my hands, shaking my head. I step back from him. "I don't know what came over me." I walk back over toward my desk, avoiding his peering eyes. I am feeling embarrassed. "I think you should leave. And, *please*..." I pause, swallowing back the shaky sound of my voice. "Don't come back."

He looks at me for a second as if he's trying to decide. He walks toward the door, then opens it. I watch him as he walks out. My hands tremble. My heart aches with disgust and anger and unexpected lust. And I'm fucking pissed that my panties are soaked.

Ohmygod! What the fuck did I almost do?

The answer comes rushing back in, shutting the door, then scooping me up into his arms, holding the back of my neck, his mouth on mine, his tongue darting into my mouth—catching me completely by surprise.

Thirty

A thick hard dick does the body good…

"Fuck, Pash! Aaaaah, shit." Stax groans as my hand strokes his long, hard dick. It's ten inches and as thick as my forearm. A thick drop of precum lingers at the tip. And then I am down on my knees, his jeans wrapped around his ankles, my tongue lapping his slit, swirling over and around it. I try not to relish in the beauty of Stax's enormous dick; the thick vein that runs along the smooth thick curve of his mocha-colored cock, its bulbous head. My tongue travels over it, leaving wet streaks as I glide up and down the length of it. I cup his juicy plum-sized balls. Bounce them in my hand. They're smooth-shaven and heavy. *My God! The gossip whores weren't lying when they said this nigga had a big dick and big, juicy mouthwatering balls.* I lick underneath them, then twirl my tongue over each one before gently sucking them into my mouth.

I can already feel my pussy starting to churn. Heat sweeps through my insides, causing my clit to engorge. My mouth waters.

"Aaaah, shit, yeah…fuck, Pash…yeah, suck them balls…Mmmm… just like that…" I continue sucking his wet balls into my mouth and hum as I use both of my hands to stroke his shaft. He dips at the knees. His dick vibrates in my hand with each stroke. It swells harder and thicker than I imagined. I kiss the head of his dick, sticky strings of precum wetting my lips. I tickle the head with my tongue, flicking over its piss slit, until I have him quivering.

In my head, I hear Booty cheering me on, imagining her saying some shit like, "Yessss, goddammit…Do that shit, sugah-boo. Suck him right, goddammit! Eat the snot outta that nigga's big ole juicy dick, Miss Pasha, girl…"

I slip Stax's dick into my mouth, sucking on the head as if it were a ripe, juicy fruit. My mouth becomes a hot wet vessel for his cock to get lost in. I suck his dickhead feverishly, my lips suckling the rim with my lips, teasing and taunting the nigga. I suck the length of his dick in long, lascivious pulls, drawing him deep and then out again to the head, swirling my tongue over it, before taking him back in. I suck Stax like it's my last dick suck. Suck him like it's my last day here on earth. Greedy and desperate.

"Goddamn, yo…oooooh, shit…fuckfuckfuck…" His hand cradles the back of my head. His fingers dig into my scalp. "Shitshitshit… mmmm…motherfuckgoddamnshit…"

My lashes flutter upward as I glance up at him. Eyes closed. Bottom lip pulled in. Head tossed back. I know I got the nigga going through it. My jaws unlatch. My cheeks swell with dick as I lightly tug on his balls, massaging them, every so often allowing the head of his dick to hit the back of my throat. I lick and suck and slurp him close to orgasm without taking him completely over the edge.

"Aaah, fuck, yeah, Pash…wet that shit, ma…"

My heart is thumping in my chest. Sucking this nigga is wrong. I know it is. But it's necessary. This is what I tell myself. *Fuck Jasper! Fuck what's right or wrong!* It's a means to an end.

Shit! His dick tastes so fucking good.

I try not to enjoy the delicious sensations that ripple through my pussy as Stax's dick pushes past my tonsils and stretches my neck, shutting my airway, but I can't help myself. My panties are soaked from the ravenous dick sucking I'm putting on his ass. I give him my porn-star special.

I give it to him wet and sloppy, gulping and gurgling and gasping as I neck bob back and forth over every thick, throbbing inch of him. Down into my neck, up to the head, my lips nursing the tip before plunging it back down into my throat.

My eyes tear.

But there is no gagging. I gulp him in deeper, extending my tongue to allow more room for his throat fuck. His dick pulses down in my throat as he nears orgasm. He grabs my head and fucks my face.

Stroke for stroke my pussy spasms. I slink my hand up under my skirt, but I am already coming before I can even touch myself. My panties are drenched in my steamy juices. I groan, gripping the back of his muscled thighs.

"Damn, you suckin' the shit outta this dick…aaah fuck…yeah, ma, handle that shit, yo…ooooh, goddaaaaaaaamn…Yeah, you got that shit all down in ya neck, Pash…fuck, yeah…mmmm…"

His left leg starts to shake. He is on the brink of unloading his cock. I pick up the pace. Suck, slurp, suck. Gulp, gurgle, slurp.

"Uhhh…uhhhh…motherfuckshit…" I keep sucking him, bringing him closer to the edge, then retreating back to the tip—teasing him until he can no longer take it—until he is slamming himself into my mouth, until he is swabbing my throat in deep urgent thrusts. I loop my fingers under the edge of my panties and into my pussy, embedding them knuckles deep as I grind down onto them.

Stax gasps. I grunt and groan, urging him on. Encouraging him to give it to me good. To feed me his thick, heated, creamy seed. And he does.

But Stax isn't finished yet. He wants more. I've snapped open Pandora's box. And now this nigga wants to rifle through its treasures. "I wanna taste you, Pash. Let me eat that pussy."

He pulls me up off my knees, lifts me up on the top of my desk. I hike my skirt up, raise my hips and he slides my soaked panties over them. I reach for the lace garment, bringing it to my nose and inhaling the sweet muskiness of my pussy as I spread my smooth legs for him.

He cradles himself between my smooth legs. Leans in, kisses the back of my thighs, then licks up to the edge of my asshole. I shiver. This shit isn't supposed to feel this good. No, no, no! Not with Stax. But there's something in the way he is touching me that causes everything inside of me to melt. Loose heat swirls around in my pussy. I want this nigga to fuck me. But that's not a part of the plan. Then, again, neither is him eating my pussy. But here he is. His face buried between my legs, his hands opening me like a jeweled oyster as he sucks on my pearl. The stage has been set. The plan is in motion. There's no turning back now—for either of us. I don't want him to stop. But it's not supposed to feel like this. Oh, sooo right when it's fucking wrong.

We are both in a heated frenzy.

He slowly licks my glistening clit, then pushes my legs back further, gliding his tongue along the slit of my pussy, then sticking it into my ass. He snakes it back up to my pussy, tongues it, then slithers it back into my ass. He alternates, tongue-fucking me, ass to cunt. He probes and thrusts and licks, tasting the river of juices that are flowing out of me.

I am moaning his name.

He pushes two fingers into my slick heat, arching upward, pressing against my G-spot. I thrust my hips upward, my pussy walls clutching and contracting around his fingers. "Yeah, motherfucker… work my pussy…oooh, yes…mmmm…"

He glances up at me. "You like that shit, ma…?" I moan out my response. "Yeah, give me that sweet nut…you taste so fuckin' good…" He curls his tongue back into my ass while fingering my pussy. My juices drench his hand. I am being tossed into the throes of another orgasm. I buck my hips.

I fight back the urge to scream out, "Give me the dick! Fuck this pussy!" I bite down on my bottom lip. *No, fucking me is out of the question.* But I want to feel him inside of me. I am so confused. I am torn. Aching with lust.

I clench my pussy tightly around his finger.

I shut my eyes and cry out as a rush of heat shoots out of me. I am literally seeing stars as my body convulses. But Stax isn't done. He pulls me up from the desk, carries me over to the sofa, his tongue slipping into my mouth. I suck his cum-scented tongue, lick around his cum-slick lips before sucking on his bottom lip, savoring my juices. He lays me down on the sofa.

"You're so fuckin' beautiful, Pash…"

I stare up at his towering frame, his dick hovering over my face as he fingers my pussy. One finger, then two fingers, then three… he stretches me. Smears my juices over my pussy lips, then strums his fingers over my clit. He rubs circles on it, causing my pussy to throb.

I reach for his bouncing dick. Grip it by the base and pull him toward me, raising my head and taking the head of his dick into my mouth.

His breathing quickens. "Fuckfuckfuckfuck…" he chants.

"Aaaah, shitmotherfuck!" he shrieks, his voice rising to a shrilling roar. "I'm comin', Pash…fuck…oh shiiiiit…here it comes, Pash…

get that shit, ma…" He pounds my pussy with his fingers. Knuckles-deep, he finger-fucks nut after nut out of me as I suck him into my mouth, matching the rhythm of his finger-strokes.

I'm so fucking horny. So fucking blinded by lust and heat and anger. I give Stax what I'm most known for—one of my deep throat specials.

I get real nasty with it. Sucking and slurping and making wet smacking sounds with my mouth while gently squeezing and tugging on his balls. The muscles at the base of his rock-hard dick contract and he is dipping at the knees. And then a burst of hot cum fills my mouth. I gulp it down. Continue sucking on his dick as another wad of nut shoots out into my wet, waiting mouth. There's so much of it. It's thick and gooey and warm and surprisingly tasty. It slides down my throat.

"Aaaah, aaaaah, aaaaaah, aaaaah…mmmm…mmmm…" He is still shooting, flooding my mouth. Some of his cream escapes from my mouth and runs freely down my chin. But I am not one to waste a drop. I keep swallowing and sucking him. I don't stop until his dick calms and begins to go from rock-hard to semi-hard. I skim my lips and tongue over the length and width of him, cleaning his dick, then taking my fingers and scooping up the rest of his nut from my chin into my mouth.

A shiver rises through my pussy.

I am moaning again, my body shaking.

"Yeah, Pash…that's it, ma…come for me…grab my fingers with that hot pussy…yeah, like that…"

I come again, coating his fingers, soaking his hand. I grip his wrist. Grind onto his hand, fuck my pussy onto his fingers. He waits for me to catch my breath, then removes his hand from between my thighs. I grab it and lick his fingers clean. Then stand up. Stax puts his arm around me to steady me.

"What the fuck have we done, Pash," he whispers as he holds my stare.

I push him down onto the sofa, keeping my eyes locked on his as I straddle him. A satisfied smirk on my face, I narrow my gaze. Reach back and start stroking his dick until it thickens and stretches out. "It's too late to worry about that now. I've already had your dick down my throat and swallowed your babies. Do you wanna stop?" My soft hand glides over the crown of his cock. Stax stretches his long legs out.

"Fuck, Pash...aaah, shit..."

I repeat the question. "Do you wanna stop?"

"Nah...shit."

"Then we've just sealed our fates." I lift my hips, positioning the head of his dick into the back of my pussy. I ride its tip, gripping it and slicking it with my wetness. My pussy begins making swishy-sounds as I fuck the opening of my slit with the head of his dick.

He grasps my hips. "Sit all the way down on it. I wanna feel you on my dick, ma. I want you to take all this dick." He tries to thrust up into me, but I lift up, popping his cockhead out.

My lips flush to his ear, I whisper, "You want this pussy, Stax? You wanna fuck?"

"What you think, Pash?" he says breathlessly. "I wanna bust this nut. I wanna feel your wet pussy all over this hard-ass dick."

"I need names, Stax." I reach in back of me, grab his dick and squeeze it, then press it downward, sliding my wet slit along the length of his shaft. I coat him with my juices, then slide down between his legs. His dick bounces up into my face. I glance up at him. "Give me the names of the niggas who kidnapped me. And you can get all the pussy you want."

I gently squeeze his wet balls, then lick them. He moans. "Tell me who Jasper had kidnap me." I take his pussy-scented dick back into my mouth. And for the first time in—I don't know how long—a sense of calm washes over me.

Nigga, you gonna give me want I want 'cause I'm about to suck your balls inside out!

"Fuck, Pash...aaaah, shit...motherfuckgoddamn...I *got* you, Pash..."

Thirty-One

There's a fine line between contempt and compassion…

"Mona, how are you *really* holding up, girl?" I ask, eyeing her over the rim of my flute. This is the first time I've seen her since last Monday. We're out having brunch in the city. I had called her late last night, when I'd finally gotten home from sucking down Stax's dick, to check in on her. He'd mentioned as he was pulling his boxers up over his long dick that she didn't seem herself. That she seemed real distracted and jittery lately. And that he was worried about her. Shit, I wanted to tell him I was worried about her, too. The last thing I need, or want, is for her to start confessing shit. Or having a damn nervous breakdown.

So here I am…on a Sunday afternoon, sitting in a private booth at a swanky restaurant in Tribeca with my dearest friend—and the cousin of the man I'm planning to shut down, trying to assess whether or not she's going to be an asset or a liability in all of this. Because the wheels are starting to spin and once this shit starts rolling full speed, it's going to get real ugly. So I need to be absolutely sure whether or not she's going to be able to keep it together or end up fucking us all over in the end. Bottom line, friend or not: if Mona needs to get knocked in the head, then I'll let Booty take it to her skull. That's not something I'm willing to do.

She casts her eyes down to her half-eaten Cajun shrimp salad, then over toward the huge glass window, the early afternoon sun streaming in and basking the room in a golden glow. She blinks. Clearly her mind is somewhere else besides here.

I reach over the table and touch her hand. "Hello? Hello? Earth to Mona."

She looks at me. "Huh? Did you say something?"

I smile. "I asked you how you were holding up." I decide not to mention what Stax had said, or anything else about my unexpected *meeting* with him. I think that information will throw her over the edge for sure.

She lifts her fork and starts picking over her salad. "I don't know, Pasha. Some days, I think I'm good. Like I can do this. Like I can put it all behind me. And go on with the rest of my life, unmoved by it all. Then other days, I feel like I'm coming undone. Like my emotions are in overdrive and I'm about to crash." She shakes her head, blinking back tears. "Lately, I don't know if I'm coming or going."

I nod, knowingly as I take a slow, deliberate sip of my Mimosa. I wait for her to say more.

"I'm so fucking torn. I know he fucked my life up. I know I should have told someone what he was doing to me. But I *liked* it. I *wanted* it. Then other times, I hated it. And didn't want it. I loved him and *hated* him at the same time, Pasha…"

Suddenly Jasper comes to mind. Before he had me kidnapped; *before* he fucking tried to have me killed, when we were both so in love—or at least my version of it. His face, his smile, the way he used to touch me. The way my body always responded to him—even after what he'd done to me.

Fucking bastard!

She stabs a large shrimp with her fork, lifting it to her lips and taking a tiny bite. "Pasha, I hate this feeling. And I feel so guilty for having wished him dead. Now he is. And I feel even more ashamed for feeling relieved that he is. That I will no longer have to look in his face and be reminded of…"

I lean over and squeeze her hand.

"I've never forgiven myself for giving up our baby, Pasha…"

I gasp, covering my hand over my mouth. *I thought she'd had an abortion.* Before I can open my mouth to ask, she's already explaining. She tells me a month after she told her parents she was pregnant, that they shipped her off to a private home for unwed mothers in Indiana, where she stayed until after she gave birth. Two weeks later, her parents flew down to bring her home. Because she hadn't been showing when she left, she was able to come back to her life, leaving behind her darkest secret, like nothing ever happened. And her having ever been pregnant was never talked about again.

"I erased that entire part of my life from my memory. I blocked it. Hid it—from myself, from Avery. Well, at least I thought I did… until now. Until Cassandra. Until JT's death." She wipes a tear from her eyes. "You are the only person, besides my parents, who knows about my son. I don't think you or anyone can ever understand the hollow feeling of being forced to give up a *baby* that you know you'd never be able to care for, or love, because of how it was conceived. No matter how badly I *thought* I wanted to keep him…JT's *baby*…I couldn't without looking into his innocent face and it being a constant, burning reminder that I was sexually molested by my own cousin and that my son was the result of that sick, twisted shit. And I did nothing to stop it."

"Mona, what JT did to you was *not* your fault. JT was a sick bastard."

She blows her nose in a napkin, then takes a sip of her drink. "I know he was. And, deep down in my heart, I *know* he got exactly what he deserved. I can only imagine how many other girls he'd molested. Sometimes I wonder if that's the real reason his mother sent him to live with us. Because he'd done something to his younger sister, Trisha."

I'd only met Trisha once, so I don't really know much about her. But I wouldn't put shit pass him. At this point, nothing would surprise me. I toss back the rest of my drink, flagging over the waitress.

"Mona, I'm sorry you had to go through all that. I wish I could have been there for you so you wouldn't have had to carry that burden alone."

She gives me a faint smile. "Thanks. I appreciate that." She releases a heavy sigh. "Talking to you, and you just being here for me, has really helped—a lot. All these years of carrying this around…" She pauses when the wiry blonde with the perky breasts comes to the table. I tell her we'd like another round of Mimosas.

We eye her as she walks off toward the bar. "I never knew how toxic holding all this shit has been for me. How it's affected my relationships with men, why I never trusted them. How it has even affected my marriage in some ways. By pretending that it never happened, I really thought I could go through life and be okay. And I was okay. I *thought* I was okay. But the noose was still there. Dangling over my head. I have spent most of my life waiting for it to finally drop around my neck and slowly tighten. And it has. I guess I have Cassandra's messy-ass to thank for that."

I shake my head. "How did she even find out about it?"

Mona shrugs. "I have no idea. Shit, who knows how that crazy bitch knows half the shit she does." The waitress returns with our drinks, placing them in front of us, then asks if we'd like anything else. Mona waves her on. "No, we're good. Thanks." She waits until the waitress is out of earshot and leans in. "I didn't even want to tell you this. But, do you know that sick bitch had the audacity to call me and threaten to put what she did to JT on *me* if I ever slipped up."

My mouth drops open. "She did *what?*"

"You heard me. That *bitch* said if the shit ever hits the fan and it gets out that she had anything to do with his disappearance, that she was going to tell them that I"—she lowers her voice to a sharp whisper—"hired her to *kill* him."

I stare at her in utter disbelief. "Ohmygod…what the fuck is wrong with her? Cassandra is really out of control."

"Miss Pasha, girl, I do whatever I gotta do to get the job done, god-dammit. A nigga-bitch tries to fuck me over, I'ma fuck 'em first. And, trust, sugah-boo. I'ma tear they asshole out the frame. It's gonna be rough 'n' goddamn dirty…"

"Pasha, I'ma tell you like this: I think there's a whole lot more to Cassandra than we need to know."

Yeah, I think you're right. I nod, knowingly, keeping my thoughts to myself.

She shoots me a warning look. "All I can say is, *don't* ever get on that bitch's bad side. She's more gangster and grimy than some of them hood niggas out there in the streets. I'm convinced that bitch is treacherous."

I sigh. "She's a loose fucking cannon."

"Yeah, and that, too. Don't tell her I told you what she said to me, though. I don't want that crazy bitch jumping up in my face."

"Don't worry. Not a word. Knowing her, she'll blab it out at some point when she thinks one of us is trying to *do her.*"

"Fuck her. I don't want shit else to do with her ass. If I can help it, I'm staying the hell away from her and all of her ghetto-ass fuckery."

I take two long sips of my drink. Mona does as well. She sets her flute down, glancing around the restaurant. She leans in. "Has she mentioned anything to you about where JT's"—she mouths— "body's at?"

I shake my head. "Not a word." In all honesty, I'm glad she didn't tell me when I asked. Knowing what she did to JT's corpse, or who helped her dispose of it, is something I don't need to know. It's bad enough I know *she* killed him.

Mona shudders. "Regardless of what he did to me, or to…anyone else, his wife and family still deserve some sort of closure. The waiting, the not knowing, is the worst part for us all. Him missing is driving everyone crazy. And the longer he stays gone, the worse it gets. Leticia and his mother are really going through it."

I nod understandingly. Yet, I have mixed feelings about the whole thing, but I keep it to myself. She's right. They do deserve some type of closure. But, niggas like him turn up missing all the time. Niggas like him get dropped all the time. So they should already know. A nigga like him is dead. There isn't going to be a body, so they might as well slap a 16-by-20 picture of his grimy ass up on an easel, toss a bed of flowers up on a closed empty casket, and grieve their loss.

Then they can all stand up, teary-eyed and broken, at the foot of his coffin and lie about how fucking wonderful he was; how much of a loving husband and father he was; how he loved his family and friends. No one will stand up and tarnish their memory of their beloved. No. They wont dare stand up and say how he was fucking Mona, or how many times he gave his wife STDs and beat her ass. They'll be no mention of him trying to rape Cassandra, or whomever else. And they'll definitely be no talk of how he was one of the niggas who eagerly forced my mouth open and shoved his dick in it. No. That nigga would go to his grave, taking every one of his dirty little secrets with him. So for that, fuck closure for them. And fuck him!

"Oh, I forgot to tell you," Mona says, bringing me out of my fog, "They're going to offer a reward to anyone with information leading to his whereabouts."

I blink. "A reward? For how much?" I ask, surprised. But what I really want to say is, "for what?" I almost fall out of my seat when she tells me fifty thousand dollars. "You have *got* to be fucking kidding me?" I hiss. "A *fifty*-fucking-thousand-dollars. Really?"

She nods.

"Mmmph. I wonder whose bright idea that was. Let me guess. Jasper's?"

"Yeah, and I believe Stax's."

She drinks her Mimosa, and after a brief moment, quickly scans the restaurant, then turns her attention back to me, sighing. "And the irony of it all is, I don't know where his body is. But *I* know exactly what happened to him. And I can't say shit about it."

I swallow back the memory of his dick and nut in my throat, hard. I blink back the frozen image of his sliced-off dick sealed in a Tupperware dish, tucked down in the bottom of Booty's freezer. I reach for my glass and take a greedy sip, then say, raising my flute, "Here's to secrets."

She rolls her eyes. "This shit's not funny, Pasha."

I set my flute back on the table. "I never said it was. But understand this: we all have them. You. Me. Jasper. JT. Cassandra. All of us. Shit we've said or done that we hope like hell no one else ever finds out about. Or shit we've done with others that bind us. Secrets, girl; the kind that'll make some of us cringe, or give us nightmares, or have us losing our minds over. The kind that'll keep a bitch paranoid and have a nigga putting a bullet in someone's head if the shit ever got out. The kind of secrets that if they ever crept out and got into the wrong hands could cost us *every*-thing. So, *no*, Mona, there's nothing funny about it. But it's real. So here's to secrets. And lies. And pretending.

"At the end of the day, you and I both know. *Payback* is a bitch. And the one thing that has always stuck in the back of my head is my grandmother always saying, 'the knife you wield at someone else is the same knife that'll do you in.' Now I don't know where she got that shit from and I've never asked her. But I *knew* what she meant. What comes around goes around, whether we like it or not. So judgment day is somewhere around the corner waiting for *all* of us."

"I know it is…" She goes silent, looking down at her plate. She plucks another shrimp with her fork, then bites into it. I sip my drink as she chews, allowing a momentary muteness, strained and unchartered, to sweep around us.

She finally looks up from her plate and asks about my situation with Jasper. "What do you plan to do?"

I give her the update, purposefully ignoring the question. Tell her how about him putting his hands on me down at the shop. About me trying to chew his balls off, about the restraining order against him. "And his ass still keeps calling me and leaving crazy-ass messages, like it's nothing."

She shakes her head, then quietly says, "Jasper's never been good with letting go; unless it's on *his* terms. He's always been like that. I guess *before* I tried to force you to meet him, I should have warned you that he was kind of possessive—"

I cut her off. "*Kind of?* You think?"

"Okay, he is possessive."

"And obsessive."

"Okay. *And* obsessive."

"Yeah, bitch. I'm thinking a heads-up would have been nice." I shake my head. "Then again, ten, twelve, years ago, it wouldn't have really mattered what you would have told me about his ass back then. You knew I had a thing for bad boys..."

For the first time today, she laughs. "And thug love."

I wave her on, playfully rolling my eyes. "What. Ever. But you're right. And Jasper's hood swag was on ten. So I would have most likely dismissed anything you had to say about him back then. I would have stuck my hand in the fire, anyway; just to see how hot it got."

"Yeah, you're right. Your ass had it bad for them street niggas; that's why I *knew* you'd like him."

You also knew his motherfucking ass was crazy! I sigh. "Yeah, I sure knew how to pick 'em. Sadly, at that time, Jasper was everything I craved for in a man, everything."

She reaches over and places the top of her hand over mine. "And, believe it or not, Pasha, you were *everything* he needed in a woman."

I roll my eyes up in my head. "Then reality hit and we both learned the naked truth."

"And what was that?"

"That he's a psychopath. And I'm a whore."

"Ohmygod, girl, stop. I can't believe you'd say that. That's not true."

I tilt my head, eye her seriously. "Which part, him being a psychopath? Or me being a whore?"

"Both." She slides her hand away from mine, toying with the platinum Tiffany's pendant hanging around her neck.

I raise my brow. "I don't know why it's *not* true. I *was* a whore.

His whore. Then, over time—with him in prison, I suddenly became everyone else's whore as well. The difference is, I take full responsibility for what I've done. He won't."

She shakes her head. "This whole shit is crazy. I really thought the two of you were in love; that what y'all had was real. You both seemed so happy."

I suddenly feel a slow aching in my chest. "We were...in love; and, *maybe*, even happy. But then the streets, and the whores, and the lies stripped that shit away. What Jasper and I shared is what it is. I'm not going to sit and say we didn't have our share of good times, because we did. But we had a whole bunch of bad times as well. And I'm not going to lie or deny that I didn't really loved him through it all, because I did. Through all the disrespect and the fighting and the streets and the bullshit I put up with, I loved him."

I feel my eyes welling up with tears and my blood starting to boil. "On the outside looking in, Jasper and I were everything. We were the perfect fit, the power couple. I was the beauty to his beast. But all that shit really was is an illusion. There was nothing ever perfect about the two of us. Jasper's ass went to prison. His *beauty* went off and sucked a string of other niggas' dicks. And the *beast* came home and had me kidnapped. So there was never going to be a happy ending for the two of us. Whatever love I *had* for Jasper died the day I opened my eyes in that hospital bed—all bandaged and wired up—and realized that *he* was the one who did that to me."

I swipe my tears away, then reach for my flute, gulping down the rest of my drink. I decide not to mention to her my six A.M. flight tomorrow morning leaving for Los Angeles to spend the day with my son. I don't know how much information I can trust her with. Right now, she seems too emotionally fragile.

I take a deep breath. "Jasper may be my son's father. And—at first, even after he threatened to beat him out of me if I told anyone what really happened to me—I still wasn't willing to ever keep him from being in Jaylen's life. But, now, after that motherfucker threatened to put a bullet in my head, then turned around the next day and had one of his goons shoot at me, the only way he'll ever see my son is through a court order."

Shock washes over her face and her jaw drops. "Ohmygod! What? When?"

I fill her in, then say, "I'm done with pretending that I don't spend every waking moment hating his ass, and wanting him to pay for what he did to me." I lean in and lower my voice. "After what he's done, his ass is as good as dead."

Mona gives me a pained look. Her eyes fill with tears. "Has Jasper no fucking shame, no conscience? I know he's my cousin. But I truly fucking despise him for what he's done to you. I can't stand to look at him, or be anywhere around him right now. And now to hear him threatening to kill you and having you shot at." She shakes her head, choking back tears. "Jasper is going too far."

"And you *still* don't think he's a *psychopath*?"

She lets out a disgusted grunt. "After everything you've told me, I don't know what to think. I'm still having a hard time digesting everything. And, honestly, a part of me doesn't want to believe it. But I know it's true. Still…" She shifts her eyes around the room, then looks back at me, exhaling deeply as if she's struggling to keep things in perspective. "It hurts knowing it's true. It hurts knowing Jasper's more cold-blooded and heartless than I ever imagined. Seems like all of them niggas on my father's side of the family, with the exception of Stax and Sparks, have a screw or two loose. Jasper, Jaheim, Dez…"

I blink. *She can't possibly be talking about Desmond, my cousin Paris' man.* "Dez? Your cousin *Desmond*?"

She nods. "Unfortunately, yes. Why you think he spent six years in prison?" I give her a blank stare. By the expression on my face she knows I had no clue he'd been locked up.

Locked up for what?

"Dez is happy-handed," Mona continues as if she's read my thoughts. "He's beat up at least three of his girlfriends; that *I* know of. There's no telling how many others." I blink, wondering if Paris knows this. "The last girlfriend he had, he beat the shit out of her so bad she was in a coma for almost two weeks. They tried to get him for attempted murder, but somehow his high-priced attorney got it down to an aggravated assault charge, and something else. I think it was a weapons charge or something."

I'm stunned by this news. And I'm even more surprised that she's sitting here telling me as much as she is. Whenever it's come to members of her family, especially when it has anything to do with her brother, Sparks, and her male cousins, she's always been guarded and extremely protective of them, of what she says.

She looks away for a brief moment. "I know every family has their share of secrets. And you already know mine is no exception. But from what other family members have said, and from what I've gathered from overhearing some of Sparks' hushed conversations over the years, all of them niggas, Jaheim, Jasper, Dez, and about six other cousins of mine have done some real scary shit."

Yeah like…

Kidnap, beat, and sexually assault me.

Molest you.

And attempt to rape and kill Booty.

My heart leaps in my throat. "Um, why'd Desmond beat her, his girlfriend, up like that?" The question is stammered. I bite the inside of my cheek, holding my breath.

Mona shifts in her seat. "I'm not really sure of all the details. But, from what I remember, he caught her in bed with another guy."

I swallow back a wave of emotions pulsing through me as I look her in the eyes and ask, "And what happened to the nigga he caught her cheating with?"

I watch as her eyes shift nervously around the room before she finally lands them on me. She whispers, "They never found his body."

My voice catches in the back of my throat. I open my mouth to say something, but nothing comes out. Frantically, I start scrolling through my memory bank, drudging through snapshots of my last horrible night down in that basement, where I'd lost track of time, lost hope, lost every last piece of me—tied up, used up, and beaten up.

The basement door opens at the top of the stairs, and a bunch of loud, rowdy niggas come stomping down the stairs. In my mind's eye, I can see all of them, standing there in their different colored basketball shorts, talking shit and cat-calling as they grab their crotches and stroke their dicks.

As I'm sitting here quickly sorting through that sordid night, I'm now wondering why they didn't keep me blindfolded, why they'd allowed me to see as much of them as I did. Did they think I'd be too traumatized to remember anything else? Did they think I wouldn't get out of there alive? Or did they just not really give a fuck?

Red Shorts comes to view. His large hand is squeezing my face. A blunt dangles out of his mouth, smoke blowing in my face. *"Yo, ma, you pretty as fuck. But I will beat you the fuck up if you scrape, cut, or bite my shit, ya dig?"*

Ohmygod…what if…?

I swallow. "Mona…w-w-what *if*…" I try to shake the thought out of my head, but it sticks to the surface. Somehow it fits. Somehow it makes sense. Mona said it herself. She's practically admitted it. Her cousins, the *three* of them, are capable of almost anything. Jasper's already proven that. Jaheim's proven it.

"Bitch, I will fuckin' kill you…"

I can feel the blood draining from my face.

"What *if* what?" Mona pushes, her stare intently locked onto mine. Her eyes taking in the look of shock, then dread, plastered all over my face. "Pasha, what is it? Are you okay? You look like you're about to faint."

I swallow hard. A burning feeling of panic slowly rises up in the pit of my stomach. "What *if* Desmond is…*was*…there, too? What if *he* was another one of those niggas forcing me to suck his dick?"

She gasps. Behind her stretched open lids, I think I see a flicker of possibility behind the fear in her eyes. She falls back in her seat, the color in her face draining.

"Ohgod, no."

Thirty-Two

A bitch caught in a fire will either end up burnt,
or eventually rise from the ashes...

"Hey. Thanks for calling me back," I say, flipping through tomorrow's appointments. I glance at my watch, checking the time. It's a little after eight-thirty in the evening. It's been a long day, but I'm energized. Having lunch in the city with Mona earlier was exactly what I needed. It gave me life. It gave me perspective. And most importantly, it gave me validation.

That my anger is justified.

That my need for justice is warranted.

That I've suffered long enough.

That reconciliation is not an option.

That retribution is the *only* way I'll ever be free.

"Ohmygod, no," Mona shrieked when I told her that if I found out her cousin Desmond was also involved in any way with what had happened to me, that he was going to catch it, too. She did everything she could to keep it together. But the possibility of him being there is real. And I meant what I said.

I narrowed my eyes. "For his sake, Mona. I *hope* he wasn't involved. But if he was, he'll suffer the consequences along with everyone else. He's going to wish he'd never pulled his dick out and shoved in my mouth."

She leaned forward. "Pasha, please tell me." She blinks twice. Her hand goes up over her mouth, a look of terror in her eyes. She takes several deep breaths. "Ohmygod, Pasha," she pushed out in a whisper. "You're *not* thinking about having any of them… *killed*, are you?"

I took a deep breath, mulled the question over in my head, then blew out my answer. "I don't know."

"Ohmygod, Pasha. This is going to become one big bloody mess. It's bad enough JT's considered *missing* and his body might not ever be found." She wiped tears, shaking her head. "I don't think my family will be able to handle any more tragic losses. I don't think *I* can. I love my cousins, Pasha—all of them. But I know they've done some grimy shit. I wasn't the one down in that basement. I can't even imagine what that was like for you."

"It was *fucking* horrible, Mona. And something I'd never wish on anyone." My eyes become narrow slits of rage. "What Jasper had done to me was brutal. Only a fucking wild animal would orchestrate the shit he pulled. And *anyone* who was callous and cold-hearted enough to want to participate needs to fucking pay, Mona. And they will. By whatever means necessary."

"Why won't you just go to the police? Tell them everything you know. Let them niggas go to prison for what they did; especially now that he's threatened to kill you."

My face was expressionless, my tone low and chilling. "No; I'm not trusting the police, or some jury to decide what any of their fates should be. From here on out, I'm going to become the judge and the jury. So going to prison for any of them niggas isn't an option until, *after*, I'm done with them; until every last one of them suffers so bad that they *beg* me to put them out of their misery. So the less you know, Mona, the better."

She reached over and squeezed my hand, fighting back tears. "I'm scared to death, Pasha."

I knew she was scared. I knew what she's scared of. Yet, she trusted me enough to show me her wounds, to spill open her hurt, and place her own secrets into my hands. Confirming what I already knew I *needed* to do. What I *had* to do.

Once we finally left the restaurant and got into the comfort of my car, Mona broke down. She cried for almost half the ride before she was finally able to pull herself together. I let her be. She needed to purge. Needed to cleanse, to rid her self of whatever guilt she harbored. She needed to mentally prepare herself for the emotional storm that was about to come.

By the time I pulled in front of her house, she had calmed significantly. Fortunately, no one was home to see her swollen, bloodshot eyes. She sat still for several moments, before slowly opening the door. She leaned over and gave me a hug.

"You might as well…" Her voice cracked as she choked back tears. "…finish what Cassandra started. Whatever you have to do, Pasha. Make *all of them* niggas pay." With that, she got out, shut the door, then walked toward the house. I waited for her to open her door, then hit the horn twice, driving off as it shut behind her.

Mona, unknowingly, lit the flame in my spirit.

And, right after I dropped her off, I made a quick call to Felecia to confirm our meeting tonight, then drove straight here to the salon with a renewed fire, with a burning conviction, tearing up my office until I found what I was looking for. The business card… *his* business card.

James Larson.

A tall, delicious, dark-skinned nigga with—what I recall—deep, piercing brown eyes and full lips, with a neatly trimmed goatee and dreads framing his chiseled face with its high-cheekbones. An IT tech who'd strolled into the salon *twice*, both times with his fiancée—a new client that messy-ass Shuwanda had brought in. He sat right here, in this waiting area for her to get her hair done.

The minute our eyes met, I *knew* who he was.

My worst fear realized.

That, one day, one of the niggas who'd respond to my Deep Throat Diva ads on NastyFreaks4u.com, in search of some slow, wet head, would somehow find their way into my salon. And—on that very day, the day he walked toward Shuwanda's workstation to get his fiancée's car keys, it happened.

My indiscretions had finally greeted me at the door.

I can remember feeling relieved, *hopeful*, when he didn't seem to recognize who I was. Or realize that I'd recognized him. But that quickly changed two weeks later when he walked out of the salon behind me, glanced over his shoulder toward the salon's door, then licked his lips and told me I looked familiar to him; that he couldn't put his finger on it at first, until he got home, then it hit him. "I'd never forget a face or set of lips like yours."

My knees almost buckled.

He sensed my uneasiness, quickly reassuring me that he wouldn't expose me. "Don't worry…your secret is safe with me. I just wanted to let you know, I remember who you are. Shit. I actually haven't stopped thinking about that night in the park."

I swallowed my nerves as he told me how I'd given him the most mind-blowing head job he'd ever experienced in his life. I had no idea what park I had sucked him at. I'd had my share of park 'n' suck action in more than one park, so it didn't matter where I'd done it. The fact was, he remembered me. That he'd sent me an attachment of his hard dick. And I slipped out of my home in the middle of the night, met him at some park, then greedily sucked him in the backseat of his car.

"I have to admit," James says, cutting into my reverie. "I was pleasantly surprised to hear your voice. I thought you might have tossed my business card out after I'd given it to you." I tell him for some reason I held on to it, not really knowing if I'd ever have a reason to use it. "I won't lie and say I didn't hope you were calling to offer me another, you know…round of—"

I roll my eyes up in my head, stopping him. "No, no. I assure you that *that* definitely wasn't the purpose for my call."

He chuckles. "I figured as much. Hey, can't knock a guy for dreaming. But, uh, anyway…your message said you wanted to know if I would be able to track down an email IP address for you."

"Yes, that's right," I say, logging back into my MacBook, then clicking on AOL. I log into my Deep Throat Diva account to retrieve my emails. My hands start to shake. My heart starts racing. It's been well over a year since I've signed into this email account. I'd had no reason to. Not after what I went through.

I'd shut down my Deep Throat Diva page, and cancelled my membership on NastyFreaks4u.com a few weeks after my release from the hospital. But still held on to this email address, saved every last email from anyone I'd met online and ever sucked off. Or intended to suck off, but then got to the designated location and changed my mind when a nigga misled me; when he pulled out a teenie-weenie dicklet instead of the long, luscious dick— that lured me out into the still of the night in the first place—he'd attached in his email; or because he was dirty, fat, disabled, disfigured, handicapped, a burn victim, excessively ugly, or all the above. Had them all categorized in folders. BIG DICKS. SMALL DICKS. STUMPY DICKS. UGLY DICKS. PRETTY DICKS. QUICK NUTS.

PIGLETS. DIRT BAGS. CRAZIES. ONE-TIME SUCKS. DOUBLE ROUNDS.

I don't bother concerning myself with any of the 138 unopened emails. It's not what I'm on here for. I click on BIGDICK&CRAZY, then scroll through the folder until I find the email I'm looking for. MydikneedsUrtongue2@gmail.com.

I take a deep breath as I open the last email I received. It's an attachment. A picture of his thick, veiny dick. I shut my eyes. Behind my lids, I sort through the hard dicks stubbornly embedded in my mind; the dicks of every last nigga I was forced to deep throat. Forced to suck the nut out of. Forced to swallow. Nothing registers. His long dick, the bulbous head, his low hanging balls…aren't attached to any of the niggas. Niggas who have now become high-priority targets.

"That won't be a problem," James says confidently. "I'll need for you to forward whatever emails you might have."

I open the previous email received from him. *U sucked me off about three weeks ago. I haven't had my dick sucked like that since. Wanted to get at u again but got locked up. But I'm home now and ready for another round, tonight or sometime this weekend. U really know how to handle a dick. The whole time I was in the county, that's all I kept thinking about.*

Then I open the email prior to the one I just opened. The subject heading reads: U GOT ME FEENIN'! I click it open. *Hey, baby. Wats good withcu? I wanna feel ur tongue on my dick again. Let's meet up.*

I know I'm going out on a limb here. Know I'm taking a risk allowing this…this stranger…this man who—other than the size of his dick and the way it felt in my mouth—I know nothing about. Yet, I feel like he is trustworthy. Feel like he has something to lose as well as I do if discretion isn't exercised. And, if I have to get my knees dirty one last time with this nigga to get the job done, then I'm willing to do *what*ever I need to do, to ensure this is handled with care. So if that means pulling open my bag of dick-sucking tricks to get what I need, then so be it. After all, it's not like I've never had his dick in my mouth before. Besides, the horny nigga's already stated he'd like another round of this deep throat.

I smirk. "I can do that." I ask him for his email address, pressing the FORWARD tab for the emails I plan to send him. "However, I need to tell you that what I'm sending you is extremely personal and an extremely delicate matter that I need handled discreetly." I lower my voice to a seductive whisper. "Can I *trust* you to do that for me, James? Be *discreet?*"

"No doubt, no doubt. I got you. Whatever it is, you can trust me on this. Like I told you the day we spoke outside your hair salon, I won't put you out like that."

"Thank you. I appreciate that. And I appreciate you being willing to help me. Now tell me, James, *what* will this cost me?"

"Oh, no worries, beautiful. There's no *cost...*" He clears his throat, then lowers his voice. "But, uh, listen. I still think about... you know, that night."

I smirk, forwarding him the emails. *Of course you do. They all do.* "Do you now?" I decide to fuck with him. Tell him to tell me what he still thinks about.

"The way them pretty lips felt wrapped about my dick. And how wet, warm, and juicy your mouth was. How tight your throat was. How you swallowed my whole dick. Then was able to lick on my balls. I think about that whole experience. I'ma be honest with you. The minute I heard your voice on my phone, my dick got hard. Hell, it's still hard."

I shake my head. I think to ask him about his fiancée, if they'd tied the knot or not, then decide against it.

"Okay, I got the emails."

"Good." I breathe a heavy sigh of relief.

"Listen. I know you said you didn't want to go another round, but I was thinking, uh, maybe…you can show me your appreciation by…you *know*. Letting me get some of that head work again."

"*Miss Pasha, girl, do whatever you gotta do to fish them no-good nigga-coons…It's time to take it to them nigga-bitches' skulls…*"

Oh, yes it is. And this motherfucker right here will be the first one to get gutted.

"*Yo, u think u can get all up in a nigga's head, then dismiss him? That's peace. Stuck-up bitch!!!!!*"

Buckle up, you psycho motherfucker! I'm about to fuck *you good!*

I stare at the computer screen, narrow my eyes at the address, then click to compose a new email.

Hey, boo. I'm not sure if you even remember me. You responded to one of my ads on NastyFreaks4u a while ago. We met and I sucked your dick once. Anyway, I was going through old emails and stumbled on one of yours. The one you sent me of your big, juicy dick. I've been sitting here staring at it up on my computer screen with no panties on, fingering myself. Mouth watering. Throat tingling. Tonsils aching. I'm so horny to feel a long dick stretching my neck out. Would love for it to be yours. I know the last time you emailed me looking for some of this bomb-head service, I told you I wasn't interested. Well, I've had a change of heart. I've been out of commission for a while, but I'm back now with a throat load of new tricks. And I'm eager, ready, and very hungry to suck some good dick. Hope you have something good for me, daddy. Can't wait to taste you…

Deep Throat Diva

I reread the email, then press SEND.

Now, let the games begin…

"So, uh, we good on that?" James asks. "I look out for you. And you *bless* me with one more round."

"I tell you what, James. I need to know exactly where those emails were sent from. You get me that info, and I promise *you* a nice, slow, wet…very *personalized* thank you."

I can practically see him licking his lips and grabbing his hard dick. "All I need is a few days."

A sly grin eases across my lips. "And all I'll need is that thick hard dick."

"I got you, sexy. Damn. You got my dick so…"

"Exactly how I like it." He groans in my ear, then quickly says he has to hurry off the phone to jack his shit before his wife gets home. I hang up, laughing just as I'm greeted with the "you've got mail" voice. I click on my inbox. "Well, well, well…look what we got here," I say as I'm opening the email.

MydikneedsUrtongue2. *Oh, shit, yo! Word? Ya whore-ass back on dick patrol? That's what it is. Yeah, u can cum hop down on dis dick. I gotta three day load u can suck outta deez balls. When u tryna meet up? My dick def could use some of that tongue n throat work. I ain't met a bitch yet who suck dick as good as u. Holla back, baby. I wanna fuck dat throat raw.*

Nigga, please!

I look down at the calendar on the desk, then open the schedule book, flipping through the pages to see which day or night this week I can meet this crazy fucker to finally serve his ass a deep dish of street justice. My way!

I reply back. *Oooh, yes, big daddy, talk that dirty shirt to me. Reading your email got my mouth wet and my pussy juicing. Let's meet next Friday night. I'll shoot you an email sometime Thursday afternoon with the exact time and place. Please, let's keep this on the low.*

I glance up at the time. It's five minutes to nine. I'm pissed at myself for telling Felecia that I'd meet her here at nine o'clock. *Fucking with this bitch is going to have me missing tonight's episode of* The Good Wife.

It takes less than three minutes for Mydik to reply back. *Aiight no doubt. Yo, long as u don't front on a nigga, we good. Bring me dat wet throat n let me skull fuck u til I bust this nut down in ya neck…in't gotta worry about me sayin shit. I wanna keep ya sexy dick suckin ass on speed dial, yo. Run me dem digits.*

I smirk. *Nigga, when I'm done with you, you're going to regret the day you ever laid eyes on me.* I forward James the remaining emails, then sign out. I shut my laptop down just as Felecia knocks standing at the door. I get up from my seat, making my way over to open it, stepping aside to let her in.

"Hey," she says, stepping inside. "It's good to see you." I pull the door tight behind her, willing myself from yanking her by her long blonde weave and swinging her face right through this motherfucking glass window.

I glare at her. "Bitch, this *isn't* a social call." I slam both hands up on my hips. "All I wanna know is, did you *fuck* Jasper?"

Thirty-Three

The day of reckoning comes when a two-faced bitch finally gets knocked on her back!

"What*?*" Felecia scowls.

"*Bitch*, I didn't stutter. Did *you* let Jasper run his dick up in you?"

She shuffles her weight from one heel-clad foot to the other; shifting her Michael Kors bag over to her right hand as she glances around the salon. Doing everything possible to avert my glare. But the bitch can't hide. And there's no running. Not this time. She needs to own her shit; admit the fuck what she's done. So we can move on.

I eye her as she pulls in a breath. She looks at me. Calmly states, "No, Pasha. I didn't *sleep* with Jasper, if that's what you're so worried about." She doesn't bat an eye when she says this. Doesn't even flinch. Still, after all the lies I've told, after all the things I've tried to cover up, I *know* when a bitch is lying.

"Bitch," I sneer, shooting her an icy-glare, "be clear. *That's* not what the fuck I'm so worried about."

She frowns. "Then why are you even asking me about it then? And why the hell would you listen to shit some low-budget ghetto bitch would tell you? You let that bitch get all up in your ear and got *you* turning your back on *me*."

I *tsk*. "No, hun. Get it right. *You* let Jasper's dick get all up in your guts and got *you* standing here lying to me. So save it. You're a lying, *sneaky*, conniving bitch."

She huffs. "Look, Pasha, I didn't come here to fight with you. But it's obvious that's what you have in mind."

"Well, I *know* you didn't come here expecting me to roll out the red carpet for your snake-ass and offer up a tea party. So why the fuck are you here?"

"Because you called *me*. And I was *hoping* we could talk this out like two mature, civilized adults. That we could work things out and not let all the bullshit going on right now come between us. But I see all you wanna do is hurl insults and point fingers."

I hear Booty's instigating voice in my head saying, *"Oooh, Miss FeFe is so full of hot skunk shit. Greasy-ass nigga-bitch! Fish this messy bitch, Miss Pasha, girl. Then gut her ass real good."*

"Bitch, you let Jasper's dick come between us the day you spread open…" I take a deep breath. Bite down on my bottom lip. Remember my real purpose. Remind myself to stay on track. I rewind. Switch gears to reel this ho in. I stare at her. "You know what, Felecia, you're right. I did call you. We're family. And we've been through too much together to not be able to at least clear the air. I'm fucking pissed at you. I still love you. But I'm hurt that after *everything* we've been through, you can't even be honest with me."

Her eyes quickly dart around the room again. "And, *I'm* hurt that you'd believe some ghetto-trash *bitch* like Cassandra over *me*—your flesh and blood."

Blah, blah, blah…bitch, please!

I feign a pained smile, placing my left hand in back of me, feeling along the small of my back. "Then I guess we *both* have shit to get off our chests. C'mon, let's go into my office." I drop my hands to my side, walking toward my office, smirking as she follows behind me. *This dizzy bitch must really think I'm retarded.* I wait until she walks all the way inside my office, then shut the door and lock it.

"Have a seat." I point to the two leather chairs that are normally positioned in front of my desk, but are now placed in the center of the room, facing each other.

Her eyes open wide, noticing the nearly empty space. "What happened to all your furniture?" The only furniture still in my large office is my mahogany desk, which I have pushed up against a wall. And matching bookshelf that is pressed up against one of the sidewalls, where it's always been. Everything else has been temporarily shifted over into the staff lounge.

I toss her a dismissive wave. "Oh, I had it all moved out. I'm having my office redone."

"Oh," is all she says as she pulls a chair back, and eases her ass onto the seat. She sets her bag on the carpeted floor beside her. I plant my chair directly in front of her, then sit.

I cross my legs, and tell her my reason for having us sit like this, face-to-face. "It's a face-off." She blinks her eyes, giving me a confused look. "I have shit to say to you. And obviously you have some shit you want to say to me as well. All I want is the truth. So in order for me to trust that that's what I'm going to get, I want to be dead in your face, looking you in the eyes as we talk." I widen my eyes for effect, then blink them twice, tilting my head. "So why don't you go, first, Felecia. Whatever you have to say to me, get it off your chest, now. And you can *start* by giving it to me raw and uncut. Tell the fucking truth."

She shifts in her seat. "Okay. I don't appreciate how *you* fucking humiliated me in front of everyone. You had *no* fucking right to slap me in front of clients like that. You had *no* fucking right to fire me! And you had *no* fucking right to tell other salon owners to not fucking hire me! Then you still block my unemployment claim! Who the fuck are *you* to fuck with my money, Pasha, huh?"

It takes everything in me to not leap up and knock her head back. I give her an incredulous look, gripping the sides of my chair to keep my ass planted in my seat.

"Bitch!" I snap. "And *you* had no fucking *right* to be talking shit about *me* behind *my* back. But you did, didn't you? Fucking dirty bitch! You wanna know who I fucking am? I'm the *bitch* who trusted you! *I'm* the bitch who loved you like a goddamn sister! I'm the bitch who gave *you* a motherfucking job! And paid *you* seventy-thousand-a-goddamn-year. That's *who* the fuck I am. I did that shit for you, Felecia. *For what?* So you can turn around and stab me in the motherfucking back?! Bitch, please!"

She blinks. Opens her mouth to speak, but I put a hand up in her face, shutting her ass down.

"So yeah, bitch, I blackballed your ass. I shut your shit all the waaaaay *fucking* down. You wanna work in another hair salon, sweetie, then you had better take your ass up to Bergen or Hudson county where bitches don't know you. Or drive your two-faced ass way down to the shore to work. Because—*unless* you plan on working in some white-owned salon or up in some home-based makeshift salon—you will *not* be working *any*where in this area. Not in a black-owned shop, that's for sure. You *think* you can talk about me, fuck my man, then turn around and smile all up in my goddamn face and *think* I'm gonna be good with it? You got me the fuck confused."

Her chest starts heaving. Her nose spreads. Her eyes narrow to slits. I can tell she's ready to go off. And that's exactly what I want. "Yeah, go 'head and blow your stack, *bitch*. Let's see your true colors."

"Look, *bitch!*" she screeches, leaning up in her chair, slamming a hand on her hip, snaking her neck and pointing her finger at me.

"I've been trying to keep my cool with you, trying to not bring it to you. But you keep testing me. You got shit you wanna say to me, then say it. You got shit you wanna ask me, then ask. But what you not gonna do is think I'm gonna keep sitting here and let you keep calling me all kinds of bitches and shit. For the last time, *bitch*, Jasper and I've never fucked! End of discussion! And if we did, so the fuck what! You have a lot of fucking nerve to sit there and call me out on shit, like you're so fucking perfect. Bitch, ain't shit perfect about you!

"But you always somewhere tryna act like you so much fucking better than me when *you're* the one who was out there sucking all kinds of different niggas' dicks in dark alleys and fucking abandoned buildings and wherever else you could go to drop down on your slutty-ass knees. So don't toss shit on me *unless* you're ready to toss it on yourself as well."

I almost laugh. Almost. *There you go, bitch. All I have to do is keep pressing the right buttons. Tell me how you really feel!* I narrow my eyes.

I imagine Booty saying some shit like, *"Oooh, Miss Pasha, that messy bitch is really tryna do you, goddammit. Don't take it to her face, yet. Keep fishin' this bitch, sugah-boo. Gut that bitch when she least expects it."*

I uncross my legs, shifting back in my seat and crossing them at the ankle, folding my arms across my chest. "Bitch," I calmly state. "I *never* said I was perfect, nor have I ever *thought* I was. Obviously, that's some of your shit, that's what *you* think." I smirk. "You wanna talk about *my* dick sucking, then let's. Yeah, I *sucked* a whole lot of dick, sweetie…lots of it. And many of 'em I swallowed, okay. But I've *never* sucked a nigga's dick in an alley, abandoned building or any other shit. So get it right."

She blinks, shifting in her seat. Her eyes flicker a hint of surprise by my candor.

"I *sucked* niggas outside in their cars. *Sucked* them in parks. *Sucked* them in parking garages. *Sucked* them in hotels and motels. I'm a slutty, dick-sucking whore, okay, who *sucked* every last one of them niggas to sleep. And *sucked* a few other niggas right out of their minds until they *stalked* me.

"And, yeah, bitch. I did it *all* behind Jasper's back. And why did I do it? I did it because that's what the fuck I wanted to do. I did it because I thought I could get away with it. Did I know there might be consequences? Yeah, I knew it. Did I care…*obviously* not because I kept on doing the shit. I made those choices. And I suffered the consequences for them. Now riddle me this, since we confessing our sins: "How many times did *you* suck Jasper's dick?"

She blinks, frowning. "W-w-what?"

"Mmmph. Here you go again stuttering again." I stare into her, letting a silent pause eat through her skin. She starts to look slightly uncomfortable. *Good, bitch!* "Answer the question. How many times did you have your fucking greasy-ass lips wrapped around Jasper's dick? Speak now or forever hold your piece, *bitch*, because I promise you. *This* will be your *only* chance to make amends with me before I beat the fuck out of you. So you had better confess what the fuck you did."

She jumps up from her seat, starts talking shit with her hands. "What? *Bitch*, are you fucking serious?! You're fucking going to sit there and threaten *me?* I'm not tryna fight you, bitch, but don't think I'm going to let you jump on me, either."

"Felecia, admit it. You sucked Jasper's dick. *Why?* Because you're a jealous, hating-ass, miserable bitch who wishes she could be me."

She huffs. "Oh, give me a fucking break, Pasha! You're fucking delusional, bitch, to think some shit like that. I don't wanna be you, or anything like *you!*"

"Bitch, lies. You've been jealous of me ever since we were kids.

Why? Because I was everything you wanted to be then. And I'm *everything* you wish you could ever be now. You *wish* you could have half of what I have. And that includes having Jasper. But, newsflash, *bitch:* You could *never* be me. And you will *never* have what I have. You wanna know why? Because bitches like you are only good for a wet fuck. You ain't nothing but a bottom-feeder, bitch. Jasper would never be with your dumb ass. Yeah, he might let you eat the nut out his dick. And he *might* even drop a few dollars on you. But you'd *never* have my spot. The only spot you'd ever have is down on your knees either sucking his dick or getting fucked in your ass, bitch!"

She shoots me a dirty look, walking a hole in the carpet. "Pasha, *think* what the fuck you want, okay. Since you seem to have all the answers, why the fuck you sitting there asking me, huh?"

I let out a disgusted grunt. "You're fucking pathetic. You're pacing back and forth, like some caged animal, trapped and scared, tryna figure out a way to escape the truth. Bitch, there's no way out. And here's the truth: you wanted a piece of me. And all that nigga tossed you were a bunch of scraps.

"You *thought* you were gonna get the mansion, and the Benz, and the long dollars that come with fucking with a nigga like Jasper. But it didn't happen that way for you, did it? No. It never does, especially for a backstabbing bitch like you. At the end of the day, you *still* wasn't good enough. You'll *never* be good enough. Even after you sucked that nigga's nut out and snitched on me, you still end up right where the fuck you started. With nothing! Stupid bitch!

"What, did he toss you a few fucking dollars for wetting his dick? Did he promise to keep you laced in handbags and shit? Bitch, admit it. You sucked his fucking dick. Admit *you* betrayed *me*—the bitch who always looked out for you—for a hard goddamn dick and a wad of hot cum!"

Finally, I hit the right nerve. Push the right buttons, and the truth starts shooting out of her mouth, hot and angry. Everything she's ever felt roars out of her mouth like a wild burning fire.

"Bitch! You *want* the fucking truth? Then here it is *raw and uncut:* I love you. But I fucking *hate* you more! And, *yes*, I sucked Jasper's dick! There, you satisfied! I sucked his dick, okay! Why? Because I fucking wanted to! You didn't fucking deserve a nigga like him! Bitch, you had it good. Jasper gave you *any*thing you wanted, and that shit still wasn't enough for you. You still went and shitted on him. It's always about *you*, bitch! Pasha this, Pasha, that! The fly bitch who always gets what she wants. Who always gets all the right niggas eating outta the palm of her goddamn hands!

"And bitches like me, who know how to treat a good man, gotta stand on the sidelines and watch bitches like *you* fuck over all the good men. You fucking slutted yourself out on Jasper and that nigga *still* wanted *you!* The nigga still stayed with *you*. I fucking told him what the fuck *you* were—" She catches herself before she finishes what I already know. She stares at me, gauging my reaction as if she's waiting for me to jump up and start hooking off on her.

But I simply sit, still. Emotionless. Staring at her, through her. And I'm surprisingly calm…*too* calm. I can tell she's taken aback by how composed I am, how unmoved I am.

I let my stare and the stillness in the room slice into her soul before finally saying, "I already *knew*. So there's no need to stop. Finish telling me how you backstabbed me; how you told Jasper shit I told, *asked*, you to keep between us. You told that nigga shit hoping he'd leave me for you. So, tell me. How'd you make out with that?" I shake my head, feeling my anger boiling up through the pit of my stomach. "You hated me *that* much, knowing how fucking crazy Jasper was, to shit on me. Because of *you*, I was almost beaten to death. Because of *you*, my son almost lost his life."

She scowls. "No, bitch! You were almost beat to death because of *you*. Not *me*. Had you kept your lips off of other niggas' dicks, none of that would have happened to you. *You* did that, bitch…" She cast her eyes downward, pausing. She swipes a tear. "You got what the fuck *you* deserved."

I count to ten in my head. Inhale. Exhale. Then slowly rise from my chair, looking dead into my cousin's eyes. My heart aches. Not for me. Not for her. But for our Nana. Tears well up in my eyes. I fight them back.

I clench my teeth, glaring at her. "You have *no* fucking idea what *you* did to me, what Jasper did to me! Maybe I did deserve it. But, bitch, I *didn't* deserve to be snaked by *you*. Your loyalty should have been to *me*. Unlike *you*, I have *never* hated on you. Have *never* disrespected you, or talked shit about *you* behind your back. I couldn't care less about you sucking Jasper's dick. And I don't give a fuck if he fucked you or not. But, *bitch*, what I do give a fuck about is the fact that *you* fucked me over. And what I find most interesting, is that not *once* did you apologize for stabbing me in the back."

"Because I didn't fucking care, Pasha, okay! I didn't fucking care! And I still don't! Fuck you, bitch! After everything and *you* still landed on your feet, bitch!" Her lips quiver. "I wish I could tell you that I feel sorry for what I did. But I don't!" A tear drops from her eye.

I leer, taking her in. Disgusted. Saddened. To think, it's come to this. Emptiness. Whatever I've felt for her is gone. Dead. Buried.

I look at this bitch and feel *nothing*.

The more she talks, the longer she's in my face, the more tears she sheds, it becomes painfully clear what will become of her, of us. This is how it will end.

And my mind is made up. After tonight, this bitch is literally dead to me!

She reaches for her bag. "And you wanna know something else, Pasha, since it's finally all out in the open. I lied. I *did* fuck Jasper. I'm *still* fucking…" I don't let the rest of her sentence roll off of her slimy-ass tongue. In one swift motion I hit the bitch dead in the throat, causing her to gasp for air as I wrap my hands in her weave and swing the bitch into the wall.

I don't give her a chance to recover from the blow to her throat. I knee her in the stomach. Finally her voice comes in a loud piercing scream as she hunches over, clutching her stomach. I swing her into the bookcase.

"Ohmygod! Nooooo! I-I-I'm preg…" She gasps for more air. She heaves loudly. The bitch doesn't even see it coming when I snatch the crystal paperweight from off the bookcase and smash it in her face. She howls like a wounded animal. Blood gushes out of her mouth and nose.

"Bitch, I don't give a fuck about you being pregnant! You didn't give a fuck about me when you were running your motherfucking mouth to Jasper. I was pregnant, bitch, when I almost ended up dead, thanks to you and Jasper and all the rest of those niggas." I crack her in the face again, causing her to hit the floor. Now I am crying. Snot and spit is flying everywhere along with Felecia's spurting blood.

I stand over top of her, stomping and kicking the shit out of her. She curls up in a ball, screaming and yelling and begging. I stomp her in the head. "Bitch, you can scream all you want. Why the fuck you think I had these walls soundproofed over the summer, huh, bitch?" I kick her in the back. "To keep nosey bitches like you from hearing what the fuck goes on in here. So scream all you want!"

I grab a handful of her weave and yank her head back. She tries to fight me off of her, but her blows are weak. I've knocked the bitch's wind out of her. Caught the bitch slipping. "Bitch, you have no idea what the fuck you've done! You have no idea who the fuck I've become!"

I drop the bloodied paperweight. It hits the carpet with a loud thud as I reach in the back of me in one smooth motion and pull out the gun I have tucked in the waist of my jeans. The minute she sees the shiny chrome in my hand, she starts trying to scurry away, pleading.

"Bitch, go cry me a river some-fucking-where else. The minute you got in Jasper's ear, *you* tossed me to the fucking wolves. And for that, I will *never* fucking forgive you. So save the Oprah special. *You* have fucking sealed your fate!"

"No, P-P-Pasha, p-p-please. Y-y-you don't have to do this. I'm t-t-two months' preg…" I bang her in the mouth with the butt of the gun, knocking out teeth. She cries out, covering her mouth with her hands. Tears and blood and snot are smeared all over her face. Her nose and mouth are still bleeding.

I hit her upside the head, knocking her back.

There's no turning back now. The line in the sand has already been crossed. This bitch made her choice. Now I'm making mine.

I slam the tip of the silencer in her mouth, shoving it as far down as it'll go. She gags. I lean in, then say in a voice that does not sound like my own, "I'm going to show you what you helped Jasper do to me. You wanna live, bitch?" She rapidly nods her head. She tries to speak, but I ram the gun further down into her throat. "Then suck this shit like a dick, bitch!" I slam the barrel in and out of her bloody mouth in deep, fast strokes. She gasps and gags as I pistol-fuck her face.

When I am sure I've knocked all of her front teeth out, I ease the gun out of her mouth and point it at her head. "I'm going to ask you this one time, Felecia, so don't fuck it up. You understand me?" She frantically nods. "*Whose* baby are you carrying?"

She blinks. Hysteria floods her eyes. I stare into them until the answer slowly rolls out along with her tears. "That's too bad, then." I pull back the slide ejector, chambering a round, then slam the gun back into her mouth. "I loved you, Felecia. Trusted you." My eyes burn with tears and anger and hurt. My lips curl into a sinister sneer. "Bitch, you *wanted* to be me. You *wanted* my life, to take my spot. You tried to take something from *me*."

Her eyes widen.

"Now I'm going to take something from *you*." For a split-second I think I see a sliver of guilt and regret swimming behind the pools of her pupils. I don't know. I don't care. I lean in, press my face inches from hers, clenching my teeth. "You crossed the *wrong* bitch!"

I count to five in my head.

Then pull the trigger.

To Be Continued…in *Ruthless: Deep Throat Diva 3!*

ABOUT THE AUTHOR

Cairo is the author of *Slippery When Wet, Big Booty, Man Swappers, Kitty-Kitty, Bang-Bang, Deep Throat Diva, Daddy Long Stroke, The Man Handler, The Kat Trap* and the e-book, *The Stud Palace*. His travels to Egypt inspired his pen name.

ONE

You ready to cum? Imagine this: A pretty bitch down on her knees with a pair of soft, full lips wrapped around the head of your dick. A hot, wet tongue twirling all over it, then gliding up and down your shaft, wetting that joint up real slippery-like, then lapping at your balls; lightly licking your asshole. Mmmm, I'm using my tongue in places that will get you dizzy, urging you to give me your hot, creamy, nut. Mmmmm, baby...you think you ready? If so, sit back, lie back, relax and let the Deep Throat Diva rock your cock, gargle your balls, and suck you straight to heaven.

I reread the ad, make sure it conveys exactly what I want, need, it to say, then press the PUBLISH tab. "There," I say aloud, glancing around my bedroom, then looking down at my left hand. "Let's see how many responses I get, this time."

Ummm, wait…before I say anything else. I already know some of you uptight bitches are already shaking your heads and rolling your eyes. So I know that what I'm about to tell ya'll is going to make some of you disgusted, and that's fine by me. It is what it is. And I know there's also going to be a bunch of you closeted, freaky bitches who are going to turn your noses up and twist up your lips, but secretly race to get home 'cause you just as nasty as I am. Hell, some of you are probably down on your knees as I speak, or maybe finishing up pulling a dick from out of your throats, or removing strands of pubic hair from in between your teeth. And that's fine by me as well. Do you, boo. But, let me say this: Don't any of you self-righteous hoes judge me.

So here goes. See. I have a man—dark chocolate, dreamy-eyed, sculpted and every woman's dream—who's been in incarcerated for four years, and he's releasing from prison in less than nine months. And, *yes*, I'm excited and nervous and almost scared to death—you'll know why in a minute. Annnywaaaay, not only is he a sexy-ass motherfucker, he knows how to grind, and stack paper. And he is a splendid lover. My God! His dick and tongue game can make a woman forget her name. And all the chicks who know him either want him, or want him back. And they'll do anything they can to try to disrupt my flow. Hating-ass hoes!

Nevertheless, he's coming home to *me*. The collect calls, the long drives, the endless nights of sexless sleep have taken a toll on me, and will all be over very soon. Between the letters, visits and keeping money on his books, I've been holding him down, faithfully. And I've kept my promise to him to not fuck any other niggas. I've kept this pussy tight for him. And it's been hard, *really* hard—no, no, hard isn't an accurate description of the agony I've had to bear not being fucked for over four years. It's been excruciating!

But I love Jasper, so I've made the sacrifice. For him, for us!

Still, I have missed him immensely. And I need him so bad. My pussy needs him, aches for the width of his nine-inch, veiny dick thrusting in and out of it. It misses the long, deep strokes of his thick tongue caressing my clit and its lower lips. I miss lying in his arms, of being held and caressed. But I have held out; denied any other niggas the privilege—*and* pleasure—of fucking this sweet, wet hole.

The problem is: Though I haven't been riding down on anything stiff, I've been doing a little anonymous dick sucking on the side from time-to-time—and, every now and then, getting my pussy ate—to take the edge off. Okay, okay, I'm lying. I've been sucking a lot of dick. But it wasn't supposed to be this way. I wasn't supposed to become hooked on the shit as if it were crack. But, I have. And I am.

Truth be told. It started out as inquisitiveness. I was bored. I was lonely. I was fucking horny. And tired of sucking and fucking dildos, pretending they were Jasper's dick. So I went on Nasty-freaks4u.com, a new website that's been around for about two years or so. About a year ago, I had overheard one of the regulars who gets her hair done down at my salon talking about a site where men and women post amateur sex videos, similar to that on Xtube, and also place sex ads. So out of curiosity, I went on their site, browsed around on it for almost a week before deciding to become a member and place my very own personal ad. I honestly wasn't expecting anything to come of it. And a part of me had hoped nothing would. But, lo and behold, my email became flooded with requests. And I responded back. I told myself that I'd do it one time, only. But once turned into twice, then twice became three more times, and now—a year-and-a-half later, I'm logged on *again*—still telling myself that *this* time will be the last time.

I stare at my ring finger. Take in the sparkling four-carat engagement ring. It's a nagging reminder of what I have; of what I could potentially end up losing. My reputation for one—as a successful, no-nonsense hairstylist and business owner of one the most upscale hair salons in the tri-state area; winner of two Bronner Brothers hair show competitions; numerous features in *Hype Hair* magazine, one of the leading hairstyle magazines for African-American women; and winner of the 2008 Global Salon Business Award, a prestigious award presented every two years to recognize excellence in the industry—could be tarnished. Everything I've worked so hard to achieve could be ruined in the blink of an eye.

My man, for another, could…will, walk out of my life. After he beats my ass, or worse—kills me. And I wouldn't blame him, not one damn bit. I know better than anyone that as passionate a lover Jasper is, he can be just as ruthless if crossed. He has no problem punching a nigga's lights out, smacking up a chick—or breaking her jaw, so I already know what the outcome will be if he ever finds out about my indiscretions. Yet I still choose to dance with deception, regardless of the outcome.

As hypocritical and deceitful as I've been, I can't ever forget it was Jasper who helped me get to where I am today. He's been the biggest part of my success, and I love him for that. Nappy No More wouldn't exist if it weren't for him believing in me, in my visions, and investing thousands of dollars into my salon eight years ago. Granted, I've paid him back and then some. And, yes, it's true. I put up with all the shit that comes with loving a man who's been caught up in the game. From his hustling and incarcerations to his fucking around on me in the early part of our relationship, I stood by him; loved him, no matter what. And I know more than anyone else that I've benefited from it. So as far as I'm concerned, I believe I owe him. He's put all of his trust in me, has given me his heart, and has always been damn good to me. And, yes, *this* is how I've been showing my gratitude—by creeping on the Internet.

He won't find out, I think, sighing as I remove my diamond ring from my hand, placing it in my jewelry case, then locking it in the safe with the rest of my valuables. Jasper had given me this engagement ring and proposed to me a month before he got sentenced while he was still out on bail. He wanted me to marry him before he got locked up, but I wanted to wait until he got released. Having a half-assed wedding was not an option. But, they'll be no wedding if I don't get my mind right and stop this shit, soon! *I'll stop all this craziness once he gets home.* This is what I tell myself; this is what I want to believe.

How many dicks have I sucked over the last year? Ummm, honestly, I wish I could tell you. Truth is I try not to give it much thought. Thinking about it would make me feel guiltier than I already do. Every time I walk back up in this spot and crawl back up into bed with thoughts of Jasper, every time he calls me and tells me how much he misses me and loves me and can't wait to get home to me, every time I sit in front of him at a visit, or when he looks into my eyes and he kisses me—it fucks with me. It eats away at my conscience. But, is it enough to make me stop? It should be. I swear I had hoped, wished, it would be. But it hasn't. Something keeps luring me right back on my knees sucking down another nigga's dick.

I sigh, remembering a time when I used to be so obsessed with being a good dick sucker that I used to practice sucking on a dildo. I had bought myself a nice black, seven-inch dildo at an adult bookstore when I was barely twenty. At first, it was a little uncomfortable. My eyes would water and I'd gag as the head hit the back of my throat. But, I didn't give up. I was determined to become a dick-swallowing pro. Diligently, I kept practicing every night before I went to bed until I was finally able to deep throat that rubber cock balls deep. Then I purchased an eight-inch, and practiced religiously until I was able to swallow it, too. Before long, I was able to move up to a nine-inch, then ten. And once I had them mastered, it was then, that I knew for certain I was ready to move on to the real thing. And I've been sucking dick ever since.

Funny thing, I've always prided myself on being a phenomenal head giver; on knowing how to take care of a man's dick—to not only suck it, but to make love to it. To slob it because I love it; because I adore it. There's something about slobbering all over a dick, twirling my tongue all over it—its slit slick with sweet precum, gliding my lips and mouth up and down its length, engulfing it—that makes my pussy wet.

The only difference is, back then I only sucked my boyfriends, men I loved; men who I wanted to be with. But now…now, I'm sucking a bunch of faceless, nameless men; men who I care nothing about. Men I have no emotional connection to. And that within itself makes what I'm doing that more dirty. I know this. Still—as filthy and as raunchy and trifling as it is, it excites me. It entices me. And it keeps me wanting more.

As crazy as this will sound, when I'm down on my knees, or leaned over in a nigga's lap with a mouthful of dick while he's driving—it's not him I'm sucking, it's not his balls I'm wetting. It's Jasper's dick. It's Jasper's balls. It's Jasper's moans I hear. It's Jasper's hands I feel wrapped in my hair, holding the back of my neck. It's Jasper stretching my neck. Not any other nigga. I close my eyes, and pretend. I make believe them other niggas don't exist.

The *dinging* alerts me I have new Yahoo messages. I sit back in front of my screen, take a deep breath. Eight emails. I click on the first one:

Great ad! Good looking married man here: 42, 5'9", 7 cut, medium thick. Looking for a discreet, kinky woman who likes to eat and play with nice, big sweaty balls, lick in my musty crotch, and chew on my foreskin while I kick back. Can't host.

I frown, disgusted. *What the fuck?!* I think, clicking DELETE.

I go on to the second email:

Hey baby, looking for a generous woman who likes to suck and get fucked in the back of her throat. I'm seven-inches cut, and I like the feel of a tight-ass throat gripping my dick when I nut. I'm 5'9, about 168lbs, average build, dark-skinned. I'm a dominate brotha so I would like to meet a submissive woman. I'm disease free and HIV negative. Hope you are, too. Hit me back.

Generous? Submissive? "Nigga, puhleeze," I sigh aloud, rolling my eyes. *Delete.*

I open the next three, and want to vomit. They are mostly crude, or ridiculous; particularly this one:

Hi. I'm a clean, cool, horny, married Italian guy. I'm also well hung 'n thick. I'd love to put on my wife's g-string, maybe even her thigh-highs, and let you suck me off through her panties, then pull out my thick, hot cock and give me good oral. I'm 6'2", 180lbs, good shape. Don't worry. I'm a straight man, but behind closed doors I love wearing my wife's panties and getting oral. I hope this interests you.

I suck my teeth. "No, motherfucker, it doesn't!" *Delete.* What the fuck I look like sucking a nigga who wears woman's panties? *Straight man, my ass! Bitch, you a Miss Honey!* I think, opening up the sixth email.

Yo, lookin' for a bitch who enjoys suckin' all kinds of cock. Hood nigga here, lookin' to tear a throat up. Not beat to hear whinin' 'bout achin' jaws and not wantin' a muhfucka to nut in her mouth. I'm lookin' to unzip, fuck a throat, then nut 'n bounce. If u wit' it, holla back. Delete.

Ugh! The one downside of putting out sex ads on the Internet, you never know what you're going to get. It's hit or miss. Sometimes you luck up and get exactly what you're looking for. But most times you get shit even a dog wouldn't want. Truth be told, there's a bunch of nasty-ass kooks online. And judging by these emails, I'm already convinced tonight's going to be a bust. Try to convince myself that it's a sign that it's not meant to be, not tonight anyway; maybe not ever again.

Then again, who am I fooling? I am a dick-sucking, freaky-ass bitch. Dick sucking has become my weakness. Long dick, short dick, it makes me no never mind. As long as it's thick, and cut, and loaded with warm, gooey cream, I want it. I crave it. I love swallowing hot cum and licking a dick clean. And the fucked up thing is that as hard as I have tried to get my urges under control, there are times when it overwhelms me, when it creeps up on me and lures me into its clutches and I have to sneak out and make a cock run.

My computer *dings* again. I have three new emails. My mind tells me to delete them without opening them; to log off and shut down my PC. But, of course, I don't. I open the first email:

5'11", 255lbs, trim beard, stache, stocky build, moderately hairy, and aggressive. Always in need to have my dick sucked to the extreme! I love a woman who is into my cum. Show it to me in your mouth and all over your tongue, then go back down on my dick and try to suck out another load.

That's right up my alley, I think, deleting the note, *but not with you. Your ass is too damn fat!* I move on to the next email:

6'3", 190lbs, 6"cut. Black hair, brown eyes. Here's a pic of my dick. If you like, hit me back. Before I even open his attachment, I'm already shaking my head, thinking, "no thank you" because of his stats. Don't get me wrong. I'm by no means a size whore, but let's face it…a nigga standing at six-three with only a six-inch dick. Hmmph. He better have a ripped body, a thick dick, and be extra damn fine! I click on the attachment, anyway. When it opens, I blink,

blink again. Bring my face closer to the screen and squint. I sigh. His dick is as thin as a No. 2 pencil. Poor thing! I feel myself getting depressed for him. *Delete!* I click on the third email:

Do u really suck a good dick? If so, come over and wrap your lips around my 8 inch dick until I bust off on your face or down in your throat. 29, 6'1, decent build here. Horny as fuck for some mind blowing head.

I smile. Maybe there's hope after all, I think, responding back. I type: *No, baby, I'm not a good dick sucker. I'm a great one! Send me a pic of your body and dick so that I know your stats are what you say they are. And if I like what I see, maybe you can find out for yourself.* Two minutes later, he replies back with an attachment. I open it, letting out a sigh of relief as I type. *Beautiful cock! Now when, where, and how can I get at it?*

I know, I know, aside from being risky and dangerous, I am aware that what I am doing is dead wrong. No, it's fucked up! However, I can't help myself. Okay, damn…maybe I can. But the selfish bitch in me doesn't want to. I mean I do try. I'll go two or three days, even a week—sometimes, two—and I'll think I'm good; that I've kicked this nasty habit. But, then, it's like something comes over me. It's like the minute the clock strikes midnight— the bewitching hour, I become possessed. I turn into a filthy cumslut. In a local park, dark alley, parking lot, public restroom, deserted street in the back of a truck—I want to drop down low and lick, taste, swallow, a thick, creamy nut. Either sucked out or jacked out; drink it from a used condom or a shot glass—I want it to coat my tonsils, and slide down into my throat. Not that I've gone to those extremes. Well, not to *all* those extras. But, I've come close enough.

And tonight is no different. Here it is almost one a.m. and I should have my ass in bed. Instead, once again, I'm looking to give some good-ass, sloppy, wet head; lick and suck on some balls; deep throat some dick, gag on it. And maybe swallow a nut. Yes, tonight I'm looking for someone who knows how to throat fuck a greedy, dick-sucking bitch like me. I'm looking for someone who knows how to fuck my mouth as if they were fucking my pussy, deep-stroking that pipe down into my gullet until my eyes start to water.

See. Being a seasoned dick sucker, I can swallow any length or width without gagging, or puking. I relax, breathe through my nose, extend my tongue all the way out, then swallow one inch at a time until I have the dick all the way down in my throat. Then I start swallowing it to give a nigga a nice, slow dick massage. The shit is bananas! And it drives a nigga crazy.

Ding! He replies back: *You can get this cock, now! No games, no BS, just a hot nut going down in your throat. I'm at the Sheraton in Edison. Room 238.*

I respond, practically drooling: *I'm on my way. Be there in 30 mins.*

I get up from my computer desk, slip out of my silk robe, tossing it over onto my American Drew California-king sleigh bed. Standing naked in front of my full-length mirror, I like…no, love, what I see: full, luscious lips; perky, C-cup tits; small, tight waist; firm, plump ass; and smooth, shapely legs. I slip into a hot pink Juicy Couture tracksuit, then grab my black and pink Air Maxes. I pin my hair up, before placing a black Juicy fitted on my head, pulling it down over my face and flipping up the hood of my jacket. I grab my bag and keys, then head down the stairs and out the door to suck down on some cock. I glance at my watch. It's 2:24 A.M. *Hope this nigga's dick is worth the trip.*